The Absence of Friends

Darren
Usted siempre será
nuestra Moncho.
El amor y la amistad para
siempre
Andrew
xxx

Andrew R. Hamilton

authorHOUSE®

AuthorHouse™ UK Ltd.
1663 Liberty Drive
Bloomington, IN 47403 USA
www.authorhouse.co.uk
Phone: 0800.197.4150

© *2014 Andrew R. Hamilton. All rights reserved.*

No part of this book may be reproduced, stored in a retrieval system, or transmitted by any means without the written permission of the author.

Published by AuthorHouse 10/08/2014

ISBN: 978-1-4969-9146-1 (sc)
ISBN: 978-1-4969-9147-8 (e)

Any people depicted in stock imagery provided by Thinkstock are models, and such images are being used for illustrative purposes only.
Certain stock imagery © Thinkstock.

This book is printed on acid-free paper.

Because of the dynamic nature of the Internet, any web addresses or links contained in this book may have changed since publication and may no longer be valid. The views expressed in this work are solely those of the author and do not necessarily reflect the views of the publisher, and the publisher hereby disclaims any responsibility for them.

ACKNOWLEDGEMENTS

Maximilion Von-Clarke – thank you for putting up with my months of craziness as I changed plotlines, character profiles and tested out the authenticity of scenes and conversations. Your catchphrases will now be eternally placed in print. Without your encouragement and belief in my abilities, I might never have a finished manuscript to submit. You have a special place in my heart and I will always love you x

Clare Marshall – thank you for being my proverbial 'guinea pig', as you were the first person to read my finished manuscript and offer me some invaluable advice through your proof-reading. Your feedback was the encouragement I needed to realise I did have the ability to become a published author x

Darren Bertram – thank you for your advice on the prologue and epilogue; the whole novel read so much better after your input. Aunque mi español no es muy bueno, que ha sido amigo mío desde hace muchos años. Vive tus sueños, como que estoy viviendo la mía. Mucho amor para siempre...un amigo para siempre x

Friends old and new – thank you for your encouragement and belief in me. Your words have meant so much to me. This has been a dream of mine for many years and I am glad to share it with you.

Readers – I hope that you enjoy reading my debut novel as much as I have in writing it.

PROLOGUE

Committing a flagrant act of unadulterated murder had begun to invade my mind almost as soon as I entered the room and dominated all other thoughts I had. The craving from deep within me was growing stronger with each passing moment; so much so, that an execution of my impalpable desire was going to be nothing short of an inevitable conclusion in order to quench the thirst that was becoming almost too unbearable to control.

My mouth had started to water with the sheer anticipation and excitement of what lay ahead of me, as I could almost taste the sweet satisfaction of the end result.

This was *not* going to be the sort of murder that would entail me killing another person deliberately, even though it was the perfectly premeditated plan that had been formulated and would be ever so simple for me to carry out without any fear of retribution, which would give me cause to have second thoughts. Nor would this entail me engineering an unambiguous scenario where self-defence or any other extenuating circumstances could be claimed because even to the most amateur of sleuthing eyes, it would be far too obvious that I was the one who was responsible for carrying out the deed.

No, my deadly intent would be nothing quite so heinous.

This was going to be far more simplistic a deed and so much more rewarding, as there would be no trace of a corpse to be discovered and certainly no trace of blood for any forensic experts to analyse and build a comprehensive picture of the events that had potentially occurred.

I had absolutely no qualms and certainly no inclination to even attempt to hide any of the obvious clues, as there were far more pressing matters for me to attend to than a few of the so-called tell-tale signs. Besides, if I were unfortunate enough to be actually caught in the act, there would be next to nothing that could be done to alter what was so perfectly obvious, other than holding up my hands and confessing my discernable guilt, making it game over. I was quietly confident that nothing quite so drastic was going to occur within the next few minutes, much less a potential full-on interrogation.

What did baffle me though, was how on earth my objective could ever possibly be defined as murder and even though this would probably remain an eternal and unrequited mystery, it *was* the initial word that had first entered my mind.

The time had finally come for me to put into action my murderous lust and I really didn't see any point in prolonging what I had already planned to do.

A heavy switch clicked, as I gave an intimation of a mouth-watering smile.

As soon as I had walked into the room, I had *that* apparently homicidal thought where I could so easily *murder* a strong, black cup of coffee, as I waited querulously for the kettle to complete its regime of coming to the boil. To say you could murder a coffee, or kill for a cup of tea is rather dramatic and misleading, don't you think? However, life *is* dramatic and misleading...you find you're being drawn into believing something, when in fact, it's the total opposite. Things are never quite what they seem, when you are deliberately being led away from what is ultimately true and genuine.

It was the rain lashing hard against the windows, in a torrential downpour, that made it difficult for me to see anything that was actually going on outside. But gazing out of the window was always a prerequisite to the task that lay ahead, in order to adequately clear my mind and reorder the day's thoughts into some form of clarity and perspective but on this occasion, it was proving that this was not going to be a viable option.

On the mid-morning weather forecast, it had predicted a fairly pleasant evening, with the possibility of a shower. It was true that it *had* been a pleasantly mild evening but this was certainly not what could be described as a simple *shower*. The rain had steadily built up to this ferocious crescendo for most of the day. In the weather forecaster's defence, the report was not actually broadcast in English so, with my knowledge of the language being rather limited, it was highly likely and actually quite probable that I had misinterpreted what was essentially broadcast as, verbatim, *wird der Tag mit etwas Regen, aber bis zum Abend zu beginnen, obwohl die Temperatur wird eine milde zehn Grad sein, gibt es eine hohe Wahrscheinlickeit einer längeren, heftigen Regenschauern*. If I had the ability to wholly understand the language and translate it with flawless perfection, I might have realised that the report was actually saying: *the day will begin with light showers but by evening, although the temperature will be a mild ten degrees, there will be a high probability of prolonged, heavy showers.*

Not that a great deal of notice had really been taken of the weather in the later hours of the evening, as my attention had been caught up elsewhere.

I wondered if this was, perhaps, the ominous storm that was predicted to hit the UK, as I recalled reading the headline of the *Daily Express* in the airport that morning - though this was not the paper I had chosen to buy for my journey - that read '*Worst Storm Of Year On Way*', which went on to explain that 100mph gales would hit the country by Friday night in one of the most violent storms of the year so far, as well as suggesting that two inches of rain was to be expected; this was apparently then meant to be followed by a similar storm on the Saturday. I remembered, at the time, looking at my plane ticket, which read a return journey of Saturday 8 February 2014 at 4.20pm, hoping upon hope that the flight wouldn't be cancelled. Still, that was three days away, I thought positively and anything was capable of happening within that time. After all, weather reports *had* been wrong in the past.

The entire day had been absolutely ghastly and disastrous, although nothing that a hot, strong cup of tea hadn't fixed in that typically idiosyncratic British way of solving those minor calamities. Ghastly, that was, in terms of the weather and not, what I had been involved in for the past few hours; that, had been nothing short of wonderful, especially as the day had begun with a high level of trepidation. I was fairly confident I was not the only one in the group that had begun their day feeling this way.

The headlights from the occasional passing cars hit the window panes in such a manner, it made the raindrops appear as if they were colourful prisms; like beautiful, miniature crystals cascading slowly, only to find themselves ending their short lives by shattering on the already sodden ground. The incessant but rhythmic tap-tap-tapping the rain created against the windows made it sound as though a band of drummers were playing somewhere in the far off distance.

The large digits looked excessively vulgar on the equally ostentatious alarm clock, which stood with irrepressible arrogance upon the nightstand. It changed its time, quite conspicuously, with the faintest of clicks that would have been far more audible had it not been for the rain outside. It read 12.23am, as if quietly emphasising the point, with its eerie, red luminosity - making it far more eccentrically dramatic, that it had been a long day.

It *had* been a long day. A *very* long day, that had begun for me not that much shorter than twenty four hours ago.

I had long since passed being tired but there was still plenty for me to do before I could permit the enticing invitation from the double-bed to whisk me away into the welcoming and wonderful world of dreams. Although having been reminded of past events, I was reticent that I might be cruelly dragged into the darkened world of nightmares instead and there was absolutely no way I wanted to relive those vivid memories.

Not again!

I had relived those memories far too many times already.

Quickly shaking the negative thoughts out of my head before they were too deeply imbedded once more, I concluded the only way to achieve that was to indulge in the task that lay ahead of me.

Switching on the bedside lamp, with nothing more than a voice command, light flooded the area, illuminating the entire desk where I had elected to sit. I hurriedly pressed the on-switch of my laptop, to begin the protracted task at the keyboard. I had never been one to work under the fiercely illuminated conditions that the ceiling lights offered, especially not when I was typing but far preferred the soft, condensed lighting of the bedside lamp, which I had purposefully towered proudly above the laptop screen. I felt that the undiluted area of light that the bedside lamp created was so focal – like a spotlight upon a stage actor – that it only served to help with my concentration so as to lessen the potential for any distraction.

Concentration was definitely what I was looking for right now.

As the laptop began to whirr and hum in its opening stages of being *booted up*, I took an evanescent moment to ponder upon what I was actually going to write. There was certainly a great deal for me to write about and I wanted to get it as perfectly accurate as my freshly-made memories would allow.

The laptop that I was about to work from had been a Christmas present from my partner and it went just about everywhere with me. If, for any reason, I was unable to take it with me somewhere, I at least had the luxury of USB flash drive as the next best thing. The flash drive had been a total godsend, as all of my important documents, as well as my writings were contained within it. A computer or laptop would be quickly sought out; at whatever location I was at, allowing my usual activities to once again be resumed.

It has been almost six years to the day that I had begun writing my diary electronically, rather than by hand. I had been keeping a diary for many more years before that and just because modern technology was taking over from good, old fashioned writing, there was absolutely no way I was going to let a small thing like advancing technology get in the way of keeping a daily record of my occurrences. However, speed would always triumph over style in my eyes, even though I had beautiful and legible handwriting.

It was all very nostalgically thrilling, transferring the previously written diaries onto computer as events, emotions and long-since forgotten conversations were catapulted from the deep, dark recesses of my memory, making them prominent once more.

When I had received the invite to meet up with everyone, to say there was a little reluctance from my side would have been an understatement. Apart from one or two people, I hadn't spoken to or seen anyone from the rest of the group in all that time.

How long had it been?

Had it really been over ten years since we were all last together?

It *was* good to see everyone again though. The fear, trepidation and reluctance that I had allowed to build up within me, in anticipation of the reunion, quickly dispersed and was replaced with abounding pleasure.

The Absence of Friends

The last time we *had* all been together, it ended in circumstances that would have better been forgotten than remembered, although the diary would be an eternal and constant reminder of the pain, anguish and horror I had felt at the time.

No, it would rather have been better if those circumstances had *never* even happened!

The evening had, to put it in a nutshell, been quite simply a wondrous adventure. The hours appeared to melt away like mere minutes upon hearing what everyone had been up to over the past few years. By the end of the enchantingly delightful evening, it was as if those superfluous years absent from everyone had magically been reduced to mere months.

The dinner, which had been a veritable feast of various styles and flavours of food, was enough to satiate twenty people, rather than the eight of us who were seated at the table. That, together with several glasses of České Slámové Víno over the course of the evening, had certainly taken its toll on me. I had been one of the first to admit defeat and announce that I was retiring for the evening. My significant – but not necessarily better – other half said that they were going to finish off their drink first, before coming to the room.

This would give me the small window of opportunity I needed, in order to write up the events of that evening.

The laptop had finally finished its *booting up* and so I selected the icon entitled *Diary*, clicking on it with the mouse-pad. As the first page of the diary met with my eyes, a cold shiver of remembrance ran down my spine, making me shudder, as well as causing the hairs on the back of my neck stand to attention.

It was from *that* period of time; the period that should never even have existed at all in time and never, *ever* created the memories that still haunted me.

I found I was being drawn into reading the entry, although I already knew every single word by heart. It read:

"It's over," I whispered softly, "It's finally over."

Dressed smartly in a dark blue suit, I knelt beside the grave. It was an unusually warm day for the end of January and the sun beat down ferociously upon my back, causing little beads of sweat to roll down my face, which met with the tears coming from my deeply bloodshot eyes. Everything seemed to participate in my sorrow. Birds were watching from tree branches, expressing their sympathy through sad singing. Flowers had their heads hung as a symbol of their reverence; even other animals seemed to stop what they were doing as if accustomed to this ritual whenever somebody visited a grave.

Pulling out the weeds and wrapping the dead flowers from a previous visit in newspaper, I laid a wreath of fresh carnations: yellow, pink and white,

Andrew R. Hamilton

> *by the headstone. Wiping the tears or the sweat from my face, I didn't care which; I stared at the flowers just laid. "They were our favourite. We always had to have some in the house. We never bought anything else, especially roses. It always had to be carnations."*
>
> *Opening my partner's briefcase, a leather-bound diary with the owner's initials on it, in gold lettering, was produced. "Do you remember this? I've re-read it all. We had some good times together, but there were a few dark secrets in our shadows of fear."*
>
> *I lovingly touched the diary, caressing the letters with my fingers, clutching it close to my chest, as though the person were with me at the graveside. I kissed it before replacing it back into the briefcase.*
>
> *"I couldn't accept what happened to you, but you would have wanted me to go on as normal. You did help me find peace in myself, but now it's over for the both of us. You have to believe that I've never stopped loving you, not for a moment. I really wanted to ask for your forgiveness after the way I thought of you.*
>
> *"I really wish that none of this had ever happened, as nobody deserved to die in the awful way you did…especially not you…and certainly not by…I just cannot bring myself to say their name!"*

I continued staring at the screen for quite a few moments, perusing the entry several times over, unable to force my eyes away from what I was reading. The expression on my face was almost as if I had been frozen within that period time from my past, caught within a continual loop of my macabre nostalgia, unwilling to be permitted back into the present.

I could recall every single word and detail of the inscription of the headstone; not just because there was a permanent record in my diary, but because my lucid flashbacks of seeing the headstone was like a permanent photograph profoundly etched deep within my memory.

I quietly cursed the fact that I had drunk too much earlier that evening, giving a self-reprimand for allowing the recollections of the night to become clouded through the effects of the alcohol. I had come upstairs with the sole intention of recording the night's events, whilst they were still supposedly fresh in my mind but it was going to be a while before I sobered up enough to be able to begin, which in my current state, posed an arduous task, rather than ardent.

As I sipped on my drink, hoping the effects would be quick-working, my mind began to wonder back to what I had just read. I fidgeted around in my chair, attempting to get comfortable; closing my eyes, for what I hoped would only be an instant. It was as if I were the star of a supernatural programme, where, against my will, I began to slip back in time, as I started to drift off. The

The Absence of Friends

strange and intricate events of the past became my present time, as I recalled with crystal clarity, what had led me to be at that graveside.

That grave.

The grave that had become an eternal resting place for somebody I had loved so very much.

Someone, who had been inextricably taken from me, by being victim to a brutal murder.

And murdered by a person I never thought capable of such a cruel and vicious act.

CHAPTER ONE

Elliot Hayden and Kristian Irwin walked confidently into the nightclub, hand-in-hand, with Luke Faraday following closely in their wake. Tonight, Saturday 24 October 1998, was the opening night of *Secrets*; Putney's newest gay club. They had, circumstances permitting, never been ones to miss out on an exciting opportunity of trying out a brand new venue on its maiden voyage into the gay scene. The venue had been advertised in the gay press as '...*why spend your weekends at home? This is the best place for you to be. A nightclub to beat all other nightclubs and with cabaret acts so lascivious, you won't be able to prevent yourself returning week after week*'. They were only too glad to be out of the bitter night air, into somewhere warm. The music had hit their ears before they reached the entrance to the club which, if they hadn't already been of the mind-set of doing, would have drawn them into the club. Paying their five pounds entrance fee, they made their way toward the direction of the music, which required descending a flight of stairs that enchantingly lit up whenever someone walked on them.

"Do you know, I could easily picture myself as one of those leading ladies from a classic 1950s film, slowly and dramatically descending the never ending great staircase; the hordes of adoring guests awaiting my grand entrance," said Kristian. "Just without the heels and the long flowing gown...obviously."

"...*and* the hordes of adoring guests," added Elliot, with a cheeky grin.

"Really, Elliot? Must you shatter the ambiance of my moment?"

"Moment? *What* moment? You don't have the class or the style to carry off being a leading lady."

"Well, my handsome prince...with you as my leading man I am, by default, always destined to play the leading lady. Ergo, I return to my original image of descending the great staircase...blah, blah, blah...in order to greet my adoring guests."

"Again, I hate to shatter your *moment* but the only person here that actually adores you is me...and even then, that's sometimes questionable."

"Humph," snorted Kristian, defeated by Elliot's last comment. "Maybe I should have just left you wallowing as a frog, rather than taking the risk of turning you into a prince."

"Oh dear," sighed Elliot, shaking his head. "Just get in there, will you?"

"The music sounds really good," said Luke, ignoring the repartee from his two friends. He rubbed his hands together with childish excitement, as his friends agreed with his statement, with a nod of their heads. "I've never heard of the act they've got on tonight though," he said, making his way through the swing door that led through to the main dance area.

"Why? Who is it?" asked Kristian with interest, following through the door which Luke had held open for him and Elliot.

Luke recalled the advert he had seen in the paper earlier on in the week. "Someone called Queen Michaela, I think."

"Ah, it's actually Queen *M'kay-La*," corrected Elliot, with a smirk.

"*Who?*" Luke questioned, not believing he had heard correctly.

"Queen M'Kay-La," repeated Elliot. "As far as I'm aware, it's apparently a play on Michaela. Goodness only knows where and how he came up with the name but I've long since given up trying to figure out how that one's mind works."

Kristian smiled knowingly. "That's our Michael! Even though he seems to come across as unique, really, he's quite far from it. Knowing him, he probably stole the name from some magazine that he read, or a television programme he watched. You won't know this, Luke, but Michael's quite infamous at plagiarising material, altering it slightly and then, after having convinced *himself* it's all his own work, tries to convince everyone else around him of the same! I'm probably not doing him any justice but underneath it all, he really is quite a lovely chap."

"I guess that you two know him away from his alter ego, then?" asked Luke.

"Yeah," said Kristian, the smile still plastered across his face. "He was my best friend in college; we both studied on the same course together and became roommates in the Halls.

"Actually, he did write to me not so long ago, saying that he would be moving from Kent shortly to Sheffield…why on earth he's chosen Sheffield to move to is beyond me! I can't see him lasting long there before he'll be on the move again.

"Anyway," he continued, trying to get back on point, "he did say that he was going to be doing a show at a new club in London, although he didn't tell me where it was going to be. It's so unlike him not to try and persuade me to come and see him though, especially when he is performing in London."

"Is he any good though?" Luke questioned. "I mean, I've seen a fair few drag queens in my time, like I guess we all have and to be honest, some don't even seem to put any real effort into their whole appearance. If you're going to be marketing yourself on the circuit as an entertaining drag queen *and* be taken seriously, don't make yourself look like a man who's just thrown a frock on in their first attempt at transvestism!

The Absence of Friends

"Oh, and don't even get me started on those ones who just mime! Not that I would, but I'm pretty sure I could slap a decent bit of makeup on and mime better than some of these supposedly *talented* acts."

Kristian looked at his friend quizzically. "For someone who really should be spending their Saturday evening being happy in boogieing their tits off to Kylie, Madonna and Steps, that's quite a deep and profound thing to say."

Luke shrugged his shoulders. "It *does* happen…occasionally."

"What? Boogieing your tits off to Kylie, Madonna and Steps?"

"No, you fool…having profound things to say!"

"Anyway," said Kristian, "we're probably biased but I'm pretty sure you'll love his act. Unless he's changed his material that much but I very much doubt that he has. If something works for Michael, he's quite loathe to change any of it."

"Good. I'll watch him intently, especially as he now comes so highly recommended."

Elliot didn't feel he had very much to offer this conversation. Drag queens had never particularly been a strong factor in enticing him to a certain venue. However, as this one was a very close friend of Kristian's, he was aware that he would have to pay very close attention to the entire act. He knew he would be interrogated later about the whole performance, literally word for word. If the topic of conversation didn't change direction in a hurry, he felt, Kristian would begin telling Luke about every single show of Michael's that he'd seen. *Now that would bore the poor bugger senseless*, he thought. He piped up: "Right, I think a visit to the bar is long overdue. Everyone want the usual?"

"Abso-bloody-lutely," came the reply from Kristian, clearly excited at the prospect of seeing his old chum again.

"Please," came the simplistic reply from Luke.

They ordered their drinks at the bar and surveyed the surroundings. Around the edges were comfortable sofa-esque looking seats, with what appeared to be velvet covering; although, the plum and custard colour scheme looked somewhat garish and out of place. Kristian commented that a soft shade of grass green, or a subtle, royal blue would probably have been more suited to the surroundings. There was no pattern to the few tables and barstools that were scattered around various parts of the room. It was the dance floor that caught the attention of the three men's eyes. It looked like individual squares of Perspex flooring, giving the illusion that it was made of glass, with lights underneath it that changed colour with each beat of the music.

The room was already filling up with people. Groups were talking animatedly by the edge of the dance floor. There were the bodies, who felt that they needed to prop the bar up all night, fearing it would tumble to the ground should they move. The young, energetic ones who would only stop dancing to buy themselves a drink, or go to the toilet, hoping to waste as little of their precious dancing time as possible. Finally, there were those who were on their own, either cruising with the intent of sharing a bed with someone for the night, or just having a fun evening by themselves, as a chance to get out of the house for the evening.

"Well, isn't this plush," stated Kristian.

"Mmm," commented Elliot and Luke, which was more of a simple affirmation to Kristian's observation.

"Not at all like that awful place we went to in Clapham," continued Luke.

"It was *you* who wanted us to go there in the first place. Elliot and I didn't really want to go."

"Now, now, let's not split hairs, shall we," said Elliot. Turning to Luke he asked: "Will you be okay if Kris and I go for a little wander?"

"Oh, you know me. I'll be all right. You two go off if you want. I've had plenty of time to get over my fears. I've got to learn to stand on my own two feet sooner or later."

"Okay. But only if you're sure."

"Go," ordered Luke.

"We're going," said Kristian, grabbing Elliot's arm and leading him off. "We won't be far. Probably somewhere near the lounge bar if you need us."

"Fine." Luke didn't really want to be left on his own, but he couldn't depend on his friends forever. He moved to the edge of the dance floor and tried desperately to hide his nervousness by continually running his fingers through his hair. Without Elliot and Kristian he felt vulnerable; as if his steadfast lifeline were being taken away from him. A few minutes had passed when he noticed a rather attractive looking guy approaching him from the direction that Elliot and Kristian had gone. His heart beat faster and faster until he thought it would stop beating altogether.

"Hi. What's your name?" asked the stranger, when he reached Luke.

"Luke."

"Mine's Scott." He smiled at Luke, showing his brilliant white teeth. "I'm about to go to the bar. Would you like a drink?"

"A Kronenbourg please," said Luke, attempting to muster his best smile in return.

Scott returned from the bar with two cool cans of Kronenbourg and offered one to Luke. "Here you go."

"Thanks." Luke took the can, his hand shaking nervously, causing some of the lager to spill over Scott's straight cut, slate-grey 501's. "I'm so sorry," he said apologetically. His face showing signs of embarrassment.

The Absence of Friends

"Don't worry. There's no harm done," said Scott, brushing the wet patch of his jeans with his free hand. "It'll dry off soon enough."

Luke smiled weakly at Scott, as he quietly reprimanded himself for being so clumsy, willing his nerves, that were currently working against him, to settle down quickly.

When he had first seen Scott approaching him, he thought how good-looking and well-dressed he appeared. His dark brown hair had been styled into the ever popular Caesar cut, which looked as though it may only recently have been cut into this style. When he saw Scott's eyes, he thought they were the most alluring green eyes he had ever seen. His pupils appeared strangely dilated, which only added to his masculine, good looks. A wisp of his chest hair was revealed over the top of the subtle pink V-neck t-shirt, that he wore under a heavy-cotton, blood-red shirt which had been left unbuttoned. The shirt was hanging loosely over his jeans. Luke really liked Scott's shoes and commented so; a light reddish, brown suede. He remembered the indelicately put comments that he had heard guys make, when he worked at *Jumbos* nightclub, such as *I fancy the arse off of him*, or *I'd like to give him one*. Even though these were exactly the feelings he had about Scott, he would never be so crass as to vocalise his inner, most private thoughts.

"So, are you here on your own?" asked Scott, with raised eyebrows, praying to whatever God would listen to him, for the answer to be *yes*, but thinking more realistically that the good looking guy in front of him was bound to say *no*.

Luke shook his head, as Scott watched him point out another smartly-dressed and attractive looking man deep in conversation with someone. "No, I'm with my…"

Scott could feel his smile fading, the disappointment setting in at an alarming rate. "Oh, I'm sorry. You already have a boyfriend? I can't say that I'm at all surprised."

Luke laughed at the presumptuous statement. "No. *I* don't have a boyfriend. That's Elliot and the guy he's talking to is *his* boyfriend, Kristian. They're just really great friends of mine…but that's who I came here with."

Scott breathed a heavy sigh of relief, as though, after a dramatically-infused pause, he had just been told that he had got the sixty four million dollar question absolutely right. When he had found himself drawn to Luke, he had hoped neither of the two men, with whom he had seen him arrive with earlier, were his boyfriend. Although he had mentally prepared himself for the possibility of disappointment, it was clearly not good enough, as his recent reaction proved.

Andrew R. Hamilton

The introduction to Rozalla's *Everybody's Free (To Feel Good)* came booming at full force, from the speakers. "I really love this record," said Scott, suddenly. "Do you fancy a dance?"

"Sure," came Luke's reply.

Moving some of the empty cans on the table, to make room for their own, they placed their drinks on the newly cleared space before negotiating their way onto the already crowded dance floor.

Elliot and Kristian were standing at the opposite end of the room to Luke, surveying the various goings-on. Elliot had undone most of the buttons on his shirt, due to the repressive heat in the club. His nipples were clearly exposed, much to Kristian's delight and incessant tweaking. As Elliot had trained professionally in dancing, he had bulging Pecs, rippling muscles and an attractive, smooth, washboard stomach. *And, oh that waistline of his*, Kristian would think. Although he was born in England, of indigenous parents, Elliot had an almost inexplicable Mediterranean look about him, with his permanently tanned-look skin. Kristian would often joke that he must have been on a sunbed or rubbed fake tan all over his body.

"Jealousy, my darling, will get you absolutely nowhere," Elliot would say in reply.

His eyes were a deep hazel, which to Kristian, made him look incredibly sexy whatever mood Elliot was in and nearly matched the colour of his neatly parted, straight hair. It was Elliot's buttocks that Kristian liked most about him; taking any opportunity he could to manhandle them. Whatever Elliot wore, whether it be bottom-hugging jeans, or a smart suit, Kristian would just gaze at Elliot's backside and say, "You really *do* have the most gorgeous bum I've ever seen." Kristian's hands constantly and magnetically appeared to be drawn to Elliot's buttocks, which on occasion was not the most appropriate or opportune of times. He couldn't, or wouldn't, stop touching, stroking or squeezing him, despite Elliot's repetitive protestations, making his own justifiable excuse that it was Elliot's fault anyway.

Kristian, on the other hand, had neglected his body recently, showing signs of putting on a little extra weight; more than he was happy with. He didn't mind cooking meals - in fact, he really enjoyed it, finding it highly therapeutic - it was the thought of eating what he had just prepared. When he cooked a main meal that would require a lot of planning and preparation, he generally found that by the time he and Elliot sat down to eat, he was no longer hungry and therefore, he would dispose of his serving. Elliot would question why he didn't re-heat his dinner in the microwave but Kristian would balk at the thought.

"I may as well get myself pre-packaged meals in that case," he would reply to Elliot. Of course, when he was eventually hungry, he would more often than not snack on junk food or order himself a takeaway.

Elliot would constantly taunt him time and again with the phrase: "Do you eat to live, or live to eat?" Kristian would only ever respond with a twist of his face.

Unlike Elliot, Kristian had pale skin, with his light-brown hair gelled into a swept back look. As he hated most of his own clothes, he would be prone to continually wearing Elliot's, even though it was himself that had purchased practically every garment he possessed. In the earlier stages of their relationship, Elliot thought this to be really romantic, although he was often perturbed when it came to searching his wardrobe for a favourite shirt or a particular pair of jeans that he wanted to wear, only to find Kristian had already worn them.

Both men had turned thirty earlier in the year, with all of ten days separating the two of them. Kristian was finding it hard to accept that he was "so old now", whilst Elliot had absolutely no issue with himself having turned thirty. The reasoning for the extreme reactions was due to people saying that Kristian looked all of his thirty years of age - much to his chagrin - whilst most were genuinely surprised when they were told of Elliot's age, swearing that he had to be in his early twenties.

Elliot occasionally stole a glance in Luke's direction, at where he was standing by the dance floor. "I do hope that he'll be okay."

"Stop fussing, like an old mother hen, will you? He'll be absolutely fine."

"Oh," said Elliot, suddenly remembering he had something to tell Kristian. "I forgot to tell you, I got a call from the lovely Chloe today."

"Oh my goodness," Kristian suspired. "How are she and Patrick?"

"They're both fine. They said they might actually come down later on, after Patrick has finished his meeting. Chloe didn't really fancy the idea of coming out without him."

Kristian rolled his eyes. "*If* they come at all. I mean, talk about being tied to the apron strings."

"Really, they're not *that* bad."

"Oh please! You can't seriously, really believe that. Chloe won't do anything without Patrick…or him without her for that matter. If that's not being tied to each other's apron strings, then I don't know what is."

"But you're exactly the same with me," said Elliot, raising his eyebrows.

"I most certainly am not!" exclaimed Kristian indignantly.

"Anyway, they've invited us over for lunch tomorrow. They've also invited Liam too and we haven't seen him in…goodness, it must be absolutely ages."

"That's fantastic. I'm really looking forward to that 'cause it'll be great to catch up with them all again."

"Yes, it's going to be great, I'm sure."

"I wonder if Liam still dyes is hair. Do you remember he was nicknamed Mrs Slocombe in our group?"

Elliot laughed, remembering those times. "Yes, I do. Although some of the colours he chose didn't go with the mass of tattoos he had."

"And I do love Chloe's cooking, especially her Sunday roasts. Mind you, anything is better than your cooking, eh?"

Elliot eyed him suspiciously. "What do you mean by that remark?"

"Come on, darling. Remember that *wonderful* meal you cooked the other night? The one that seemed to take you forever and a day. It was a complete and utter disaster, née a total collapse! Is it any wonder that I have to do all the cooking?"

"Well," said Elliot, with a candid grin, "you didn't exactly fall for me for my cooking, did you?"

Kristian didn't respond. He had been distracted when he turned, to steal a glance at Luke, spotting him on the dance floor. Tapping Elliot on the shoulder, he said, "Hey look at this. Luke's with someone."

Elliot turned round to look at where Kristian had surreptitiously pointed and smiled. Turning back, he remarked, "but he's danced with people before, it doesn't really mean anything's going to happen. You know that he *never* swaps telephone numbers with anyone, let alone agree to go home with them…and God forbid should anyone want to sleep with him! I do wish he would forget about what happened before. It's all in the past, which is exactly where it should stay. What happened is preventing him from meeting someone whom he might actually build up a wonderful relationship with. If only he would learn to let go!"

Kristian took another glimpse at Luke and the guy he was with. "I have to hand it to him though; he's got really great taste in men."

"So have you!"

"Oh, quick, pass the sick bucket…please," Kristian joked.

The volume of the music began to slowly decrease, as the two men heard the DJ coming over the microphone, asking people to clear the dance floor. "This is your ten minute warning for tonight's act, the one and only Queen M'Kay-La, who is almost ready to grace us with her majestic presence. So, if you need to get yourself a drink, or relieve yourself of one you've already had, *now's* your time to do it."

Kristian, once again, became ecstatically excitable as he urged Elliot to make their way to the edge of the dance floor. "You know how I always want to have a front row view whenever Michael's performing."

"But you've seen his performances nothing short of about a million times by now. Surely you must know every word, every nuance, every outfit and key change by heart."

"That's not really the point, though, is it?" he questioned, with an air of defiance. "It's about supporting *our* friend."

"Wait!" exclaimed Elliot, grabbing Kristian's arm. "Hang on just a minute."

"What?" Kristian asked, with genuine curiosity.

"They're coming off the dance floor just now."

"Who is?"

"Luke…and look, he's holding the guy's hand," said Elliot, with candid optimism. "Could this be the person who will finally make him realise that…?"

Kristian glanced, like a caring older brother, as his friend was leaving the dance floor. He turned to Elliot and sighed desperately. "Each time I see him with someone, I keep hoping, like you, that this could be the *one*; that this could be the person who Luke will finally find the happiness with, that he so richly deserves. Since Matthew, I haven't seen him get any further with anyone, other than a half-hearted hug, or a subtle peck on the cheek. What will it take him to realise that not everyone was like that bastard, Matthew."

"*Bastard* is a bit of an understatement, though. He was a complete and utter psycho!"

"Can we please clear the dance floor," boomed the authoritative voice of the DJ over the microphone.

"Ah," said Scott, "this must be in preparation for the act, who's coming on tonight."

Luke nodded. Without any hint of hesitation, he took hold of Scott's hand, whose mouth curved into a salacious smile, as he allowed himself be led from the dance floor.

The DJ's next statement, confirmed Scott's belief. "This is your ten minute warning for tonight's act, the one and only Queen M'Kay-La, who is almost ready to grace us with her majestic presence. So, if you need to get yourself a drink, or relieve yourself of one you've already had, *now's* your time to do it."

Although they finished their drinks they had left on the table earlier, they had long since lost the refreshing coldness that they were both hoping for.

"I'm going to heed the DJ's warning," Luke began, "and go to the bar before the act comes on. Another Kronenbourg for you?"

Scott nodded. His throat had become a tad parched with the recent dancing and croaked: "Oh, yes please!"

"And I promise I won't throw it over you this time."

Scott chuckled to himself as he watched Luke stride purposefully to the bar.

"God, it's really hot," said Luke, returning from the bar with the ice-cold drinks and handing one of them to Scott. "I'm sweating like mad." He wiped the moisture from his forehead with his sleeve and flapped the front of his shirt in a mildly desperate attempt to cool himself down.

"I'm not at all surprised you're hot, dancing the way you did. You know, you're ever so good."

Luke laughed an embarrassed laugh, as he slid his fingers through his hair. "Thanks. You're not so bad yourself."

"Oh, I don't know. My body seems to move of its own accord and clearly doesn't do what my mind wants it to. I've got absolutely no sense of rhythm. I think my dancing was once described as…if I can remember the exact phrasing…" he paused for a moment to think. "…ah yes, I remember now. *In order for me to fully justify the quality of Scott's dancing, one must first picture a marionette that's proportionate to being operated by a highly inexperienced and ineffectual puppeteer.*"

"Well, that's a rather harsh critique. Don't you think?"

"It was from my mother!"

Luke almost failed in his promise of not spilling more beer over Scott, as he tried to choke back a laugh.

The DJ's voice came over the microphone once more. "Okay guys and gals, it's *that* time…are we ready?" The thunderous cheer from the crowd, eagerly anticipating the arrival of Queen M'Kay-La, was all the motivation he needed to continue. "She might be a Queen, but she's also a diva…her tongue is quicker and sharper than a butcher's cleaver and she isn't afraid to use it… and only she can put the Whore of Babylon completely to shame…I love her, you love her, so let's all put our hands together in a frenzied round of applause, as we welcome the beautiful and majestic Queen M'Kay-La."

Queen M'kay-La, to her promised deafening round of applause, made her grand entrance on stage dressed in a flowing baby pink and pale cream wedding gown, singing a satirical version of *It Should Have Been Me*. During the performance, she took off pieces of the wedding outfit to reveal a sultry, tight-fitting, red dress, and immediately broke into the strains of Cliff Richard's *Devil Woman*.

The Absence of Friends

"This is actually quite good," said Scott.

"Yes, it certainly is. I was told that I would probably love the act."

Queen M'Kay-La sang several more songs from her repertoire, which were generally parodies, often rude, crude and vulgar ones, of well-known pop songs or musical numbers. The grins and chuckles from the audience made it obvious that this was the kind of act that they enjoyed watching. Scattered randomly between these musical hilarities, a joke or anecdote would be recited, usually at the expense of an audience member that, by the end of it, would have the victim resembling a beetroot and the remainder of the crowd doubled-over in hysterical laughter.

Spotting Elliot and Kristian, literally an arms stretch away from him whilst he was on stage, he looked directly at them. "With all this singing and burning of extra calories through a vigorous cardio workout from eyeing up all you gorgeous boys…that will get the heart pumping better than any gym session can…I am absolutely starving! I have to say, seeing you two fine specimens of men has really put me in the mood for having a Manwich. So, if you want to make yourselves scarce and scurry along with haste to my dressing room, you can be the slices of bread and I'll be the hot cock and crispy bollocks filling."

The crowd whooped with delight at the overtly sexual connotation and began chanting, "We want a Manwich!"

During the course of Queen M'Kay-La's act, there had been a crowd of around half a dozen young lads, who had been heckling throughout, with varying degrees of ferocity. She had already decided she was going to pick on one of the group at random, to subtly show them at their own expense how she could easily handle this type of character who rarely recognised when their overactive mouth had exceeded the point she believed was acceptably comical. She would certainly ensure that they would regret ever thinking that they could get one over on her.

In the softest of purrs, she invited her chosen victim on to the stage with her. "Aren't you just a total cutie-pie? And by the looks of things, you're clearly the better looking one of your group…by quite some margin. I'd even go as far as to say that, certainly within the looks department, you're a total god amongst the mere plain mortals that are your friends."

The man turned and smiled broadly at his friends, most of whom had contorted their face as if to disagree with the summation that had just been made.

"What's your name, sweetheart?" she asked.

"Ritchie Head."

"Ooh, a sexy name for a sexy man. I like it. Very befitting if I may say so."

Ritchie again turned to his friends and somehow managed to broaden his smile even further that would have made a Cheshire cat look as though it were scowling.

"I'll have to sack the author of my scripts now, as you just couldn't write this," she giggled. "You've handed me a golden platter of opportunity."

Ritchie frowned, as his grin began to vanish.

"I knew it. I just knew it. There had to be a dickhead somewhere within your group, though I personally wouldn't have limited it to just the one. I suppose it's too much to ask that your brother is here with you and his name his Norbert…then it would make sense that there was not only a dickhead in the family but a nobhead too."

Ritchie's eyes widened and his mouth dropped open, as the crowd roared with laughter.

"So Ritchie," said Queen M'Kay-La, as she continued in a dulcet purr. "You and your chums seemed to have quite a lot to say this evening, which I'm taking a wild guess is no big feat really because you all seem to have rather big gobs…I'm just hoping that your mouths are the *only* orifice that's wide and gaping!"

Ritchie giggled nervously, as he could feel his cheeks redden. He thought he would take one last attempt at upstaging the sharp tongue of his immediate tormentor. "I could be a great filling though, if you wanted me for a Manwich."

"You want to be a filling for my Manwich?" she asked, raising a pencilled eyebrow.

"Oh yes," said Ritchie, the huge grin returning once again to his face. "Besides, as you said earlier, I'd be a far better looking filling than any of my friends."

"Oh, my darling boy…as handsome as you may be, I'm what you would call a ravenous carnivore, which means I'm somewhat of a huge meat eater." Whilst pointing a gloved finger in the direction of Ritchie's crotch, she continued, "There's absolutely *no way* I'm turning vegetarian…not for *any*body!"

The colour drained from Ritchie's face, as his friends roared with laughter and would no doubt continue to taunt him for the remainder of the evening about the size of his manhood.

Shooting a glance, through narrowed eyes, toward Ritchie's friends, Queen M'Kay-La couldn't let them get away without a quip from her razor sharp tongue. "Laugh as you may, oh dearest friends of Ritchie's, I'm pretty sure that the only meat any of you could hope to bring to my sexual table is a smorgasbord of crustaceans…and to be honest with you, I'm certainly not willing to share your crabs as a filling!"

The whole place roared with laughter, as those nearest to Ritchie's friends watched them hang their heads in embarrassed mortification.

"So," she said, driving the final nail into the proverbial coffin, "if anybody *does* fancy a crab salad for a snack, you know exactly where to come!"

"So, this is the quintessential inner sanctum of Queen M'Kay-La," said Kristian, as he and Elliot made their way into Michael's dressing room. "The Grande dame of London's social scene, if you will."

Michael waved a discerning finger at Kristian. "Oh no. The Queen has been deposed for the evening. Once the dress, the make-up and the wig come off, you're just left with plain, old, boring Michael."

Elliot allowed himself to quietly chuckle. "Plain? Old? Boring? Hardly the adjectives I would have used to describe you, Michael! I would be more inclined to have gone with flamboyant, perpetual and unorthodox…and just to add that little bit of extra spice into the mix, 'cause I know you like that kind of thing, I would even go as far as to say sexually lurid."

"As ever, young Mr Elliot, you're being just too kind. You always seem to have this wonderfully rousing ability to finger my best bits." He sighed, raising an evocative eyebrow. "Oh, but if only…a girl can dream though."

"But this dream of yours has lasted for…well, for years though, Michael, hasn't it? Isn't it about time you woke up from it?" laughed Elliot.

"But I don't want to wake up," Michael replied, with mock petulance.

Michael had held a romantic soft spot for Elliot for almost ten years. He would continually profess that Elliot was his one and only true love that got away, although nothing further than a friendship had ever developed between the two of them. Neither Elliot nor Kristian would ever deny the solidity or importance of the friendship they had with Michael but when it came to matters of romance, Michael's allegiance would change from day to day about who he was supposedly in love with. On one occasion, he was allegedly in love with three different men at the same time, none of whom had actually developed any kind of rapport with him. Michael's string of fantasy partners were always evolved from a safe distance and more often than not, without even the recipient of his affections ever having any knowledge.

Even though Michael didn't believe he was particularly attractive, he was aware that he had plenty of admirers, who made it perfectly obvious that they would like to spend a night of totally debauched and unadulterated fun with him. He was convinced that they were more drawn to his alter ego than to himself but he couldn't have been further from the truth, as Michael was a very handsome man.

After all traces of Queen M'Kay-La had been packed away, Michael would often stay at the venue he was performing in for a couple of drinks before making his way home. When he wasn't smiling at hearing his victims' friends quoting lines from the jokes he had told that evening, serving to prolong their humiliation further, he could hear the suggestive comments they were making.

"The man behind Queen M'Kay-La is hotter than a summer in Egypt and I wouldn't mind raising the temperature even further, with him," a punter would say.

"Michael," another punter said, "the guy who's the drag queen, is absolutely gorgeous and if I didn't already have a boyfriend, I would be asking him home with me."

"If Queen M'Kay-La happily does Manwiches, do you think *Michael* would make a Manwich with us?" one half of a couple would say to his partner.

Yet another punter was heard to say, "I don't think there is anything I wouldn't let him do to me, especially if he's as filthy as Queen M'Kay-La."

It was *always* Queen M'Kay-La who was actually the one who got noticed, Michael thought. He often wondered to himself whether he would receive even half of the innuendoes and audible attention, if she didn't exist.

When Michael wasn't masquerading as his alter ego, he could easily be recognised as her creator, simply by his sheer height. He stood at a very proud 6'5", even without the added advantage of the extra three inches of Queen M'Kay-La's heels, which he could walk in better than a lot of women; his superior, upright posture would make his height, at times, quite intimidating. Even though he had a 34" waist, he still appeared very slim. His long, slender and shapely legs were the envy of nearly every woman, who would say that they would kill for legs like his. His platinum blond hair gave him a masculine maturity that caused some to believe he was older than his thirty years of age; whilst his smooth and vibrant skin exuded a glow that caused other's to believe he was much younger than his age. This manly exterior would so easily be shattered as soon as he opened his mouth to speak.

"I really don't know how you manage to go through all this rigmarole each time you do a show," said Elliot, with curiosity.

"It's a case of having to, my darling," he replied. "How else am I going to drip myself in diamonds and pearls? Unless I get myself a very rich husband… and that's not really gonna happen anytime soon, right?"

"I'm sure someone out there is waiting for a 6'5" drag queen to come knocking at their heart's door and sweep them off their feet in a flurry of powder puffs and false eyelashes," Kristian said, trying to keep a straight face.

The Absence of Friends

"Now, now, Kristian…there's no need for you to be such a jealous bitch; green just isn't your colour. Just because *your* claws have well and truly harpooned a perfect piece of man candy, it doesn't mean the sweet shop has closed its doors on me."

"Your *man candy* can't be anyone so blandly generic. He's got to be the right balance of sweet and sour to compliment your unique outlook on life," offered Elliot.

"Indeed," agreed Michael, hoping that Elliot's statement was actually intended to be a positive remark. He pointed a pragmatic finger in Kristian's direction, "exactly what he said."

"You know I'm only playing with you," said Kristian, as he put a friendly arm around Michael's shoulder. "Your Mr Perfect is out there somewhere but your paths just haven't crossed yet."

"Talking of Mr Perfect," began Michael. "I have another of my unrequited lovers coming over tomorrow for a totally tantalising tête-à-tête and a delectably delicious dinner, prepared by my magically wonderful hands."

"Who?" replied his friends, in interested unison.

"None other than the masculinely moreish Max…but of course, he's accompanied by the Minxy Madam, Maxine. Otherwise known to you and me as *Max Squared*. You know, you're both more than welcome to come and join us…I've got enough food to feed the five thousand!"

"We would have loved to," said Kristian "but we're already going to dinner with Chloe and Patrick…and they've invited Liam as well."

"Mrs Slocombe, with the mass of tattoos?"

Elliot nodded. "One and the same."

"Oh, give him a huge, sloppy kiss from me. I miss the old days, where we all used to stay up 'til the early hours of the morning, drinking and talking complete and utter nonsense but thinking we were intellectually profound."

"We'll have to arrange another time where all of us can get together and relive the old days," suggested Kristian.

Both Elliot and Michael nodded, with enthusiasm.

"So, what did you think of the show?" asked Michael, totally cleansed of his character. "I know that you two will give me a *fair* critique."

"Nothing short of sheer perfection…as always," offered Kristian, mimicking his best critique voice over. "She doesn't honour herself with the designation of Queen for no reason. Although, once you experience her acerbic comical genius, you will understand why she could never settle for being *just* a Princess."

"I can't give as classy a critique as Kris," said Elliot, "but yes, you were suitably filthy, especially to poor Ritchie and his mates. I think I've given myself jaw ache from all the laughing."

Michael embraced his friends and gave them a kiss on their cheeks. "Thanks guys. I knew there was a reason I loved you both…but please *don't* feel sorry for Ritchie or his chums, 'cause they were all total bitches throughout my entire act! They weren't even being particularly funny. I could see people around them giving them filthy looks, so I knew that I just had to step in."

The three men continued to talk, until Michael had vanquished any trace of Queen M'Kay-La's very existence. Her outfits, wig and excessive amounts of make-up were packed neatly away into a large suitcase that sported QML in bold lettering.

Several times, when a stranger enquired as to the meaning of the acronym on his suitcase, he would feign a thick Australian accent and reply "Queensland Medical Laboratories."

"You're a medical scientist?"

"Of sorts," he would continue with his lie, as he willed his inquisitor to be drawn into his own shrewdly spun web, like an excessively intrusive fly deserving to receive its penance. Michael didn't particularly relish the idea of strangers prying unnecessarily into his personal affairs and so, would combat their line of questioning by being disingenuous in his own inimitable style. "I'm more into, what you might consider I guess, as facial reconstruction." With his confident stance and adeptness to deliver fast-paced, impromptu anecdotes, he had the steely nerve to throw overtly misleading words into his lengthy explanations such as *epigrams*, *fallacious* and *dramaturgical* and still manage to successfully fool them.

"Do you fancy a drink before you have to go?" asked Elliot. "Then we can introduce you to our friend Luke, if he isn't otherwise occupied."

"That would be lovely," said Michael, "but I think I'll have to pass. I'm just going to have a very swift half a shandy at the bar whilst I pick up my danger money and then I will have to get a cab home. Unlike you two, I *do* need my beauty sleep and I can't have that little minx, Maxine looking better than me tomorrow!"

"Please make sure that you give Max and Maxine our love," said Kristian, as he and Elliot said their goodbyes to Michael. "Tell them that we would have loved to have seen them tomorrow but do pass on our apologies."

"I definitely will," Michael said. "And we will definitely have to make sure that we try and arrange a time very soon that all of us can get together."

"We'll also try and pin Liam down tomorrow to a time when he might be free for a get together, to reminisce over old times," Elliot said.

The Absence of Friends

"I'll look forward to that. I'm going to have that quick drink now before I get my cab home and hopefully, I won't bump into wee willy Ritchie and his band of crab-infested friends whilst I'm there."

Both Kristian and Elliot raised a corner of their mouth, in a wry smile.

"If I don't see you before I go, I love you guys a great deal and we'll have to arrange a time for drinks ourselves very soon."

"Sure thing," they both said, as they pecked Michael on his cheeks simultaneously and made their way downstairs into the main bar area.

As Queen M'Kay-La was singing the final song of the evening, *Bugger Off* by The Pogues, which she had deliberately altered the lyrics in order to suit the crowd she was performing to and was fast becoming renown as the swan song of her act, Luke turned to Scott and continued with the conversation from earlier.

"How old are you?" he asked.

"Twenty eight. And yourself?"

"Twenty six."

Scott took a very discreet step toward Luke, hardly moving at all, but to Luke it seemed like a huge stride. He backed away, visibly beginning to shake. He ran his fingers nervously through his blond hair.

"What's wrong?" asked Scott, looking at Luke with concern.

"Nothing. I'm fine...*really*."

Luke was reasonably confident that Scott liked him, as he was aware of the growing length of his manhood, as it became quite prominent through his jeans. Nonetheless, due to the memories of the past that continually haunted him, he was unable to let his mind be free of them. He wanted to speak to Scott, craved to get to know him better, longed to tell him that he really liked him; but his nerves were holding his heartfelt desires back like an invisible tether taunting him with the knowledge that never the twain should meet.

"Don't be nervous," Scott said gently, sensing Luke was exactly that.

Luke attempted a smile, hoping it would hide the fact that he was as nervous as hell.

"Tell me," began Scott, as he smiled warmly hoping this would calm Luke down sufficiently to break the ice further and allow the conversation to continue to flow. "What do you do for a living?"

"I'm a professional singer. Not like Queen M'Kay-La though. I sing as me."

Scott's face showed signs of being impressed. "Really? Where do you sing?"

"Mainly the pub and club circuit, though I've appeared in a couple of musicals, as I do enjoy a bit of acting too." Luke was slowly starting to get his flow back and continued: "I write all my own material and hope to get an album produced one day. What about yourself?"

"Oh, nothing as exciting as being a singer. I'm a teacher."

"I don't know. Exciting singers wouldn't exist without the help of teachers. You don't teach Music do you?"

Scott smiled at Luke's ego-booster. "No, I'm actually a Deputy Headteacher in a primary school, so we teach everything. But, I majored in English and Maths, I'm afraid, so I was right when I said my job wasn't as exciting as yours."

"English and Maths!" Luke showed his disdain of those subjects with a twist of his mouth. "You know, you should be teaching Music. I would have enjoyed having you as a teacher." As he realised what he said, he let out another of his infamous embarrassed smiles.

"You've got a really cute smile."

Luke came over all shy, not knowing how to act or what to say when he received compliments. As normal, he would automatically reach for his drink, or run his fingers through his hair.

Realising that Luke was beginning to dry up with the conversation because he was embarrassed, Scott spoke again, "I like writing poetry. I guess it's similar to writing songs."

Luke nodded. "It's lyrics without the melody really. That way, the reader can give their own musical interpretation to it."

They talked more about their jobs and how Luke had become interested in singing, what musicals he'd been and places he'd sung at; why Scott took up teaching, stories about some of his pupils and about other staff. Luke appeared to relax after a while and the more he talked to Scott, the more he grew to like him. He had talked to plenty of other guys on various visits to pubs and clubs, but he never seemed to reach the point where he could fully relax. For some reason, Scott was different. He was gentle, kind, polite and fun; not pushy and arrogant like a lot of the others.

"I'm just gonna go to the toilet," said Luke, as Scott finished his story about the member of staff who had introduced him into the world of the gay scene. "I'll be back in a minute," he said, with a reassuring smile.

Scott nodded. "Okay. I'll be right here...I won't move a single muscle."

Without any hesitation, or premeditated thinking, Luke leant over to Scott and kissed him on the lips. Scott wrapped his arms around Luke's waist, as they both allowed themselves to be devoured by the other.

Luke was the first to break away. "I'll be back in a sec," he said, running his fingers through his hair. Not only could he feel himself becoming flushed from the passionate kiss, but visibly aroused as well. The more he relived the kiss in his mind, the more self-conscious he became, which wasn't helped at all by the vivid picture he mentally conjured of the two of them in bed together.

Scott smiled wantonly at Luke, giving him a shameless wink as he watched him leave.

Luke was washing his hands at the sink, when a hand grabbed him on the shoulder. He spun around to find Kristian standing there, grinning like a Cheshire cat at him. "Jesus Christ, Kris! You scared the shit out of me."

"Sorry," Kristian said, trying to contain his laughter. "How are you anyway? Are you having fun?"

Luke continued the conversation to Kristian's back, whilst he was standing at the urinals. "Yeah, I'm okay. I've been talking to this guy, Scott."

"What's he like then?"

"He's quite nice. He's…"

"*Quite nice?*" Kristian questioned incredulously, fastening his button flies and belt. "He's obviously more than just *quite nice*, or else you wouldn't have tried to eat him alive."

"Kris, *please*!" Luke looked mortified, as two lads entered the toilet, one of them pursing his lips, silently giving his response to Kristian's last comment.

Kristian might have responded quite tersely to the pursed-lipped lad, had he noticed him and not been concentrating on obtaining enough soap from the poorly maintained soap dispensers. "Come on Luke, there's no need to be embarrassed. If I was young, free and single, I wouldn't mind a really cute guy trying to sweep me off my feet."

"Kris, stop it," pleaded Luke.

"Okay, I'll stop. Did you manage to see any of Queen M'Kay-La's act? Or were you otherwise engaged in the lustful desires of…" he feigned a cough "…the heart?"

Luke wasn't going to allow himself to rise to Kristian's obvious baiting. "Yeah, I thought she was really good and actually, very funny. She's definitely one of the better drag queens I've seen a long time. Where did you say you knew her from?"

"From my college days. Michael and I studied together."

Luke smirked.

"What's so funny?" asked Kristian with some confusion.

"Well, didn't you do a degree in engineering and mechanics?"

"Yeah. So?"

"Sorry. I was just trying to picture a drag queen doing that kind of degree, that's all."

Kristian sighed. "There's a lot more to Michael than first meets the eye, you know. So tell me, how *are* you getting on with Scott?"

"Yeah, fine, I think. Although it took a while, I feel surprisingly calm and relaxed with him. I'm pretty sure he isn't the kind of guy who's just looking for someone to bed for the night, or else he wouldn't be making the kind of conversation with me that he is."

"Oh, what *is* she like?" said the pursed-lipped youth to his friend, in an overly emphasised effeminate voice, as they were leaving the toilet.

"Fancies herself as some kind of Mary Poppins, no doubt…I bet she's probably a right filthy whore though!" replied the friend.

"*Why don't you choke on your own shit, bitches? That's all that's capable of coming from your foul mouths,*" Kristian yelled at the closing door but hearing the boys' laughter to his angry retaliation.

"Thanks," said Luke. "I really do hate those bitter and twisted queens, who make your mood turn sour."

"Fuck 'em," said Kristian, as he put an arm around Luke's waist. "They're really not worth wasting any time and emotion on." His tone softened considerably, as he continued. "Listen Luke…I wouldn't be surprised if Scott might want to ask you back with him tonight, if he likes you that much. Don't be afraid to say *yes* if you want to but if you choose to say *no*, and he really is genuine about not using you just for sex, then he'll happily wait."

Luke looked his friend straight in the eyes. "I know what you're saying is right. I just can't stop myself thinking about Matthew. The memories still really haunt me and to be honest with you, Kris, it scares the absolute hell out of me."

Kristian's expression changed to one of real concern. "Look," he sighed. "I know this might sound harsh but Matthew is history. None of us could have anticipated what he was going to do. You know, if you allow the memories of Matthew to keep a hold of you, you will never get to meet anyone else. You have your own life to live…do what *you* want to do."

Luke kissed Kristian on the cheek. "I know. I know you're absolutely right. Thanks Kristian. I'm really glad that I've got such amazing friends like you and Elliot."

Kristian returned the friendly kiss. "That's okay. I'm only telling you this 'cause both Elliot and I really care a lot about you. After all…what are friends

The Absence of Friends

for? Now, get yourself out there, as you have a sexy, gorgeous guy waiting for you and he's probably wondering where the hell you've got to."

He watched, as Luke left, hoping that he would heed the advice just given. Matthew had already tried to destroy Luke's life once, for which Kristian would never forgive him but hell would have to freeze over first, before either he or Elliot would allow that to happen again. They both tried desperately to support Luke and help him to regain his self-respect after that calamitous saga. Kristian was hopeful, after the short conversation, that Scott might be the very person who could entice Luke away from his painful world of hellish memories.

Damn that bastard, Matthew, if he ruins this for Luke. Damn him to the depths of hell, he thought.

"Hi."

"Hi," said Scott with a broad smile, when Luke returned to the table. "I didn't think you were going to come back. I'm glad you did though, 'cause my muscles were beginning to ache in this static position. I promised you I wasn't going to move a muscle and I didn't."

"Sorry about that," Luke grimaced, not really knowing whether to actually believe that Scott had stood statuesque for those few minutes. "I got talking to Kris."

"Ah! No doubt he wanted to know all the low-down, nitty gritty and gory details about me," he joked. He could tell he had hit the nail on the head when Luke ran his fingers through his hair. "I suspect he probably thinks I'm a boring, old school teacher, who talks nothing but shop all night long."

Luke looked up. "No. He said he thought you looked really…"

Scott smiled broadly, as he cut in on Luke's sentence. "Ah, so you *were* talking about me." *He's so cute when he's embarrassed. I'd love to just give him a really big cuddle,* he thought. "Do you fancy a dance?" he asked, as a quick way of relieving Luke of his embarrassment of being caught in the act.

"Sure. I like this song."

They waded through the mass of people, attempting to find their own private space within the crowded dance floor, passing Elliot and Kristian on their quest to do so. The place looked like a sea of drowning bodies, with flailing arms and violent shaking of heads. Some people had clearly been sniffing Poppers, as the pungent aroma wafted across to the two men, as they found a suitable spot to join in with the other drowning bodies. Luke was pretty certain that there were two or three of the thrashing bodies that had taken drugs, which he would normally try to avoid, as they would irritate him no end but nothing could have been further from his mind, as he allowed his body to move with the rhythm of the music.

The DJ's throaty voice came over the microphone, as he began to mix in the next track. "Okay guys, we've had a special request, for all you young lovers out there."

A dance version of Whitney Houston's *Greatest Love Of All* played. Even though it was a dance record, there were some people who had their arms around their respective partners, stealing a kiss every so often. Scott took the opportunity to follow suit, taking Luke into his arms and holding him tightly to himself. He rested his cheek against Luke's, who drew his head back to meet with Scott's. Slowly, Luke edged his face towards Scott's, as their lips met in a gentle but passionate kiss. Moving his hands down Luke's back, Scott stopped at his buttocks, following the contours in a circular motion, pushing him gently against his own hardness. He longed to touch Luke all over, to taste him and to feel him naked in bed, beside him.

The moment felt perfectly right for Scott to take the ultimate plunge, as he asked Luke: "Would you like to come back with me?"

Without the slightest hesitation, Luke found himself agreeing, involuntary, to Scott's request. Since his conversation with Kristian, he had attempted to rationalise his fears and convince himself that Scott wouldn't be anything like Matthew. *Why would he be anything like Matthew? After all, they are two completely different personalities*, he thought. All Luke ever wanted, was to fall in love with somebody. *Was that too much to ask?* He had been unlucky in love with Matthew but was adamant that history should never repeat itself, which was primarily the reason why he never agreed to go back with anyone before tonight. A few of his very closest friends, including Elliot and Kristian had told him that he was far better off without Matthew. After all, it wasn't his fault what happened.

Was it?

Luke couldn't seem to accept that it wasn't his fault. He constantly blamed himself, as he truly believed that he was the sole cause of Matthew's death.

CHAPTER TWO

Scott Delaney was born on 1 May 1970, in the City of Bath, Somerset, although by 1974, it had become a part of the newly created county of Avon.

His father was a highly experienced neurologist, who was one of the most renown and revered in the country. Many of his nationwide subordinates would often seek out his professionalism, valuing and respecting any opinion he might offer them.

His mother was the Principal of a private school, where the girls and boys sat their lessons and ate their lunch in separate buildings. They were only permitted to mix during the fifteen minute morning break and even then, that was only under the hawked eyes of the teachers.

Scott was the youngest of the three Delaney children. His sister, Eve, was six years older and his brother, Marcus, was older by four years. The entire family adored Scott from the moment he was born. He had huge cartoon-like eyes, which women oddly cooed over and stated that if his gorgeous eyes were anything to go by, he was bound to have a string of broken-hearted women at his feet when he was older. Eve, who was actually six and a half years old and took great umbrage when people failed to take note of that all-important extra half year, wanted to be Scott's *'sorrow gut'* mother and look after him like one of her dolls. She couldn't actually get her head around why anyone who wanted to be a substitute mother, like herself, would ever be full of sorrow; unless it was something to do with the baby not coming from their own tummy. Still, this would be just another one of those unexplained conundrums to add to her rapidly increasing list that she would present someday to her mother or father for the answers. For many hours at a time, she would sit alone with Scott, constantly telling him that she was his *'sorrow gut'* mother, how much she loved him and that she would always look after him, just like a real mother would. Marcus would refer to his brother as "my little Scottie", which annoyed Eve incessantly. She held no shame in not hiding the fact from Marcus, who, when he discovered the kind of reaction it elicited, took great delight in teasing his sister and making her jealous.

Scott obtained excellent results at school. His teachers kept his parents informed of all of his *outstanding achievements*. At the age of sixteen, he had no idea of what he wanted as a career, even with his four grade A 'A' levels. He often accompanied his mother to her school, sitting in on classes and helping other teachers when activities became a little uncontrollable. He enjoyed working with the children and felt good when he achieved something positive with one of them. This was a major factor that prompted him into undertaking a part-time B.Ed. course, after which, he secured a job at his mother's school. Teachers and pupils alike seemed to take to Scott; he had a very attractive nature which many people found hard to resist. His mother was proud of his achievements with the children and that he had become very popular with all the other members of staff. The parents of the children welcomed his appraisals and criticisms about their offspring, as Scott had the ability to put whatever point he had to make across without appearing rude or false. This excellent work of his continued for three years and would have probably continued for several more had it not been for the fact that he was dismissed, without explanation, almost six months after his twenty first birthday, by his own mother.

"Scott, I cannot have you working at this school anymore. I am, therefore, dismissing you," stated Deborah pragmatically; the Principal and Scott's mother.

Scott jumped up from his chair with such force it caused the legs to creak. He stared deep into his mother's eyes, who was perched sternly behind her desk. "What!" he screeched, his voice rising an octave higher than normal, as he felt the anger swelling inside him. "Why in hell's name are you doing that? I'm the best teacher you've got at this school. You've even said so yourself. I'm making good progress with the children and I'm well-liked by the other staff. So, what the bloody hell is going on?"

"Sit down!" commanded the Principal with hard authority as she pointed to the chair which had just been vacated. Scott took a deep breath hoping it would calm him down and complied with his mother's instruction. "I run this school and have the right to employ or dismiss anyone I damn well choose. Your attitude leaves a lot to be desired, Scott. I may be your mother, but you do not raise your voice to me in a rage of temper.

"Furthermore," she said, leaning nearer to him, clasping her hands together on the desk in front of her to drive her point home much harder. "It is your father's wish that you remove all your belongings from the house and live elsewhere."

Scott was stunned. He felt as though he had been as good as slapped across the face by her. "Mother, tell me what's going on. Please?" he pleaded.

Deborah retained her expressionless face. "You can go now, Scott. Please make sure you are out of the house before either your father or I return home from work."

Scott searched his mother's eyes, intensely, for any hint as to why she and his father were banishing him from their lives, but all he found was a cold and stony-faced woman staring back at him. Without a further word, he rose from the chair and left the room. No sooner had he closed the door to his mother's office, she broke down in tears. Deborah had not wanted to let her son go from the school; it was true he *was* the best teacher she had, but her husband had told her they didn't need perverts such as homosexuals in their lives. She loved Scott dearly, but now she had lost him.

Scott had heard his mother's sobbing, so he left her a note at home where he knew only she would look, telling her he was going to move to Bristol in a few days. He also wrote that he would contact her at the school as soon as he found somewhere to live. He was fairly sure that the reason all this had occurred was because he was gay. How the hell they had found out baffled him completely. The only explanation that he could come up with that made any sense, was that maybe Daniel King had said something.

When Scott first admitted to himself that he was gay, at the age of nineteen, he was terrified and thought he was the only person who had these - *abnormal* was what his father had called them - feelings for other men. Daniel King, one of the teachers at his mother's school befriended him very quickly, soon revealing he too was gay. Daniel took Scott to a youth group to meet other young, gay men in the hope it would help him feel comfortable and at ease with his sexuality.

Scott had his first sexual encounter with Daniel, having an affair with him which lasted all of four weeks. Daniel was not the sort of guy who stayed monogamous for too long, as he liked to sample what was on offer too much. Learning the ways of the gay scene came quickly to Scott. It didn't take him long to find out there were the bitches, who liked to spread malicious gossip and hurtful rumours and the bastards, who only showed interest in someone for their self-centered pleasures. For the first few months, he was often on the receiving end of both these types, but with experience, he learnt how to cope with and avoid them.

Now, his deepest fear had surfaced: the assumption that his parents knew he was gay. In the note to his mother, he wrote that he still loved her and hoped she would continue to love him. He finished by saying: *You loved me before you knew I was gay. I haven't changed. I'm still the same person. I'm really sorry if the fact that I'm gay offends you, but it's who I am and I hope you will accept me for who I am. I'm still your son and always will be. I love you, mum. Scott.*

It did anger him that his parents were still quite naïve and rather conservative to his way of life, refusing to let him live under the same roof. He had thought that times were changing, with the eternal ongoing fight for equality but this had clearly not hit his family household. He was pretty confident that his mother had been coaxed into agreeing with her husband that, due to his lifestyle, he should be banished from being a part of the family. Scott decided that he didn't want to live within the same city as his father, whilst he refused to let go of his negative and quite frankly archaic attitude, which he appeared to hold on to like a lifeline.

Maybe it was the fact that it was far enough away from his father to be able to live the way he wanted to and still near enough to retain some close familiarity of his upbringing but he had absolutely no idea what led him to choose Bristol to move to. However, when he had decided that was his course of action, he was extremely excited about the prospect of leading a whole new life.

A couple of weeks after Scott had arrived in Bristol, as promised, he rang his mother at the school. Every day that had passed without any communication, since Scott had left, had only served to increase the concern and anxiety that his mother was carrying. It was true that she was a very formidable woman, when it came to matters of the psyche, but even she was finding it increasingly difficult to mask her true feelings from her husband. She confessed to Scott that she had never wanted him to leave the school, or home and begged unashamedly for his forgiveness. She explained that his father still refused to compromise or back down from his reasons - even when she had pleaded with him to allow her to keep her son on at the school - as he could never be able to live with the shame it would bring upon his family by having *an abnormal son*. Scott reassured his mother that he completely understood why she had to hold on to the cold and hard façade she had portrayed that day because they both realised that if there were the slightest crack, or hint of her true emotions, Scott would have fought tooth and nail to stay both working at school and living at home. If that had happened, Scott knew it would only go on to cause continual problems for his mother, who rarely triumphed against her husband, especially when he was so rooted in his obstinacy regarding a particular issue. His mother would never come to realise that Scott knew exactly what her real emotions had been. When he asked her if it were Daniel King that caused all these knock-on events, she refused to comment. His mother ended the conversation with a plea to him that he never tell his father that she was still in contact with him; nor ever reveal the fact that she was sending him money on a regular basis, genuinely fearing what her husband might do if he should ever find out. Scott could hear the panic in her voice and promised he would respect her wishes.

After three months of living in Bristol, just before the start of a new school term, Scott managed to find himself a job as a teacher at the local primary school, which was literally only a stone's throw away from where he lived. His performance and reputation built up just as quickly as it had at his mother's school. It was toward the end of the summer term, at the age of twenty five, when Scott had been at the school for three and a half years, he was promoted to being Assistant Headteacher, with responsibilities for English and leading Key Stage 1. The reaction from his colleagues, as well as parents, was overwhelmingly positive, as they congratulated him on his richly deserved promotion.

Simon Ashworth took an instant liking to Scott when they met at the *Roundtable* nightclub, shortly after Scott had moved to Bristol. Simon was twenty-seven years old, five years Scott's senior. He was a fairly stocky-looking lad, without appearing overweight, as he took a great deal of effort and pride in keeping his body as well-toned as possible without overdoing it, with regular trips to the gym for a rigorous work out. His face had taken on a slightly weather-beaten look, maturing his whole physical appearance by several more years than his actual age dictated. It was his sparkling blue eyes that Scott was completely transfixed by, totally oblivious to the fact that he kept staring at them; almost hypnotically put under a spell by their translucence. Scott appeared to take pleasure with his insouciant dishevelling of Simon's thick, brown hair, which was easily sculpted into an artistically tousled look due to the amount of wax or gel he would use; not that Simon particularly minded, as he far preferred having his hair with a slightly unkempt appearance.

When Simon, at the end of the night, asked Scott to go home with him; from the limited amount of questions that he was asked that weren't revolved in some way or another around sex, or his sexual proclivities, his initial thoughts were that it was going to be nothing more than a one night stand. These initial first impressions were soon proven to be totally misjudged, as they continually phoned each other and arranged evenings out to the cinema, theatre or to a restaurant. Three years on, they had built a very solid and almost inseparable relationship. To all their friends, they appeared to be very much in love.

It was around the time that Scott was successfully promoted to Assistant Headteacher at the school, that Simon was also successful in his application for Manager of the Human Resources department within the Bristol branch of a national company. They decided to go out for a romantic meal in the evening, making it a triple celebration: three years together and both being successful in their respective promotions.

Scott had never been happier, since he had been forced to move out of the family home; something which he had told Simon all about. Simon had met Scott's mother several times on her frequent *holidays with a friend* - the excuse she gave, for the benefit of her husband - and they instantly both got on well together, which pleased Scott.

Deborah had long since come to terms with her son's sexuality, although she denied the fact to her husband whenever it rose within conversation. She had taken a few of her very close friends into her confidence regarding Scott and they agreed, wholeheartedly, to cover for her whenever she took off on one of her *holidays*, should her husband ever check on her whereabouts, which he invariably did. Knowing that her son was very content in his relationship with "a very helpful and charmingly pleasant young chap", made her more than happy and she was pleased that her son's life was, at last, taking a turn for the better.

Unbeknown to Deborah though, it was all about to drastically change for Scott.

For a supposedly mild spring morning, it was a bitterly cold day, with a biting wind that went right through to the bones. The miserable weather conditions didn't help matters for Scott, as he had developed symptoms of the flu and was struggling to keep himself warm. He was feeling particularly unwell that morning and would have far preferred to have just stayed in bed, cocooning himself within his quilt and sleep the flu right out of him. The first thing he was going to do when he arrived home, was to have a long soak in a hot bath; as hot as he imagined he could stand. Simon had taken the day off work in order to do some DIY around the house, so Scott was looking forward to an empathetic cuddle from him, which would mark the beginning of his recuperation. Although he was feeling under the weather, Scott wasn't opposed to a little humorous prank, so he chose to prolong his element of surprise by creeping quietly into the house, just in case Simon was working downstairs. As there was no sign of him, Scott gave up on the idea of having a bath and opted to go straight to bed instead.

When he marched into the bedroom, his mouth dropped open, temporarily losing the ability for any words to be found, as he found Simon in their bed with another man. His mother's ability to have a solid self-composure must have rubbed off on to Scott, as he stood bolt upright, allowing his illness to become a secondary issue.

"You bastard!" Scott yelled, trying not to let his coarse throat overrule his anger at being betrayed. "Is *this* your idea of DIY?"

The stranger opened his mouth, about to speak but Scott glared evilly at him, with daggered eyes, daring him to make even one sound come

The Absence of Friends

from his mouth. The stranger decided not to take up the challenge, feeling uncomfortably conspicuous under the watchful eyes of Scott, as he sank as far into the bed as he could.

Simon, with deeply flushed cheeks that matched Scott's in his anger, spoke with a duplicitous tone in his voice: "Scott, if you can just let me explain…"

"Don't you even dare say one fucking word," Scott hissed at him. Pointing an accusing finger at the intruder in his bed, he screamed: "You! Get the hell out of my house and take that cheating, little rat with you if you enjoy screwing him so much!"

As the stranger audaciously attempted to reclaim whatever of his clothing he could physically reach and endeavoured to get himself dressed under the duvet as best he could, Simon's eyes pleaded with Scott. "Please Scott, will you let me explain…"

Scott laughed, with a hint of hysteria. "Explain *what*, Simon? What feeble excuse are you going to come up with to explain this? Oh wait…hang on, don't tell me…let me see if I can guess what insipid excuse my cheating twat of a boyfriend is going to attempt to try and fool me with…You're going to try and tell me that it's not what it looks like…aren't you?"

"No, Scott. You've got it all wrong," Simon said haughtily.

"Have I?" Scott said incredulously.

"Yes, you have. You see, we…what I want you to understand is…let me get dressed first and then I can explain to you," Simon pleaded.

Scott snarled incongruously and let out a heavy smile. "No, Simon! I don't think there is anything for you to *explain*. It looks perfectly obvious what the two of you have been up to and nothing you have to say will make the slightest bit of difference." Taking another deep breath, to calm his fraying nerves, he said, in a low rasp: "In fact, I want you and that son of a bitch out of here…and don't bother coming back either. You are nothing more than a lying, fucking creep. God, you make me sick." He picked up the remainder of the clothes on the floor, not caring whose they were and threw them out the door. "Out," he croaked, aware that his throat started to feel like razors. "Get out, you bastards!"

The two men darted past Scott, as they hurried out of the bedroom, scooping up their clothes. Scott slammed the door behind them and paced the room for several moments, not actually realising that his relationship had suddenly come to an end. He looked out of the window, until he saw them leaving the house. "Bastards!" he yelled after them, through the open window.

He threw himself on to the bed and thumped it angrily with his fist, unable to hold back the tears that had been stinging his eyes. "Damn you, Simon. I thought you loved me. You can rot in hell for all I care."

It would be an emotional time for him, having to leave a job that he loved but he knew he needed to get away from Bristol and from the possibility of running into Simon. What he needed was a whole new start somewhere else but even with the prospect of a new chapter about to be written in his life, it would take him a long time to turn the proverbial page on the one that had just finished.

Reaching for a pen and paper from the bedside table, he proceeded to write his letter of resignation.

Caroline Faraday had always longed for a daughter, ever since she became pregnant with her first child. She knew this would be her final opportunity in getting her wish, as she was only a few months away from turning forty and it wouldn't be too long, she realised, before her biological clock would stop ticking permanently. Although she wasn't able to mask her disappointment, she didn't love her latest child any the less when she gave birth to a third son on 19 April 1972, whom she named Luke.

Luke had two older brothers: Oliver, who was seven and Samuel, who was ten.

Anthony, Luke's father, was the landlord of the local pub *The Bull And Bush*, where the family resided in Southampton, Hampshire. In public, Anthony came across as the perfect father, who doted upon and idolised all his sons, seemingly unable to do enough for any of them. Behind closed doors, however, it was a completely different story. Anthony was heavily into the gambling scene, with his drinking addiction becoming more of a concern as the years went by. It was only his wife and his sons who knew of the Jekyll and Hyde style personalities that were beginning to develop within him.

The family were never told where Anthony went to whenever he went out, as he felt it was none of their business who he saw and what he did when he saw them. If anyone had the courage to question him, he didn't hold back in telling them exactly what he thought of their impudence. His clandestine encounters began with innocent Poker games "with the lads", which quickly degenerated into major gambling tournaments, where the stakes were high and his losses were frequent. Whenever he suffered a particularly heavy financial loss, he would begin to seek solace in the arms of the nearest woman who didn't reject his advances and straight into their bed. Invariably, he would always return home - whether it be the early hours of the next morning, or a day later - completely drunk and usually in a raging temper.

Caroline, Oliver and Samuel would usually receive the brunt of Anthony's violent temper from the moment he walked through the door, to the moment he passed out, which was practically anywhere other than his own bed. Luke would often hear the screaming and uncontrollable sobbing of whoever was unfortunate enough to be at the receiving end of his father's unquenchable wrath.

When Luke witnessed a particularly violent and disturbing episode of his father's, where both his brothers were the unwilling participants, the graphic scene was indelibly locked within his subconscious, where it stayed and haunted him for years to come, through horrifically vivid nightmares. No sooner had Luke reached the age of five, he too was included in the nights of terror from his father.

Black eyes and visible bruises were always given a cover-up story in order to placate any inquisitive minds, which were for the benefit of the gossip-mongers of the town, who didn't help matters for the Faraday family. The usual lines of: "*I can't understand how accident-prone one individual can be*", "*the boys tend to become excitably rough when they're playing*" or "*I don't know how many times I keep telling them to tidy up after them…and this is the consequence. When will they ever learn?*" would roll from Anthony's tongue with such ease of conviction and usually affirmed by the bearer of the bruise or black eye.

Concerned neighbours and friends, in the earlier years, thought that they were being helpful to the family by intervening with the added weight and help of the police and social services. Anthony thought it was more a case of interfering busy-bodies who had nothing better to do with their time but poke their unwanted noses into circumstances that really didn't concern them. Like an animal that's survival instincts kick in when it becomes desperately cornered, Anthony was exceptionally quick at thinking on his feet to ensure the preservation of his own survival, when anybody of an official nature came knocking at the door. He had the unnerving aptitude to sweet-talk himself out of practically any compromising position he might have found himself in, having the ability to know exactly what to say and what to do, with nobody ever really disputing that he was nothing but "a charming man, who loves his family unreservedly". It helped his case that the rest of the family feared any reprisals - which to them, was ultimately the value of their lives - and therefore, denied any allegations that had been made against their father or husband.

Anthony's sons never received the fatherly love and attention from him that they all still so often craved and hoped he would eventually show. The only times he even deigned to acknowledge their very existence, was when he dealt them a right-hander on one of his drunken rampages, or in giving them a terrible beating for misbehaving. Caroline, naturally, would intervene, trying anything and everything that wouldn't send her to prison, in order to defend her children.

Caroline's closest friends had desperately urged her to divorce her husband, or take the children and flee but she knew that both of these options could never really be acted upon, as there was no knowing what Anthony would do to her, or worse, to the children, if she had ever acted upon this advice. Only once, did she ever contemplate taking her children and running as far away as she could but even though she had gone as far as packing a couple of small bags of the barest and basic essentials, she didn't have that all important final bout of courage she needed, in order to walk out the door for the very last time.

Although she was happy when the focus of the beatings was taken away from her children whenever she did intervene, it would only result in her husband venting his anger out on her. As the children grew older, they often begged their mother not to intervene anymore. They were all becoming progressively fearful for their mother's life, as their father would sometimes deal her a particularly heavy blow, which would inevitably send her crashing to the ground and cause her head to knock forcefully upon the stony floor. Likewise, the children learned not to intervene on each other, as they would pay the price, heavily, should they have chosen to do so. The three boys thought that the lives of the others, including their mother, were far more precious than their own, so none were willing to pay the ultimate price of having that permanently taken away from them.

Samuel had found this out the hard way, being made an example of to the others.

On this particular occasion, when Caroline had been knocked unconscious from one of her husband's blows, Samuel couldn't contain his boiling anger any longer. He rushed as his father, with the intention of punishing him by releasing the years of built up frustration he had carried, with a large serving of his father's own violent dish. What he actually succeeded in doing was dealing a pathetically weak blow to the stomach. This was the mistake which he lived to regret to within only an inch of his life and his mother and brothers made him promise *never* to do again.

Although Samuel never dared to challenge his father with violence again, things didn't improve for any of the members of the Faraday household. From the very first day he was able to get out of bed after his near-death beating, Samuel's subsequent actions caused a sinister chain of events, the consequence of which, would shake the entire country to its very core.

It began with Samuel regularly going around local businesses and private residencies, where he would offer his services with chores he knew would fit his capabilities, in return for a small fee. The earnings from his secretive enterprise would automatically be saved in order to execute his final plan. By the time Samuel had turned sixteen, he surprised himself that he had managed to earn nearly £4,000.

When Oliver accidentally stumbled upon his brother's covert savings, it took him a great deal of coaxing to get Samuel to confide in him that he was planning on running away from home and these savings would be crucial to that plan. Oliver incessantly begged Samuel to take him with him, saying that without the both of them living under family roof, it may make things easier for their mother and younger brother.

After weeks of planning and whispered conversations, it was the day of truth for the two brothers. What they had failed to do within their plans was read any of the newspapers, or watch the news, as if they had, they might have decided against running away or indeed, reconsidered their entire strategy.

There were a string of emotionally televised pleas, usually with Caroline doing the majority of the talking, asking for her sons to return home where they belonged. Fighting through the flow of tears, she apologised for anything she might have done that could have driven her boys away - knowing *exactly* what the boys' reasons would have been - but all she wanted to do was to have them back in her arms and never let them go. It wasn't until nearly a month after the boys' disappearance, that most of the national newspapers had the screaming front page headline that read: *'Two Teenage Lads Found Dead In New Forest'*. These articles would go on to describe how the boys' bodies had been discovered in the New Forest, brutally murdered, and most likely at the hands of the serial killer who, the newspapers had reported previously, had struck several times before.

It was during the month of March, when Luke was twelve years old, that his father died from alcoholic cardiomyopathy, leading to congestive heart failure, that had been brought on by his excessive drinking over a protracted period of time. Although both Luke and Caroline despised the man they were finally putting to rest, they both reacted to his death in very different ways. Luke felt a sudden sense of real freedom that was totally overwhelming and for the first time in his life, he understood what peace and tranquility really were.

As the brewery was suitably impressed with Caroline's work at the pub, they offered her the chance to retain the tenancy, as well as the residency. Her name, naturally, would replace that of her husband's over the pub door. Caroline couldn't believe that luck was finally smiling down on her and graciously accepted the brewery's offer.

Caroline was unarguably and an exceptionally beautiful woman with a range of very enigmatic smiles that she could always use to her advantage.

Luke loved his mother dearly and since the loss of his two older brothers, she was the only person who remained precious to him in his young life. He would never forget her different styles of smiling and had long since learnt how to read his mother's *true* emotion by whichever of her smiles she hid behind at the time. Even after a horrific night of violence at the hands of his father, he remembered his mother would never fail to come into his room, with her compassionate smile, as she placed a vase, with a single red rose in it, on his bedside table. She would sit on his bed and gently stroke his hair, telling him that everything would eventually turn out fine. Although the soft strokes of his mother's touch wouldn't take away the physical pain, it certainly helped with the healing of the emotional scars that he had already begun to build up. She would suffer through her own pain, which showed clearly in her eyes, to sing angelically to her last remaining son, until sleep finally took him over. He fought desperately hard not to allow himself to drift off, as he adored listening to her sing; it took him into a world where no violence, no pain and no fear could ever be allowed to exist. His passion for his mother's singing seemed to be the only thing that mattered to Luke and he promised himself, one night, that he would follow in her footsteps.

When Caroline wasn't spending her time pulling pints behind the bar, she showed off her talent for singing, which welcomed in a whole new clientele to the pub. She put on a regular Friday night show, much to the appreciation of the pub, where she performed sultry jazz numbers, heart-wrenching power ballads and infectiously rhythmic swing. Luke would occasionally sneak out of his room and as far into the bar as he possibly could without being detected, just to watch his mother perform. Luke was fortunate enough not to witness any of the raucous scenes from the male population of the bar, when they would begin to heckle Caroline with drunken obscenities, like: "*get your tits out for the lads*" and "*fuck the singing, start the stripping!*". Some men would even point to their crotch and invite Caroline to "*sing into their microphone*". The women just sat there quietly and envied her shapely figure.

To those who weren't within Caroline's diminutively intimate group of extremely close friends, it appeared that she had taken the shocking murder of her two sons a little too well. Many of her friends rallied around to give Caroline support with her loss, even though she gave the impression that she was very strong in character, with a strength of optimism in the difficult times. With the histrionic goings-on behind the family closed doors, Caroline had ceased wearing her heart on her sleeve a long time ago. In public, she learnt how to retain a stoic look upon her face, which would not draw too much unwanted attention to the pain or despair that she truly felt deep within her; this only served to give the local gossipers the opportunity to suggest that any maternal instinct she ostensibly had - though if she had any, they believed, it were only to be a mere scrap - had been totally quashed by her obvious air of aloofness. What these people didn't realise was the loss of her sons had affected her far deeper than they would ever realise, as she had secretly booked herself in for some intense sessions with a psychiatrist; fearing that if her husband ever discovered that not only had she bought a complete stranger into their private family matters but paid for it too, he would bring a fatal finality to her life, or even worse, to Luke's.

Upon the death of her husband, though she had despised him for many years, she became bitterly depressed. She felt the only true solace she could find, was at the bottom of a bottle of brandy or bourbon, where every emotion that she couldn't, or wouldn't deal with, would be drowned within the copious amounts of alcohol. This, unfortunately, was only the beginning of a totally drastic change in Caroline's entire character.

On her nights off from working at the pub, she took to going to seedy bars. She would dance provocatively to the pleased male clientele, some of whom were so aroused by such a confident and personal display of eroticism, they would slide money into her licentiously visible cleavage, with the hope that it would encourage her to continue even further in fulfilling their lustful desires. It didn't take Caroline long to allow herself to succumb to her self-loathing, in her manipulation of these men, when it was clear that their minds weren't doing the thinking. She found it easy to entice them to part with more of their money by obliging them with an exclusively private strip show, or the opportunity to relieve themselves of their sexual frustration.

The path of self-destruction that Caroline was so precariously travelling came to an abrupt halt shortly after Luke's eighteenth birthday. A particularly harsh and intolerant court judge wanted to make an example of her by sentencing her to serve the maximum seven years in prison for possessing Cocaine, a Class A drug.

Although it tore Luke up inside, he knew he didn't ever want to emotionally abandon his mother, despite her continual protestations to the contrary. She had managed to coax her son into escaping the memories of the last few years by finding happiness for the both of them, and making something of his life far away from the surroundings he had grown up with. She knew there was nothing left for him in Southampton, especially with the pointing fingers and accusatory eyes of the local community. She had managed to preserve a small amount of savings, stashed away, that would at least see him through a few days and urged him to take it with her blessing.

As Luke began his journey of fleeing to London, he knew it was time to overcome the past by looking toward a positive future; what he wouldn't be able to realise was the nightmares that were awaiting him in his first few years in London were going to be far worse than the last eighteen in Southampton.

Luke wasn't that naïve to think that life on his own in a big city would be anything other than extremely difficult. The stresses of the past couple of years had taken its toll on him, ageing him by several years. Nobody would have believed that he was a frightened eighteen year old boy, with no idea of what he was going to do, without any family member to guide him along. If anybody had wanted to give it a moment's thought, they might have assumed he was a nervous young adult, who had recently left home to start the exciting journey of life away from the family nest.

His entire world now consisted of whatever he had managed to cram into his suitcase and a backpack, which included a couple of photographs of his mother.

As an eighteen year old, very much on his own, he knew that London would be rather intimidating and foreboding. The little money that his mother had managed to save wouldn't last him as long as he might have liked, but he desperately needed some time to be able to recollect his thoughts and decide what on earth he was going to do next. The promise he had made to his mother, to find happiness for the both of them, played in the forefront of his mind and there was absolutely no way that he was going to allow this promise to go unrealised.

After purchasing himself a train ticket, which took him to London's Waterloo, he surprised himself by managing to successfully negotiate the underground to Kings Cross; the only place in London that he remembered his mother ever mentioning.

Wondering around for what seemed like several hours, Luke stumbled upon a rather quaint looking bed and breakfast, which, from the weather-beaten and faded lettering seemed to be called *Grace Dwellings*. After investigating the price - although he had nothing to compare it with - he concluded it was relatively inexpensive for his immediate needs. The establishment was owned by a very warm and welcoming elderly woman, called Lillian Grace, whom Luke assumed to be in her mid-seventies. Lillian enjoyed fussing over people, especially those who were young enough to be her grandchild. At the very least, Luke thought, this would ensure a few comfortable night's sleep, with the ability to have a hot shower and begin the day with a hearty breakfast. The deal was finally sealed for him, when he discovered that Lillian didn't have any

The Absence of Friends

guests booked in, as undisturbed solitude was what he believed he needed to get his quality thinking into motion.

Luke counted the money that he had remaining, which totaled £750. He initially booked a room for five nights but upon reflection, he didn't believe that this would give him enough time to arrive at any positively tangible conclusions and therefore, decided to extend it to ten nights. This would only leave him with £400 as his capital to use in whatever decisions he finally came to, which meant he would have to act very wisely but more importantly, with some form of sensible haste. His hesitancy in not knowing exactly what he wanted to do didn't go unnoticed under the astute eyes of Lillian. With a few carefully worded questions, so as not to alert any suspicions in him, it didn't take her long to decipher that he was much younger than he claimed to be, nor was he a typical tourist coming to discover the delights that London had to offer its youthful inhabitants.

With a small but thankfully crucial reprieve from his disastrous *fait accompli* being set permanently in stone, Luke didn't have the first idea of where to start in thinking about how he might be able to shape his future into the direction that he ultimately wanted.

For the first couple of days, Luke spent a great deal of time talking to Lillian about London, what it had to offer and questioning her about what activities she believed he might enjoy involving himself in. Even though he felt magnetically drawn to her grandmotherly qualities, he was cautious not to reveal too much information about himself or his history when she questioned him about what had bought him to London and what his long term plans were. He believed he was successfully achieving in keeping his past concealed but what he hadn't banked on, was Lillian's ability to listen to what *wasn't* being said, that revealed a lot more information about him than he would have otherwise willingly disclosed.

On both of the first two mornings, when breakfast was being served, Luke asked Lillian if it were too much of a cheek to have second helpings of bacon, sausages and eggs; he believed that if he could at least gorge himself heartily at breakfast, it may see him through until the following morning. Without hesitation or question, Lillian silently carried out his request. On the third morning, Luke had easily concluded that one meal a day was definitely not sufficient enough for him and so, that morning and the next, he asked if Lillian would mind terribly if he could make himself sandwiches with the leftover bacon and sausages. Again, without any question, she offered to make the sandwiches up for him, whilst he was putting together his rucksack in order to spend the day exploring the local area. The nature of these unusual requests only further compounded Lillian's suspicions that all was not what it appeared, as far as her young guest was concerned. She felt she needed to bide her time in carefully finding the right opportunity to discover what pain and troubles were being kept a dark and hidden secret on such young shoulders.

On the afternoon of the fourth day in London, whilst Luke was tentatively familiarising himself with his local surroundings by retracing exactly the same route as he had taken the previous day, a middle-aged man propositioned him to perform lewd, sexual acts with him. Although Luke believed himself to be gay, a fact which he never dared reveal to his mother, let alone his father, he had never had the opportunity to experience any physical contact with another man, though he had often allowed himself to sink into his own fantasies.

"How much are you asking?" enquired the middle-aged man.

Luke looked at the man, confused. "What?"

"How much do you charge for a blow job?"

Luke didn't know what to answer, so he decided upon picking a figure at random. "Five quid, I guess," he responded weakly. *At least that could buy me a reasonably decent meal tomorrow*, he thought, *so I won't keep being an imposition on Lillian's very kind hospitality.*

The man laughed. "That all? I guess you spit rather than swallow for that amount! What about anal? Do you fuck or like to be fucked? Or," he said with a salaciously raised eyebrow, "do you like it both ways?"

Luke was rendered momentarily speechless, as he was being bombarded with questions that he had absolutely no idea on how he should answer. All he could muster was a very quivering, "I…um…I…er…I don't know. I've… ah…I'm…I've never actually been with anyone before."

The man's smile broadened. *If he isn't lying, I've managed to hook myself a lovely little fresh piece of meat, with a nice, tight, virgin arse*, he thought. "Okay," said the man definitively, "here's what we're going to do…we're going to go back to my place, which is literally around the corner…*but* if anyone asks you, you're my nephew, right?" He looked Luke up and down, with a ravenous smile developing on his face, as he continued, "If you swallow and then let me fuck you, I'll give you twenty five quid…that's twenty quid more than you wanted. So not a bad deal for a couple of hours of fun for you, right?"

Luke didn't have the slightest clue as to whether this was *a good deal* or not, but nodded anyway and followed the man. He questioned himself the entire way to the man's house if he was doing the right thing, feeling the nerves steadily becoming more obvious. The man was very well groomed, dressed in a dark grey, pinstripe suit and carrying what looked like a very expensive leather briefcase. Luke guessed he might have been anywhere between his early to late forties. He noticed that the man was wearing a gold band on his wedding finger but thought it prudent not to question him on whether he was married or not.

The Absence of Friends

He came to his own conclusion that if the man *was* married, his wife, more than likely, would be totally unaware of her husband's double life and he would hardly want to be reminded of that fact, if he was planning to gratify his sexual needs that could only be found with another man. Luke didn't think the man looked particularly handsome, but at the same token, he was not unattractive. He just appeared to be an average run-of-the-mill businessman.

Luke had very mixed emotions about what happened but true to the man's word, he received twenty five pounds for *services rendered*, which is what he recalled the man had said to him as he handed over the money. He found the experience to be quite cold, as there was no real emotion involved from the man, other than him being solely concerned about his own climatic gratification, during his animalistic lust. The fact that Luke benefited by receiving a financial reward, outweighed the temporary negative feelings he had, whilst the acts were being performed. He believed he could keep doing this until he managed to secure himself a proper job. He thought back to the man being surprised at the small amount of money he was asked for, so over the next five days and nights, with each man he provided *services rendered*, he asked for a little more money than the last, until he was greeted with: "How bloody much? You've got to be joking!"

It took Luke four days to find the most reasonable *rent* - he constantly found himself being referred to as a *rent boy* - to charge his clients for various acts. He also learnt that the more bizarre the acts he was willing to do for his clients, the more they were willing to pay. As the days passed, he found he was able to switch off emotionally and treat sex like a mundane chore that had to be tackled and completed in order to keep a regular income.

It was the final evening of Luke's stay at *Grace Dwellings* and he was no nearer in making any real concrete decisions about his future plans for his life. He walked with fearful despondency into the building, resigning himself to the fact that his earnest contemplations would have to continue whilst the streets became his new home. He did wonder, from the £365 he had earned from his carnal activities, if he might extend his stay at the bed and breakfast for a further ten days. He gave a silent prayer, to any god that he thought might listen to him, for a miracle to happen someday soon.

"Good evening, Luke," called Lillian, in her cheery manner, as she poked her head around the kitchen door. "How was your day?"

Trying desperately to shed himself of his dejected appearance, he forced a smile. "Yeah, it was a fun…and interesting day, I guess," he lied, wandering into the kitchen to find Lillian cooking what smelt like a roast chicken dinner. *Oh my goodness, that smells wonderfully delicious*, he thought, as his stomach agreed with a rumble.

As if reading his mind, Lillian interrupted Luke's desperate thoughts. "Oh really, I am quite a silly, old goat," she exclaimed, "I honestly don't know what's wrong with my brain today…I clearly didn't switch it to think mode this morning."

"Why? What's happened?" asked Luke with concern.

"Well, I appear to have cooked far too much food and there's absolutely no way that I could possibly eat it all by myself. I wonder if you might want to join this daft, old woman for some dinner."

For the first time in days, Luke let a heartfelt smile come across his face. "I would," he said. "It smells absolutely gorgeous…it's making me really hungry." Luke didn't want to reveal the fact that he was already hungry before he had even smelt Lillian's divine cooking.

"Lovely," she said, with a duplicitous grin forming, as she turned her attention once more to the meal. "That's that little conundrum resolved. All's well that ends well, as they say." In the twenty five years or more that Lillian had been cooking dinner for herself, she had never once cooked too much; this was nothing short of a calculated ploy to get Luke into a situation where she could talk properly with him.

"I'll just have a shower and change first and then I'll be down," Luke stated, clearly looking forward to another decent home-cooked meal, without having the stench of his afternoon's activities lingering under his nose. "Oh, and Lillian," he continued, as he was leaving the kitchen, "you are anything but a silly, old goat or a daft, old woman. In fact, I think you're kind, caring and absolutely wonderful."

Luke savoured every single mouthful and complimented Lillian on a truly delicious roast dinner.

"I've really enjoyed having you around these past few days. You've injected some youthfulness into the place, which I've really missed," she said. "It will be a shame to see you go tomorrow. Do you know where you'll be going next?"

During the dinner, Luke had allowed the issues regarding his future direction to be pushed to the back of his mind but now, with Lillian's question, they had cruelly been dragged right back to the front of his thoughts, where he had no choice but to confront them. His face drained of colour, his eyes lost their sparkle and his lips curved downwards, as he came to a split-second decision. "I thought I might like to stay on for a few more days," he said, hoping that the slight waver in his voice wasn't noticed by Lillian. "I like it here and there's still so much more to discover about the area."

"I thought you might say that," Lillian said, as she watched Luke getting up from the table and making his way over to the sideboard to look at two framed photographs that had caught his eye.

The Absence of Friends

"Who are they?" he asked with intrigue, as he studied the photos, hoping that the quick change of subject would stop him feeling like a cornered animal with the inquisition that was no doubt coming his way.

One of the photographs, he noted, must have been taken a very long time ago. It was of a very handsome man, whom Luke thought must have been somewhere between his mid to late twenties, dressed in a military uniform. Upon closer inspection, Luke could decipher that it was an army uniform. Although it was a very official photo, there was still an obvious warmth that could be seen behind the man's eyes.

The second photograph, albeit still quite old, wasn't as old as the first one. Again, it featured a reasonably good looking man that Luke guessed was a similar age to himself. The lad was dressed far more casually but still with that same warmth behind the eyes. There were other striking similarities between the two pictures and Luke surmised that they must be related to each other.

"They're photos of both my husband and my son," Lillian said, with a hint of pride.

"I have to say, they come across as two very striking men," Luke offered. "Where are they now?"

Lillian's confident demeanor deflated slightly, as she got caught in her past. Letting out a prolonged sigh, she said: "I've lost both of them."

"Oh," gulped Luke, as he took his seat back at the table. "I'm really sorry to hear that. Whatever happened to them, I bet they were both really amazing people who made you a very proud wife and mother."

The sharp glint reappeared in Lillian's eyes. "Yes, you're absolutely right. I *was* incredibly proud of them both. To be honest with you, Luke, I can see traits of both of them in you."

"Really?" asked Luke, taking the compliment as a much needed boost to his dampened ego. "Tell me more about them, please." He began to fiddle with his napkin ring, as Lillian agreed to take him on the journey of her past.

"Paul William Grace," she began deferentially, "was born at the beginning of July 1914, literally days before the First World War. I, on the other hand, was born a few days after war had broken out, at the end of July 1914.

"We became childhood sweethearts at the age of fifteen. Back in those days, you finished school at fourteen, so we had both already left.

"My parents owned a haberdashery on Upper Street in Islington, where we lived in the flat above. Naturally, upon leaving school I began working straight away, with my mother in the shop. As the business was going from strength to strength, my father began to realise that he needed to employ a strapping, young lad to help him with the ever increasing manual work."

"Which is where you first met the man who was to become your husband?" Luke questioned.

"Exactly," Lillian confirmed. "Paul was in the right place at the right time and my father decided he was exactly what he was looking for and so hired him literally on the spot. It wasn't very long afterwards that Paul began writing me little love letters and poems. I've still got every single one that he wrote me, in a box upstairs.

"So as not to bore you with a long, drawn out story, we were eventually married in the autumn that we were both eighteen. I remember the day with total clarity, as if it were only yesterday, 10 September 1932. My mother had made my wedding gown and my father had already interrogated Paul until there were no more questions that he could possibly ask, that he hadn't done already."

Luke stifled a little laugh. "Goodness, how different things were back in those days."

"Oh yes! In the 30s, things were very much different. My father was very proud of Paul when he announced that he was going to join the army, into the Royal Fusiliers, as he thought that was a very worthwhile career; to serve King and country.

"We had seven perfectly wonderful years as husband and wife before Paul, who was now a Captain, went to serve in the Second World War. Nobody would have believed that history would so cruelly repeat itself after the previous war had finished only twenty one years before."

"Oh God," said Luke, as he felt a cold shiver go up his spine. "You're not going to tell me that he was killed in battle?"

"I'm afraid that's *exactly* what I'm going to tell you. As with my wedding day, I can remember the day I received the telegram as though it were, again, only yesterday. All the women who had family serving in the war would always dread the mail coming and being handed a telegram, as they knew it would more than likely be bad news; it would either say that the person had lost their life within the line of duty, or that they were missing in action and presumed dead.

"When I received mine, it said that he had lost his life on 5 March 1943 whilst serving in battle. He was only twenty eight."

Tears had already filled Luke's eyes. "I really can't imagine what you must have been feeling," he said between sniffles. "I've got goose bumps just thinking about it."

"It wasn't easy, I can tell you that much. Especially with having a young child to bring up by myself."

The Absence of Friends

"Oh," cried Luke. "Please don't tell me that your husband didn't even get the opportunity to see his son."

Lillian smiled at Luke, at his show of concern. "He *did* get the opportunity to see him.

"Thomas William was born in February 1940. I was already pregnant with him before my husband went off to war. However, in the three and a half years that he was away, he managed to get shore leave three times to be able to spend a few days together with us, as a family. Needless to say, by the time I was used to having him home again, he had to return.

"Thomas was a really good lad, who had a beautiful caring nature about him and really, couldn't do enough for those he cared deeply about. I actually still receive the occasional letter from a lad whom Thomas had befriended when he was about ten or eleven, after quite a sordid affair that is just too awful for me to go into detail but it involved nasty, wicked boys who thought it would be fun to torment those who were younger than them. However, if it hadn't been for Thomas intervening, this lad might not have been fortunate enough to be around today. I know I keep calling him a lad because he must be about fifty by now but I will always picture him and Thomas as young boys, playing together."

"No wonder he made you so proud, if he was like that," said Luke, who had been hanging altruistically onto Lillian's every word. "It would have been wonderful to have known him. If only I could have had someone like him as a friend whilst I was growing up, I might not be in the mess…" *Oh my god, I really need to be careful what I say*, he thought, *if she knew the whole truth she wouldn't want me here. I hope to God she didn't notice*. Luke believed he was stealthily shrewd in realising his error quickly enough to rectify it before it was too late to prevent Lillian noticing and begin to interrogate him for further information.

It *hadn't* gone unnoticed by Lillian that Luke had momentarily allowed his guard to drop, surreptitiously permitting the frightened young lad with no direction in his life to briefly emerge as the *real* Luke. She felt that it probably wouldn't be too much longer before he did eventually open up to her but she wasn't going to press the matter further, just yet, as he clearly felt very conscious about revealing too much.

Before she continued telling Luke about her son, she shot him a warming maternal smile. "Thomas, despite his good natured side, had his father's impetuous temperament and would always become involved in things without really weighing up any of the consequences. It was this impulsive side to him that was ultimately his undoing."

There was the slightest pause, as Luke could see that Lillian was fighting an ephemeral battle with the emotions that were rising within her throat. Her hard cough was the power weapon that claimed the victory, as she continued. "It wasn't that long after his seventeenth birthday, he was involved in an horrific motorbike accident with several of his friends. Silly, silly, silly boys who all thought they were invincible and indestructible…"

Luke could feel the hairs on his arms, neck and the back of his head all stand on end, as several shivers went up his spine in anticipation of what was coming next.

"…Thomas was the only fatality within the group. The other boys had, apart from a few broken bones, only suffered fairly minor injuries. I think that one incident changed all those boys' outlook on their lives, as I don't think I saw any of them ride a motorbike again.

"I suppose you could say that with the loss of both my husband and son, I opened this bed and breakfast as a memory to them, where it gave me the opportunity to look after people and, some might say, fuss over them. So, that brings me to the here and now…"

Lillian's train of thought had been mentally building up to this exact point throughout the course of the evening. *It's now or never*, she thought, believing that this was the perfect time. She had long since determined already that Luke would not be the type of person to accept a charitable hand-out, as he would allow pride to stand in the way of what might be considered as his better judgment. *No, that would not be the best way to handle this. I need him to believe that he's doing me a favour, rather than the other way around.*

"…I'm seventy six years old now and need to start realising that I'm not as agile as I used to be. I'm way too old to be running an establishment such as this all by myself and so I need to find someone whom I can rely on, who wouldn't be afraid of hard work and long hours. I need to ensure that it's someone who will understand, treasure and uphold the legacy that I've set up."

Although Luke found himself praying several times throughout his short life, he had never thought of himself as particularly religious or spiritual. However, he *did* ask God for a miracle to happen and he thought, perhaps, that this was exactly what was being offered to him. He would be a fool not to jump at the chance of a permanent roof over his head, as well as the assured decent meals every day.

"Why do you need to look for someone else?" asked Luke, taking in a deep breath as if he were sucking in extra courage. "What about me? I'd be more than happy to roll my sleeves up and get involved."

Lillian rubbed her chin, with her eyes fixed onto one spot, as if contemplating Luke's offer. "I *could* trial you I suppose but I would expect total honesty and full commitment at all times. I didn't expect anything less

The Absence of Friends

from my husband or my son and I don't see why you should be any different… but then, I don't want to impose on whatever your future plans are."

"My future plans?"

"Yes. I understood you were only planning on staying for a few more days, to do a bit more sightseeing of the area before you were off to do whatever it is you have lined up to do."

"I…um…I thought…" Luke was unable to think of something quickly enough to respond satisfactorily to Lillian's statement but before he could stop himself, he found himself blurting out: "…I don't actually have any future plans."

"So indeed shall the truth finally become unleashed for those who choose to persevere, for others, in helping to overcome the greatest of life's misgivings and thus bestowing upon them the rewards of their labours, whence they shall rejoice in twain," Lillian said softly, as though she had reached the crux of a personal testimony. "I may be an old woman, Luke, but I am certainly no fool.

"You know," she continued, her face softening, "you actually remind me of my husband when I first met him; with his steely determination and the laboured decisions he felt he had to make alone. However, though you possess the maddening impetuosity of Thomas, you do also have his decorous and genteel traits and I certainly don't wish to see yet another man's life destroyed by silly mistakes and grossly miscalculated judgments that could so easily have been avoided.

"It *will* be hard work though, Luke." Her eyes narrowed as she carried on, "There will be no time for any extraneous, extracurricular activities…"

Luke swallowed hard, as he felt his cheeks become slightly flushed, wondering exactly what Lillian meant by that last remark. *Does she actually know what I've been up to over the past few days?* He quickly dismissed this notion, as there was no way on earth that she could possibly know. She was an extraordinary woman though - there was no doubting that - but he couldn't decide whether he should be delighted or unsettled by this prospect.

"…Still," Lillian went on, "we *have* got on very well together over the past few days and I have to say, it *is* lovely to have a young man around the house again. I really want you to make something of your life, Luke. Don't allow yourself to become trapped in the past but look to the future and concentrate on living your dreams. Find happiness for yourself."

Making something of your life! Find happiness! It was his mother's words all over again. All the torment he had carried, all the pain he had suffered and all the struggles he had faced suddenly hit Luke like a hard, stinging slap across the face, as his stoic demeanor crumbled dramatically and he yielded to the emotions that he had bottled up for so long.

For the next hour, Luke found himself pouring his heart out to Lillian amidst the constant flow of tears that seemed as though they would never cease. He confided in her about his father's brutality, his brothers' tragic death, his mother's acts of true love, as well as the rapid decline of her character after his father's death and how he longed to follow in his mother's footsteps to become a singer.

"Well then," Lillian said positively, "let's decide to make today the first day of your new life, shall we?"

"I don't quite know what you mean," he said, taking the box of tissues that she had offered him and wiping his tear stained face.

"I want you to live here, with me. You will have a place that you can call your home and your meals will all be provided for you. All I ask for in return though, is if you can help me with the general day-to-day running of the B&B."

Luke almost tripped over his legs as he ran around to Lillian and flung his arms around her. "I won't let you down. I promise. You've a very kind heart and I will *not* disappoint or betray your trust and faith in me."

Lillian's eyes sparkled, lighting up her entire face. "You've got yourself some dreams, Luke. If you're going to realise those dreams, then let's do it together."

CHAPTER THREE

Kristian Irwin was born on 7 May 1968 in the City of Leicester.

He and his sister Phoebe, who was three years older, experienced very disruptive childhoods as their parents Sean and Anna-Leigh were involved in a very tempestuous relationship. Neither could apparently live without the other, even though verbal fireworks were often a main feature of their partnership. The principal cause of the majority of their arguments were centred on trust issues, mainly stemming from Sean's insecurities.

When Anna-Leigh had announced to her parents that Sean had asked her to marry him, they quizzed their daughter incessantly, ensuring that she was making the right decision. They pointed out that Sean was considerably younger than her, where his immaturity shone through more often than not. Ignoring her parents' protestations, Anna-Leigh married Sean a mere fortnight before she turned twenty-six and two months after Sean had turned eighteen.

There was rarely a day that went by that Anna-Leigh and Sean weren't locked in a heated quarrel for some reason or other, usually revolved around who the other had been socialising with, what they had been up to and finally degenerating into dragging up historical spates. Woe betide the individual, when it was unearthed, who had chosen to socialise with a sole member of the opposite sex, as this was guaranteed to be the fuse that caused the most prolonged of their arguments. On the rare occasions that they weren't sealed in an argumentative battle, they were giving each other the silent treatment in the cataclysmic aftermath. In spite of the odds being stacked against their relationship standing the test of time, they managed over ten years together, as husband and wife. They might have seen a further ten years, had Sean not committed a cardinal sin, causing Anna-Leigh to walk out on him and file to set divorce proceedings in motion.

"So, remind me, which one of your string of fancy men is it that you're going to be seeing today?" sneered Sean.

Anna-Leigh sighed hopelessly at the repetitive line of interrogation she faced each time she was invited to have lunch with one of her male friends; not that she had that many, as Sean had made sure of that on many an occasion. "I don't know where you get these fantastical ideas from. I *do not* have any fancy men, Sean!"

"Russell. Craig. Martin. Daryl. I know I could list plenty of others but do I really need to go on?" He didn't give his wife the courtesy of waiting for a response; not that she would have graced him with one anyway. "You seem to have a lot more time for *them* than you do for me."

"Let it go, Sean…just let it go, 'cause I can't take your crap anymore!"

"*My* crap?" Sean almost choked on a forced laugh. "Oh, honey, if you weren't out and about gallivanting and goodness knows what else with any old Tom, Dick and Harry, there wouldn't be *any* crap for us to deal with! You know, this could all be ended now if you cancelled your *lunch* date."

"Who the hell do you think you are, telling me who I can or can't see?" Anna-Leigh screamed at Sean.

"I'm your bloody husband, that's who I am! And I don't particularly relish the thought of having a tart as a wife!"

"*Nothing* damn well happens! Certainly not what you're thinking of," she spat. "How many times do I need to tell you that? If I say I'm having lunch, then that's *exactly* what I'm doing!" Her eyes glared right through him, stinging with an angry mist. "And how dare you insinuate that I'm a tart."

"Methinks the lady doth protest too much, 'cause the cap certainly fits and it fits very well!"

Anna-Leigh elicited another disparagingly exasperated sigh. "God, you're pathetic, you really are. I sometimes wonder how on earth you managed to create the two beautiful children we have, as you are nothing but a disgustingly weak excuse of a man!"

"Well, sometimes I wonder if they *are* actually mine!"

"What?" Anna-Leigh croaked.

"Do I have to spell it out for you?"

"Please do," she said tersely, pursing her lips and adopting a defiant stance with her hands on her hips. "But I warn you…tread very carefully with what you say!"

"Think about it," he said, pausing for a moment before continuing. "When you're with me, we argue. The times when we don't argue, we're not *actually* talking to each other! You don't hide the fact that I apparently make your skin crawl at times…and of course, you spend more time whoring with other men than you do with me. Is it any wonder that I have my doubts that the children are mine?"

Anna-Leigh's blood began to boil to a point where she found herself begin to perspire. "You've gone too far this time, Sean. I have put up with a lot of your bullshit over the years, with your constant interrogations of the hows, the whys and the wherefores just to satiate your juvenile insecurities…"

Sean began waving a finger as he opened his mouth to retaliate.

"…Don't you *dare* say a word," she hissed slowly, whilst the proverbial daggers were being shot from her acrimonious eyes. "You've said more than enough already. You know, my parents were always against us marrying because they thought you were too immature to handle being a husband, let alone a father. I can see now that they were absolutely right in their assumptions."

"But I..."

Anna-Leigh's glare cut him dead before he could finish his sentence. "I have put up with being humiliated by your name-calling, smothered by your petty jealousies and have even suffered with, although god knows why, your overbearing and controlling nature. What I will *not* stand for, is being thought of as a tart and a whore and I am mortally offended and hurt that you would ever consider suggesting that the children are not yours. I am bitterly ashamed of you."

"If I can..."

She continued ignoring him. "To be honest, I'm sick to the back teeth of you and your puerile indoctrination of my worth as a wife and mother. In fact, I'm not even sure I can truthfully say I love you anymore. Sean, I want a divorce!"

Anna-Leigh closed the front door of the Irwin household for the final time in the summer that Kristian had turned three years old. She agreed with her soon to be ex-husband that they would have fortnightly custody of both Phoebe and Kristian.

In the early years, both children found it quite thrilling that they were able to make two sets of friends at their respective schools, which was especially exciting at birthday times, as it meant that they would always be assured of two parties and double the amount of presents. In the later years, however, they both hungered for some stability in their lives and often found themselves talking together about which parent they would prefer to live with on a more permanent basis.

Whenever they stayed with their mother, she would take them on outings to theme parks, zoos, funfairs and other fun-filled activities. Although Kristian didn't deny that he enjoyed all these outings, he far preferred the time that he spent with his father. He would often spend hours watching, with interest, whilst Sean was mending the car or doing various odd jobs around the house. Phoebe would just stay in her bedroom and play with her dolls, upset that her father was not paying her all the attention; she always made sure that she reported back to her mother the lack of interest her father was showing her.

By the time Kristian had reached the age of eight, instead of just watching his father, he decided that he would rather help out with the jobs. He enjoyed the satisfaction he felt when a job was completed, especially when it had something to do with mending the car. The more that he helped his father, the more he knew what he wanted to do as a career when he left school.

Kristian hated his years at school. He found it extremely difficult to make anything but a handful of friends and became somewhat of a loner in the times when his friends were otherwise occupied. The other school children would poke fun at him and call him hurtful and spiteful names. He no longer hated school, he loathed it. No, he detested it with a passion that he never thought could exist within him. He wished the other children would just leave him alone, to be alone to do his own thing. The only two things that he enjoyed in his life was to spend time on his own, or helping his father out with chores.

At sixteen, he was glad to leave his school years behind him, as he looked forward to starting the long-awaited course in Mechanical Engineering. All his efforts were put into his studying. Every spare minute he had was spent with his head buried in books on mechanics and engineering. When he wasn't swamped with books and papers for his coursework, he had his head under the bonnet of his father's car.

Kristian was amongst the top ten percent of those who had passed the course. His desire to better himself remained unquenched, as he wanted to go further in his studies and become the best of the best within the trade. He found himself a three year course to register himself on, in London; so at twenty years old, he tried hard to fight back the tears, as he bid an emotional farewell to his father, in order to move to London. Sean was more than impressed with Kristian's achievements thus far and sent him on his way to London with a manly hug and pat on the back, together with all the luck in the world to do the best that he could.

The three years' that he studied in London were far more draining and tiring than the four years he had done in Leicester. Now that he was much older, he found it a lot easier to make friends, but he would still make little to no effort to socialise like the rest of the students. This was all about to dramatically change when he was introduced to Elliot Hayden, two years after enrolling onto his course.

He liked Elliot instantly.

Perhaps, he thought, a little more than he first cared to admit.

Elliot Hayden was born on 27 April 1968 in London's Walthamstow.

He was an only child; not that his parents didn't often try for a brother or sister for him but as the years rolled by, this was looking increasingly unlikely as a possibility.

His father, Peter, was a gym instructor at the boys' secondary school that he would be attending; not that Elliot would ever get the chance to see him at

The Absence of Friends

the school, as Peter had secured himself a new post within another school the year before Elliot was due to start. His mother, Judith, was the Manager at one of the local big superstore food chains, where the family's groceries were always purchased.

Elliot took a great deal of pride in his physical appearance, where he would challenge himself every other day to an intense workout programme at the gym. On the days that he wasn't to be found at the gym, he was at his local swimming pool, where he would spend anywhere between ninety minutes and two hours on completing one hundred laps. Several times his father would accompany him, in order to keep track of the time he spent in order to finish and encouraging him to better the previous time. Both his parents were convinced that Elliot would go into swimming professionally and maybe even work at possibly competing at a future Olympics. They were genuinely surprised when this turned out not to be the direction that Elliot actually wanted his career to go.

As a tangent from his exertive workouts and swimming, he found himself drawn into taking up dancing. The older he became, the more serious he found that he was taking his dancing and this, he decided, was direction he wanted to go into professionally. Whilst being very intent to succeed in his dancing abilities, which he was certainly doing with great gusto, he also wanted to turn his talents into acting.

At the age of fourteen, he joined an Amateur Dance and Dramatics Society, setting his mind on achieving the goal that his standard be considered good enough to be recommended by his coach and put forward for an audition, which was to be held in Birmingham. Six weeks before his fifteenth birthday, he made his professional acting and dancing debut in *Footloose And Fancy Free*, at the Royale Theatre in Birmingham. Elliot was over-the-moon that he had received highly acclaimed reviews by the media critics, where one newspaper described him as '*an excellent talent - watch out for this rising star, as he will go far*'. By the time he reached his seventeenth birthday, the offers were flooding in, whereupon he asked his parents to be his manager and agent. At nineteen, he had performed in theatres all over England, Scotland and Wales. No matter how hard the critics tried, they just couldn't find any flaws within his performances to injure his ever-rising and successful career.

Surprising both his parents, Elliot coped very well with his stardom, not allowing the fame and financial rewards to go to his head. Over the following two years, his talents stretched into Europe and his parents would always travel with him wherever he went.

It was at the lavish party for his twenty-first birthday that he first met the woman who would eventually go on to become his fiancée. Elliot strongly believed in old-fashioned traditions, so was somewhat taken aback when she was making all the advances on him.

"I know it's an open bar," she said coquettishly, "but I'd really like to buy you a drink."

Having been caught slightly off-guard by the offer from the beautiful woman in front of him, Elliot was momentarily stunned into silence. He quickly recovered and in the boldest tone he could muster said, "that would be lovely. I'd like a champagne please."

The woman confidently grabbed two flutes of champagne from a passing waiter, nodding her head graciously as she did so and returned to Elliot, who was patiently awaiting her return.

"My name's Maxine," she said, with a flutter of her eyelids.

"Thank you, Maxine" he said, taking the flute from her, as she took the opportunity to touch his hand for a little longer than was necessary.

"I've seen you in a couple of shows that you've done," she said in a self-assured tone. "I have to say though, that being up close and personal with you, you are far more handsome than the photos in the programmes would lead you to believe."

Elliot blushed. "Thanks again…I think."

They talked for nearly an hour before Maxine hoped that she had made enough of an impression on Elliot to leave him wanting more, especially as she had, without verbally saying so, shown her exact intentions by giving him a couple of lingering kisses. "This is my telephone number," she said, writing on a piece of paper, "and I would love for you to give me a call some time…maybe we could go out on a date, far from the maddening crowd."

Maxine, who was herself not far from turning twenty-one, rarely escaped without at least a second glance from most men. She often heard the comments that these men made to their male friends, such as: "God, she's absolutely stunning," or "she's so beautiful, she could easily make millions for her looks," or even, "she looks as though she should be a model." For those who didn't actually know her, they couldn't appreciate the irony of her words, as Maxine *was* a model.

Maxine had actually been christened Siobhan Katharina Darlington, being the daughter of Lord and Lady Darlington, but due to her modelling career, a pseudonym was needed. The name change was helped by the fact that she hated her real name from the outset, as some people couldn't or more likely wouldn't pronounce it correctly, so decided to be known as her alias; she felt it mirrored her personality perfectly: plain and simple but with fashionable elegance.

The Absence of Friends

It was nearly four months after Elliot's twenty-second birthday that he and Maxine announced their engagement, much to the delight of both his parents. Over the course of the past few months they had both met her several times and fallen in love with her almost immediately, both longing and praying that their son would honour them by making Maxine their daughter-in-law.

Maxine's parents, on the other hand, tried to persuade her against the marriage as they thought that she was marrying beneath herself. "You should be marrying aristocracy," her stepmother had told her.

Although Elliot truly believed he was in love with Maxine, he thought that something was amiss with their relationship but couldn't quite work out what it was.

Working as a model, Maxine would often mix with a lot of gay men, many of whom went on to become her very good friends, who would invite her to parties, pubs or clubs; she enjoyed and valued their company much more than some of her straight friends. It was only a month after the engagement had been announced that Maxine was invited to a flamboyant party of one of her closest gay friends and she was literally ordered to bring Elliot along too, as more men at the party would certainly make it all the more merrier. Some of Maxine's gay friends didn't hide the fact that they found Elliot incredibly attractive and there were those that would even go as far as to reveal to her, in the greatest of detail, exactly what they would like to do with him. Many of them tried their luck in asking Maxine to give Elliot their telephone number, should she ever see the light of day and finish with him. Maxine would always respond by rolling her eyes and letting out an exasperated sigh.

Maxine had the enviable ability to persuade just about anyone to do almost anything that she asked, so it came as no surprise to her when Elliot eventually agreed to go along to the party with her.

To those who knew Kristian, trying to persuade him to go along to the party would seem like a totally hopeless task that would best be written off before it had actually begun. Not to Michael though, as once he had set his mind on achieving something, even if it were to take an eternity, he would persist until he reached a successful conclusion. He certainly wasn't going to let a small issue such as time constraints intimidate him into so easily giving up.

Michael Hart was Kristian's closest friend at college and even though he knew that Michael was gay, this didn't bother him in the slightest, as he had already begun questioning his own sexuality. On the rare moments he allowed himself to relax - Michael constantly told Kristian that he needed to relax more - he would seek Michael out and ask him what it was like to be gay, about the places he went and the people that he met and mixed with. Michael told him about the different kinds of gay people on the scene, the places to go to for casual sex, with no strings attached and the best clubs in town.

Michael had already set himself an almost unfeasible challenge of somehow getting Kristian to go to a gay club, or at least a gay pub, as he knew that Kristian was itching to experiment with gay life. Whenever he asked, Kristian would always decline, saying that he was too busy with his studies. *How on earth is he ever going to know what team he is batting for*, thought Michael, *if he isn't even prepared to participate in the try-outs?* However, the opportunity was being handed to Michael on a platter of gold, which he would ensure was laced with all the glitz and glam that he could muster. If Kristian wouldn't go to a pub or club, he would more than likely go to a party and the place would be teeming with gay life. Michael was genuinely surprised at how little effort it took to persuade Kristian to go, as he thought that hell would have frozen over first before Kristian ever agreed to part from his precious studies.

The big night had arrived, where Michael was looking forward to seeing exactly how Kristian would react and cope with being thrown into the proverbial lion's den; directly into the iniquitous epicentre that featured a mass of voracious gay men, who would be waiting to devour anyone who might smell like fresh meat. Michael had taken Kristian out shopping for a whole new outfit for the party, so he felt confident that they were both dressed to impress.

"Hey Max! You're looking absolutely and disgustingly gorge tonight," squealed Michael.

Maxine rushed over to him, flinging her arms around his neck as she kissed him. "How ya doing, sexy?"

"Not so bad. Studying hard, but bearing up under the strain, if you know what I mean. I couldn't miss tonight. Really, I couldn't, not for anything. I thought, come hell or high water, I would be the belle of the ball. Do you know what I'm saying?"

"Absolutely," said Maxine. Taking hold of Elliot's hand, she continued, "Remember I told you about Elliot? Well, Michael, meet Elliot. Elliot, meet Michael."

Michael eyed Elliot thoroughly, drawing in his breath. "Wow!" he exclaimed, "You're one hell of a bitch Maxine Wyatt, a total harlot without a heart! The only person here who is worthy of a second glance is not only straight, but he's with *you*." He pretended to sob. "How could you be so callous?"

Maxine tittered like a schoolgirl.

Elliot appeared bemused by the whole charade that was unfolding before him.

"If this woman ever comes to her senses and leaves you," he said to Elliot, "you'll find me waiting for you at the aptly named *Studs* bar."

Elliot smiled nervously, unsure of what to make of this effervescent character in front of him and whether he was genuinely flirting with him.

"I know how to treat a real man. I wouldn't drag you around the likes of Mothercare and Chelsea Girl." He paused for effect. "Well, actually, on second thoughts, I probably would," he giggled cynically.

Maxine cut in, "Michael! You're one hell of a rude, little boy."

With false surprise he asked: "Who? Little, old me?

"Yes, you."

"I've said nothing." He looked at Elliot and raised an eyebrow suggestively before adding, "yet!"

"I'm not on about that, if you will only behave for one moment," she winced, slapping Michael playfully on the arm. "You haven't introduced us to your friend."

Michael grasped delicately at his throat, in mock horror. "Oh God, will you just clutch my pearls? How could I be such an ignorant bitch?"

Kristian, who was standing behind Michael, was stunned by the whole scene he had just witnessed.

"Max, Elliot, this is Kristian." He took a dramatic step aside so Kristian could move in closer. "He's studying with me on the same course, which is a real boon."

Both Maxine and Elliot greeted Kristian with a polite handshake.

"He's my roommate too," continued Michael. "Terribly shy, if you know what I mean."

"Shy? More like shell-shocked!" Maxine turned to Kristian and said: "How could someone as charming and prudent as you have a friend like him? And living with him too! I have a great deal of admiration for you."

"Now, now Max," said Michael, before Kristian had a chance to say anything, "don't be so catty, it doesn't become you nor does it go with what you're wearing! Those claws of yours are obviously too long. I will rip them off viciously if you can't use them sensibly."

Maxine grinned at him.

Taking her by the arm, he murmured, "Let's leave these two alone to some much needed betty talk whilst I introduce you to Roger. He's a real scream."

"Sure."

Michael touched Elliot's shoulder and winked at him. "I'll see *you* later."

Elliot and Kristian watched in amazement as the two most talkative of their group skipped through the crowds on their quest for Roger, both men wondering if Roger would be up to the challenge to verbally compete with Michael.

Elliot took a step closer to Kristian. "Well, he was certainly one hell of a character."

"There's never a dull moment with Michael around."

"I can imagine."

"So, Maxine's your girlfriend?"

"Yes. Well, no, actually she's my fiancée."

"She's very beautiful."

Elliot nodded. "She certainly is."

They talked for a while before Elliot offered to buy Kristian a drink, where they spent the rest of the evening talking, laughing and exchanging stories about the respective people with whom they came. Both men found themselves to be quite comfortable in each other's company and began to open up to each other about rather personal issues.

"I've really enjoyed myself tonight," said Elliot.

"Me too."

"Would you like to go out for a drink sometime?"

"Sure. Why not."

"Are you on the phone?"

"Yeah. Do you have a pen and paper?"

Elliot nodded and handed Kristian a pen and paper he had inside his jacket pocket. Kristian returned the pen and paper, with his telephone number written upon it.

"Bring Maxine along too if you want."

"Sure."

"I really must go and find Michael and think about going home," said Kristian, sneaking a glance at his watch. "God only knows who he is attempting to offend now. If there is anybody left for him to offend!"

Elliot smiled at the remark, thinking many people could be easily offended by Michael's acerbic sense of humour if they didn't know him. "Would you like a lift?" he asked.

"I've got my car, but thanks anyway."

They parted company with a warm handshake. Kristian wondered if Elliot may have held onto his hand a little longer than was necessary; not that he would have minded if this were the case. But in spite of his attraction toward Elliot, it was never going to get any more physical than a handshake, despite its warmth.

"It was really nice meeting you, Kristian."

"Likewise…and please, call me Kris. It's really only Michael…and my parents who call me Kristian."

"I'll give you a call."

"Please do." Kristian smiled a little too fervently at Elliot, as he turned to begin his search for Michael.

"Tell me you're joking. You *are* joking, aren't you?"

"No! I'm deadly serious"

Michael screamed. "You bitch, Kristian! He was supposed to be mine."

"I'm sorry, Michael but what could I do?"

"All *I* want to do now is drown myself in a bucket of gin!" Michael sighed.

"It just happened," sputtered Kristian, trying desperately to hold back the laughter at Michael's response.

"Things like that don't *just* happen." He looked at Kristian through narrowed eyes for a few moments before continuing. "Ah well…you win some, you lose some, I guess."

"I knew, if anyone was going to understand *los dramas del corazón*, it was going to be you."

It may have been Kristian's use of the Spanish language but, as if it were merely a veil being lifted, Michael's chagrin vanished and he was back to his usual self. "Oh, darling you know me just a little too well. Dramas. Me. Glove. Hand. So, tell me everything. The whole nitty gritty, unless it's too gruesome, then I don't want to know…oh, who am I kidding? Yes, of course I want to know. Don't leave *anything* out…I want to know everything…every sordid and disgusting minute detail!"

"There's not much to tell really. We've met several times and then…"

"You've slept with him! Haven't you?"

"Michael!"

"I thought so. I always had my suspicions about the gorgeous, *straight*, Elliot."

Kristian revealed to Michael how it had all stemmed from the party. He had actually been surprised, albeit pleasantly, when Elliot had asked for his number. He had received a telephone call from Elliot several days after the party, thanking God that Michael hadn't been around that day. He wanted to keep whatever happened between him and Elliot a close kept secret, a word that was conveniently not apparent in Michael's *extensive* vocabulary, as he had sorely discovered on several occasions. Elliot had never bought Maxine with him on any of their first few "liaisons", which is what Michael said they were: "a sneaky and sleazy meeting, unnecessarily clandestine". She was allegedly busy doing other things, or so Elliot had always told him.

The two men began meeting up nearly every day, with Elliot finding it quite easy to come up with excuses for Maxine, so he could be with Kristian. The more they saw of each other, the more they enjoyed each other's company. It was the Saturday before Christmas that Elliot opened up to Kristian, telling him he liked him more than just a friend. They ended up in bed for the first time together that afternoon, not wanting their time together to finish. Elliot finally realised exactly what it was that was missing from his relationship with Maxine. He never wanted to hurt Maxine but in the long run, it would be better to break off the relationship with her sooner, rather than later and he attempted to explain to her in the easiest and most sensitive way he could. She appeared to take it a whole lot better than Elliot thought she might and said that she had expected something like this to happen, as aspects of their relationship just didn't add up.

Not long after Christmas, Kristian couldn't keep his growing relationship with Elliot a secret any longer from Michael, who couldn't believe what he was hearing when Kristian confessed that he was falling in love with Elliot.

"Tell me you're joking. You *are* joking, aren't you?"

"No! I'm deadly serious."

Elliot and Kristian's relationship continued to go from strength to strength. It appeared that nothing could separate the two of them, as they finally sealed their commitment together, buying a house in Ealing in October, at the mark of their third anniversary of when they had met at the party.

Kristian set up his own DIY business, advertising his services, which covered most things from painting and decorating to mechanics, although the embryonic stages of his business was not without its teething problems. On a few occasions he found himself threatening to give up "the whole crazy venture." Elliot's confidence in him kept him going through the difficult periods. By the turn of the new decade, Kristian's business actually showed signs of profit and he began to look into hiring new staff.

Elliot made his television debut shortly before he was due to turn twenty-four, in a television-made version of a West End musical. He recorded the programme, refusing to let Kristian record over it.

"It has to be kept for posterity," Elliot told him.

"You'll live to regret it," Kristian responded.

"Why?"

The Absence of Friends

"God, can you imagine watching it in twenty years' time and thinking to yourself, *Jesus, did I really look like that?*"

"That's not the point, as well you know."

It didn't worry either of them that they had very few friends, as they enjoyed each other's company too much and preferred to keep themselves very much to themselves.

However, that all changed when they met Luke Faraday.

It was in the height of summer, after Luke had been working with Lillian for just over two years, that his emotions underwent a convoluted turn of events. He felt he was trapped in the middle of a tumultuous whirlwind of emotions, where the mêlée of joy, fear, anger and pain he felt simultaneously were all waging a covert battle within him.

"Live the dream, Luke. For your mother and for me," were the final words that Luke would hear Lillian say to him. He had already telephoned for an ambulance, as he held on to her sallow and ice-cold hand; his eyes already red-raw from the endless tears he had shed. He wanted to stay brave for Lillian's sake but she had emerged as somewhat of a grandmother figure to him, rather than his employer and therefore, it proved difficult to falsify what he truly felt. When she was pronounced dead from a massive coronary, after the paramedics had arrived, Luke refused to believe that he would never get the opportunity to see her again.

He opened the letter that the executor of Lillian's estate had given him and began to read:

My dearest Luke,

Over the short period of time that we have known each other, I have become incredibly fond of you, as you have often reminded me of Thomas when he was your age. My one regret in life was that I never got the opportunity to have a grandchild, as you would have been exactly the grandson I would have wanted.

Believe me, I know it's never easy to lose someone who is very close to you and whilst I do not wish to disparage any emotion that you may be feeling at the moment, I don't want you to dwell on the negative side for too long.

You have fast become the closest thing to family for me. I know that Paul and Thomas had dreams of their own, which they never got to realise and I certainly don't want you to end up in a position where you would end up neglecting your own dreams.

I wish to bequeath you the bed and breakfast, which I know was my own personal dream, so I would hope that you sell it and not feel obliged to hold on to it, just in the belief that it will keep my memories alive. The house does not retain the memories of the times we shared, you hold them within yourself.

I have complete faith in your artistic abilities, so I wish to stand by my convictions and as a final gift to you, bequeath the sum of £10,000, which I know will set you travelling on the road to stardom that you so richly deserve.

Leave the past exactly where it belongs, Luke and go and live your dream for yourself, your mother and for me.

With eternal love, Lillian.

The tenacious flow of tears seemed as though they would never come to an end, as it finally dawned on Luke that he was once again all alone. At least, as a twenty year old, he was significantly more astute, cognitive and worldly-wise. As an act of sheer defiance against the odds that history might repeat itself when he first came to London, he tenaciously vowed to pursue his passion for singing and dedicate his debut album to Lillian, with a personal eulogy to her expressing his heartfelt thanks for her belief in him.

He reluctantly sold the bed and breakfast, although he knew he had no other option than to do so and bought himself a flat in Islington. He took with him a solitary treasured item that would become a constant source of inspiration to him. It was a painting of Lillian, her husband, Paul and her son, Thomas. Lillian had commissioned an artist friend of hers to innovatively create the picture from two separate photographs she had, making it appear as though it had only ever been created from a single one.

He tastefully furnished his new flat, injecting some youthful exuberance into his styling. Whilst organising his new homestead, he registered himself onto a course at the Royal Academy of Music and Performing Arts. It took two years for Luke to reach being known as *'an exceptionally outstanding talent'* at the Academy, where many people envied both his singing and acting abilities.

He knew that the money he had wouldn't last him an eternity, so he secured himself an evening job, working behind the bar in a gay club called *Jumbos*. Having turned into adulthood, his facial and physical characteristics had begun to determine that he was a very good looking young man and heard such comments from some of the guys at the bar.

When the Manager of *Jumbos* was made aware of Luke's singing and acting abilities, he decided to offer him the chance to do an evening's entertainment. "If the guys like you here," said the Manager, "then we'll talk about offering you a regular slot and what sort of money we can offer you." On the evening that Luke took to the stage at *Jumbos*, it was to be a turning point in his life,

The Absence of Friends

as well as that of the club. The guys loved and admired Luke's singing just as much they did his body; and *Jumbos'* clientele dramatically rose in number after his performance. True to the Manager's word, that night, the both of them were discussing his future at the club. Luke accepted the offer he was given and the Manager found that his latest business transaction was of great financial benefit to him; never had he seen his club so busy on the nights that Luke was performing.

Even though life was beginning to settle for Luke, after losing Lillian, he never stopped writing regularly to his mother, keeping her informed of what was happening. He found himself sitting in his flat one afternoon, reading a letter from his mother, telling him that he should stay in London and continue with his new found life. She was more than a little embarrassed about her past and didn't wish Luke to return to Southampton after her release and witness the state in which she had become. Although this letter saddened Luke, he could understand how difficult it must have been for her to write this.

It was one night in December that a Casting Director of a newly written musical that was hoping to be debuted in the West End later the following year, spotted him performing at the club. "I'd really like you to come and audition for this musical," he said, taking a card from inside his jacket pocket and offering it to Luke. "This is my card. Please be in my office at 10.00am sharp tomorrow morning." Luke was, by far, the most outstanding of those who were asked to audition and he was instantly offered one of the leading roles. Several months later Luke made his long-awaited acting and singing debut to the world. He thought of how proud both his mother and Lillian would have been and cried out: "I've done it. I have really, really done it."

Luke's friendship with Kristian Irwin and Elliot Hayden developed entirely through an innocent accident, whilst he was performing his final number at *Jumbos*. He would always pick on someone from the crowd to come on stage and help him for his spectacular finale, which all the punters loved. This particular evening, which was several weeks after his twenty second birthday, he picked Kristian from the crowd. "C'mon guys, let's give him some encouragement…give him a round of applause." As Kristian walked on to the stage, to the round of applause, he tripped over the wire of the microphone, causing him to fall. Even though Kristian was doomed to fall flat on his face, no doubt costing him to feel mortified for several minutes afterwards; his inevitable ending appeared to occur in slow motion to him. His instincts naturally led him to grab Luke for support but he only succeeded in knocking Luke's drink from his hand, spilling it all over the both of them. Luke was caught completely off balance and fell to the floor, with Kristian landing on top of him. Kristian was the first to recover and quickly returned to his feet, offering his outstretched arm to help Luke up from the floor, who instantly picked up the microphone and thinking of a joke, spoke into it: "If you wanted to take me home young man, all you needed to do was ask!" The crowd roared with laughter. "What's your name?"

Luke held the microphone closer to Kristian so he could speak. "You mean to tell me, after a year together, you *still* don't know my name?" he joked. Luke laughed with the crowd, as Kristian continued, "I'll tell you again, it's Kris."

"Well, Kris, shall we get on with it then? The show, I mean."

Luke and Kristian's finale was a show that would not be forgotten in a hurry, literally being the best finale in both humour and style that Luke had done with an audience member. Many of the punters couldn't stop talking about it; even after some weeks had gone by, their act was still mentioned in conversations.

"A huge round of applause for Kris," called Luke, in a manner that was designed to get the crowd whipped up into a frenzied, almost hysterical round of applause. The crowd responded, as Luke had expected, with a deafening reception of applauding, yelling and whistling. Switching off the microphone, Luke turned to Kristian and said, "I'm really sorry about earlier. Let me buy you a drink after I've changed."

"Okay," replied Kristian, not expecting to see Luke at all, as he thought he was only being polite, so was very surprised when, twenty minutes later, he received the promised drink.

"I really am sorry about earlier."

"That's okay. Anyway, I think everyone presumed it was part of the act. They seemed to love what we did."

Kristian and Luke continued to talk for the remainder of the evening. "Would you like to come back for a coffee?" Kristian asked. "I'm not trying to come on to you. Elliot, my boyfriend, is at home. He loves your singing and will be ever so jealous that he didn't come out tonight."

Luke tried to conceal the apprehension in his voice, even though he thought Kristian to be genuine. "All right, you've got yourself a deal." In the two years Luke had been working at *Jumbos*, he had only gone off with one guy, and even that had resulted in an emotional nightmare. He didn't want to make the same mistake again. True to Kristian's word, Elliot was fuming with himself, but delighted that Luke had come round. They talked, laughed and sang, before they fell asleep in a drunken stupor.

The emotional nightmare had begun within weeks of Luke starting his musical career at *Jumbos*. He had finished his stint of vocal entertainment for the evening and decided to have a quiet drink at the bar before heading home,

The Absence of Friends

when a good-looking guy who introduced himself as Aaron Howard approached him. Aaron was twenty-nine years old and worked as an independent painter and decorator. Luke was mystically drawn in by the aromatic smell of the sensually potent aftershave that Aaron was wearing, which matched the expense of the designer clothes that he was dressed in. Aaron was very hasty in revealing that he was more than a little turned-on by Luke and in suggesting that he should come back to his place for some fun. Even though Luke turned down the tempting offer, Aaron was incredibly persistent and wouldn't take "*no*" as a viable answer. He did find Aaron very attractive and desirable, but he was put off by his slightly aggressive and overbearing personality. Eventually, more out of hopeless realisation that Aaron seemingly would never give up on his incessant pursuit of him than because he really wanted to, Luke half-heartedly agreed. He would have much preferred to have gone straight home and to the comfort of his own bed, than back with someone else.

As Aaron owned a car, he suggested they should drive back to his house. Luke, in the future, would never make the mistake of getting into someone's car again without at least memorising the car's number plate first.

The car stopped by a woodland area, as Luke needed to relieve himself. He made his way into the thick of the trees, unaware that Aaron had followed him. After Luke had finished, Aaron grabbed him, making Luke jump. Aaron pinned him forcefully to a tree and kissed him; not passionately, but with forceful aggression, biting him on his lips. Luke struggled to free himself, but was no match for Aaron's strength. He managed to pull himself away from Aaron's face and said forcefully: "All right, you can stop now. Enough is enough!"

Aaron leered at Luke, striking him hard across the face. "Oh no," he hissed. "You've gotta be joking. I'm not stopping until I've had some fun!"

Luke's nose had begun to bleed from the blow. Aaron forced Luke to his knees as he undid his jeans, pulling his underwear down. He pushed his thickening cock into Luke's face. "Suck my dick!" he said coarsely.

Luke kept his mouth firmly shut. Aaron held Luke's nose so he couldn't breathe and would therefore be forced to open his mouth. When he achieved this, he grabbed Luke's hair, causing his head to tilt backwards as he thrust himself into Luke's mouth and continued thrusting, fast and furious. Luke did think about causing Aaron a lot of pain by biting down hard on him and making a quick getaway, but he feared that if he tried, unsuccessfully, he would only come of worse for it. Luke began choking and pulled his head back further in order to get Aaron to withdraw from his mouth. This didn't please Aaron at all, as he hadn't achieved climax, but he didn't relish the idea of Luke throwing up all over him.

Luke rose from his knees, gasping for breath. Aaron leered maliciously at his victim as he thought of another way he could climax and this time he would not be stopped. "Take your clothes off," he demanded.

Luke realised what Aaron intended doing and yelled, "No!" He started to walk away, but Aaron grabbed him and threw him against a tree so hard, that even though Luke was winded, he still managed to scream out in pain.

"You'll do as you're damn well told, pretty boy," snarled Aaron. "Now, get your bloody clothes off, you little shit!"

"Go to hell."

"I'm only going to tell you once more. Get those fucking clothes off!"

"Go fuck yourself, you weird bastard!"

There was another strike across Luke's face. "The only thing that's going to be fucked around here, is your pretty, tight, little arse, you goddamned prick teaser." Another blow, another, and another. Tears were streaming down Luke's face, meeting the blood from his nose and the cuts on his cheeks, made by the rings on Aaron's fingers. "If I can't persuade you," began Aaron, "maybe my friend can." He produced a flick-knife that was concealed in his jacket.

The fear for his life was clearly shown in Luke's face. "Jesus! You're a fucking maniac!"

Luke received two more blows across the face. Not caring what happened anymore, he let Aaron tear the clothes from him. He threw Luke to the ground, taking the rest of his own clothes off, as he entered Luke, who screamed as he did so. Aaron was not small, but very well endowed and thrust like a wild animal. Due to his corpulent manhood, the pain which Luke felt was excruciating; not that this bothered Aaron in the slightest, as the only thing on his mind was his own pleasure. Whenever Luke had the strength to yell, "Stop", he received a blow across the head from Aaron. Safe sex had never been a concern to Aaron, as he spent himself inside Luke, and enjoyed hearing his own groans of climatic ecstasy.

"I hope you're better next time round," sneered Aaron, as he got dressed and returned to his car leaving Luke bruised, bleeding and cold. Not that Luke could feel anything, as he had long since passed out.

It was in the early hours of the morning, when an elderly gentleman, taking his dog for an early morning run in the woods, found Luke. He was physically sick, when he thought he had stumbled upon what appeared to be a dead, naked body. His dog was sniffing around Luke with huge amount of curiosity, while the man hurried himself off to the nearest public telephone box to inform the police and ambulance.

It took Luke several weeks to fully recuperate physically from his ordeal, although the emotional scars would never leave him and always remain locked within his memory. The police were not holding much hope of finding Luke's attacker, as nobody at *Jumbos* had ever seen Aaron before. They were more than a little convinced that Aaron Howard was probably not even his real name. Still, they had told Luke that they would hold the details on file; not that this was much of a consolation to Luke. He was desperate to get Aaron for what he had put him through but it was highly unlikely that their paths would ever cross again. *If they ever do*, he thought, *I will be more than ready for that bastard and things will turn out so much differently.*

Elliot, Kristian and Luke's friendship grew rapidly and more solid as time went on. They were forever telephoning each other, asking if they wanted to go out to the cinema, to a bar or some other social event.

When Luke auditioned and got the part in his second stage musical, Elliot and Kristian were there to offer him moral support at the premiere.

Although the three of them had other friends, none matched their own unique friendship. Elliot and Kristian became totally trusting of Luke, taking him fully into their confidence and vice versa. They shared their good and bad experiences with each other, with Luke opening up wholly about his family background, his frightening introduction to London, the amazing person that Lillian was and his ordeal of being raped.

Nothing or nobody seemed able to come between the three of them and ruin their very solid friendship, until it was put to the ultimate test when Luke met Matthew Sylvester.

CHAPTER FOUR

Lady Veronica Darlington was pronounced dead shortly after she had given birth to her premature, miracle daughter, Siobhan Katharina on 18 July 1968, in a hospital in St Albans, Hertfordshire. Throughout the term of her pregnancy, complications had arisen with the high blood pressure disorder, Pre Eclampsia. When she had given birth to a stillborn son two years earlier, the doctors had strongly advised her against trying for another child but when she did fall pregnant again, she was adamant in seeing the entire term through. With only several weeks of her term remaining, she collapsed and was immediately rushed to hospital. As the baby's life was in danger, a caesarean operation was performed. The relief that Lord Darlington felt was completely overwhelming when he was told that the operation was a complete success and he was now father to a beautiful baby girl. Unfortunately, this euphoric state was short lived, as his wife never recovered from the anaesthetic.

Lord Darlington, due to his continual work engagements, knew that he wouldn't be able to focus on his parental responsibilities alone and so hastily set to interviewing and appointing a live-in governess to look after Siobhan. Not only did he have a rigid set of questions to ask potential candidates but he also watched to see how they interacted with his daughter. All of the candidates, out of the dozen that he interviewed, didn't fail to disappoint him in any of the short-listing criterion.

Except one.

Elisabette Dahlström, an ex-school teacher from Sweden, was the only candidate that stood out on every single level for Lord Darlington, especially as she continued to play a variety of fun but educational games with Siobhan whilst comprehensively answering any question that he threw her way. At twenty-eight years old, she looked as though she would have been far more comfortable on the cover of a beauty magazine. Her shoulder length, golden hair was soft and shiny, which would always dance lightly in a breeze, when it wasn't being played with by Siobhan, who always took great pleasure in running her fingers through Elisabette's hair. Her eyes were a deep sapphire, that appeared translucent whenever a bright light caught them. If it wasn't her well-structured features that caught people's attention, then her eyes certainly did. Her shapely, feminine figure was one that most women would absolutely die for. All the clothes that she wore looked expensive; almost Chanel, Dior, Gucci or Laroche, although they were far from it. Perhaps it was because she wore them like a model.

The Absence of Friends

Siobhan's adoration for Elisabette was unyielding and she rarely wanted to leave her side, other than at the obligatory times when she had to go to school or to sleep. Whenever they were going to be apart for more than a few minutes, Siobhan would always demand a hug before they parted company and again, when they reunited, along with a kiss for each hour that they had been apart. Elisabette, in turn, grew to love Siobhan as though she were her own daughter. She would spend many a long hour in the early years, ensuring that Siobhan understood, memorised and carried out her stringent rules on how to be nothing short of exemplary in her decorum at school, as well as setting her demanding educational challenges that she knew were slightly above the expectations of her age.

As the years rolled by, Elisabette not only ensured her protégée was taught how to speak with graceful eloquence but also the art of sophisticated deportment and etiquette. There was no way on god's earth that she was willing to tolerate any lazy talking, disgraceful posturing and inappropriate posing; certainly not from someone with an aristocratic background.

During her limited free time, Siobhan would sometimes request that Elisabette teach her some Swedish phrases, where she quickly learnt how to say *"I will always love you"* so that when any opportunity arose and with the accent perfected, she would declare to her guardian: "Jag kommer alltid att älska dig." Elisabette's robust reply of "Och så kommer jag" would always ensure a hearty beam from Siobhan.

Had it not been for the unexpected actions of her father, Siobhan and Elisabette's relationship might not have suffered a precipitous U-turn from reciprocal doting of each other, to one of complete hatred. On 28 July, ten days after Siobhan's eleventh birthday, Lord Darlington announced his engagement to Elisabette Dahlström.

Prior to her father announcing his engagement to Elisabette, Siobhan couldn't contain her irascible impatience at wishing the day's school to finish, so she could tell Elisabette every single detail and indulge herself in the activities that had been set for her. Had Elisabette been aware of the irascibility and the impatience of her charge, she would have made this negative behaviour an immediate issue to address and correct. Now, however, Siobhan would try every trick she could think of to delay going home too quickly, such as deliberately misbehaving at school in order to be detained by the professors, or socialising with her friends without telling her father or Elisabette where she was going. The arguments that ensued as a result of her actions would undoubtedly end with Siobhan being reduced to tears, screaming at Elisabette that she hated her and hoping that her father would soon come to his senses and not marry her.

After a particularly intense and heated argument, Elisabette attempted to explain to Siobhan that she had tried her hardest to be as near to a mother figure as she could to her, as well as understanding the difficulties she had been experiencing in coming to terms growing up without her actual mother. Siobhan was having none of this and refused to listen to anything Elisabette had to say.

Siobhan laughed manically. "A mother figure?" she hissed venomously. "You are *not* my mother, Elisabette and you never will be," she screamed.

"As hateful as you are trying to be, young lady, if you want me to turn against you," Elisabette said with majestic poise, "I will, as you are travelling that definitive path to ensure that it will happen."

"I am going to work so incredibly hard at school and prove to my father that I'm far better than any Swedish bitch," she said with indomitable vehemence one day to a school friend. The passionate anger that she felt toward Elisabette and her father were directed toward her studies. Any spare moment that she had was devoted to studying, making her hatred for Elisabette and the determination to succeed become increasingly more of an obsession.

It was in the August, thirteen months after their engagement had been announced, that Lord Darlington and Elisabette were married. The fact that Siobhan's plan hadn't worked out as she would have liked, did not deter her from continuing to work as hard as she could. From the time that her father had announced the engagement until two years later, she steadily worked her way up from being at the bottom of all her classes, to the top of every single one of them.

If Siobhan hadn't been captive to her own negative feelings and been truly honest with herself, she would have readily admitted that the wedding was nigh on perfect as one she had often fantasised about for herself. However, as this was Elisabette's wedding she thought it to be extremely lavish, overly decadent, with a pretentiously grandiose and expensive garden party afterwards. She thought that the cost of the entire affair must have been astronomical; catering for around three hundred guests. It was easy for her to successfully slip away unnoticed amidst the sea of unfamiliar faces and excitable mêlée, with neither her father nor Elisabette being aware of her absence. Back in the seclusion of her own bedroom, she couldn't wait to rid herself of the ghastly pink bridesmaid's dress that her father had been so intent on forcing her to wear. It was her narrow-mindedness that wouldn't even make way for her to consider the reality that her father was thoroughly overjoyed that his daughter was being a bridesmaid at his wedding - in Siobhan's blinded perception of what was tangible, all she could see was that Elisabette had manipulated this

The Absence of Friends

scenario in order to rub her nose into the fact that she hadn't prevented the wedding from taking place.

Pouring herself into a pair of faded, worn jeans and equally dated sweatshirt, she looked at herself in the full-length mirror, finding herself caught in a daydream where she was romanticising that it was herself in the wedding dress that Elisabette had worn. With palpable unwillingness she had to admit that Elisabette did indeed look beautiful, which angered her. She felt threatened when her father was taken in by Elisabette's ironically skin-deep beauty and in doing so, believed that she was therefore pushed mercilessly aside in his affections.

She continued to look at herself in the mirror, speaking in a hauntingly evil drawl as if Elisabette were in the room with her. "You are one hell of a vindictive and odious, stuck up little bitch, Elisabette! You may feel as though you have fooled my father with your superficial beauty, but certainly not me. I can see right through all your sanctimonious and conceited ethics. You think you're really something, don't you? But we'll see who the clever one really is, when I become rich and famous…just with *my* looks."

Persuading her father to send her to finishing school in Switzerland would not pose as the most unachievable of feats for Siobhan, as she had long since learnt how to play to his weaker traits in order to get what she wanted. With Elisabette now being included as a new element to the equation however, this would only serve to be more of an enigmatic threat to her success. When addressing her husband, it was Elisabette's vindictively caustic comments, delivered in an eminently deadpan fashion, that were designed solely to antagonise Siobhan and hopefully cause a cavernous rift between her and her father.

"Think of the expense, Rupert," she would say with a rational tone. When her husband would respond by saying that expense didn't matter when it came to his daughter's education, she was not easily defeated. "We will miss her terribly if she goes away for such a long time," she would retaliate or, "she doesn't really need to attend finishing school - don't you think she's too good for it already?"

"Oh, you insidious little witch," Siobhan would snarl underneath her breath, whenever she caught wind of Elisabette's faux concern. "But I will ensure that my father is not beguiled under your wily spells."

Elisabette's maliciously introspective ploy to prevent Siobhan from attending finishing school failed miserably, as six weeks after her sixteenth birthday, Siobhan was packing her suitcases in order to fly to Switzerland. Had Elisabette been aware that her husband had surreptitiously opened a Swiss bank account for his daughter, regularly depositing generous amounts of money, she might have been more adamant in winning that particular battle.

When Siobhan arrived in Switzerland, the first few days were spent familiarising herself with the local area and window-shopping for potential outfits for her wardrobe at school, even though she had brought a suitcase full of clothes with her. She promised herself that she would only purchase her ultimate favourites, which ended up being nearly everything that she had laid her eyes upon. The dormitory that had been assigned to her was pitifully small in comparison to her bedroom at home but what was even more incredible - and she didn't hide her horror - was that she was sharing with two other girls: Delores Freeman, also from England and Francesca Sacchetti, from Italy. It didn't take long for the three girls to develop very strong bonds with each other but only two of them would remain good friends for many years to come.

At sixteen years old, Siobhan was already capable of bedazzling men, who would always turn their head for more of a prolonged second glance. As the years passed, she became adept in fixing her long, wavy auburn hair into a variety of different styles, as skillfully as if she had just been to a salon, in order to suit the outfit she had selected to wear, or an occasion she had been invited to attend. Her perpetual ruddy complexion served to accentuate her full, rose-coloured lips and deep hazel eyes that brought a curious intensity about them. It was her curvaceous femininity that added further aesthetic indulgence to her many male admirers. Most of these men would be rendered momentarily mute or paralysed, mentally struggling to find the most favourable words in order to strike up a conversation with her, that wouldn't leave her thinking they were totally incapable of being in a woman's presence.

Delores and Francesca were always eager to point out any men who were so obviously entranced by Siobhan, whenever they went out together. Siobhan would just smile at her friends, having no inclination of ruining her chances of getting her revenge on Elisabette by falling in love with someone, no matter how handsome they might have been.

Delores, on the other hand, was notorious for her sexual exploits with any man who engaged with her for more than a few minutes or paid her the slightest hint of a compliment. She disgraced herself by quickly earning the defamatory nickname *The Mantis* from the few obstreperous students, who were keen to spread their creativity like wildfire. Whenever Siobhan or Francesca were in earshot of these malevolent comments, they were quick off the mark to defend their friend. Delores would spend many a long hour sobbing uncontrollably upon Siobhan's or Francesca's shoulder when one of

The Absence of Friends

her numerous suitors had given her the cold shoulder, refusing to see her again after they had managed to get her into bed, which, with Delores, was not really any major challenge.

It came as an unexpected shock, therefore, that it was Francesca who was the one to fall pregnant at seventeen years old. Both her roommates were stunned to learn this was the case, as Francesca rarely went out by herself and on the odd occasion that she did, she never once mentioned to the others that she had been having clandestine liaisons with a young man. Both girls felt different levels of betrayal from Francesca, as they had all agreed and were of the belief that no secrets were ever going to be kept from one another. For Delores, the troubling paradox was that it was always Francesca who was keen to assert her compliance for taking precautionary contraceptive measures and safer sex.

Siobhan was quick to put aside her selfish opinions at being let down, asking her friend's forgiveness and offering support in the current dilemma but Delores took a little more persuading to be able to see things from Francesca's perspective. Having only completed eight months of the first year, Francesca found herself being expelled from the school, where she was instructed to pack her bags and return to Italy.

When the two years of schooling had been completed, the two girls were sad to be leaving, as they had become very fond of each other. They promised that they would keep in touch, as they had with Francesca. Siobhan wrote to her father, telling him that she was visiting Francesca in Italy before returning to England.

Francesca's parents, with whom she was still living, found Siobhan to be an extremely pleasant and affable young woman. They were left under no misapprehension as to why, when Francesca had been sent home from Switzerland, she was incessantly talking about her new friend, Siobhan.

"I really can't believe that Antonio is already ten months old now!" exclaimed Siobhan.

"Yes," agreed Francesca. "It's frightening how quickly the time has passed. I'll blink a few more times and he will be eighteen."

"He's so beautiful," cooed Siobhan, cradling Antonio in her arms. "He's got your eyes, nose and mesmerising smile."

"Do you really think so?" she questioned.

"For sure," Siobhan said, unequivocally. She couldn't believe how much Francesca had matured since leaving Switzerland as a frightened and discredited young girl.

"How's Delores?" asked Francesca, quizzically.

"She's absolutely fine. She went straight back to England when I came here. As far as I'm aware, she thinks she is going to find fame and fortune in her non-existent beauty salon. Heaven only knows why because she never really had a head for strategic thinking."

"Do you think she will? Find fame and fortune, I mean."

"Oh, I very much doubt it," Siobhan sighed wistfully. "You know what she was like. She was far too fond of the *occasional*…" she coughed demonstratively, to highlight her generosity in what was the exact opposite of the actual truth, "…dalliance with all the potential Casanovas to be able to concentrate on the longevity of her career. I think I lost track of all the men she had on the go at once. I often had to keep biting my tongue, so I wouldn't laugh when she was crying on my shoulder every other night, about how each man who spurned her, was her true love and how she was destined to never have her love returned!"

"Me too."

"I really wouldn't be at all surprised if she married before long and tried to create her very own football team!"

Francesca giggled unashamedly. "You're probably not wrong."

Francesca felt that Siobhan was like the sister she had craved so many years for. She had found it somewhat easy and remarkably therapeutic to confide her deepest secrets, her perplexing fears and her audacious aspirations to Siobhan, that she had otherwise so easily kept to her bosom. This only made more of an emphasis to Siobhan that she herself had missed out on the joys and tribulations of growing up without a sibling.

Allowing Siobhan to be drawn deep within the heart of the Sacchetti family didn't just stop with Francesca. The invitation also extended from her parents, Armand and Gabriela, who treated Siobhan like a second daughter and not purely the friend to their own.

Gabriela was a trained masseuse with her own parlour, which proved to be a huge success with the tourists for some unknown reason. Not that Gabriela was complaining; as long as she had enough money to feed her family and treat herself to an occasional new dress or pair of shoes, she was more than happy. Not only did the salon offer massages but the whole beauty experience, where a woman could easily spend the entire day having her hair, nails and makeup done whilst literally parting with a small fortune. Gabriela took Siobhan to her salon, where she found the entire experience to be invigorating and rejuvenating, telling Gabriela that it was the most worthwhile profession to be in, as people would always want to be pampered.

Armand, with his profession, kept the theme running, as he was a director in beauty and fashion, being a powerful name within Italy's fashion industry.

He would often use the services of his wife's salon to get the hair and makeup done for any models that he needed to employ for a specific shoot or fashion show. Siobhan really couldn't believe her good fortune, as Francesca had rarely talked about her parents before, or if she had, she must have been too preoccupied with Delores to have heard. Many hours were spent between Siobhan and Armand, discussing her ambition to become a model and how she might go about it.

"I have many influential contacts within the industry; some in very high places," he told her candidly. "More than you can probably imagine. I have to say, you certainly have the qualities and markings to take you all the way. If that's really what you wanted."

"Really?"

"Yes, of course. However, I do warn you, it is an incredibly tough industry to be in, so you would have to be strong in mind, as well as determination because one is nothing without the other."

"My determination, Armand, is driven *because* of my strength."

"The fashionista wars can make or break an individual and at times, these wars can become very, very ugly."

Siobhan telephoned her father to explain that she would be staying in Italy for several weeks longer and she would return to England as soon as she could. Although he accepted his daughter's independence, it didn't stop him missing her a great deal. A few weeks holiday here and there over the past two years were not a suitable consolation in his eyes.

Armand would spend many hours, over many days, tutoring Siobhan on adopting and perfecting her own unique walk for the catwalk. Had it not been for the excellently stringent tutelage under Elisabette, there would have been additional work needed on Siobhan's posture and composure; something which she begrudgingly but quietly thanked her adversary for. He asked one of his close friends, who was a professional photographer that had worked with many well-known celebrities, to help compose a truly comprehensive but enticing portfolio, covering a variety of looks and poses: from plain housewife, to girl-next-door, to femme fatale, to the virginal bride and finally, to the glamorous Hollywood movie star of the 40s and 50s.

Even though there were hair and makeup stylists employed for each of the various photo shoots, he asked the cosmetologists to explain to her the art of how to apply her own makeup in such a way as to prominently highlight certain areas of her face with various tones of light and shade, without it appearing to have been applied by an overzealous drag queen.

Siobhan was most surprised - and slightly bemused at first - that there were several lessons devoted on how to wear an outfit in such a way that it would speak volumes to perspective buyers.

"Young girls nowadays," he said disdainfully, "not only wear some ghastly choices of outfit but," he paused "and this is a big but, they just do not know *how* to wear an outfit properly."

"Oh," was all Siobhan could say.

"There is a real art to wearing an outfit properly and correctly to make not only woman wearing it even more beautiful, but also make the article itself far more pleasing to an individual's eyes."

"Oh," repeated Siobhan.

"I don't believe in all this *a good model can be quite cosmopolitan and will be able to wear anything* nonsense. There will be styles of outfits and certain colours that you will need to avoid, as they will do you absolutely no justice at all."

"Oh."

"Yes, oh indeed. I have met many young girls over the years who thought that they could just choose modeling as a career but really, they aren't what the industry needs at all. If you do well and get to meet the right people, Siobhan, there's nothing to stop you going all the way to the top. All I can do is to start you off on your path, what you do when you get there is entirely in your hands."

Siobhan hung onto every word that Armand spoke to her.

"However, the first thing you need to do," he said, "is change your name. With respect, I'm afraid Siobhan Katharina Darlington really is not a very good one. You want something plainer but catchy; not too fancy, nor too boring."

"Oh God," said Siobhan with excitement in her voice, her mind already trying to work on a new name for herself.

Siobhan walked with a natural, expert elegance along the catwalk, catching Armand's eye within the crowd. He had taken her to Rome, to unleash her into the fashion world in one of his own organised catwalk shows. She was unable to pinpoint either Francesca or Gabriela from the crowd, as she gracefully showed off the latest in Italian eveningwear. She had listened exactly to what Armand had told her about what her eyes should be revealing to various people within the audience; even to how she held her gown, pivoted on her heels or curved her lips, would say so much more than a thousand words ever could. He had gone through with her, several times, before she went onto the catwalk, exactly the people with whom she should have eye contact and the expression she should have on her face at that particular moment. Above all, he told her, it was of the utmost importance that the length of time that eye contact should be maintained should be neither a second more nor a second less.

"It is imperative that you get everything absolutely perfect because there is no room for error. If there is something amiss, or you do something incorrectly, it will cost you dearly. I don't want to put any extra pressure on you but there are some highly influential people in the hall, who will be watching your every movement with a great deal of interest and potential criticism. Do not give them *any* excuse to belittle you in any way, because believe me Siobhan, that is exactly what they will try to do. So many girls' careers, who had amazing potential, were short-lived because of this."

Siobhan spun slowly and expertly on her heels, catching the eyes of all the people Armand had instructed her to, while the commentators described each of the gowns she was wearing, in perfect detail, disbelieving that she didn't feel in the slightest bit nervous.

After the show had ended, she made her way to Armand. "So, how did I do?"

"Maxine, mia Cara, sei stata perfetta. Perfection. You are a natural! Un bel talento," exclaimed Armand, hugging her tightly.

"I still can't get used to that name. Maxine Wyatt."

"It's got a down-to-earth purity about it, whilst sounding slightly grand without being overtly gratuitous."

"However did you think of it?" asked Francesca with interest.

"I may be a natural on the catwalk, but not when it comes to choosing names. Armand chose it for me."

"I must admit," said Gabriela, I did have reservations about you carrying it off, but seriously, you were so much better than some of these so-called professionals."

Maxine's face shone with the compliments. "It's such a shame that it's only a one-off show. I really did enjoy myself."

"Non pensare in fretta. Don't be so hasty in your assumptions," said Armand with a smile. "Remember I was telling you that it was imperative that you look at certain people in a particular way?"

Maxine nodded, clutching at her chest, in excited anticipation of what Armand was going to say.

"Well, I've already had two people come up to me, telling me how impressed they were with you. Believe it or not, they too are very big names in the world of fashion. They've asked me if you would consider being a part of their teams. One is in Paris, the other in Lisbon."

"I don't believe it." Tears of joy flowed from Maxine's eyes. Forgetting momentarily that she was wearing waterproof mascara, she asked Gabriela to lend her the compact mirror to check herself.

"Believe it. It's true. Remember, if you get in with the right people, you will go far. This, my girl, is the start of your career. Carpe diem. Seize the day. Seize your moment. Questo sarà il vostro momento di brillare."

Maxine's new career took her all over Europe. Her photographs appeared in beauty magazines across Europe and she appeared at many public, as well as private, functions. Armand continually received telephone calls from her, as she thanked him time and again for launching her career and telling him where in Europe she was going next.

Maxine first met Michael Hart at a Christmas party, when she was twenty-one years old. She had met many gay people within the fashion world, a lot of whom became good friends. When she first came into contact with gay life, she was extremely wary of it and totally naïve, though she accepted their lifestyle as their own choice and often helped defend them when they were faced with homophobia. She had been invited to a party in London by one of her gay friends, and Michael was there.

"God," he screamed, "will you just look at those tits! Aren't they just the most? They would look totally gorge and right at home in my bedroom."

"I beg your pardon," said Maxine defiantly.

"What?" asked Michael, with a start.

"You were saying something about…um, tits."

"Yes, these china blue tits are beautiful, don't you think?" he asked, picking one up and showing it to Maxine.

Maxine apologised. "I thought you meant…"

"Hmmm, I suspect you did! Listen sweetie, as gorgeous as you and your tits may be, do you really think I would want them in my bedroom?"

"I'm really sorry."

"Don't be sorry, my little cupcake, it's only me." He giggled to himself. Placing his hand around the base of his neck, he said: "Oh, clutch my pearls, will you!"

"What?"

"Well, I'm such a dozy mare! You don't know who *me* is, do you? Unless of course, you are psychic. Are you psychic? 'Cause that would just be something, if you were."

"No. On both accounts."

The Absence of Friends

"Well, let me introduce myself then," he said with a curtsey and bow in unison. "Darling, I am the one, the only, the incomparable Michael Hart. Lifelong homo and eternal best friend in waiting to the right applicant…and let me tell you something, my dear…I am not just any old Hart but to the right person, I will be all heart."

Maxine stifled a giggle, with a bite of her lips. "Hi, Michael. I'm Maxine Wyatt."

Michael took Maxine's hand and was about to kiss it in a chivalrous manner. "Jesus Christ! Will you just look at those claws! Thank God I'm gay is all I can say, or you could do someone a nasty injury with that arsenal of weaponry!"

Maxine laughed nervously, as she watched Michael kissing her hand, not really knowing how to react to this unusual behaviour. They spent a lot of time talking about Michael, though he found it in his heart to ask Maxine a few questions about herself. This was the beginning of what was to become a very close and lasting friendship.

They would often buy each other small gifts as a way to show their *sisterly love*, as Michael had called it, for each other. One particular occasion they bought each other the same gift: a leather-bound diary, with their initials in gold lettering on it."

"Great minds think alike, don't they sweetie?"

"They sure do. And just because we share the same sisterly intuition, this doesn't give you the automatic right to sneak a peak in my diary."

"Moi?" he said, with mock defiance. "As if."

They both absolutely adored their diaries, religiously setting aside time every day, so as to inscribe their inner most thoughts into their respective entries. It quickly became an annual event for the two of them to exchange exactly the same diary, necessitating Michael in turning it into a vivaciously flamboyant ceremony. Maxine didn't wish to break Michael's heart when, several years later, it would be her husband that took on the tradition of presenting her with the same leather-bound diary with her initials in gold lettering on it. She would ensure that, come hell or high water, this secret would be taken with her to the grave.

Maxine not only attended functions around fashion and beauty, but was also drawn into the world of film and theatre functions. A friend asked her to accompany him to the twenty-first birthday party of Elliot Hayden, a colleague of his who was a dancer and actor. When she was introduced to him, she thought him to be undoubtedly talented, intelligent and remarkably handsome. She came onto him somewhat strong, allowing him to be aware in no uncertain terms, exactly how she felt about him. By the end of the evening, she had not only given him several lingering kisses but persuaded him to agree to take her out on a date.

To say that Elisabette was so outraged that her blood was almost boiling was a total understatement, when Maxine eventually publicised her engagement to Elliot in September of the following year. She attempted, unsuccessfully, to hide her extreme jealousy of Maxine's recent good fortune but didn't with her shock, when it was revealed that she had changed her name and the utter disgust in discovering that she had been consorting on a social level with homosexuals.

"You'll be marrying beneath yourself, Siobhan," Elisabette sneered. "If you feel you have to marry, then you should be marrying aristocracy."

"What?" Maxine spat, poised like a viper and ready to strike a deadly blow into her prey. "Just like my father did with you?"

Elisabette slapped Maxine across the face so hard, that she winced at the pain lingering in the palm of her hand.

"I'll marry whom I damn well choose," Maxine yelled, slapping her equally as hard in return.

Soothing her stinging cheek with her hand, Elisabette sneered, "Not if I have anything to do with it you won't."

"You will never manipulate me as you have done with my father."

"How dare you," Elisabette said fiercely.

"The truth hurts, doesn't it *mummy?*"

Although Elisabette remained silent, she leered triumphantly when she learnt that the engagement between Maxine and Elliot had been called off because he was gay. Maxine, whose floods of tears hadn't eased the pain she felt to her devastating news, craved solace within the arms of her father. Elliot was completely oblivious to the emotional turmoil that Maxine was going through, as she had been more than magnanimously altruistic, calmly accepting what Elliot had told her, marking the end of their romantic relationship.

Four years later, when Maxine was twenty-six years old, she met Maximilian Beresford through an impromptu and innocent encounter. She didn't rush into marriage but let him make all the advances. Elisabette, again, was totally against Maxine's relationship with Max, as she thought it was abhorrent that someone with a highly respectable ancestry should deign to contaminate that purity by dating someone from a mixed-race background. Nothing that Elisabette could say or do would stop Maxine pursuing her

The Absence of Friends

relationship with Max and they finally announced their engagement a year after they had met, marrying in the summer of the following year.

As Maxine was continually out socialising with her gay friends - sometimes even asking one of them to be her 'date', prior to her meeting Max, as part of her professional public relations exercises - she would occasionally ask Max along with her to a party, official function or even a good old fashioned boogie on the dance floor at a nightclub. Max had never had any real interaction, as far as he was aware, of gay people but being around Maxine opened his eyes to a totally different lifestyle. Maxine was more than pleased that Max was not the judgmental kind of man. His motto was: *I'm neither judge nor jury, in order to decide what's right or wrong - if that's who they are then who am I to argue?*

Maxine couldn't contain her joy when she finally fell pregnant three and half years into her marriage, as she and Max had been trying for a baby for months. If it was a boy, Max suggested on calling him Pierson but if it was a girl, Maxine wanted to call her Thalia. With only six weeks of her term remaining, Maxine collapsed suddenly and was rushed into hospital.

"I'm going to lose the baby, Max, aren't I?"

Maximilian Beresford was born in Huntingdon, Cambridgeshire on 6 January 1970, although he was expected to come the week between Christmas and New Year. His two older brothers, Nathaniel and Ferdinand were born on exactly the dates that they were due, 9 November 1965 and 27 March 1968 respectively.

His mother, Catherine, was a reporter for The Times newspaper and had many interesting stories to relay to her sons, which she never tired of recounting, much to their dismay. His father, Lamarr, who originated from Jamaica, was a solicitor, specialising in matrimonial law and was surprised at the increasing number of divorces that were taking place in recent times.

Max had a very short concentration span and he was often prone to procrastination, which would ultimately lead him into many-a-strife throughout his early years. His grades at school were markedly poor in comparison to that of his brothers when they were his age, which had been head and shoulders above the rest of their classmates. With the high standards that his older siblings had set, the expectation from his parents was equally as high. It constantly upset him that he felt he couldn't meet these expectations, although it wasn't for the want of trying. His parents continually demanded better results than his report cards showed, explaining that he should actually be concentrating in his classes and not allowing his mind to wander into a dreamland. Nate and Ferdy would often ridicule him, saying he was a "dunce" or "an idiot" and letting him know in no uncertain terms that he was letting the family down. The distress that his caused Max went totally unnoticed by his parents.

Letters were frequently sent home to his parents, outlining that Max was constantly misbehaving and often ending up in fights, which usually stemmed from his own frustration rather than a deliberate act of mischief. Max was easily led astray by his so-called friends, who dared him to carry out deeds that they knew would land him into trouble.

When Max left school, the only exam he had worthy of a mention was a B in Mathematics 'O' Level. His CSE qualifications were grade 2 in Economics and 3's in English Language and Literature. His parents scoffed at his lack of decent qualifications, telling him he would never get himself a decent job with his current grades unless he went to a night school or at least studied for a qualification. Ferdy was studying to be a computer analyst and Nate was in law school, studying to be a solicitor like his father.

After leaving school, the following three years were spent taking holidays with friends around Europe with the money that he had saved from various temporary employment contracts, mainly working within the finance industry. He found that figure work interested him a great deal, sometimes spending hours a day entertaining himself by setting himself challenges in solving complex arithmetic.

At the turn of his nineteenth birthday, he had finally set his mind to take up a career in accountancy, applying to polytechnics around England. It was Brighton Polytechnic that was the first to offer him an interview, though Max knew that he would have to work extra hard at the interview, as they normally only accepted students with 'A' Levels. Although the panel could see that he was nervous, his performance at the interview was outstanding, with his drive and ambition shining above the nerves. The polytechnic chose to waver their normal entry requirements, allowing him a place on the one-year foundation course, which would begin in the September of that year. His parents were keen to show their pleasure that he was at last doing something worthwhile, urging him to study hard and keep his concentration sharp.

Moving into the halls of residence whilst he was studying was not going to pose as any problem to Max and by far the easiest option available to him. He was sure that he would manage to cope, as it was only going to be for a year. The first two weeks were the worst, as he didn't know anyone in Brighton, finding it difficult to make the first move in making himself some new friends. As he progressed in the course, he naturally began to build up a rapport with his fellow classmates, though he tried hard not to let his social life interfere

The Absence of Friends

too much with his studying. He was fairly confident that he would pass with at least a Credit and found himself being nothing short of surprised when he actually passed with a Distinction.

Around four months prior to the foundation course being completed, he had already begun the arduous task of applying to large and medium sized firms with the hope that he could secure a four year contract with them. It didn't come as any surprise to him that all the large, prestigious firms turned him down, as they only usually took on graduates but he took the view that there would be no harm in him trying just in case. All his classmates had been accepted into companies before the wind of good fortune finally decided to blow in Max's direction. He was eventually accepted by a medium sized firm, in London, called Levy Partners, which he was appointed to in the middle of June. Being a junior accountant, he would accompany the senior accountants to help with the auditing of various firms' accounts.

Whilst working at Levy Partners, he was required to undertake a correspondence course to achieve his PE1, which would be the first stage in him becoming a bona fide Chartered Accountant. The PE1 exams could only be sat in the June or December, which were taken on completion of the year's correspondence course. In order to coincide with sitting the exam the following December, Max decided to delay starting the course for four months, as he thought it would be an unwise move to have such a lengthy gap between finishing the course and taking his exams. Had he been taken on by Levy Partners a few weeks earlier than he had been, he could easily have undertaken the course immediately and still managed to sit the exam the following June. Under the terms and conditions of the contract with which he had been taken on, he was permitted to three weeks annual leave per year and twenty-one weeks study leave for the entire four year period.

Eight weeks before sitting his PE1, he had to attend the tuition centre full time, for revision of all he had learnt on his correspondence course. He decided upon taking two weeks leave prior to the revision course; in order to do his own revision. He set himself a stringent timetable: beginning a day at 8.30am, allowing himself two half hour breaks for lunch and dinner and rarely finishing before 9.00pm. He allowed himself four ten-minute breaks through each day, just to stretch his legs and make himself a cup of tea, forcing himself to stick to his rigorous programme.

The PE1 exams spanned over three days, with five exams in total to sit, each of which lasted three hours. The results were posted approximately three months later, though students would undoubtedly be at Victoria Station for the first edition of the Financial Times to see if their name was in print. Max breathed a heavy sigh of relief when he eventually noticed his name printed clearly on the page for all to see. He witnessed the shocked and disappointed expressions of those whose names had not been printed, watching them scan the page several times over, willing their name to suddenly appear. One of the disappointed faces was his best friend, Charlie Johnson. Charlie phoned him a couple of days later, telling him that he had only marginally failed one paper and was therefore able to sit that specific paper again, the following June.

At Levy Partners, Max was now a senior accountant, knowing exactly what the juniors were going to be letting themselves in for. In order to become a fully qualified Chartered Accountant, he needed to sit his PE2 exams, which meant going through the entire process once again. He sat his PE2 in June of his penultimate year with Levy Partners, which he again passed. As he was under a four year contract, he was unable to finish at the firm until the following June.

Max had managed to secure himself a permanent post at Lewis (UK) Ltd, which would begin in the September after he had left Levy Partners. Before taking up this position, he decided to use the few weeks he had free to catch up on some fun that he had sorely missed out on in the previous four years. He would continually go out with his friends, getting ridiculously drunk with typically youthful drinking games and embarking on a string of one-night stands.

Max stood an impressive and erect 6'3", always retaining a perfectly rigid and straight back regardless of whether he be standing or sitting. He couldn't quite fathom those individuals who would permit themselves to languidly slouch, taking a degree of dignity away from their majestic height. His slender physique, with not an ounce of fat to be found upon him, was only one of his numerous attributes that would lead many a romantically inclined woman to instantly fall in love with him. Unlike a lot of his friends, Max wasn't one to be fussing around with hair gel or wax for hours on end, ensuring that every strand of hair was in exactly the right place, so he would clipper his hair twice a week and occasionally, even shave it completely bald. To add further charisma to his masculine ruggedness, he liked to preserve a subtle hint of stubble. His teeth were beautifully shaped and a brilliant white, where his entire face would light up whenever he smiled and his deep, hazel eyes would crease in the corners whenever he did so, giving his smile a hint of cheekiness.

As he entered into his latter teenage years, his skin tone became slightly darker, proving to be an aphrodisiac to potential female admirers. The velvety mystique of his deep, resonant voice typically ensured that any woman, even those with the coldest of hearts, would melt and become weak at the knees upon conversing with him for several minutes, leaving them totally at the mercy of his articulative charms.

The Absence of Friends

His dress sense was nothing short of impeccable, as more often than not, he preferred to wear immaculately sharp suits. Even on the nights that he went out drinking with friends, he would don a pair of smart trousers and a shirt with the collar open, as if to emphasise that this was his casual look. On occasion, he would wear a pair of jeans, although they would have to be Armani, Hugo Boss or Paul Smith. He was loathe to disgrace himself in public by wearing anything ill-fitting or even worse, with the supposedly fashionable rips or patches.

Louisa Kennedy became a large part of his life when he met her six months after finishing at Levy Partners. They had an intense and passionate affair and even contemplated marriage, though Max felt that at twenty-three years old, he was too young to permanently settle down. At twenty-five, Louisa was already an established Chartered Accountant in the Dublin branch of Lewis (UK) Ltd. They had only been in their relationship for approximately five months, when Louisa was offered a prestigious position in Dubai, which she was extremely excited about. She tried to persuade Max to come with her, which he refused to do, as any concrete commitment such as that, scared him. That simple refusal was enough to close the chapter on that particular part of Max's life, as both he and Louisa mutually agreed to part ways.

It was in Luxembourg, several months after his relationship with Louisa had ended, that Max met the woman who would become his future wife. He had already begun his employment with Lewis (UK) Ltd, who also had subsidiary companies all over Europe, Australia, Canada and America. His first duty was auditing the books for a new client, who was within the fashion industry. Their work had taken them to Luxembourg for a few weeks and Max had been given the responsibility for this new client. His colleagues were extremely jealous that a new employee's first job was not only a new client, but abroad too. However, as they were already involved in projects of their own, Max was the only person available and therefore, the most reasonable and obvious of choices.

After arriving in Luxembourg, the next few hours were spent in a preliminary meeting with his new client, which incorporated a hearty lunch and several bottles of wine, though Max thought it prudent not to consume any more wine than what would be considered polite. Despite the insistence from his client to eat, drink and be merry, there was no way that Max was going to allow himself to become intoxicated and jeopardise a new business relationship and possibly even his job.

"You are more than welcome to come along to the show this evening and view some of my work. It might not necessarily be *your thing* but it will give you some sense of what I'm about," his client said, jovially. Max immediately recalled one of the many golden rules of his firm: *Occupational obligations can at times be your bête noire - the onus is upon you to slay the beast*. With this thought in mind, he had no choice but to accept the invitation.

Although his client was right in suggesting the show wouldn't be Max's *thing*, he surprised himself by being genuinely enraptured by watching the array of couture gowns being displayed by the models strutting and sashaying down the catwalk. He even found himself wondering how some of them managed to walk so solidly on their ridiculously sized heels. If truth be told he was, by far, more interested in the actual models than the clothes that they were wearing but there was one in particular that he couldn't take his eyes off. If only he knew who she was. He furiously flicked through the pages of the programme to find her name but all he came across was names of the designers, names of the sponsors and a comprehensive explanation of each of the outfits, together with the heart-stopping price tag associated with each of them. There was absolutely no mention of any of the models' names other than a line at the back of the programme which read: *Models provided courtesy of Second Glance Model Management.*

When the show had finished, he was urgently called to the phone to discuss a matter related to work. In his haste to get to the telephone, which was inexplicably the only one in the building and located within the deep, dark recesses, he bumped headlong into some poor, unsuspecting woman, spilling his drink over her. As he looked up, he realised it was the model from the show whom he couldn't take his eyes off. *Oh God*, his first thought was, *she looks even more beautiful than before*. He could feel his heart racing with every second that passed, unaware that all he was doing was staring at her, without even saying a word.

The model was the first to break the silence. "Well, aren't you going to do the gentlemanly thing and offer me a handkerchief, or something, so I can dry myself?"

"Oh..oh...," Max stuttered, unable to get any coherent words to come from his mouth. "Sorry...I am...um...I'm really, really sorry." When he had helped her back to her feet, he offered her his handkerchief.

"It's okay,' she said, sensing his discomfort. "Accidents happen." Leaning nearer to him, she whispered, "Between you and me, I didn't particularly like this dress anyway."

Max smiled. He had already made up his mind that he was going to take the plunge with this girl - it was going to be now or never and never really wasn't a viable option in Max's book. Even if she turned him down, at least he would have tried and not spent an eternity wondering *what if*. "Can I buy you a drink? As way of an apology, if you like?"

"Okay. But only if I can buy you one too."

"Sure. It's a deal." *At least*, Max thought, *if nothing else, I will get the time it takes to finish two drinks to spend alone with her*. "By the way, my name's Max."

The model smiled. "No kidding. Mine's Max too. Well…Maxine, really."

What was going to be a pleasant evening's conversation over two drinks in a bar, also turned into a meal at an Italian restaurant, with champagne and a night of dancing and talking at a popular nightclub. It was more than obvious that they were attracted to each other and Max couldn't contain his delight when Maxine agreed to meet up with him again.

"As long as you promise not to spill your drink over me next time," she grinned.

It was over a year later that Max eventually proposed to Maxine, having whisked her away on a romantic holiday in Czechoslovakia and booking them into a luxurious hotel, The Golden Palace, in Prague. Each evening, Max would dress in his customary tuxedo, whilst Maxine tantalised his never-ebbing passion by wearing low cut gowns that showed off every perfect curve of her body.

Having been in residence at the hotel for a few days, Max had arranged for a dozen bunches of flowers to be sent up to his suite, via the doorman, Andrej Lukáš. Maxine, as was her wont, was still in the suite applying the finishing touches to her makeup and hair. She had told Max that she would meet him in the foyer when she had finished and so he used this opportunity to make certain arrangements without her knowledge.

Andrej was dressed in the hotel's customary green livery, with gold braid around the jacket and the rim of the top hat and in brilliant sun-gold lettering, The Golden Palace, was sewn into both the jacket and top hat. He obviously had a penchant for fattening foods, as his jacket looked as though the buttons might pop off at any moment due to the size of his stomach. Andrej, at best, was in his mid-forties, sporting a plain but friendly look with a grin that seemed as though it were permanently there. Even the most obnoxious and self-important of guests, with their never-ending requests that were usually idiotically pretentious and nigh on impossible didn't seem to faze Andrej in the slightest and he would usually respond with: "As you wish, Ma'am" or "Not a problem, Sir." Max found himself wondering, on occasion, what it would be like to be a fly on the wall after these guests had disappeared from view or earshot - would he see the grin from Andrej's face vanish and the lines on his forehead become more prominent?

"Will you be able to do all that for me please, Andrej?" asked Max, continually looking over his shoulder to see if Maxine was in sight.

"Not a problem, Sir. Is Sir anticipating a special occasion with Miss Wyatt?" Andrej's English was near perfect, with only a slight trace of an accent in his pronunciation of certain words. He liked Max and Maxine, as they always stopped to talk with him for a few minutes on their way out for a day's sightseeing or shopping, and again upon their return. He looked forward to hearing about their day's exciting outing and other little details that either of them might care to volunteer.

"Yes. I'm going to ask her to marry me."

Andrej looked like an excitable child being told he was about to be given a gift. "Congratulations to you, Mr Beresford. You'll be wishing me to get roses for the lovely lady, then?"

"No!" Max said firmly. "It can be anything *but* roses."

"I don't think I quite understand," said the doorman, his expression briefly flickering to one of confusion, before the grin once again returned. "Most women adore roses being given to them. Don't they?"

Max sighed. "Okay, Andrej. You're dying to know, aren't you?"

Andrej nodded, with a cheeky glint emerging behind his eyes.

"It's quite simple, really. Maxine can't stand roses. She never has done."

"Oh," said Andrej simply, disappointment now reigning within his eyes. He thought there might be some wonderfully elaborate explanation attached to the reason of not wanting roses as part of a romantic occasion, such as a marriage proposal.

Max couldn't help but feel sorry for Andrej, with his sad puppy dog eyes at the obvious disappointment and confessed. "Actually, there *is* more…"

The eyes lit up and the cheeky grin returned once more.

"Maxine is allergic to roses." He paused for a response from Andrej but as there was none forthcoming, he continued. "She comes out in a terrible rash if she gets too close to roses and woe betide if she even chooses to sniff them! Don't ask me why."

"Bizarre," was all Andrej could manage to say.

"Exactly. Doctors were baffled for ages. They made her change her diet, washing powder, cosmetics and many other things but the problem still persisted. It was quite by chance, when the doctor had his wedding anniversary, that they realised what the problem was. There were roses in his office, either from or going to be given to his wife and naturally, with Maxine being so close to them, she came out in a rash within a matter of minutes."

"Okay," said Andrej with purpose. "So no roses."

"You got it," Max stated. "And not a word to…"

The Absence of Friends

"Max!" Maxine emerged from the opening elevator. "Good morning, Andrej," she said breezily, wafting past him - allowing the scent from her favourite perfume to linger beneath Andrej's nose - and linking her arm through Max's.

"And a very good morning to you, Miss Wyatt," Andrej said, touching the rim of his hat. "I trust that you and Mr Beresford will have a lovely day," he continued, in his customary fashion.

"Thank you," she said with a smile. "I'm sure we will."

As they left the hotel, Andrej gave Max a wink, as if to seal the deal on his silence and to confirm that the details of the little surprise would be fully carried out.

Upon their return, in the early evening, they treated themselves to a Jacuzzi in the sunken bath of their en suite bathroom. The flowers that Max had ordered were beautifully displayed around the side of the bath. Max smiled inwardly as he knew Andrej would have made a special effort for them and his efforts were nothing short of exceptional.

Maxine hadn't stopped smiling as soon as she had set sight upon the mass of flowers adorning the bathroom. "They are absolutely gorgeous," she said.

"There's a card, I believe, somewhere within the mass of flowers."

Maxine hunted for the card and opened the envelope when she managed to find it. The card read: *Maxine, I love you with every single beat of my heart. I'm not complete without you and need you in my life to make me whole. Will you make me the happiest man in the world by becoming my wife? Will you marry me?*

"Yes, yes, yes!" Maxine said, with excitement, throwing her arms around Max's neck and planting a kiss on his lips.

"Andrej is ever so nosy," Max said, after he had allowed himself a moment to let Maxine's answer sink in and for his psyche to acknowledge that he was soon to be a married man. "Did you know that?"

"No," said Maxine with a look of confusion developing on her face. "Why do you ask?"

"Well, he wanted to know the reason behind why I was asking for all these flowers."

"And so you told him that you were going to ask me to marry you?"

Max nodded. "He also wanted to know why I wasn't filling the room with roses. *Most women adore roses being given to them*," he mimicked. "Naturally, I had to tell him the story of you being allergic to them."

"It doesn't matter. So what are our plans for this evening?" she asked, as Max stepped out of the Jacuzzi.

Without uttering a word, Max picked Maxine up in his arms and lifted her out of the Jacuzzi. He took a towel from the rail and dried her body slowly and deliberately, taking his time over the places where he knew she would derive the most pleasure. She, in turn, dried him, dropping the towel halfway through, as he had swept her off her feet and carried her to the bedroom, placing her gently upon the bed.

She watched Max as he looked under the bed. "What are you doing?" she asked curiously.

Max stood up and placed a finger on her lips. He lay down beside her and took her into his arms, kissing her passionately. Maxine closed her eyes, allowing herself to drift away on her emotional sea of desire. She pulled Max's head down, to allow herself the opportunity to unleash the hunger within her and was, with a sudden start, bought back into reality not by feeling Max's lips against hers but something strange and cold. She broke away, taking a moment to focus on the object that was clasped between Max's lips. It was the most beautiful diamond ring she had seen.

"Oh, Max," she gasped, her breasts still heaving with the passion that remained burning inside her. "It's absolutely beautiful." She slipped the ring onto her finger.

"I love you, Maxine."

"I love you too."

"Do you know what I want to do now?" he asked, curving his lip like a cheeky teenage boy that was about to engage in something that would likely be deemed as up to no good.

"What?" asked Maxine, raising an inquisitive eyebrow.

"I want to make non-stop love to you for the next week."

Maxine positioned herself comfortably on the bed. "Do with me what you will, Mr Beresford. I'm all yours and totally at your whim," she said in a suggestively erotic manner.

"I'm afraid, though, that our wanton lust will have to be put on hold."

"Why? What *have* you done?" she asked, glaring at him through narrowed eyes.

Max bit his lip. "I had it all planned…a wonderfully romantic proposal, leading into an equally romantic dinner and ending with a night of seductive passion."

"And you clearly hadn't factored into your planning how a woman's mind would actually work!"

Max frowned in frustration that his miscalculation had taken away from what he wanted to be a totally perfectly planned experience. "I suppose that's as good a way as any of putting it."

"So how long have we got before we're going out to dinner?"

The Absence of Friends

"That's just it...we're not going out. I already had everything arranged with Andrej and pre-ordered room service to arrive at 7.30pm. So that gives us..." he looked at the clock, "ten minutes!"

Maxine sighed vociferously, as she slipped herself into her nightgown and Max, into a pair of pyjama bottoms and a t-shirt.

"This is not over, Mr Beresford," she said, as a soft rap at the door and a muffled voice announced room service. "You still owe me a night of seductive passion."

Max grinned broadly. "Rest assured, Miss Wyatt, you *shall* get your night of seductive passion," he said, opening the door.

On one of the frequent occasions that Maxine hadn't come down to the foyer with Max, he had pre-selected the menu with Andrej. Max had ensured that oysters, lobster, asparagus, champagne and chocolate truffles were all a part of the wonderful and memorable day that he had planned; as if they really needed the added power of an aphrodisiac now. Maxine, having been caught up in the whole romantic whirlwind, found herself drinking quite a lot of champagne, making her a lot more light-headed than she would have liked.

They made love three times that night, each one more passionate and sensuous than the last.

Their wedding took place in July of the following year, almost two years after they had originally met. Had they held it off for another three weeks, it would have coincided perfectly with the anniversary of the first time they had *literally* bumped into one another, in Luxembourg. Even though Elisabette had been eventually convinced to attend the wedding by her husband - though Maxine had only addressed the invitation to her father - they sat near the back of the church and she refused to attend the party afterwards. Maxine had convinced one of her friends to distract Michael for at least an hour, so that she and Max could have some photographs taken together, without Michael wanting to be in every single one.

Maxine was kept in the dark as to where the honeymoon would be, right until the last minute. It wasn't until they were making their way to the airport that Max finally conceded and revealed to her that they would be spending three glorious weeks in The Bahamas. Maxine couldn't contain her excitement and squealed with delight.

Michael Hart's flamboyantly gregarious and uninhibited nature usually got him exactly what he wanted. People would either instantly hate him or be magnetically drawn to his decadent personality; not that he particularly let it bother him what people actually thought. Whenever anybody attempted to put him down, he would continually retaliate with an acerbic response as his own defense mechanism. Not many people seemed capable of getting one over him, as he would always have a quick-witted put-down.

Michael was an illegitimate child. He was born on 20 February 1968 to Julie Cooper, a fourteen year old girl, from a strict catholic family. The father, himself only being only fifteen at the time, was in no position to help out financially, still being at school and scared Julie into not revealing his identity to anybody. His family involved Social Services and between them and Julie's parents, they opted to put the child up for adoption, not wanting the family name to be disgraced if it were ever to be discovered that they had a bastard child within their family.

Michael was placed with a childless couple in Birmingham, Paul and Maria Hart, who were desperate to have a son of their own. They chose to formally adopt him when he was seven years old and were always proud to call him their son. Even though it broke Maria's heart to do so, they believed that they needed to be honest with Michael, when he was older, about his natural background. Although they revealed the sole reason to be that that Julie was too young to be able to properly care and provide for her child, Michael was shocked to discover that this was not entirely true. He came across some paperwork on his adoption that his adoptive parents thought they had secured away, which revealed that Julie had taken her own life three years after Michael was taken into care due to a variety of reasons which led her to believe that she could no longer cope. Julie may have been just a name to Michael, but he felt extremely sad because of her untimely and unfortunate death and also, because he would never gain the chance of ever meeting the mother he would never know.

Paul and Maria provided everything that Michael could ever need but their money couldn't buy him the love and warmth of a real family that he truly craved. He felt empty without the encouraging pats on the back from a father, or a reassuring cuddle from a mother and often thought of himself as an *odd ball*. Michael never truly settled in with his adoptive family, running away several times but always being bought back home by the police. A few weeks after his sixteenth birthday, he succeeded in his bid to run away. He spoke to Maria on the telephone, several days later, telling her that he was alright and not to worry about him, nor attempt to look for him and persuade him to come back. After a lengthy discussion, mostly on Maria's part, she reluctantly agreed to Michael's wishes.

Each time that Michael ran away, he would usually head straight for the city centre but he anticipated that this would be the first place Paul and Maria

The Absence of Friends

would try, especially as they would no doubt try and trace the call that he had just made. Instead, he took the first available train to Manchester with the money that he had regularly stolen from Maria's purse.

Once he had arrived in Manchester, he found it easy to pick someone up, using his powers of persuasion to take him home with them and eventually getting them to agree to keep him under their roof. He promised that he would do the housework as payment, instead of paying any rent. The man whom he had picked up was called Dexter Carter, a thirty-two year old American, who worked as a Department Manager in a city bank and known to his closest friends purely as DC, especially as he originated from Washington.

Dexter was a very astute individual who, rather than see a vulnerable young lad tread firmly upon the cruel path of danger that society was all too capable of paving, offered a meal and a bed for the night, with the chance of a friendly ear if they needed one. He listened intently to Michael's string of obvious false tales as to why he was in Manchester but never once belittled him by questioning their authenticity. Dexter could not abide the types of men who would take advantage and prey upon those who were considerably younger than themselves and therefore, treated Michael with the utmost respect. Even though Michael was totally expecting it, though not particularly wanting it, Dexter never once forced himself upon Michael to have sex with him. In fact, he treated him better than the average landlord would their tenant.

The moment Dexter would arrive home, he would transform from a very professional city worker in a perfectly pressed suit, starched shirt and suitably co-ordinated tie, into one of Manchester's best-loved drag queens, under the name of *Dinah Mite*. Michael was more than a little fascinated by the extreme personalities of Dexter and his alter ego and would often accompany him to the pubs and clubs where he was performing. Whenever Michael was introduced to any of Dexter's friends, he would usually say that they were cousins. Though none of them actually believed this story, they would just nod their head in quiet acceptance.

Michael had been living with Dexter for almost a year and even put in an occasional appearance in some of his shows as *Dinah Mite*'s Scandinavian friend, *Mel Strøm*, when he was approached with the suggestion that they should become a more permanent double act. They went under the name of *The Krystal DeCampers*. Michael quickly became renowned for his catchphrases and completely over-the-top effeminate characteristics. It didn't take them long to become established as Manchester's hottest drag act, attracting large crowds wherever they performed.

Michael embraced most of his camp mannerisms from his love of the Eurovision Song Contest, as it was one of the events of the year that he simply could not miss. No matter what, he would ensure that nothing or nobody would ever prevent him from revelling in his annual extravagance. The entire contest was nothing short of several hours of pure kitsch, where he adored drinking in the grandiose costumes, the whimsical makeup and the flamboyant stage performances. Sometimes, he would just sit at home watching videos of previous contests, so he could perfect the various movements and somehow use them in the shows with Dexter. On occasion, the both of them would indulge in a Eurovision sketch, where they would poke fun at the contest, with Michael changing the lyrics to either the British entry or a previous winning entry.

It was around the time that Michael had been living in Manchester for four years that he fled to London. He had finished his act with Dexter and they had decided to go straight home.

"Actually Dex," said Michael, "I'm starving. Let's go for a burger first."

"Sure. I fancy a hot fudge sundae too."

"Sounds good to me."

"With lashings of cream."

"Stop! You're making my mouth water in more ways than one."

"Michael! You're insatiable."

They were about to turn the corner, where their favourite burger bar was, when they heard a man shout out: "Oi, you!"

Dexter spun around. "Are you talking to us?"

"Who else would I be talkin' to?" asked the man sarcastically, catching up with Dexter and Michael, with his friends following closely in his wake.

Michael counted seven men of various shapes and sizes and could sense they were not there for a friendly chitchat. "C'mon Dex, let's go."

"Go?" the man snarled. "You aint going nowhere."

"What do you want?" asked Dexter.

The man turned to his friends and made an obscene gesticulation to them. "The poof asks us if we want anything, lads!" His friends laughed, as he turned to Dexter again. "Well, I suppose *you* want to give us a snog, or a blow job, don't you?"

"What about the kid?" asked one of the man's friends. "He a fuckin' poof too?"

Michael's eyes were wide with terror. "Please, just leave us alone."

"Shall we show 'em what we do to shirt-lifters, Gary?" The man leered, grabbing Michael viciously by the arm, swinging him around to face his other friends, throwing his arm around Michael's throat in a headlock.

Gary, who couldn't have been much older than Michael, looked at him and seeing the terror in his eyes, said: "Rob, leave him alone, he's just a kid."

"What? Are you a fucking queer as well?"

The Absence of Friends

Gary, not wanting Rob to start on him, answered: "Piss off! Just leave him alone."

Rob beckoned another of his friends over, and shoved Michael toward him. "Tom 'ang on to this 'un. We'll deal with him later."

Tom took Michael's left arm, forcing it behind and up his back.

Michael screamed. "Stop! You're breaking my arm."

Tom snarled. "I'll break more than your fucking arm if you don't shut the fuck up."

Rob walked menacingly over to Dexter, with an evil and possessed look on his face. "We fuckin' 'ate queers! Do ya know what we do to 'em?"

Dexter, already witnessing what was happening to Michael, felt more afraid for himself now, as he knew there would be no assistance from Gary this time, to stop any violence towards him. With every approaching step of Rob's, Dexter took a step back until he was forced against the wall, with nowhere to run and nowhere to hide.

"Answer my fuckin' question, poof," Rob screamed, right into Dexter's face.

Dexter, smelling the putrescent stench of fetid alcohol on Rob's breath in his face, cowered, wishing the wall would open up and allow him the chance to escape. His voice trembled as he managed to find the words to say, "I...I...I d-d-don't know."

"If he d-d-doesn't know," Rob mocked, "maybe we should show 'im. Eh lads?"

Rob's friends were clearly out for blood that night and their approving gestures and comments were all Rob needed to throw the first punch, hitting Dexter hard in his face. Dexter's immediate response to the first blow was pure self-preservation. He cowered lower, almost crouching, bringing his arms up over his head and face to protect as much as possible, to prepare himself for the expected onslaught of blows from the mob.

"Beat the dirty bastard," called one of the men.

"Give the fuckin' gay boy what he deserves," cheered another.

"Kick the shit out o' the bum bandit," cajoled yet another.

The chorus of encouragement from Rob's followers spurred him on, launching him into a tirade of punches, with his arms flailing around like a mad man. As he gained rhythm with his punches, he could have been mistaken for someone in a drama lesson pretending to be a windmill.

The faster and more frequent the punches came, Dexter gripped around his head tighter, praying to himself that the attack on him would soon stop. One particular blow from Rob caught Dexter off balance and threw his head backwards, hitting it against the wall with such force, it caused him a slight blackout and to slump slowly to the ground.

Had Dexter believed in a God, he might have been cursing their name right now, wondering why this was being allowed to happen to him - *what have I done so wrong in my life to deserve this punishment*, he thought, *I've never knowingly hurt anybody*. Paradoxically, he wished that he had been taught how to defend himself properly from such an attack. Although even if he had, with the odds stacked against him in the number of assailants he was facing, he would have been lucky to get any more than a couple of blows in. The anger that was rising within him didn't stop him wishing that he could retaliate with some severely damaging strikes of his own to the bastard who was attacking him but then, the fear that was dominating his anger made him wonder that if he had done so, would the result have been any different.

Michael watched the scene with horror and disgust, witnessing the blows his friend was receiving from Rob. His innocent eyes had never beheld such unprovoked violence before and he wouldn't allow himself to be tormented or tortured further by continuing to watch any more. Each time he attempted to turn his head away from the distressing scene, Tom would grab a handful of his hair, forcing him to carry on watching.

"Watch, you little bastard, 'cause you're next. Hope you can put up more of a fight than your boyfriend."

"He's not my…"

Michael didn't finish the sentence as Tom had struck him across the back of the head. "Shut your fucking mouth!" He wondered if it had been Gary who was restraining him, he might have shown a little more compassion by not forcing him to watch the horrific scene unfold before him. Michael's attempts to detach himself from the reality of what was actually going on by forcing himself to believe what he was watching was a carefully constructed, though convincingly acted, gratuitously violent scene from a movie and not his friend being beaten to a bloodied pulp, was proving to be almost impossible. He couldn't dismiss the thought from his mind that, unlike watching a movie, he was unable to fast forward, pause or even stop what was playing out before his eyes.

His hope that this technique would at least cease his constant flow of tears was proving to be in vain. The tears, however, continued to stream down his face, as he heard his friend's pained and anguished pleas for help. He wanted to scream out exactly what he thought of the bastards who were hurting his friend but the terror held him back. He watched helplessly as he saw trickles of blood forming upon the ground.

The intensity of his trepidation built like a volcano that was about to erupt at any moment, with nothing being able to prevent it from doing so. He screamed "No!" so loudly and so sustained, he thought that his throat would finally give up on him and cut off all sound. It was a blood-curdling scream and one filled with sheer panic, as Michael truly believed that they had succeeded in beating Dexter to death.

Gary, who had only watched the scene, as he couldn't bear to allow himself to participate in adding to Michael's torment, shouted out to the others: "C'mon we need to go. There's probably people on their way here, if not the police."

Each one of the remaining lads had a final kick at Dexter before they ran off into the night.

Michael collapsed to his knees beside Dexter, as he heard heavy footsteps running toward him. "Leave us alone! Haven't you done enough harm?" he shouted through his tears at the approaching bodies.

"It's okay," a woman's soothing voice said. "We're here to help."

Michael didn't even allow himself to register who she was, as he jumped like lightning to his feet, threw his arms around her and let the tears run free. He was thankful for the soothing strokes to the back of his head from the woman.

Both Michael and Dexter were taken to hospital, as Michael was suffering with severe shock, whilst Dexter had numerous fractures and broken ribs. Michael stayed with Dexter until he was well enough to be able to look after himself. He decided upon moving to London, although promised to keep in touch with Dexter and agreed to write often as he could and visit whenever he was able.

Michael never really knew what led him to sign up for a Mechanical Engineering course. He would give the answer to inquisitive people that he enjoyed a good screw and liked fiddling with nuts. Other students would wonder how on earth he managed to pass the selection interview, but Michael never revealed how he was accepted. He would just answer: "It's amazing what you can get if you sleep with the interviewer." The reputation that Michael built up for himself was one of promiscuity and constant flirting. He held no shame in not hiding his sexual activities. Most students became tired of his boasting and would often turn a deaf ear to his continual ravings. Only one person took any notice of his exploitations:

Kristian Irwin.

Michael never completed the course, as he dropped out with only a few weeks of the syllabus remaining. He had built up a really strong friendship with Kristian but when Kristian began a relationship with Elliot - someone with whom Michael had taken a particular liking to himself - he wanted to leave London and try his luck elsewhere. As he had done with Dexter, he promised to keep in contact with Kristian because he didn't wish the strong bond that had formed between them to break.

Michael was never very good at facing up to and dealing with his problems and so he would continually run away from them. He never seemed to settle in one place for very long and over the next few years, moved from London to Cardiff, on to Kent, then Sheffield and Hampshire before finally moving back to London, where he eventually settled permanently. Wherever he moved to, he found himself indulging in many one-night stands, which sometimes developed into a short or even longer-term relationship but when these broke down, it would be time for him to move on to somewhere new until he moved to Hampshire. He met Steven Cronje at a nightclub in Portsmouth and was caught off guard by him making all the moves. They didn't sleep with each other that night but arranged to meet again the following evening. It didn't bother Michael that he hadn't slept with Steven, as over the next few weeks he began to realise that Steven meant more to him than the possibility of a mere casual fling. It wasn't until the seventh week that they actually slept together and Michael admitted to himself that it was well and truly worth the wait.

It was a few weeks before Michael was about to turn thirty three that he visited Kristian and told him all about Steven and how he was fast becoming the true love of his life. The biggest surprise was when Michael revealed that they would be house-hunting whilst in London. He knew that he would have to find himself a source of income reasonably quickly but the only job that Michael seemed to enjoy was being a drag queen on the gay circuit. He felt that even though Queen M'Kay-La had only been around for five years, she still had plenty of life left within her yet. Michael and Steven insisted on having a house-warming party when they eventually found a property and bought it. It was a chance for Michael to have all his close friends together in one place: Dexter, Elliot and Kristian and of course, Max and Maxine, whom he collectively and constantly referred to as *Max Squared*.

CHAPTER FIVE

It took Scott a long time to come to terms about what Simon had done to him. When he initially moved to London, he spent the first three months confining himself to his own flat, not caring to go out at all. If he wanted a drink, he would go to the local supermarket and buy some alcohol to drink by himself.

Whenever his mother phoned, he would be brusque with her, not really wanting to engage in idle conversation. "Scott? When is all this going to stop?" asked his mother with concern one day. "You are not achieving anything by cutting yourself off from everyone and everything."

"I loved him, mum. I was really happy and things were going really well for us," he sobbed down the phone. "What went wrong?"

"You are better off without someone like him. Their sort only succeed in dragging you down with them. Now's the time to focus on yourself again and bring back the old Scott that we all know and loved. You *will* find someone who will treat you right and respect you, when the time is right. Until then, concentrate on *you* and only you."

"I can't mum. It's too difficult."

"Now, these are *not* the words of my son. You would never let anything get in the way of what you wanted. You would not be so easily defeated because you would fight and fight until you got what it was you were after. I'm sorry to be so brutal, Scott, but Simon's in the past now and you have to get on with your own life. If you continue like this, he will have succeeded in ruining your life. Don't let him think that he has got the better of you because I'm sure that, if he could see you now, he would be laughing."

"You're probably right, mum. He *is* screwing my life up."

With those final words of his mother's constantly ringing in his ears, Scott went out that night for the first time in three months. Over the following few weeks he began to make a few new friends and this began the healing process to help him take his mind off Simon and allow him to begin living a normal life again. Many of Scott's friends enjoyed his company, as he had a very magnetic and confident personality. They found it very easy to talk to him and off-load any problem they might have had. Although Scott might not have always been able to offer any advice, he would always make himself available to be a willing ear when needed.

Finding himself a new job was proving to be very difficult, as Scott had hoped to have secured himself a post within a couple of months of his arrival in London. He had long since lost count of how many intensely gruelling interviews he had been to for potential teaching posts. If the memories of Simon were not hard enough to cope with, the fact he couldn't manage to get himself a job depressed him even further. Knowing that his savings would probably not last much longer than a couple of months at a real stretch, Scott resigned himself to the fact it would be unlikely he would find himself a teaching job within that space of time. Therefore, he turned his concentration into finding himself another job until he could back into teaching. Purchasing himself a newspaper, he circled any job that he thought might be within his capabilities.

He couldn't actually believe how difficult it was to get himself into a job; not even a job that was far below his skilled capabilities. The responses were always nearly along the lines of: "I'm sorry, Mr Delaney, but I feel you're far too over qualified for this post and would therefore not stay in our employ very long." *You're absolutely damn right I wouldn't*, Scott would think, *but I don't have the luxury of choice at the moment*. The sometimes adverse reactions and hostile responses that he received from potential employers shocked him, where he often left the building feeling more than a little sorry for the other employees who had to work for such mindless and ignorant individuals.

In September 1993, Scott managed to secure himself a permanent job, as a Kitchen Assistant in a rundown East End restaurant. His duties comprised of little more than washing and drying dishes, cleaning all the kitchen equipment and scrubbing the floors. The wages were pitiful in comparison to the salary that he was used to but at least, he thought, it was a regular source of income.

The Head Chef instantly resented Scott's popularity with the other members of staff and began to make life very difficult for him. He demanded that he stay well after the restaurant had closed to repeatedly scrub the floors and cookers, which were not even dirty. Scott never once complained about the treatment he received from the Head Chef but did everything that he was asked to, without any question or hint of retribution.

He did find himself thinking a couple of times how easy it would be just to walk away from the job and find another one but he had two reasons for continuing. The first reason was because he didn't relish the idea of going through all the newspapers again and having to be put through the whole rigmarole of false enthusiasm and contrived answers to the myriad of questions thrown his way, only to be turned down for a whole host of jobs before he eventually found one. The second reason was more to strengthen his personal character and help him rebuild his self-confidence and respect, as there was no way he was going to let some shallow and narrow-minded lowlife drive him away. He had made up his mind at this point that he was no longer going to run away from the little problems that life threw at him, but challenge them by facing them head-on. He attempted to convince himself that part of life's fun was all about facing the challenges and defeating them. Many would disagree with Scott's theory and even told him that if something wasn't particularly going his way, then he should just give up and move on. *Not anymore*, he thought, *there is no way anybody is going to get the better of me again.*

"Vince is one hell of a mean guy," warned one of Scott's colleagues, of Vince Shepherd, the Head Chef. "Be careful that you don't put a foot wrong, or he'll make your life absolute hell. One guy was given the boot just 'cause he questioned Vince's authority once."

"But surely if you all…" began Scott, about to offer a potential solution.

"If you're about to suggest that we should go en masse to him with our grievances, or something more drastic like a collective walk out, these ideas have been broached before. As keen and as quick as people are to bitch about Vince behind his back, or offer their critical opinions on his management skills, nobody will do a damn thing about it because they're all shit scared of him."

"Well, thanks for the friendly warning, I guess."

Scott tried to do everything right by Vince, but even though his efforts were pleasing to the eye, Vince never seemed to be fully satisfied.

After four months at the restaurant, Scott became thoroughly fed up with the way that he was being treated and decided to confront the problem head on with Vince. Even though he didn't breathe a word of his intention to a soul, somehow word broke out that he was going to have "have it out with Vince." Comments exchanged between the other staff: "He's digging his own grave" or "Vince will kill him, for sure" or "When he does the deed, I'm sure he won't be here the following day".

Whilst everyone was giving their various opinions on what fate might befall Scott, he assumed it would be a bad idea to confront Vince whilst the rest of the staff were there, so he decided upon doing it the next time he was ordered to stay behind. He didn't have long to wait, as that very night, Vince demanded that Scott scrub the floor again and again until he could see his own face in it. Scott could feel the adrenaline flowing throughout his entire body, as he glanced up at Vince, who had his gaze transfixed back down at him.

He asked: "Why do you hate me so much, Vince?"

"Oh, do shut up and get on with your work," snapped Vince.

Throwing the scrubbing brush angrily to the floor, Scott jumped suddenly to his feet. "No! I won't shut up. You've treated me like crap ever since I started here and for what reason? I can't see any real reason, other than you enjoy throwing your weight around. So, no, I'm not going to shut up until you tell me why you're so intent on making my life a misery."

Vince advanced towards Scott, who flinched slightly as if anticipating that Vince would raise his hand to strike him, though he was ready to block his fist from ever reaching his face with his arm.

"Oh, that's right," yelled Scott, the anger within him reaching boiling point. "Show me that you're a real man by punching me. Do you seriously think that's the answer to whatever problem you might have? In fact, what is your problem? You clearly seem to have one."

"Firstly," barked Vince in return, "I have never raised a hand to anybody and I'm certainly not about to make an exception to that rule for you. Secondly, in order to answer your question, *you* are my problem!"

"If that's the case then, let's take this opportunity to sort it out once and for all. We have to work together, so I would, at least, want us to be civil to each other. You know, I deliberately waited for the other guys not to be around, so it would only be me and you."

"Why?" asked Vince, his tone softening a touch.

"Well, to be honest with you, because I didn't want them around when I found out that you're a really nice guy when we get the opportunity to get to know you."

Vince shook his head, as if this would release the confusion that he was suddenly facing. "What the hell are you on about?"

"I've noticed that in front of the other guys, you're always aggressive towards me and I was always trying to fathom out why. However, now that we're alone, like now I guess, I can actually see there's a politer and softer side to you."

Vince backed away and turned to look out the window. *It's working*, thought Scott. He had agonised for ages on how he might get Vince to listen to what he had to say and had finally decided upon taking the direct challenge but quickly following it up with a statement or comment that would bring a much calmer atmosphere in order to get to the real root of the issues.

"I'm really sorry if I'm making you miserable. I don't mean to," said Vince, still gazing out of the window. "It wasn't my intention and certainly not to get you as angry as you clearly are."

"Why do you do it then? What have I done that's so awful to offend you, or upset you so much? I try my damnedest to please you but nothing I do ever seems to be right or good enough for you."

Vince spun slowly around and looked Scott directly in his eyes. Any of Vince's other subordinates might have felt incredibly uncomfortable and awkward by the deeply penetrating look from their boss but Scott held his nerve steadfast. "It's not you," he began in a slow, awkward tone. "Your work

The Absence of Friends

is really good. In fact, you're probably the best worker on my team, actually. It's just that…"

"Yeah? Go on. It's just that, what?"

Vince could no longer maintain the eye contact that he held with Scott and broke the gaze by averting his eyes to the floor. He sighed deeply, forcing the words to come out as he continued, "…it's just that…I've seen you in the *Pink Coconut* and I…well, I like you."

So, he's clearly gay and obviously doesn't know how to handle his feelings towards other men, or he's just not comfortable with who he really is, thought Scott. *It does all really make sense now.*

Vince was on a roll and continued with his explanation in the hope that he would finally be free of his pent up frustration that he had held onto for all this time. "I was so happy when you got the job here but you never seemed to notice me. I got so jealous, I suppose, when you built up friendships with the other guys. I know this probably makes no sense but I guess the only way that I could get your attention was by making you do extra duties. For me, it was a way of assuring that it was kind of our time together. I guess I've only succeeded in making you hate me. I'm really, really sorry Scott. I never meant to make you so miserable." He turned back and looked at the window again, exhaling loquaciously.

There was silence for a few moments before Scott found himself attempting unsuccessfully to stifle a laugh, causing Vince to spin round and face him once again. "What are you laughing for?"

"Here I was, terrified of what to say for fear that you'd probably beat the hell out of me, when all along, you're really not that kind of guy at all."

Vince managed to muster a smile, finally relieved that he had got everything out in the open.

"What about this guy that you supposedly got sacked?"

"I've never done any such thing. If the guys have been telling you stories about me, then don't believe a word of what they say. They seem to take great delight in tarnishing my reputation by making me out to be a real ogre. Mind you, I can see why they make these stories up."

"Why?"

"Well, I suppose it's probably because I put on the image that I'm quite a tough guy, when actually, I'm really not. When you get to know me, you'll find out that I am anything but this supposedly tough guy…in fact, I am really a pussy cat underneath it all."

"Now, why doesn't that surprise me in the slightest?"

"You see, I would love to be open about my sexuality, like you but to be honest, I'm quite scared about what others might think of me. I know you probably think this all sounds rather silly and quite passé…you know, you've heard it all before…the old cliché of the man who finds he is battling to come to terms with who he really is and who he wants to portray who he is to the world."

Scott shook his head. "No, I don't think that at all."

"It's only since I admitted to myself that I was gay. The way I act, I mean. You know the tough exterior that I portray. I guess I wanted to believe that I wasn't really gay."

"C'mon," said Scott, putting a friendly arm around his shoulder, "let's go out for a drink."

During their in-depth conversation over a couple of pints, Scott pointed out that whilst he was really flattered by the revelation that Vince liked him, he could only reciprocate the feelings as a platonic friend. It didn't take long for the seeds of friendship to be sown between the two men; developing steadfast roots that would grow firmer over the coming years. The other guys at the restaurant were stunned when they witnessed Scott and Vince laughing and joking together the following day. They were all keen to know what happened to cause such a drastic turnaround in their relationship but Scott was keeping the previous night's revelations very much a close kept secret.

In September 1997, after having worked with Vince for a year, Scott was ecstatic that he had finally managed to find himself a teaching job once again. Not only had things improved for him on the employment front but also his romantic life had begun to blossom, as he had been dating a guy called James Talbot for almost as long. Although Vince was sad that Scott would be leaving the restaurant, he was nonetheless pleased that his life was beginning to go in the right direction for him.

"After all," he said to Scott on his final day, "this isn't the end, really, is it? You are only closing one chapter of your life but the book continues to be written…and the characters we engage with will go on to develop…"

"What a lovely way of putting it," said Scott, slightly in awe of Vince's profoundly poetic farewell speech.

"…and of course, you know this isn't really goodbye because I'm confident that whilst both our lives' books are being written, there will be many cross-over chapters in the making."

Scott's other colleagues at the restaurant, whilst confused about what they considered to be a quirky and puzzling speech from Vince and still in the dark about his drastic character transformation, endlessly thanked Scott for whatever it was that he had done to improve the working relations between them and him.

The Absence of Friends

As Scott was about to close the door behind him for the final time at the restaurant, Vince said: "Let me cook you and James an anniversary meal and maybe we can go out for a few celebratory drinks afterwards."

James Talbot was an actor, who was becoming somewhat of a household name.

He had made his television debut at the age of four and took to the screen as though it were as natural as getting up in the morning. At the age of twenty-five, he had had minor roles in three major motion pictures; two of which had been an international success, and for the past five years, had starred in a hugely popular British soap opera, typecast as a gay character. His character had been written out of the show in quite a dramatic and emotional scene, much to the chagrin of the general public, who couldn't quite believe how the soap could continue without his character. Letters had been sent to the television station from emotionally distressed women and men, who clearly had a crush on James' character, making their feelings perfectly clear about how unhappy they were that one of the best loved soap characters would no longer be gracing their screens. It had been an incredibly tough decision for James to make when he informed the producers of his intention to leave because he wanted to concentrate on films rather than television. The producers would later regret their decision in killing off James' character, regardless of how dramatic and explosive the episode had been.

However, in June 1997, he began filming what was to be his fourth motion picture but this time, cast into a major role. This was, far and away, the most promising, exciting and challenging role that he had landed to date, as it allowed him the opportunity to play a character that was the complete opposite to the one he was associated with in the soap opera.

Acting was James' life but at times, he quietly loathed the superfluous recognition and demonstrative publicity that went hand-in-hand with it. He firmly believed that no matter how famous an individual was, they were still entitled to a private life but he was learning the hard way that once in the public eye, there was very little that remained private. He enjoyed attending the obligatory television or magazine interviews because he felt they were the occasional prognosis in his line of work. He didn't even mind the long, arduous photo shoots where the cameras clicked a thousand times in order to get that one perfect photograph that they were after. It was the inexorable paparazzi, with their incessant thirst to capture a sensational or shocking newspaper headline and the obsessive fans, who verged on the psychotic side of stalking that proved to be the biggest bugbear of his profession.

Scott couldn't believe his eyes, or his luck, when James approached him at the *Pink Coconut Club*. He wasn't particularly a fan of modern day soap operas; in fact he wasn't a fan of soap operas at all, but he knew the name James Talbot and that he had a particularly large gay fan base. James had an air of luminescent confidence about him that enhanced his rugged complexion, making him handsomely attractive both on and off screen.

Scott had been by himself for nearly an hour when James approached him, as Vince had long since left the club, due to finding someone that he had liked. James' self-assurance seemed to reflect onto Scott, as he didn't feel in the least bit nervous being in the company of a celebrity, or phased by the amount of proverbial daggers being shot in his direction from would-be challengers to his position. James and Scott talked the night through about everything and anything they cared to talk about, with the occasional raucous laugh thrown in when one had said something particularly humorous. Although their careers were worlds apart, their personal interests were revealing to be very similar. Both enjoyed the athleticism and competitiveness in each other, due to their love of swimming, running and cycling. At the end of the night it seemed as though they had known each other a lot longer than just a few hours.

Having only drunk soft drinks all night, James offered to drive Scott home. Their departure was viewed by many an enviable and covetous eye.

"Would you like to come in?" asked Scott when they arrived at his home.

"Sure," James replied, already mentally out of the car and eagerly anticipating what was to come. "You don't need to ask me twice," he continued, with a wink.

Scott had craved some meaningfully intimate contact since his relationship with Simon had ended and he wasn't disappointed with the erotic closeness that he felt with James. Over the course of the next few days, there was hardly a moment when they weren't apart, either in or out of the bedroom.

One of Scott's main concerns about this newly developing relationship that he was eager to keep pursuing, was James' prominence within the public eye and the obvious publicity that came with it. He wasn't shy in coming forward about mentioning his concern to James, who was careful to respect and honour Scott's wishes to keep him out of the media limelight. If James had any religious inclination or a belief in superstitious fate, he might have thought that the gods were smiling upon his promissory intentions to Scott, as other celebrities were causing far more of a stir within their private lives, that warranted the time and energy of the paparazzi. He did, however, have a few tricks of the trade up his sleeve to give that extra assurance that he could maintain his promise to Scott, as best he could, should the media's attention be redirected once more upon him.

The Absence of Friends

James' *tricks* depended very much upon his friends' co-operation in bringing his plans to fruition, so whenever he felt he needed to distract the media attention from his personal life, he would invite one of his friends around, with the prerequisite that they had to own a car. A minimum of half an hour would pass before the friend would then depart in their car, although the paparazzi would be totally unaware that the two men had actually exchanged clothes and it was James driving the car to wherever he wanted to go. To mix things up occasionally, the friend would leave in James' car, as he would watch the media trailing his car, as he slipped away unnoticed to his pre-planned rendezvous.

As Scott and James had spent such a wonderfully intense few days together, they both felt equally sad when James had to finally start the filming of his next motion picture. He would be up at the crack of dawn and not back until late in the evening, when Scott would be working in the restaurant and not returning back home until well gone midnight. The few hours that they did get to see each other were usually spent in the intimacy of each other's arms. James had every other Sunday free from filming and therefore, the couple would do something really special together, like a picnic in the countryside, swimming in Brighton, or whatever took their fancy on the spur of the moment.

When James was nearly at the end of his gruelling filming schedule, with only a few weeks remaining, Scott had managed to secure himself his teaching post. James wasn't in any of the scenes that were being filmed over the next few days, so he was overjoyed that he had a perfectly timed and welcomed break in order to celebrate his first anniversary with Scott, as well as Scott's new job. Vince had promised to cook a sumptuously romantic feast for the two of them, so they didn't have to ponder on which restaurant to go to, where the paparazzi were unlikely to pounce upon them.

James always erred on the side of caution whenever he was tasked with selecting an appropriate restaurant on the occasions that they did choose to dine out. He naturally wanted to avoid the areas that he affectionately dubbed as *Celebrity Central*. These were the places frequented by the celebrities who would automatically attract hordes of photographers and journalists wherever they went because the media felt the public needed to know about every single item of clothing they owned, or every blink they made and were clearly in paparazzi heaven when they were treated to an occasional faux pas. What was a little more difficult to equate were those he referred to as the *Pap Potentials*, who were the fame-hungry wannabes and the celebrities desperately eager to give their career a much needed boost to put them back into the public's eye. More often than not, it was the quaint little restaurants, hidden away on the quiet side streets of the outer zones of London that were frequented by the two men.

"That was absolutely divine, Vince," James said, satiated from the culinary delights he had just eaten. "Thank you so much."

"You're more than welcome," he replied.

"You know, anyway, that I think you're a wonderful cook," offered Scott, "but yes, thank you so much for this treat. If I could think of a word that means something more than just delicious, that's what I would be telling you right now."

Vince drove them all to a newly opened pub called *The Grand Duchess*, to round off their celebrations, with James using another one of his *tricks* by laying low in the backseat, so it would appear there were only two people in the car.

In the November of the same year, each of Vince, Scott and James had something of their own to celebrate: Scott's surprisingly sudden promotion to Head of the English and Maths departments; James' completion of filming and Vince's success in opening his very own restaurant. On the night of Vince's celebration, had Scott and James left the house ten minutes later than they had, one of them would have heard Deborah's sobbing voice as she left a message on the answer phone: "Oh God, Scott. Why aren't you there? You have to phone me as soon as you get this message…I need you here! Your father is seriously ill in hospital."

When Deborah came and stayed with Scott on one of her many visits, she was often unsure of how to treat James whenever she was in his company. Being an avid follower of all the soap operas, she found herself somewhat star struck and demonstratively in awe that her son was dating a soap star; especially as it was a character she really liked. She would continually compliment her son on finding himself "such a nice boy", even though her son was twenty-seven and James, twenty-six. She couldn't seem to let go of the fact that they were fully grown men and not little boys. James would constantly refer to Deborah as "mum", which made her smile warmly.

"So, how is dad doing these days?" Scott asked of his mother.

"Oh, you know, the same as usual. He knows that I'm visiting you now."

"What!" he exclaimed, genuinely unable to hide his surprise at his father's knowledge that his mother was maintaining contact with him. "How long has he known about this?"

"Yes, I thought this might surprise you," Deborah said earnestly. "He's known about my visits for quite some time now. He always asks after you, wanting to know every single detail of my time with you, no matter how small or insignificant it might have been."

The Absence of Friends

"Why doesn't he come and visit?"

Deborah avoided answering the question and continued in her convivial manner. "He was over the moon when I told him about the promotion you got. He's really proud of you, Scott."

"And what about James?" Scott asked, not wanting this question to be avoided. "Has he learnt to accept him yet?"

Deborah gave a long, drawn out sigh. She looked at James and then back to Scott. "He's trying very hard to, darling, but you know how he is and what he's always thought when he first found out." Turning back to James, she continued. "I'm so sorry, James. It's really difficult for him but he's trying very hard. He's constantly battling with his feelings for his son against his views on homosexuality."

James gave Deborah a warmly empathetic smile. "It's okay, mum. I completely understand. I can quite believe that it's a tormenting battle, especially when it's a member of your own family."

Deborah felt that James was very good for Scott and could see how happy the two of them were together. She couldn't bring herself to shatter their happiness by revealing that her husband had developed aggressive prostate cancer. The preservation of her son's happiness didn't enter her mind when, in November, her husband was rushed into hospital. Deborah was so distraught, she felt she had to ring Scott and beg him to come and stay. Gaining no reply, she left a tearful message on his answer machine.

February 1998 became known as the month of hell and never-ending tears for Scott.

Firstly, there was Vince. Although not a million miles away, he was imminently moving to Paris, as he was to view potential venues to open his second restaurant in what he was hoping to become a European chain; the Parisian *Shepherd's* ∏. He had adored Paris for as long as he could remember and made up his mind that he wanted to live there whilst he oversaw the opening of his latest venture. It was an incredibly emotional parting for Scott, as he had become very close and hugely fond of Vince. They promised each other faithfully that they would keep in touch and although their intentions were to do so, it wasn't as much as either of them would have liked. In the early months, they maintained reasonably regular contact by phoning and writing to each other, although it was always Vince who made the effort to come and visit Scott. Vince never settled in Paris, as over the next few years, he opened further *Shepherd's* ∏ restaurants in Düsseldorf, Barcelona, Venice, Rhodes,

Valletta, Malmö and Vienna, moving to whatever area he was opening his newest restaurant.

Secondly, there was James. He had been offered a very lucrative and promising deal of a new movie, in Hollywood. This was finally his chance to make it really big and make a name for himself on the other side of the Atlantic. He wanted Scott to move to Hollywood with him, which caused many arguments between the two of them. Eventually, they came to a mutual agreement that they should go their separate ways, even though neither one really wanted that as a solution, but as neither wanted to give up their respective career, it was the only option they had left. They too kept in contact, albeit for the first few weeks of their separation but the return responses from James became less and less frequent, until they stopped altogether. He did get to realise his dream in Hollywood, as America took him to their hearts and it wasn't too long before scripts became his to turn down. He bought himself a luxury apartment in Malibu, only returning to England in order to promote his latest movie. Never, on any of his visits to London, did he ever make any attempt to see Scott.

Thirdly, there was his father. He was the only person who Scott would be unable to keep in contact with, as on 18 February, his father passed away. Since being admitted into hospital, his father's health had deteriorated at an alarming rate. Scott's visits to the hospital over the three months were nothing short of painful for both men; physically and emotionally. What upset Scott the most was the fact that he would never have the chance to claim back all those wasted years with his father. It would be a long time before Scott allowed himself any forgiveness, ruing the day he allowed himself to walk out of his mother's school and his father's life.

Scott stayed with the remaining members of his family for a couple of weeks before he returned to London. Before he departed, Deborah handed him an addressed letter that his father had written to him in the September of the previous year.

"I found this in your father's belongings. I'd completely forgotten that he had written it and I guess his intention was to post it to you. But, with everything that's…" She paused, as tears began to well in her eyes. "He wanted this to be the olive branch to bring the two of you back together."

Scott placed a comforting arm around his mother, as he bit his tongue in a bid to stop the flow of tears coming from his own eyes. He knew that the moment the first tear dropped, there would be absolutely no stopping what he was trying so desperately hard not to start. If he was going to have an emotional breakdown, he wanted to ensure that nobody else was around to be able to witness to it.

The envelope that his mother gave to him was placed tentatively at the top of his carry case, as he knew that he did not have the strength of courage to open it until he was in the solitude of his own home. When he did eventually arrive home, he put off the inevitable for as long as he could. He sat on his bed, hands trembling, as he gently opened the envelope and began to read:

Dearest Scott,

I guess it's probably far easier for me to put my feelings and thoughts down on to paper and say what it is I need to, rather than stumble over my words in a stifled conversation with you in person and more than likely make an even bigger fool of myself than I already have.

It's somewhat pathetic that it's taken me almost six and half years to realise what a foolishly stubborn, old man I have been; a trait of mine that I am ever so glad you didn't inherit.

I really hope you can believe me when I say that truly, I never, ever wanted you to become alienated from the family. I know that I must have caused you a lot of pain and heartache over these years and all because I am a pathetically obstinate fool whenever I get an idea inside my head. Whether it's a good idea, or a bad one, I end up stupidly allowing my selfish pride to get the better of me…and this is what causes me to make the ridiculously poor judgments that I have done. (I know that your mother will definitely agree with what I have just said here).

I know that six and a half years is a ridiculous amount of time to reflect upon what happened and why but I suppose, thinking about it, I was initially very hurt and angry to discover that you were gay. If only you had turned your back on that part of your life, I wouldn't have lost all these years with you. But, I brought my children up to have faith in their convictions and fight for what they believed to be true and honest, even if it entailed them having to make some very painful decisions.

I knew that your mother, brother and sister were visiting you but never challenged any of them over this, as I guess they were the only real links I had in knowing what was happening with you. I might be an old fool, Scott but I'm certainly not deaf and on many an occasion I overheard the conversations between them.

I am ever so proud in what you have achieved in your life. I did come clean to your mother one day and admit that I knew about her visits to you; she tried on numerous occasions to persuade me to come and visit you but, as I said before, you know how stubborn I can be.

I regret now that I hadn't followed your mother's desire so much sooner, then we could have been a real family again. The guilt of my mistakes will live with me for the remainder of my days.

However, the real purpose of me writing this letter to you is meant to be a positive one. I really hope that you can find it in your heart to forgive me so we can concentrate on catching up and allow me the opportunity to be the father I should have always been.

I understand from your mother that James is quite the charming and respectful young man, who makes you very happy. Well, it really would make me very happy if both you and James could come and visit some time very soon. I would like to shake James warmly by the hand and welcome him into the family.

I hope that you will forgive me and allow me to become a father to you once again. I believe a father should hug his children often, so I have a fatherly hug awaiting you.

All my love, Scott,
   Your ever loving Father.

A lump of raw emotion had built in Scott's throat, almost choking him, as he read his father's letter but he fought hard to hold back until he had reached the end, even though his eyes were burning with a bitter sting. When he had finished, there was nothing to stop the flood of tears, as he wept uncontrollably for several minutes. The tears continued to flow, as the anguish he felt over the wasted years he couldn't claim back and the years ahead that he would never be able to embrace, was mixed with realisation that his father had finally accepted him. For several hours he lay on his bed, re-reading the letter over and over, until his eyes were red raw from the tears that he thought would never end. He longed for his father to be with him right now, just so he could tell him how much he loved him too.

On Saturday 24 October 1998, a new club had opened its doors for the first time in Putney and Scott thought he would try it out, after seeing quite an eye-catching advert for it in the press. On first impression, he decided that he liked it a lot, mainly because the music they were playing was what he enjoyed dancing to.

After being at the club for a couple of hours, he spotted a lad whom he thought looked quite handsome, standing by the edge of the dance floor. He appeared to be quite shy and nervous, which, Scott thought, gave him extra appeal. Scott hadn't been with anyone since James, but found himself unable to take his eyes off this lad. He had actually noticed him a little earlier, coming into the club along with two other men but immediately concluded that one of them had to be his boyfriend, because surely someone as good-looking as he was, couldn't really be single. Still, he thought, there was absolutely nothing to lose by talking to him. The least he could hope for was a decent conversation, or potentially a friendship. *It's all or nothing*, he said to himself, as he approached the guy.

"Hi. What's your name?" he asked.

"Luke."

CHAPTER SIX

After his second successful stage musical, Luke became a much sought after performer in pubs, clubs and bars; both gay and straight alike. He would often return to his favourite venues due to "popular demand". More often than not, Kristian and Elliot would accompany their friend to these venues and offer their friendly moral support. This would often relax Luke prior to entertaining; knowing there were friendly faces in the audience for him to hone in on. He would always make a point of tracking them down from within the crowd before beginning each performance.

Most people who had seen Luke performing, would have argued until they were blue in the face that there was absolutely no way he was characteristically a shy and retiring sort of man. How on earth could someone enjoy performing on stage, being the focal point of attention to a mass of people and then not enjoy the adulation of the same attention afterwards? Luke only truly allowed himself to become relaxed when he knew that there was a friendly face within the audience, almost as if they were the anchor for his confidence. This was the key reason that he would always ensure that he met up with Elliot and Kristian beforehand, so he could determine where they were standing and use them as his emotional rocks. More often than not, after a show had finished, he would make an immediate beeline for Elliot and Kristian, involving himself into a deep conversation so he wouldn't have to face other punters and their multitude of questions, or banal and unwanted sexual innuendoes.

Knowing that his popularity was far exceeding his original expectations, Luke found that he could only manage to perform in a select amount of venues. He thought that being in this position was rather unfortunate, as he did not wish to let go of any potential for further advancement in his career, as he was putting all his efforts into his singing. After finishing his entertaining for the evening and his obligatory chat with Elliot and Kristian, he would go straight home and crawl into bed in an exhaustedly crumpled heap, aware that he would need to be up early in the morning to begin his vocal exercises. It didn't take someone of Einstein's brainpower to determine that he was in dire need of a break.

After nearly three years of continually performing, whether it be in the theatre or in the bars and clubs, with the ever-increasing fame, he realised that he was nearing the edge of a physically exhausting breakdown. He decided that it was time to take matters into his own hands and took it upon himself to cut off completely from the performing circuit for a couple of months, so

The Absence of Friends

he could take this time to thoroughly recuperate. For the first month, he would just sit around the flat, taking it easy, reading a book, or even writing some lyrics and music. On the odd occasion, he would take himself away for a day trip to Brighton, Portsmouth or Bristol, just to take in the sights and not have to think about anything that might require a degree of concentration. Disciplining himself not to sing, especially when the phone was constantly ringing and managers of his regular venues were requesting him to do a show, was exceptionally difficult at the beginning. After the first month had passed, though, he actually began to relax and enjoyed not having to continually perform.

His twenty-third birthday fell during his second month's recuperation. The phone rang in his flat and he picked it up reticently, hoping to God that it wasn't someone offering him the chance to perform in their venue.

"Hello?" he said inquisitively, through gritted teeth.

Thankfully, it was Elliot on the other end. "Hello Luke. I'm just calling to tell you to get your glad rags on 'cause we're going out."

"Why? What's the occasion?"

"Oh God, Luke. Seriously? Are you naturally thick, or just pretending to play dumb?"

"Quit with the riddles, Elliot and tell me what you're blabbering on about" snapped Luke with puerility.

Elliot, who was joined by Kristian on another extension began a raucous chorus of *Happy Birthday*.

"Thanks guys," Luke gushed, after apologising for snapping, clearly chuffed with the felicitous, though not always tunefully choral, birthday surprise.

"So, Luke…" began Kristian with an audaciously convoluted tone that a paterfamilias might adopt with his offspring before an admonishment was forthcoming.

"Yes?" replied Luke with the predictable hint of trepidation.

"…What does it feel like to be twenty-three?"

"Twenty-three? Good Lord, is that *really* how young I am? Honestly guys, I feel like a thirty year old."

Kristian spoke. "That's just wishful thinking on your part, Luke."

Elliot continued with Kristian's obvious train of thought. "…Well, that's probably a stroke of luck for you because I'm sure you'll find plenty of thirty year olds where we're taking you tonight. If that's what you like."

Luke chortled wryly. "Very droll guys. Alright then, Mr Comic and Mr Humour, what time?"

"We'll come and pick you up around seven-ish."

"Okay. I'll see you then."

All eyes turned on Luke as he walked into *Jupiter's* nightclub with Kristian and Elliot; not just because they recognised him as the newly rising star on the cabaret circuit, but because at twenty-three years old, he was one of the very few young, good-looking lads there. Luke had very classic boy-next-door looks and as he had never had a problem with teenage acne, his skin was smooth and silky, which made even the most placid eye jealous. His fine, blond hair had been styled into the latest men's fashion, which he continually ran his fingers through. His hair would always fall neatly back into place whenever he did this. His deep blue, opulent eyes seemed to sparkle and smile, even if his lips were not. When he did smile, showing his perfectly white teeth, you could have been forgiven for thinking that he was filming a toothpaste commercial. Even the clothes he wore seemed to make a positive bearing on how good looking he was: A snug, teal, thick-cotton shirt over a dazzling white, t-shirt. These were tucked neatly into his figure-hugging, slate-gray 501s, which covered the tops of his well-polished and sensible, black Dr Marten shoes.

"Well, hello there," said Kristian, turning to Luke, "who's the belle of the ball then?"

Luke went almost beetroot-red and avoided answering Kristian's question. "Quick! I need to get to the bar."

They made their way to the bar and ordered their drinks. Luke was about to pay, when Kristian looked sharply at him. "What do you think you're doing?"

"Paying for the drinks."

Elliot shook his head. "No, no, no! You're not meant to buy any drinks on your birthday." He handed a note to the bartender, and whilst waiting for his change, both he and Kristian raised their glasses, wishing him a happy birthday in unison.

"Thanks guys. And thanks again for the watch, it's really wonderful. I've been lost without one since my last one broke."

"We only got it 'cause we're fed up of you always asking us for the time," laughed Elliot.

"Let's have a boogie," said Kristian, his body already swaying gently to the rhythm of the music.

They managed to squeeze themselves onto the dance floor, but Kristian continued on up to the DJ's mixing booth and began talking with him.

"What did you say to him?" asked Luke, with his hands on his hips, pretending to be angry. "What have you got planned?"

They both looked at Luke and smiled. "You'll see."

Luke concluded that it would be futile in persisting to find out what his friends were up to, so he continued dancing, trying hard not to show he really wanted to know what they had cooked up between themselves. Lee Marrow's *Don't You Want Me* played, which was currently Luke's favourite dance track. When it finished, the DJ came over the microphone. "That was from Kristian and Elliot, to the gorgeous Luke Faraday, on his twenty-third birthday. It has been requested though, Luke, if you would do the honours and sing a couple of numbers for us."

Luke spun around to face his friends, his fingers running through his hair and his cheeks reddening by the second, whilst the club's clientele cheered on their encouragement for him. Feeling suitably mortified at being stitched up by his friends, he sighed at them. "You bastards!" Elliot and Kristian were almost in tears due to their uncontrollable state of laughter.

As Luke walked up the couple of steps to the stage, the DJ spoke again: "Here he is guys." Turning to Luke, he asked, "So, will you sing us a couple of numbers?"

"I would love to," began Luke, "but I don't have any of my backing tracks with me, so…"

Kristian came running up to the stage, with a couple of Luke's backing track CDs in his hand. Luke shook his head in total disbelief; the whole night's charade must have been entirely planned by his two friends. Over the microphone, he said to them, "I'll never forgive you two for doing this." He began with Abba's *Gimme, Gimme, Gimme (A Man After Midnight)*, which he had reworked to a more up-to-date, dance club melody and then went on to sing a song he had written himself, called *Let Your Love Be My Rhythmic Drug*.

Whilst Luke was singing his self-penned composition, he became aware of a young man who had made his way from the back end of the bar to a more prominent position at the front of the stage. He had maintained eye contact with the man throughout his short, meandering journey until he settled at his final position. Luke shot him a huge cheeky smile, together with an ominous wink, the man reciprocated the smile, with a solicitous raise of an eyebrow thrown in. When the song had finished, Luke asked the guy to come up and join him on the stage, which was met with a tremendous round of applause from the whole club, who were anticipating another of his spectacular finales.

"Well now," began Luke precociously, "as you were so eager to get to the front of the stage, one can only assume it was obviously to get the best view you could of yours truly. So, I immediately thought to myself that his man clearly has an unmet desire, why not go one capricious step further and invite him up here? Hence, we now have said eager beaver," Luke gesticulated nonchalantly toward the man, "who will now be able to go home tonight, safe in the knowledge that his desires have been fully satiated."

The man smiled awkwardly, clearly not sure whether to put his hands in his pockets, hang them down by his side or cross them in front of his chest.

"Please don't shatter my already tenuous ego and tell me that my number one fan is actually shy." Luke curled his lower lip and sighed mockingly.

A chorus of "aww" and "ahh" emanated from the crowd, obviously enjoying their chance for a bit of audience participation.

An inaudible mumble came from the man, who shook his head, even though his eyes were focused upon the floor.

"Well then, I don't suppose I can keep referring to you as *my number one fan*, or even Bashful from Snow White for the remainder of the show now really, can I? So, what to actually call you? I presume you do possess such a thing as a name?"

The DJ had given the inquisitive stranger a microphone of his own to use. "It's...ah...Matthew...Matt," came the sheepish but cautious voice.

"*It's...ah...Matthew...Matt* is not a name I've ever come across before."

Matthew laughed. Not because he thought that what Luke had said was particularly funny, but because the rest of people in the club were laughing at his expense and he wanted to cover his uncomfortable embarrassment by laughing with them. "No, that's not my name! Matthew Sylvester is my name. Or just Matt, to my friends."

"Well now, if that's the case, *Matt* Sylvester, as we've now broken the ice, I think I am going to consider myself as one of your friends. Is that okay?"

Matthew nodded, as he started to feel his nerves calm slightly and a genuine smile return to his face.

"Right...let's get on with the show then, Matt. Do you know *Summer Nights?*"

Again Matthew nodded.

"I'm afraid that I can't sing the male parts in these duets, so you're gonna have to be the big, butch man for me and sing the part of Danny, right?"

"Sure, no problem."

"This is another track I've danced-up," he said to the crowd, "so bear with us for just a moment." He turned to Matthew and in his ear gave him a quick rendition of how the tempo of the track was going to be, so he wasn't caught totally by surprise at how different it was to the original. "Are you ready?" he asked Matthew. He was greeted with a very apprehensive nod. "Okay," called Luke. "DJ, let's get down to some real summer lovin'"

The Absence of Friends

The crowd loved Luke and Matthew camping it up as Danny and Sandy, giving them a near-deafening ovation when they had finished. Luke was surprised at how well it had gone, as he thought it was going to be a total and utter travesty but Matthew had a reasonably good voice and their vocals certainly complimented each other.

Luke gave Matthew a kiss on the cheek. "Thanks for doing that. Let me buy you a drink."

"Okay," agreed Matthew.

The DJ spoke, as Luke and Matthew headed toward the bar. "Thanks to Luke for his performance and enjoy the rest of your birthday." Luke signaled his thanks with a wave of his hand toward the DJ and the dance music once again resumed.

Luke and Matthew talked the night through, until Luke agreed to go home with him. Luke would end up regretting ever going back with him. When he eventually thought about it, he would live to regret *ever* having invited Matthew on to the stage with him.

Matthew was twenty-six years old and on his way to becoming a doctor of psychiatry, having already completed four years in medical school and was now on his second year of his psychiatric residency. Both his mother and father were doctors, although they specialised in different fields. Having completed his college education, his parents were naturally delighted when Matthew had chosen to continue his studies and earn his Bachelor Degree in Psychology. Unfortunately, they were not there to witness Matthew receiving his degree and bask in the usual parental pride, as they had cut off all communication with him, in his final year, when they discovered that he was gay.

Matthew's sisters, on the other hand, did stay in contact with him but never volunteered the information to their parents, denying it when they were challenged on the many occasions. When Matthew was in his third year of medical school, his younger sister, Cheryl-Ann, was involved in a fatal car accident. This affected him a great deal more than he cared to admit or show but instead of allowing himself the time and opportunity to grieve his loss, he forced himself to harden and suppress his emotions in order to be able to continue with his studies. In the same year - a matter of weeks after Cheryl-Ann's tragic death - his older sister, Monica, had run off abroad with a much older man, whom he knew that his parents would never have approved. He never heard from Monica again.

With the loss of both his sisters, Matthew became bitter and depressed but desperately tried to suppress these feelings further. The only people who had ever shown him any love were now gone. The hatred he felt against his parents for disowning him was becoming an overwhelming obsession. He guessed they would have attempted to persuade his sisters to do the same; making him resent his parents even further. He cursed his mother and father for depriving him of his sisters' love. To prevent anyone from taking anything away from him again, he would psychoanalyse events and reactions and begin to second-guess outcomes, so as not to allow himself to suffer any further losses. He began to play emotional and psychological games with others, which became much darker and far deeper as time passed by. In the early days these games were not carried out maliciously but definitely with intent, after he found out what positive results he could achieve from them. Matthew knew that the loss of his sisters and the extreme feelings he had towards his parents was affecting him psychologically. Instead of seeking professional help from a qualified psychiatrist, he thought he could give himself the treatment that he needed to make himself better and enable him to think more clearly. In reality, with his self-diagnosis, he only succeeded in making matters, by far, a lot worse for himself.

Matthew had liked Luke for a long time but he had never dared to make a move on these feelings, as he thought that somebody like Luke would never be interested in someone like him. Jubilant ecstasy didn't really cover the overwhelming euphoria that he was feeling, when Luke had agreed to go back home with him after their little impromptu duet.

In Matthew's eyes, he thought of himself as a very plain person, with only average looks and incessantly asked Luke what he had found attractive about him. Luke would simply reply that beauty was truly in the eyes of the beholder and that he shouldn't continually keep putting himself down

Believing that Matthew was genuine was not difficult for Luke, as this was the first time anyone had shown him any real affection since leaving his mother all those years ago. Elliot and Kristian had grown to love Luke and he them, but with Matthew it was different. He was able to let his true emotions surface easily. They enjoyed being in each other's company. Over the course of the following few months, they were rarely out of each other's sight and begun to admit that they were falling in love with each other. When they weren't out by themselves, they would often make up a foursome with Elliot and Kristian, who were pleased that they were getting on so well.

In July 1995, around Matthew's twenty-seventh birthday, they had their first major argument.

"If you really loved me, you would do as I ask."

"I do love you, Matt."

The Absence of Friends

Matthew slammed the phone down on the table, next to Luke. "Okay, prove you love me. Cancel your performance for tonight."

"You know damn well that I can't do that," shouted Luke, as he jumped out of his chair. "Why didn't you tell me when I asked you the other day, that you wanted to go out? Then I wouldn't have booked anything for tonight."

"Am I not entitled to change my mind?"

"You may well be. I can't just be given a few hours' notice to cancel a show. It doesn't look very professional."

Matthew thumped his fist down hard on the table. "Do as you damn well please then, Luke. I thought I meant more to you than your singing. Obviously I was wrong."

"For God's sake," hissed Luke, "you're being totally unreasonable. How about doing something tomorrow night? I've got a free night, as I'm not performing."

"Tomorrow night isn't *to*night! You're a selfish pig, Luke," screamed Matthew, grabbing Luke with one hand and slapping him hard across the face with the other.

Luke stared at Matthew for what seemed like an eternity, as if time had frozen him with a look of horror and disbelief on his face. When the reality of what happened sunk in, Luke stormed out of the room, without any further words, slamming the door behind him.

He came home after finishing at the club he was performing at, not even stopping to talk with Elliot or Kristian, who were stunned by his hasty departure without even acknowledging them. He went straight to the bedroom and saw Matthew sitting up in bed, obviously having been crying.

Luke lay on the bed and put his arms around Matthew. "I'm really sorry, Matt. It was a silly argument that really shouldn't have happened. I do love you very much you know."

"I'm really sorry too, Luke" Matthew sighed. "You know I love you too. I just hate it that I get so angry and lash out at the people I love."

They made love. Slow, sensuous and very real.

That night was to be the first of many typical ones to follow. There would be a very heated argument, which would ultimately end in Matthew lashing out at Luke and questioning his love. It would always be Luke who relented first and apologised. Matthew would try and analyse why Luke provoked him into acting the way he did, subtly hinting that the blame was never upon his own shoulders. Finally, after the tears had flowed, usually from Matthew, they would end up making love. On occasion, Matthew threatened to leave Luke, or something equally similar. On some particularly violent rows, Matthew even threatened to kill himself, which would always lead to Luke hastily quenching the heat of the argument by immediately apologising, with a fearful tone in his voice. What Luke didn't know was that Matthew had absolutely no intention of carrying out his suicidal threats. Pure and simple, they were nothing more than a deliberate ploy in pulling at Luke's emotional strings in order to ensure that he was nothing but putty in Matthew's hands. Luke truly believed that Matthew meant it when he repeatedly told him that he still loved him but always promised he would try hard to alter his negligent behaviour that was seemingly, in Matthew's eyes, the root cause of their arguments. It never seemed to cross Luke's mind that they only ever made love after one of their arguments.

After one particularly violent argument, Luke decided that he'd had enough and threatened to leave Matthew. Matthew broke down in tears, recounting the harrowing history of his parents and sisters, failing to mention the after effects he had suffered.

"Why didn't you tell me this before?" asked Luke, with tears rolling down his cheeks.

Matthew shrugged his shoulders.

Luke truly believed this to be the real root of their problems. After they talked about Matthew's background, he began to convince himself that things could only get better from hereon in.

He couldn't have been further from the truth.

Their relationship drew into its eighteenth month. Luke had been neglecting his friendship with Elliot and Kristian, visiting and going out with them less and less frequently; not through choice but because he was ashamed of the bruises he kept receiving from Matthew. He deliberately made no attempt to return their calls, even if they said it was urgent. He felt very alone, even though he chose to believe that he and Matthew were still in love. On the nights when Matthew went out without him, he would sit in the dark and cry for hours, until he fell asleep.

The desperation he felt seemed to eventually outweigh the fear regarding the bruising; as he decided it was high time that he visited Elliot and Kristian. He kept his finger pressed firmly on their doorbell. Even after Kristian had opened the door, his finger was still pressed on the bell.

"Well, hello stranger," said Kristian with a slight smile. "What's the emergency?"

Luke took his finger off the doorbell and with desperation, asked: "Can I come in?"

"Sure."

Luke followed Kristian into the living room, where Elliot was already seated, watching television. As they sat down, he switched off the television

The Absence of Friends

with the remote. Turning to Luke, he said: "Hi there." He paused for a moment, when he had had a proper look at Luke's face and cried: "Jesus Christ, Luke! What the hell's happened to your face?"

Luke couldn't look either of them in the eye. "Um…nothing. I banged my face on the wardrobe, after sleepwalking." He ran his fingers through his hair.

"It's Matt. Isn't it?" Kristian volunteered. "He's been hitting you, hasn't he?"

"No!" lied Luke.

"We've been worried as to why you've been avoiding us."

"I haven't."

Elliot cut in. "Look, Luke, we're your friends. You know that you can trust us. If Matt has been hitting you, we want to help."

It took Elliot and Kristian over an hour to cajole Luke into telling them what had occurred over the past few months between him and Matthew, which took another further hour to explain all the little details that Luke needed to offload.

"What a bastard!" declared Kristian.

"He's not!" exclaimed Luke defiantly. "He loves me."

"Matt is playing games with you," stated Elliot. "It's affecting you deeply and your singing is suffering because of it. We know that you haven't been turning up for some of your shows. We're really worried about you, Luke."

Kristian nodded in agreement.

"I'm fine."

"You may think you're fine but you are acting like you're a hunted fox."

"Don't you believe what I'm telling you?"

"It's not a case of whether we believe you," answered Kristian. "It's whether you believe yourself. You have to realise how Matt is affecting you. If you're not careful, the way that you're going, you're not going to be able to sing anywhere, as word will get around that you're unreliable and we don't want to see that happen to you."

Luke broke down in tears. "I really don't know what to do."

Elliot and Kristian sat on each arm of the chair and put their arms around Luke.

Kristian handed Luke a box of tissues to wipe his red and swollen eyes. "Only you can decide what to do, but we want you to know that we'll help you in any way that we can. We've been friends for three and a half years and are not going to throw it away over someone like Matthew."

Luke tried to smile at his friends, knowing exactly what it was that he needed to do.

"I'm leaving."

Matthew looked shocked. "What?"

"It's over between us, Matt. You're destroying my life and I can't take it anymore."

"But I love you."

Luke shook his head vehemently. "No, you don't! You only pretend that you do. I should have done this a long time ago."

Matthew began crying. "Please don't go," he begged. "I know we can work it through this time. I really don't know what I would do without you."

"It's no use pretending to cry, Matt. You'll cope, as you have always managed to cope…by looking after the one person that means the most to you. Yourself."

Matthew could see that Luke was adamant in leaving and resorted to his pleas which always seemed to work. "If you go, I'll kill myself."

Luke sighed and drew in a deep breath. "That won't work anymore either. I know the kind of emotional games you play with me, Matt. Do whatever you like. Say whatever you want. It won't change my mind."

Matthew was becoming desperate. For some reason, Luke was not conforming to the usual threats. "But…I….love you."

"…Maybe you do. Or maybe it's the fact that I bow to your every whim and command that you love."

"Well, you *do* love me. Don't you?"

Luke bit his tongue. "No, Matt. I don't think I do anymore. I really don't know what I feel for you right now."

"Can we still be friends, at least?" asked Matthew, fishing for an opening; anywhere that he could resume the attack once more.

"I really don't think so. I'm going now, Matt and I'm not coming back."

"Well, don't bother coming to say goodbye to me," he screamed, leaving the room.

Just keep out of my way until I've left, thought Luke.

Luke tried to dial the number, but his hand was shaking like a desperate leaf clinging to its branch in a vicious wind. It took some time to dial all the digits he needed.

"Hello?" It was Kristian's voice.

The Absence of Friends

"Oh God," Luke managed to whisper, his voice shaking in terror.

He could hear crying down the phone. "Luke? Is that you?"

"Kris. Oh, God…"

"Luke," said Kristian anxiously. "What's wrong?"

"It's…it's…Matt."

Kristian became angry. "What's that bastard done to you now? Has he hit you again?"

"No."

"Luke? What is it? Tell me!"

Silence. Apart from the sobs that Luke couldn't hold back.

"Stay right there and don't move. We'll come over straight away." He put the receiver down.

Twenty minutes had passed when Elliot and Kristian finally arrived, banging furiously on the front door. Luke opened the door to them, looking pale and withdrawn. Kristian noticed the receiver off the hook and guessed it was from their telephone call earlier.

"Where is he? Where is that bastard?" asked Kristian angrily, as he placed the receiver back on the hook.

Luke pointed upwards, in the direction of the bedroom.

His two friends bolted up the stairs and flung open the bedroom door, ready to have it out with Matthew and send him packing. They were stopped in their tracks, with the blood slowing draining from their faces at the sight before them. The smell alone made the two men want to wretch, as slumped over the bed was Matthew. His face, and all around where he had been laying was covered in vomit.

Elliot scrambled to the bed, so as to feel for a pulse from Matthew's wrist, noticing what appeared to be an empty bottle of pills and an almost empty bottle of whisky. Looking up at his partner, vacantly, he whispered: "Kris, he's dead!"

Elliot and Kristian persisted with their efforts to help Luke come to terms with Matthew's death, determined not to admit defeat in convincing him that what had happened was in no way his fault.

They had managed to glean from Luke that after the argument, at the point where Luke said he was leaving, Matthew had stormed out of the room to the bathroom and grabbed the bottle of pills from the medicine cabinet; the one he had continually threatened Luke with that he was going to take. To add further effect to the drama that he hoped Luke would find himself being caught up in, Matthew also grabbed himself a full bottle of whisky from the kitchen. Several times he asked Luke if he was really adamant in leaving him, to which Luke would always answer "yes".

"Well, if you are *that* determined," Matthew said, "then I am determined to take this bottle of pills. Then we'll see who is sorry." He showed Luke the bottle, opened it and quickly swallowed a handful of the pills, taking a large swig of whisky to ensure that they were washed down. "Satisfied?" he spat.

"Oh yes…the infamous bottle of pills that you keep telling me you are going to take."

"What?" said Matthew, shocked and confused that Luke was taking this a little too calmly for his liking.

"Oh yes, Matt. I came across, quite by accident, your infamous little bottle of *pills* one day! They are nothing more than Smarties, Polo mints, or something along those lines." He sneered at Matthew before continuing: "All this time, you've been threatening to kill yourself with nothing more than a bottle of sweets! Well, go ahead then and take them…knock yourself out with nothing more than what's tantamount to a possible sugar overdose! Nothing will change my mind, Matthew…I am still leaving you."

As if he still believed that he was playing his trump card, Matthew took another handful of the pills, with a couple more large swigs from the bottle of whisky but his ploy to emotionally entrap Luke had failed miserably. No matter how many of his so-called pills that he took, Luke was not going to be fooled by these pathetically desperate games of his any longer. What Matthew hadn't realised though, was that the bottle he had grabbed from the bathroom in his haste to control the situation was not the usual bottle he used in order to trick Luke with.

When Luke was suffering with a particularly debilitating headache and couldn't manage to find the usual bottle of extra strength painkillers one day, as Matthew had kept it hidden and only placed it in the medicine cabinet on the occasions he was going to play his emotional games with Luke, he purchased another bottle. *This* was the bottle that Matthew had actually grabbed.

"I am so utterly tired of your games Matt, and the way that you have continually strived to manipulate me over the course of god only knows how long…Well, you go ahead and have all the fun you want with your *Smarties*," he cried exasperatedly, leaving the room to continue collecting his belongings from other parts of the house.

The Absence of Friends

The conversations between Luke and his two friends became more strained and often very one-sided, as he made little to no attempt of any input. Their patience, loyalty and friendship were put to the ultimate test, as Luke became extremely difficult to communicate with, often lashing out verbally as well as physically.

Even though Luke had been cleared of any involvement in Matthew's death, as a verdict of death by misadventure had been recorded through the police investigations, he became totally withdrawn, deliberately isolating himself from everyone. It was becoming far too much for him to cope with: the death of Matthew, the constant probing questions from the police and of course, the matter of Elliot and Kristian becoming nothing more than interfering busybodies in his life. They were the easiest people for him to lash out at and he would invariably find himself having arguments with one, or both of them. These arguments would generally end with Luke telling them to "get lost", "why don't you just mind your own business and let me mind my own?" or even, "when I need someone to offer me *advice*, it won't be you that I will be calling upon."

However, the bond that had grown between them in the past three and a half years had become so strong, it seemed as though it might withstand the strain in spite of Luke's ignorant and malevolent behaviour.

It was in February 1997, three months after Matthew's death, Luke finally agreed to see a psychiatrist. Both Elliot and Kristian were insistent that he should get some treatment, even though he kept telling them that he didn't need any. Luke received a year of intense psychotherapy, which helped him to finally come to terms with Matthew's suicide. Although he couldn't fully accept that he wasn't responsible for Matthew's death, he eventually believed that he wasn't totally to blame.

He began to realise and understand the effect that his behaviour had had on both Elliot and Kristian and therefore, made some positive efforts to rectify the problems he had caused amongst the three of them.

In the time which had passed since Matthew's death, Luke had not ventured out to a pub or a club nor even a restaurant or the cinema. Elliot and Kristian were persistently trying to coax him into going out but he would always make up some feeble excuse, or just point blank refuse. He had not even returned to performing in any of his regular pubs or clubs since the physical abuse episodes from Matthew, even though he had been bombarded with plenty of requests and invitations. At first, he would blatantly ignore the invitations but after the talk with Elliot and Kristian about the possibility of destroying his career, he wrote to each of the managers of the venues, explaining that he would be taking a long break and would contact them once again when he was intending to return. There were a handful of venues who wrote back telling him to take a permanent break from their establishment, which only served to make Luke all the more determined to never allow himself to get into this situation again. The majority of the replies that he received, were ones that wished him well, where the manager as well as all the punters, would be looking forward to his future return.

In the three months prior to receiving his psychotherapy, Luke would often go to Matthew's graveside, with his emotions being caught within an internal maelstrom, mixing them up so he was never sure what he would actually be feeling on each occasion. Every emotion he possessed would often surface when he knelt by the graveside, either reliving events, or desperately longing that he could have changed them, or wishing they had never actually happened at all. This ritual had ceased entirely after he had undergone four months of his treatment.

His twenty-fifth and twenty-sixth birthdays both went uncelebrated but not without Elliot and Kristian first attempting to get him to go out by calling around and inviting him to a bar. For his twenty-fifth birthday, Luke flatly refused to go out anywhere but on his following birthday, he agreed to his friends buying some cans of lager and bringing them back to his flat.

"Do you think this could be the start of the old Luke coming back?" asked Elliot to Kristian, as they were buying the alcohol to take back with them.

"Let's hope so," replied Kristian eagerly.

On Saturday 2 May 1998, Elliot and Kristian had planned to have their joint thirtieth birthday celebration. Naturally, they both wanted Luke to be there and since February, had kept asking him if he would go along, to which he would always apologise and decline. It was several days before the big celebration that Luke surprised his friends by ringing them and told them that he would be there with them at the club.

At the height of the party, whilst Elliot and Kristian were passing from person to person and thanking them for coming along, or for the gifts that they had received, Luke hurried to the DJ's mixing booth and asked to borrow the microphone. After the current record had finished playing, Luke asked for everybody's attention.

"I would like to sing a song if I may."

The cheer from the crowd gave him the answer that he was looking for.

"It's a song that I have recently written myself and it's called *No Greater Friend Than You*. I wrote it especially for Elliot and Kris, whom I love dearly.

The Absence of Friends

Through the good times…and the bad, they have always been there and never turned their backs on our friendship, even though there were times that I nearly did! Thank you guys, I love you so much."

When he had finished the song, both Elliot and Kristian joined Luke and hugged him tightly. The three of them sang *Thank You For Being A Friend*. The crowd went wild, as tears of joy, reaffirming the strength of their friendship, were in the three men's eyes.

By mid-July 1998, Luke was back to performing at most of his old haunts on the cabaret circuit, with renewed vigour. He was welcomed back with open arms, as they had missed him in the time that he wasn't performing but now, he was back…and back with a vengeance.

Luke thought long and hard about dropping his big finale act, where he would invite someone onto the stage with him but as this was the highlight of his performance for most of the crowd, he decided on keeping it in. So, whenever he invited anybody onto the stage with him for the big finale, he would only offer his thanks for being such a sport and never offered to buy them a drink afterwards; he even made a point of deliberately avoiding them for the remainder of the evening, if he chose to stay on at the bar. He didn't mind talking or dancing with people but when they made any suggestion to him of going home together, he would find an excuse to hastily finish the conversation and walk away, leaving the other person more than a little bewildered. He found that most guys who had taken a fancy to him to be incredibly pushy or very arrogant. Some he even found too difficult to maintain any interest in continuing the conversation, or the feelings were in no way reciprocated.

On Saturday 24 October, Luke phoned Elliot and Kristian, telling them of a new club that had opened in Putney and they agreed to go with him and see what it was like. Luke liked the place instantly. After an hour, Elliot and Kristian wandered off to another part of the club, leaving Luke by the edge of the dance floor, feeling nervous, shy and more than a little vulnerable. He had been on his own for about fifteen minutes, when he noticed a very good-looking guy approaching him. His heart beat faster, as he hated to reject good looking guys who might be able to hold a decent conversation, but there was no way he was going through again what Matthew had put him through; not for anybody.

The guy stopped right beside him, smiling before asking his name.

"Luke."

"Mine's Scott," he replied.

CHAPTER SEVEN

Luke rubbed his eyes, as they slowly adjusted to the unfamiliar surroundings, when he awoke the following morning. It took him a few seconds to remember that he had gone back to Scott's home with him and there was absolutely no trace of regret entering his mind for having done so. In fact, he had had a very exciting and - blushing as he thought about it - incredibly erotic time with Scott, feeling confident that, if asked, Scott would more than likely say the same. As Luke had not had sex in over two years and Scott for eight months, this only served to add to the eroticism and extreme pleasure that each of them felt. Luke felt a rousing stirring as he remembered the events of the previous night. As he ruffled the pillows and sat up, pulling the duvet up to cover his naked chest, he began to wonder where Scott actually was, straining his ears to see if he might possibly hear the sound of running water from the shower.

He could hear no tell-tale signs that might reveal where Scott had gone.

At the moment when Luke was considering leaving the comfort of the bed and seek Scott's whereabouts, he walked into the room, carrying a tray laden with various breakfast items.

"Good morning, sleepy head." Scott smiled warmly at him when he saw that Luke was awake and sitting up.

"Morning," Luke responded cheerily.

"I've made us some breakfast," said Scott, placing the tray upon the bedside table, at his side of the bed. He discarded his dressing gown and crawled back under the duvet, inching his way nearer to Luke.

"Oh my god, you're freezing!" gasped Luke, as he flinched at Scott's cold flesh, stealing the warmth from his own body.

Scott grinned. "Sorry. I'll warm up in a minute." He gestured towards the tray that he had just bought in and said, "I hope you don't mind cereal and toast."

Luke shook his head. "No, that's absolutely fine."

"I've made some tea too. I hope that's okay? I'll make you coffee if you like."

"No. Tea's fine. Thanks."

"I didn't know if you took milk and sugar, so I brought them both in."

"Milk but no sugar, please."

Scott poured some milk into Luke's cup, offering it up to him. "Would you like some toast?"

"Please."

The Absence of Friends

He handed Luke a plate with several slices of toast, putting the tray of various jams and spreads onto the bed. "Help yourself," proffered Scott.

They talked about what they thought of the club the previous night, likes and dislikes, holidays they'd been on and general small talk.

"It's a gorgeous day out. Do you fancy going for a walk today?"

"Sure. Why not?"

They had a shower together and dressed. Luke borrowed one of Scott's shirts, as his own smelt of stale smoke and sweat, and he didn't really relish the idea of wandering around for a further day with these obnoxious fragrances lingering under his nostrils.

The weather was very pleasant for October and they decided upon going to St James' Park for a picnic. Scott packed a picnic hamper, while Luke shaved and attempted to brush his hair into some kind of perfection.

They both thoroughly enjoyed each other's company, laughing, joking and feeling completely relaxed with each other. The afternoon seemed to pass all too quickly for them both.

"I must be going," said Luke, which appeared as an all too sudden announcement for Scott.

"Oh," said Scott, the disappointment clearly shown in his voice.

Luke helped Scott pack away the remains of the picnic hamper. "Yes, I'm doing a gig at *Les Hommes* tonight."

"Well, it's been a rather lovely afternoon. I've really enjoyed myself."

"Me too," said Luke. "I'll tell you what," he suggested. "Why don't you come along and see me tonight? Kris and Elliot will be there. I'm sure you'll really like them."

"Okay. I'd love to," agreed Scott, not requiring any further coaxing.

They took a slow walk to the tube station, making their arrangements for later that evening, neither one of them really wanting the afternoon to be finalised by parting company but both, very much looking forward to seeing each other in a few hours' time. On the way to the tube station, Scott caught sight of a rather attractive looking woman, who must have been roughly his own age, tending a flower stall. He could hear her yelling something out to the passersby that Scott could only assume to be her sales patter and in a spontaneously romantic instant, he rushed over to the stall. Luke smiled to himself as he watched Scott pointing in his direction, whilst he was conversing with the woman and then make his selection of flowers to buy. The smile quickly turned to one of sheer horror as he saw the flowers that Scott had bought.

Roses.

"No! Not roses," he yelled out to Scott. "Please not roses." It was too late. Scott was already making his way back with a bunch of dozen roses, clasped tightly in his hand. "Oh God," Luke said to himself, his face felt drained of colour. "Anything but roses."

Scott noticed Luke's look of horror, not quite being able to make out what he was mumbling. "What's wrong? Don't you like roses?"

"Not really," Luke gulped.

"Why ever not?"

"It's a long story."

Scott looked at his watch and smiled. "It's only four o'clock."

Luke smiled back. "Okay, I'll tell you. My mother always had roses in the house. Not, you understand that they were necessarily bought by my father. In fact, there were very few occasions when he did actually buy her flowers. Any time he did, he always grumbled about the expense for something that he thought was a complete waste of time because they died after only after a few days.

"I can always remember smelling the roses, or looking at them whenever I heard my mother singing. I used to think that her singing was like the sweet smell of roses.

"For as long as I can remember, my father always used to beat us all. I would dread him coming anywhere near me, for fear that I would be at the receiving end of one of his drunken beatings. Most of the time it was usually my mother who would receive the brunt of his anger. I hated him so much for that. Not only did he beat her but he used to throw objects at her. Regardless of who got beaten, whether it be my mother, brothers, or me, she would come into our room and sing to us, telling us that everything would be okay. She always put a vase with a single rose in it on our bedside table, which oddly enough seemed to comfort me at the time.

"It was probably when I was about ten or eleven years old, that my father was in a particularly violent mood. He had apparently lost vast quantities of money in gambling and had been drinking rather heavily. I can't remember why he started yelling at my mother, but he never really needed an excuse to yell at anyone; they only had to be in his line of vision and that would just set him off. I was in my bedroom at the time, when I heard them both shouting at each other, which made me realise just how violent the situation had become, because it was very rare that my mother raised her voice, let alone argue with anyone. I heard something smash, which, not only made me scared but caused the hairs on the back of my neck to awaken and I wanted to run into my mother's room and see what had happened. I know if I had, though, my father would have started on me and with the mood he was in, there was no knowing where he might have stopped. So, I waited for a few moments until I heard my father's very heavy footsteps going down the stairs before I had even an ounce of courage to dare to venture into my mother's room.

The Absence of Friends

"I don't know what had happened between the two of them, but my mother was collapsed in a heap on the floor, in a pool of blood. It was obvious that the vase of roses had been thrown, as it was lying smashed on the floor around her. My guess is he probably hit her with it, rather than threw it at her. She seemed to be clutching the roses to her. I remember her telling me once that she thought of us as roses. It made me smile when she told me that; to be thought of as a rose."

Scott looked intently at Luke, drinking in the scene as though he had actually been there himself. "Oh my God…please don't tell me she was dead, was she?" he asked, drawing in his breath, anticipating a terrible answer. "He hadn't killed her, had he?"

"No, he hadn't killed her. Thankfully."

Scott let out his held breath and sighed deeply, allowing himself to return to his normal breathing.

"At the time, though, I thought that she was. I lay down beside her, with my arms around her and I cried for what seemed like forever, as the tears just wouldn't end. The thorns from the roses were digging into my skin but at the time, I really didn't care. All I could think about was the bastard whom I had to call my father, had killed her. The next thing I can remember was running out of the house, screaming: *he's killed her, the bastard has killed my mother.*

"Everything seems pretty hazy after that. I just know we never had roses in the house again. I can't seem to get out of my mind that something I once thought of as so beautiful could turn into something associated with destruction and pure evilness. For me, roses symbolise pain and sorrow now; a death flower."

"But she didn't die," said Scott. "Remember, she thought of you all as roses. Why do you think she was clutching them? It seems to me that she wanted to clutch her children. In a way, by protecting the roses, maybe she thought she was protecting all of you. I guess, what she was maybe trying to do, was to preserve your thoughts of roses in comparison to her singing, but for some reason your anger for your father is blocking that out."

Luke smiled at Scott's attempt to find the positive, however small it may have been, from an episode in his life that was filled with terror and negative consequences. "I know you're trying to help, Scott and I thank you for it. I really don't think I can take the roses, it would just be too painful."

"It's okay," said Scott, with a smile, to shade his disappointment. "I understand."

Luke had already introduced Scott to both Elliot and Kristian before taking his place on the stage for the evening's entertainment. Kristian, earlier in the evening, had already interrogated Luke thoroughly about Scott, when they called around to give him a lift to Les Hommes. Elliot would show his disapproval at the barrage of questions from his partner by tutting every so often and telling Kristian not to be so nosey but this didn't serve as any real deterrent in Kristian trying to quench his hunger at attempting to find out every single detail he possibly could.

Every eye in the club was now transfixed upon Luke, where the beholders were excitedly anticipating another spectacular night's entertainment. He began with renditions of Beverley Craven's *Promise Me* and The Carpenters *Yesterday Once More*, watching as some of the audience were dreamily captivated by every note and vocal nuance that drifted their way. His next two songs were ones that he had written himself, called *Learning To Be Me* and *To Hear Your Voice*. Instead of his usual trademark finale of bringing someone up on stage with him, he meandered through the tables, until he came to one with a vase of roses on it. He hesitated slightly, before picking two of them out of the vase, with a smile to the occupants of the table. He weaved his way back to the table where Scott, Elliot and Kristian were all sitting and gave one of roses to Elliot, getting him and Kristian to hold the rose between their clasped hands before working his way back onto the stage, for the climax of his song.

All eyes were firmly fixed upon Luke anticipating his next move, as there seemed to be an eternal pause of deathly silence. It was almost like that heart-stopping moment when an actor is on stage and he forgets his next line. Luke glanced at Scott, gave him a knowing wink and then threw the rose to him as he blew him a kiss. The crowd was so intense with their thunderous round of applause, only Scott noticed the sigh of relief that Luke had let out.

When Luke eventually joined the others at the table, Scott spoke. "That was absolutely fantastic. You have such a wonderful voice…just like the sweet smell of roses." He gave another of his knowing winks.

Luke reached for his drink, brushing his other hand through his hair.

"You were, as always, superb," offered Kristian.

"One word sums it up perfectly. Excellent," said Elliot simply.

"C'mon guys," said Luke. "You're embarrassing me."

"Where on earth did you learn to sing like that?" asked Scott with interest.

"Well, I trained at the Royal Academy of Music and Performing Arts, right here in London."

"Don't you think he's just great?" beamed Elliot, like a proud parent.

"Great doesn't quite cover it. I think he's nothing short of brilliant!"

"Guys, please! You're doing it again."

"You should've seen some of the other shows he's done," Kristian said. He relayed to Scott how he and Luke had met for the very first time, on the night of their unforgettable performance. He recounted in so much detail, it was as though the event had only happened the previous evening and not nearly five years ago.

The four men continued to have an enjoyable evening together, with Luke's fingers spending more time being run through his hair than not. When Scott had gone to the toilet, both Elliot and Krisitan took the opportunity to tell Luke how much they liked him, which they had clearly been itching to do for the majority of the night.

"He's actually a very charming man," said Elliot.

"Really nice and friendly," chipped in Kristian.

"I know," smiled Luke.

It was around 11.30pm that Elliot and Kristian announced that it was time they needed to leave. "Would either of you two like a lift?" offered Elliot.

Scott turned to Luke and asked: "Are you coming back with me tonight?"

Luke nodded.

Scott turned to Elliot and said: "Only if it's not out of your way. Then, yes, please."

"Where do you live?"

"Hammersmith."

"We're in Ealing, so that's perfect for us."

"Thanks."

As they left, many people called out their congratulations and appreciation of Luke's earlier performance. When they reached the car, Luke asked: "Hang on just a second. I've just thought…which one of you is driving?"

"I am," said Elliot.

Luke sighed and turned to Scott. "You're safe, Elliot's driving."

Scott smiled.

Kristian hit Luke playfully on the arm and said: "You cheeky sod. If you're not careful, I *will* drive."

They all laughed.

"Breakfast in bed."

"Oh, this is just absolute heaven," Scott smiled. "I could really get used to this kind of treatment…especially in my own home."

Luke gently placed the tray on Scott's lap and sauntered into the en-suite bathroom to draw himself a bath. "I took the liberty of picking up the post for you. It's on the tray, underneath the plate," he called.

Scott picked up the three envelopes that were laying on the tray: one was obviously a telephone bill, which he placed immediately back down on the tray. From the handwriting, he could immediately tell that one of the letters was from his mother and the other one, from Vince.

He opened the letter from his mother first. She had written to tell him - almost commanding him - that he must come and visit sometime soon, as she hadn't seen him for quite some time and she was beginning to forget what he looked like. Scott rolled his eyes and exhaled exhaustively at his mother's wry attempt at sardonicism. He allowed his mind to wonder about when he might eventually introduce Luke to his mother, quietly confident that the both of them would instantly hit it off, like a house on fire. He knew that his mother would undoubtedly take a moment, in private, to say to her son that Luke was "ever such a lovely boy" and make some complimentary comparisons, in Luke's favour, against Simon and James. There was absolutely no doubt in Scott's mind that his mother would be suitably impressed with Luke's singing, as she was a soft touch for a heartfelt power ballad.

After he had finished reading the letter from Vince, he put both letters back into their envelopes and placed them back onto the breakfast tray. "Remember I told you about Vince?" he called in the direction of the bathroom, over the noise of the running water.

"Pardon?" came back the yell from the bathroom.

"My friend, Vince," he shouted louder.

"What about him?"

"He's written to say that he wants to come and visit us over the Christmas period."

"Pardon?"

"He wants to...Turn the bloody water off, then you'll be able to hear me."

Luke obeyed the directive from Scott, turning the water off and apologising, before Scott told him once again about Vince's desire to come and visit over Christmas.

"When does he want to come then?"

"On the twenty second."

There was an almighty splash and an "oh my God" from the bathroom, which caused Scott to violently throw the duvet off him and jump out of the bed, racing into the bathroom to see if Luke was all right. Luke looked up at him with an innocuously cheeky grin and beckoning outstretched arms. Scott put his hands into Luke's but was caught unaware by Luke's sudden tug, which caused him to be flipped easily over the side and into the bath with him.

"Well, well, well," glowed Luke. "Is there no end to satiating your ravenous sexual appetite?"

"You little bugger!" said Scott, trying to suppress his laughter. He put his arms around Luke. "I always seem to fall for your devilish pranks." He kissed him.

"It wasn't a prank." He kissed him back.

"What?" said Scott, a little confused.

"You said that Vince is coming on the twenty second, right?"

"Yes."

Luke looked at Scott, as though he should have known the answer to a simple question. After a brief pause, he said, "Well, my little dotty Scottie, your friend Vince will be here the day after tomorrow! It's the *twentieth* today!"

The splash that was caused by Scott's panicked shock caused a mini tidal wave within the bath, with a mass of water being sent over the side and onto the bathroom floor. Luke found himself laughing uncontrollably at Scott's little mishap and put his arms around him, pulling him tighter to himself. Scott got up onto his knees. "You think that's funny, do you?" He scooped up the water with his hands and aimed it straight into Luke's face.

Luke's laughter turned into a suggestive grin, as he said: "You know, whilst you're there on your knees…you could give me a you-know-what."

Scott didn't need any further encouragement and lowered his head toward Luke's crotch but as he did so, Luke slapped the water with the flat of his hand with such force that Scott ended up with a face full of it.

"You'll pay for that," spluttered Scott, as he grabbed the jug that Luke had used to wash his hair with, filling it to the brim and throwing it at him. It wasn't long before the two lads were fully locked into their own hysterical and totally messy water fight; not giving a moment's care that water was going everywhere. It wouldn't be until later on, when a major cleanup was in dire need, that both regretted their frivolous water activities.

"Oh my God, look at the mess we've made," said Scott, surveying the scene when the water fight had reached its climax.

"Don't worry," began Luke. "I'm here to save the day…yet again!"

Scott smiled. "What would I do without you?"

Kristian agreed to drive Scott to Gatwick airport in order to meet Vince, whilst Luke was left at Scott's house, having offered to wash up, tidy up, dust, polish and vacuum. He had hardly spent any time at his own flat since he had met Scott two months ago and would continually need to go back to his, so as to pick up some shirts, a pair of shoes, underwear or favourite cologne that he wanted to wear. He far preferred being at Scott's house, with him, and of course, Scott enjoyed being with him. He had helped Scott put up the Christmas decorations and had single-handedly dressed the tree, with all the intricate trimmings. Even under his own critical eye, he was pleased that the place looked beautiful.

Scott and Vince were expected back shortly after one o'clock and Luke had agreed to prepare the lunch, ready for their return. The food was simmering on the stove, as Luke slumped, exhausted, into an armchair. No sooner had he begun to relax, Scott walked in, followed by Vince and Kristian.

"It's alright for some," joked Kristian, "sitting with their feet up all day, with absolutely nothing to do."

"Cheeky sod," grinned Luke, throwing the tea towel from around his neck at him.

"Vince, this is Luke," said Scott.

Luke stood up and shook Vince warmly by the hand. "Nice to meet you, Vince. Scott has told me so much about you."

"Likewise."

Luke stole a glance in Scott's direction. "If it was good, don't believe a word of it. If it was bad, it was probably all true."

Vince laughed. "It was all good."

Kristian interjected. "Sorry that I can't stay but Elliot is expecting me back for lunch. Knowing him, it'll be a twenty question inquisition if I'm late. Lord alone only knows why, as he knows where I am!"

They exchanged their goodbyes, as Vince and Scott thanked Kristian for driving them. Kristian promised Luke that he and Elliot would be at the *Grand Duchess* later, for his performance.

Luke and Vince got on well with each other instantly, which pleased Scott. They actually talked as though they had known each other for as long as Vince had known Scott. Vince complimented Luke on his cooking, causing him to beam with pride, as he knew that Vince was an outstanding chef and was told of his long-lived passion for cooking. To an outsider, they might have been forgiven for thinking that Vince was being patronising but this was not the case.

At a very young age, Vince would constantly be found in the kitchen, helping his mother prepare the dinner, or electing himself to be her helper when she was doing some baking. At the age of ten, he began to bake cakes and make desserts by himself, which his family found to be mouth-wateringly delicious. At twelve, he had managed to win third prize in a nationwide school cookery competition, which saw hundreds of children submit entries. By the age of fourteen, he was competently cooking fanciful main courses and advising his mother on how to ensure that dishes were that little more appetising and exotic. At the age of sixteen, when he had left school with an easily achievable grade A in O Level Home Economics, he enrolled himself onto a four year Hotel and Catering Management course. He sailed through the course with ease and attained an Honour at the end of the four years.

During the evenings and holiday periods, he found himself plenty of part-time work to do, so that he could save enough money in order to travel to different countries of the world and gain first hand, authentic experience of that particular country's cooking styles.

Between the ages of twenty and twenty-seven, with the money he had saved and financial help from his parents, Vince had visited a total of seventeen countries, learning their culinary delights by securing himself employment in a restaurant. In return, he would teach them some typical English dishes. After seven years abroad, he returned to England, landing himself a job as Head Chef in a particularly run down, East End restaurant, which he was hoping to turn around within a few years. It was here, in September 1996, that he had met Scott.

Now, at thirty-two years old, he was the proud owner of two restaurants: one in London, the other in Paris. Paris was showing a deficit at present, though Vince had every confidence it would at least break even, if not actually show a slight profit by the end of 1999. London was now beginning to show signs of making a profit.

It was Christmas morning.

Scott entered the living room to find Vince and Luke deep in conversation.

"Merry Christmas," he said cheerily.

They looked up at him, returning the seasonal greeting.

"How long have you two been up?"

"Ages," replied Luke.

Scott joined Luke on the sofa and rested his hand upon his leg. He asked: "What time's Elliot and Kris coming round?"

"I told them to be here for midday."

Vince noticed Scott's hand discreetly wandering up and down Luke's leg. "Here, we'll have less of that, you two," he grinned.

They both shot Vince a cheeky smile.

"So," said Scott firmly. "What conversation did I interrupt?"

"I was telling Vince about some of the shows I've done and the musicals that I was in. Apparently you saw *The Perfect Alibi* with him."

"Yes, I did," said Scott. "Were you in that?" he asked, raising his eyebrows.

Luke nodded. "Yes."

"Oh! Which part did you play?"

"Lance Wilkinson, the son of the widow. I sang that haunting solo after I found out my father was murdered. It still sends shivers up my spine when I think about it."

"Oh, wow! Was that *you?*"

"Yes, it was really me."

"Well, I never…"

"I know," began Vince, "I was surprised when he told me too."

They carried on their conversation for a short while, knowing a good two hours were needed to get everything clean and tidy before Elliot and Kristian arrived and they were a couple not to let punctuality slip. Not for any occasion. They had built themselves up a reputation for arriving at exactly the time they said they were going to.

The doorbell rang, just as the clock in the living room chimed its seventh time out of the twelve. Scott greeted Elliot and Kristian, as Vince helped finish tidying the living room.

"Merry Christmas to you both," said Scott, as he kissed them both on the cheek. They returned the friendly greeting, following in Scott's wake into the living room, whilst Luke had already begun the preparations for the Christmas dinner.

Luke greeted his friends with a hug and a kiss, before formally introducing Elliot to Vince, who rose from his armchair and offered his outstretched hand, which Elliot took and shook firmly. "It's nice to meet you at last," said Elliot. "Being the only one left who hasn't met you yet."

Luke left the four of them to sit and talk whilst he carried on preparing the dinner in the kitchen.

"I see you've got him well trained," said Elliot.

Scott smiled. "Actually, it's nothing to do with me. He loves his cooking, so I just let him get on with it. He's usually making breakfast for us when I wake up and brings it up to me before I even have a chance to get out of bed."

Elliot turned to Kristian and asked: "Why don't you ever bring me breakfast in bed? Maybe you can take a leaf out of Luke's book!"

Kristian laughed sarcastically. "The day *you* bring *me* breakfast in bed, my darling, will be the day I consider doing the same for you."

"Now, now boys," said Scott.

A few minutes after one o'clock, Luke declared that the dinner was ready.

Kristian placed the gifts that he had bought in with him under the tree, along with the others, before joining them all in the dining room. The room was breathtakingly beautiful. Luke had worked extremely hard the previous day hanging the decorations and making the room absolutely perfect. He didn't believe in swamping the place in decorations; just enough to show that the festive season was in. Everything on the table was so neat and symmetrical, as though he had laboured for hours with a ruler to get the measurements exact. Even the flowers in the two vases seemed to have been put into a purposeful display, as if to tell a romantic story.

It seemed a shame to spoil such a beautifully laid table.

After the meal had been finished and plenty of wine drunk, they retired to the living room, where all five collapsed heavily into their seats, fully satiated. They paid their compliments to Luke on such a wonderful meal.

"I've had to undo the top button on my jeans," said Vince with mock scorn. "As if I really need to be fattened up any more!"

With that comment, Vince was unanimously elected to play Santa, as physically he was the one who most resembled the fictitious character and therefore, easily the most obvious choice. In a cheerily festive spirit, he accepted the honour with a hearty "ho, ho, ho". The more intimate of gifts brought deeply red cheeks to the recipient and raucous laughter from the others. After all the gifts had been given out, Scott brought a final one out that he had hidden under the sofa, where he was sitting, handing it to Luke.

"I had to ensure that I saved the best for last," he said.

Luke took the gift from Scott and shot him an endearing smile. He tore open the wrapping paper and produced a beautiful leather bound diary, with his initials embossed upon it in gold lettering. He held it to his chest in a possessive manner and said: "It's so lovely. Thank you." He leant over and gave Scott a kiss.

Scott gave a coy smile in response. He had enjoyed watching Luke unwrap the present and witness the exuberant expression on his face. He knew that Luke ardently kept a diary, as it had been mentioned several times in conversation since they had first met.

"I'm so glad that you like it," he said.

"Like it? I love it."

"In years to come, I want us to be able to look back on all our years together and remember all of the good times that we've shared."

"That'll come in handy, especially when we're old and grey!"

"Or when we're so old that our memories are starting to fail us…and we'll be two old, cantankerous men arguing over when a specific event happened."

"Because, of course, a diary will never lie or forget."

CHAPTER EIGHT

April 1999 was the time of celebrations for Luke.

Scott had spent the previous two months trying to organise a surprise party for Luke's twenty-seventh birthday. He had engaged the help of both Elliot and Kristian, in regular clandestine meetings, to ensure all the arrangements were carried out perfectly, with the specific instruction that Luke was never to find out.

It was agreed that they should hire a hall, as there would be around one hundred guests all told. Finding a hall suitable to accommodate all the guests was not a problem, nor was finding a willing DJ. The problem lay in the catering; firms were either charging rates way above their budget, or they weren't able to provide some of the foods requested. Eventually, Kristian stumbled upon a firm in Stratford that seemed to offer the most reasonable rates and the majority of food items that they wanted. Unfortunately, they weren't able to deliver, but they were adamant it would not pose too much of a problem.

Luke loved the diary he had been given for Christmas, by Scott and kept very stringent daily records of everything he had done. He thought he would record the events of his birthday in great detail:

> *It was the night of the party and I hadn't suspected a thing. As far as I was concerned, I was going out for a quiet meal with Scott, Elliot and Kris. It was going to be a really special night, as I had something very exciting to tell them all.*
>
> *"Kensington?" I asked, more than a little surprised. "What on earth are we going to Kensington for?"*
>
> *"There are some really lovely restaurants there."*
>
> *"Yes, that may very well be but what's wrong with good, old Ealing?"*
>
> *"Luke, I've already booked the table and made all the arrangements with the guys."*
>
> *"Okay...okay. I'm just a little surprised that you chose Kensington, of all places." Scott had told me later that keeping all the plans a secret from me was far easier than he had imagined.*
>
> *"Do you want me to drive?" he asked.*
>
> *Scott didn't have a car of his own, even though he had passed his driving test a few years ago because he felt that he never really needed one in London,*

with easy access to public transport. I had passed my driving test in January and was now the proud owner of a black and silver Montego Mayfair."

"Sure," I said. "At least I will be able to have a drink."

"We're meeting the guys first, before we go on to the restaurant."

"That sounds good to me."

"You don't need to worry about a thing. I've taken care of all the arrangements. All I ask from you is that you just enjoy yourself."

"You can count on me to do that."

If it were anyone other than Elliot who had suggested an impromptu stop-off, I might have suspected that something was awry. Elliot was the kind of person, indicative I suppose of his puritanical nature, who is rarely questioned about his actions or motives. Other than, of course, Kris but then that's the nature of their relationship...I can only describe their relationship as sobriety vs. frivolity. Elliot had muttered something that was somewhat incoherent about the need to stop off at this particular hall involving a friend and a down payment that was required before the end of the day.

The entire charade was perfectly executed between the three of them.

"This might take me a few minutes, so you're more than welcome to come in if you want," offered Elliot.

"Are you sure?" exclaimed Kris. "We don't want to get in the way of your enigmatic business transaction."

"It might be the perfect time to stretch our legs though, Kris," said Scott sensibly.

"But he's only going to be a few minutes. By the time we get out and *stretch our legs*, it will be time to get back in again."

"Come on guys," said Elliot with an air of impatience. "I need to go in there and do what I need to do. Are you coming or not?"

"Let's go," Scott commanded. "At least we can play at being the exasperated timekeepers if he takes too long!"

As if that was all the encouragement Kris needed, he was out of the car in a flash.

I didn't think I was particularly gullible but obviously I've been misleading myself all this time because I insouciantly followed the other two in.

"Surprise!" The noise from nearly one hundred people was thunderous, as I walked into the crowded hall.

"Oh God," I said, as I buried my face in my hands to cover the embarrassment. "No wonder you wanted to come to Kensington." I sighed, shaking my head in disbelief at the number of people.

From where I was standing, I could see managers of clubs that I had performed in, some members of the cast of The Perfect Alibi; I even recognised people I had got on stage, when performing some of my more memorable finales. "How on earth did you manage to get hold of all these people?" *I asked Scott with genuine surprise and intrigue.*

Scott put on one of his I've got something to confess *faces and explained that he had taken my address book, which was why he had to deny all knowledge, when I asked of its whereabouts. I had searched high and low for that address book and thought I was going mad, when it turned up exactly where I thought it was.*

"You are so bad…"

"…But you still love me."

"Of course I do. But I still think we should have gone for a quiet meal in Ealing."

"Luke Faraday!" *exclaimed Scott, as he put his hands on his hips in an overly emphasised, defensive manner.* "After all the work and planning that I've put into this for you!"

"I'm just kidding," *I laughed. Leaning nearer to Scott in a provocative manner, I continued.* "You know, you look so cute when you're angry."

Scott strained to hold back his laughter, as he gently clipped the back of my head with his hand. "Be off with you, you little trouble maker."

"So where have Elliot and Kris disappeared to?"

"I suspect they have gone into hiding, as soon as they came through the door."

"Hiding? Whatever for?"

"Well, they were my partners in crime after all."

I tutted and sighed deeply, shaking my head. "I don't know. What are the three of you like? Anyway, I will see you later, as I ought really to make the rounds," *I said, kissing Scott on the cheek.* "And thank you so much."

"What for?"

"For this," *I said, sweeping my arm across the scene.* "It's an absolutely wonderful surprise."

"Oh, that's okay. Just seeing you happy makes me happy too."

I headed off into the thick of the crowd, pleasantly surprised at who was at the party. I was reacquainted with old friends I had lost contact with in the past and therefore, there was a lot of telephone numbers exchanged. I talked with cast members of the stage musicals I had been in, catching up with what they were doing and in return, I told them what I had been up to. People who had seen me perform in pubs and clubs kept asking if I would sing that evening and if I would also do a special finale. To everyone who asked, I

The Absence of Friends

confirmed that I would, as I was sure that Scott would have anticipated this and bought along some of my backing tracks. Managers of bars and clubs were bombarding me with offers to perform at their respective venues. Sadly, I had to decline all these offers, no matter how persuasive they were or how lucrative it all sounded. Although I would not explain why, I assured each one individually, I could take up their offer at the end of the year.

Finally, I stumbled upon Elliot and Kris. "I'd given up hope on finding you two," I said languidly. "I was beginning to think the two of you had gone into permanent hibernation after your earlier performance."

"Do you really think we'd have done that to you?" smirked Kris, attempting to raise an innocent eyebrow.

"Nothing would really surprise me anymore," I replied.

Elliot moved forward and gave me a hug. "Happy birthday," he said. Kris followed suit immediately afterward, with his birthday greeting.

"I suppose I really ought to go and sing a couple of songs now, as I'm sure that Scott would have bought along some of my backing tracks. You don't know how many people have asked me if I am going to sing this evening. There have even been some people who have put in a specific request."

"Oh," began Kris like a child who had just thought of something exciting to tell. "If Scott had the foresight to bring along the backing track with that song that has…"

I shot Kris a defiant glance, which was all the prompting he needed in order to cut him short in his tracks from continuing with his train of thought any further.

"If I sang every request that was put forward to me tonight, it would take me a minimum of three hours to get through them all."

My friends smiled, watching as I took my place on stage. It was surprising how quickly the noise died down when people noticed me on the stage.

"Ladies and gentlemen," I began, as I adjusted the height of the microphone stand. "I would like to thank each and every one of you for coming along tonight. I hope that you are enjoying yourselves, as I certainly am.

"Actually, I thought that I was going to be having a very quiet dinner for my birthday but this is certainly going to be one birthday that I don't think I will forget in a hurry. I guess, if I'm honest, I didn't initially appreciate the amount of effort and organising that tonight would have taken. For that, I would like you to join me in wishing a very heartfelt and special thank you to the people who were responsible for making tonight extra special. Three people who are very close to my heart: Scott Delaney, Kris Irwin and Elliot Hayden."

The applause that ensued seemed to last an eternity and although I could not hear what was being said, I was confident everyone was agreeing in one way or another with what I had just said.

"I'd like to sing you two or three songs. I've had so many people give me requests and as you'll no doubt appreciate, I can't sing them all, else we'll be here until this time next year."

Laughter.

For my first song, I sang an up-tempo version of Céline Dion's Power Of Love, which was met with an overwhelming round of applause. The second song was from the Jekyll & Hyde musical that had taken America by storm a few years back, called This Is The Moment. My connections in the musical industry thought that the soundtrack would suit my vocal style and managed to get me a recording of the backing tracks, some of which I had reworked into more of a dance track. My final song was one that I had written myself called I'm Raining On The Inside. Some people, I noticed, had tears in their eyes due to heart-rending lyrics.

"I would like Scott, Elliot and Kris to come up here and join me on the stage."

I watched, as the three of them fought their way through the crowds and up on to the stage. When they were all eventually with me, I whispered something to them, which caused three pairs of arms to hug me and three pairs of lips to kiss me.

"There's time for that later," shouted someone from the crowd, which caused the group around him to roar with laughter.

I hushed the crowd. "I've been given so many offers to sing in various pubs and clubs and unfortunately, I've had to decline. This isn't because I don't want to, as I will be back performing at all these venues later in the year, so don't worry. I had to tell these three first that I'm going to..."

"You're going to have a baby," shouted the same voice as before.

"No, I'm not having a baby," I laughed. "I'm going to be recording an album. I found a record company who's willing to sign me up on a contract."

I had to wait several minutes before the noise had been reduced to a level that was low enough for me to carry on.

"I have dreamed of this moment ever since I was twelve years old. I know it's a cliché but it really is a dream come true. However," I said in a slightly more serious tone, "had it not been for a very special and wonderful woman who really believed in me, I probably wouldn't be here today. The album, which is titled A Vow To Grace, is dedicated to her and I know that she is looking down on me and smiling."

As the crowd cheered once more, I lifted my eyes up to the heavens and whispered a silent thank you to Lillian Grace, wishing she had been here to witness this moment.

I sang Bette Midler's Wind Beneath My Wings. *When I had finished, Elliot and Kris promptly left the stage, leaving me alone with Scott. "I'd like to sing one last song to finish up with."*

I handed Scott a microphone that the DJ had ready for me and we sang Something's Gotten Hold Of My Heart. *I took hold of Scott's hand whilst I sang and noticed that anybody who was with a partner seemed to follow suit and copy whatever I did.*

"I'd like to say a big thank you to all of you again," I said after finishing. "Enjoy the rest of your evening."

As Scott and I left the stage, there was not one person who was not applauding.

The party seemed to thin out at around three o'clock in the morning. Scott and I ended up getting to bed just after five o'clock. Neither of us coherent enough to say or do anything, so we went straight to bed, falling asleep almost immediately.

Luke spent the next four months collecting the best material for his album. Although it was incredibly hard work and emotionally very draining, he enjoyed every minute of it. He would spend many hours in the recording studio, wanting his debut album to be perfect in every way. By mid-August, it was completed to his satisfaction. He listened to the finished product, feeling totally pleased with himself. Other than the absence of Lillian Grace, only one thing shadowed his happiness; the fact that his mother wasn't around to witness his moment of triumph.

Prison had certainly taken its toll on Caroline Faraday. Anyone who had seen Caroline before she went to prison would have been forgiven for thinking that they were two different women. She was released after six years confinement and refused to let anyone from her history anywhere near her. She was too ashamed and guilty of what she had done and become. Luke never tried to give up returning back into her life, and each time he attempted to do so, he was bitterly disappointed by his mother's rebuttal. His mother was adamant that Luke should lead his own life and begged him not to destroy it by returning back to being a part of hers. Luke would have continued to persuade his mother to let him be a part of her life once more, had she not upped and moved away from Southampton, leaving no indication as to where she was going. It was her way of telling Luke that he should be free of her terrible life and the bad examples that she had shown him.

Since leaving Southampton nearly nine and half years ago, Luke never let the memories of his mother fade away and constantly thought of her. He sometimes wondered how his life might have been different had his mother never been arrested and convicted but as she had told him, he had to live his own life. Scott helped by always being there for him, though he could not always offer advice, he was certainly there to listen and offer a shoulder for him to cry on.

Luke found it extremely hard to say a mental and final goodbye to his mother, after so many years of wanting to welcome her back into his life. For several weeks after Caroline had moved, Luke spent most nights crying over what he classed as the loss of his mother. This time, the loss seemed to be final.

Luke was surprised at how well the sale of his debut album was doing as he had, deep down, felt dubious of how well the whole enterprise might have been. The first three months after the album's release were spent promoting it. Scott was always asked to accompany Luke, to which he obliged, work permitting.

At the beginning of each concert, Luke ensured he made a point of telling the audience that a percentage of monies raised from concerts and album sales would be going to HIV research. The positive reaction that followed always bought a smile to his face.

When the touring across the country had finally come to an end, he felt physically and emotionally drained. He decided to have a long rest before returning to the original pubs and clubs, not allowing himself to forget that they were the beginning of his road to fame.

By January 1998, he was back in full swing, much to the delight of the managers and punters. He also auditioned for another West End musical, called *Heaven Requires A Cupid* but failed to be selected for a call back. This upset him a great deal, after the run of success he had had. He thought the person who had got the part was awful both with their vocals and their acting ability and he began to wonder why on earth it had been given to him. He found himself hating the person who had got the part, as the rejection stuck in his head, like a pain that wouldn't go away.

Emilio Lopez.

He wouldn't forget that name in a hurry.

Scott was very happy that Luke's career had taken a turn for the better. For so long, he had been telling him things could only get better and he just had to believe in himself.

Things, on the other hand, were not so good for Scott. He desperately needed Luke's support through his difficult time, but he didn't want to shatter Luke's happiness by burdening him with his own problems. The solution Scott opted for, filled him with so much guilt, he couldn't bear to look Luke in the face until he had confessed.

It all began in June 2000.

Scott was facing the possibility of redundancy, as the Government was making drastic cutbacks in the education sector, especially within the management side.

At the end of the previous academic year, he was successful in his application for the Headship at the school he was teaching at. More hours were put into the new job and Luke occasionally commented that more and more of his time was being spent at school.

The support he received from Luke was practically non-existent, which only achieved in pushing Scott further into his work. Luke was oblivious to the fact that Scott was drowning under the pressure, as he was clearly in the throes of enjoying an almost full-on schedule of entertaining, as well as juggling mini concerts here and there.

Now that there was a question mark hanging over Scott's head, like the sword of Damocles, regarding the future position of his job, it only served to drive a wedge further into his and Luke's relationship. The lack of communication between the two was becoming more prominent, although Luke was totally unaware that anything was untoward. Scott's thirtieth birthday had come and gone, without any real acknowledgement of its significance, from Luke, if he had indeed remembered at all.

If the threat of losing his job wasn't enough to cope with, his mother was taken ill. Both his sister, Eve, and his brother, Marcus, were at his mother's house. Scott made matters worse by his presence and created arguments between himself and his siblings. His mother had contracted some rare blood disease that he could never remember the name of, even though he was reminded of it on several occasions. Marcus and Eve would try to talk to Scott, to find out what was troubling him. They only succeeded in making him more withdrawn and unable to think clearly.

Scott's mother died on 3 August 2000. Eve and Marcus had long since given up hope of getting any sense out of Scott, leaving him feeling bitterly alone; even more so, as Luke was re-touring, to promote his album.

It was at this low point in his life, when he met Ben Richards.

Andrew R. Hamilton

Ben was twenty-nine years old, working as a barman in a gay pub near Turnpike Lane tube station, called *The Golden Gate*. He had a body and looks that would make men's heads, as well as women's turn. Ben never thought of himself as particularly good looking but enjoyed basking in the compliments when others did.

Since leaving college at eighteen, he had always worked in bars, never having the motivation or inclination to work anywhere else. As his parents were very well off, they always came to his aide in any financial crises he might have had. Being an only child, many people thought Ben was spoilt. His parents had bought him a car on his eighteenth birthday; a flat on his twenty-first and constantly bought "little presents", that would have cost a small fortune, in order to help furnish his new home. In fact, practically everything that Ben possessed was bought and paid for by his parents.

He never had much success when it came to boyfriends. They all seemed to take advantage of him, treating him as though he were a toy, or piece of meat, that they could use for their own carnal pleasures, rather than someone who possessed and actually experienced any real emotions.

He decided that Scott might be the one to break the disastrous mould. "I've not seen you in here before," he said, wiping the top of the bar down.

Scott shot a glance in his direction. "No. I don't usually come to the East End much," he said, taking a seat on the barstool.

"So, what are you drinking?"

Scott scanned the bar for inspiration. Finally, he settled upon a pint of Websters.

Ben smiled as he placed the pint on the bar, in front of Scott, taking the note from his hand. He came back seconds later with the change and held Scott's hand a little longer than needed, as he slowly placed the change into his open palm. "You know," he began, "you're really good looking."

Scott smiled.

Ben leaned over the bar and kissed Scott on the lips, before scurrying off to serve the next customer, leaving Scott a little shocked although slightly aroused. No sooner had Ben finished serving his customer, he was back talking with Scott. "Do you have a boyfriend?" he asked suddenly.

Scott was about to nod that he had and stopped himself. "No."

"Oh," said Ben with disappointment.

"What?"

"Well, nothing quite beats a threesome!" He was off again.

Scott didn't have time for practical jokers and took his drink to the seats in the corner of the pub, where he ran through his mind everything that had

The Absence of Friends

happened over the past few weeks. Ben, who was collecting empty glasses, took it upon himself to sit beside Scott, interrupting his deep thoughts.

"So, would you like to wait for me to finish? We could have some fun, if you want."

Two can play at this game, thought Scott, even though he had no intention of doing so. "Sure, why not?" he said, nodding his head.

Ben smiled. "You know, you look really horny."

"Do I?" asked Scott, becoming a little bored with Ben's tiresome games.

Ben nodded, showing his enthusiasm and kissed Scott again before he continued collecting the remaining empty glasses.

During the course of the evening and a further three pints, all served by Ben, Scott was swamped with suggestive comments, kisses and even at one point, a playful slap on his backside. What made matters worse, was that if Scott had been single, he would have been sorely tempted in showing Ben just how horny he could be. *It's a shame Ben's only fooling around*, Scott thought, *as it's actually nice having some sexual attention.*

A quick visit to the toilet was called for, as Scott decided that it was time to call an end to the night and go back home. He hated the bars that had cubicles in the toilet which had broken locks and cursed the management under his breath for not taking the time to fix it. True to his fear, someone had barged into the cubicle, causing Scott to jump with quite a start.

It was Ben.

"Well, I guess you are pleased to see me," Ben chortled, staring down at Scott's exposed manhood.

Scott smiled nervously. He wasn't exactly erect but clearly that didn't stop Ben in making his lewd comments, no matter how inappropriate the time.

"So, what's happening now?" asked Ben.

"Well, I was trying to go for a piss!"

"Don't let me stop you," said Ben, taking hold of Scott's penis and feeling it grow harder in his hand.

"I wouldn't do that if I were you. I'd probably end up pissing all over your hand and clothes!"

Ben raised his eyebrows and began kissing Scott. Maybe it was the intimate physical contact that he had craved for so long, but Scott never really understood why he responded by putting his arms around Ben, allowing himself to be devoured. Scott's hand slowly moved down to Ben's crotch, feeling that he was as hard as rock through his trousers.

Ben broke away. "I ought to get back."

"Sure."

Looking down at his crotch, Ben tutted. "I can't go out like this."

Scott gave a wry smile. "I guess not."

"Look, I'm finishing soon. If you want to wait for me, we can finish what we've just started. It would be such a shame to let the night go and not have you in bed beside me."

That was all Scott needed to make up his mind. "Okay, I'll wait for you."

Ben left the toilets, leaving Scott to finish relieving himself, before he returned to the bar.

As Ben was on his final few minutes of clearing and tidying up, he asked: "Will it be my place or yours?"

"Where do you live?"

"Wood Green."

"I'm in Ealing."

Ben screwed his face up in mock horror. "Too far. It looks like it's my place then, doesn't it?"

"Okay. Do you have a car?"

He nodded.

It took a further twenty minutes before Ben was ready to leave. Throwing his coat over his shoulder, he bid his colleagues farewell. "C'mon then. Let's go." He motioned Scott to follow him.

With Ben's arm around Scott's waist, they left the bar.

CHAPTER NINE

"What!" screamed Luke hysterically.

"I'm so sorry..."

"Sorry? God, Scott! You've been fucking around with someone else and all you can say to me is *sorry!*"

Luke's eyes were bloodshot from the tears he had cried, more from anger than because he was upset. "How many times?"

"Just the once. I felt really guilty after."

"Well that's really noble of you," spat Luke.

"You're not making this any easier for me."

"Why the hell should I? You're the one who had the affair, Scott, not me."

Luke's vehement tone and expression made Scott very uncomfortable, causing him to keep fidgeting in his chair. He pained for ages on whether he should tell Luke or not, coming to the final conclusion that it was better to be honest about the whole situation. Telling him was the easy part. What worried Scott was how he would deal with Luke's reaction. So far, there had been a lot of tears and shouting but nothing more drastic than that. He still loved Luke a great deal and constantly brought that up, but Luke couldn't decide whether to believe him or not.

When Luke asked why, or rather demanded why, he had gone off with someone else, Scott poured his heart out. The negative feelings that had been bottled up and suppressed for weeks came out amidst a flow of tears. It began to dawn on Luke that he had not been there for Scott in his time of need. Upon hearing that Scott's mother had died, Luke became aware of how little he knew about Scott over the last few weeks. Although he understood why, when Ben showed Scott some attention he ended up in bed with him for the affection that he had so dearly craved, it was going to take Luke quite some time to really forgive him.

The whole scene between the two of them ended up being dramatically reversed. Instead of Luke screaming at Scott, demanding explanations, he ended up trying to comfort him and apologising for his lack of support. There were tears and hugs whilst they talked about their relationship, coming to a mutual agreement that they would work harder at it, promising to give each other the support whenever they needed it.

It was a couple of weeks after the events with Ben were revealed, that Luke sat purposefully at the table, wading through the invitations to perform at various venues and preparing an itinerary for the upcoming weeks. Scott was writing letters for the invitations Luke had decided that he couldn't take up, but offering to perform later on in the year.

The ring of the telephone cut the silence like a knife.

Luke answered it. "Hello?"

"Oh, good evening," said the voice at the other end. "May I speak to Scott?"

"Sure. Who's calling?"

"Ben."

"Not Ben Richards?"

"Yes."

Scott looked at Luke with confused apprehension. *How on earth did he manage to get my number*, he thought.

As if reading Scott's mind, Luke asked: "And how did you manage to get this number, may I ask?"

There was a pause before Ben replied: "He gave it to me when he met me at *The Golden Gate* pub."

"He gave it to you?" repeated Luke, watching Scott shaking his head violently.

"Look, why all these questions? Who do you think you are? All I want to do is to speak to Scott."

"I'm Scott's boyfriend...and to answer *your* question, *no* you cannot speak to Scott!" With that, Luke slammed down the phone.

"All I can think of," said Scott, wracking his brain to find an explanation, "is that he must have got hold one of one of my personal business cards."

"I suggest," said Luke sternly, "that we change our number first thing in the morning. I don't want that son-of-a-bitch being given the opportunity to pull another stunt like that."

The following day, Luke went to visit Elliot and Kristian, as he needed a friendly ear and some credible words of wisdom from them when he confided in them of Scott's infidelity with Ben. Neither of them were the judgmental kind and could easily understand Scott's indiscretion, as well as be compassionate as to why both he and Luke had acted in the way they did. They advised Luke that if he wanted his relationship with Scott to continue, then the effort could not be just placed on one side nor could he permit himself to allow communication to slip in the way that it had. They did note that Luke had become overly preoccupied with his escalating success and had obviously forgotten about the people around him, who really cared for him the most.

Luke made a promise to himself and to his friends that he would try his damnedest not to allow the same thing to happen twice. He loved Scott far too much to lose him on something that was so easily resolvable.

The Absence of Friends

"Well, you need to go and tell *him* that you love him," advised Kristian. "I could bet every single penny I own that you haven't told him that in a long time and to be honest with you, he needs to hear it once in a while to know you haven't forgotten about him. Likewise, he needs to do the same with you."

Elliot chipped in: "I don't think that we've allowed one day to pass by that one of us hasn't told the other one that we love them."

In late January 2001, Michael Hart had decided it was high time he paid his old friend, Kristian, a visit. "How the devil are you, sweetie?"

"I'm fine."

Puckering his lips, he asked: "And how's the lovely, not-so-straight Elliot?"

Elliot smiled, giving Michael a quick peck on the lips and then withdrawing with haste lest Michael should want to linger more than Elliot would have liked him to. "I'm not so bad, thanks. What about yourself?"

"Oh, darling," said Michael excitably, slapping Elliot on the arm with a bit more force than he had intended. "I thought you'd never ask. This bitch has found herself a boyfriend!"

"Really?" they both said in unison, not hiding their surprise with their mouths agape.

"Oh please, I don't know why you're looking so shocked. I think it's absolutely wonderful...you can close your mouths now, you know, as I might take offence by the fact you think I can't turn the impossible into the possible."

Elliot and Kristian complied with the instruction and apologised to Michael for their inappropriate reaction.

"Anyway," Michael continued, back to his effervescent self, "the only way that I can describe how I currently feel is that it's like being permanently stuck in a cocktail hour."

"I don't know why you never told me," said Kristian, quietly chuckling at Michael's unique analogy of the lucky - or would it have been unlucky? - man who had allowed himself to become ensnared by Michael's voracious need for melodramatic effeminacy.

"I'm so sorry I didn't tell you, sweetie but the whole affair would have just been way too sordid for your delicate mind and precious ears to have been infected with."

Kristian sighed resignedly.

"Anyway, changing the subject then, have you seen Maxine recently?" asked Elliot.

Michael raised his fingers to his open mouth, as if realising a cardinal sin had just been committed and then sighed impetuously at the need to correct Elliot yet again. "How many times do I need to tell you? Obviously I haven't drummed this into you quite enough. When you are talking about Max or Maxine, then you should always refer to them as *Max Squared*."

Even after all this time, Elliot still wasn't totally used to Michael's little idiosyncrasies with his own special language that he used and wondered if he might sometimes deliberately overemphasise his idioms in order to gain a specific reaction from his listeners.

"I'm really ever so sorry," Elliot said, giving Michael a look of someone who had just been severely chastised that he knew Michael would be clearly hoping for. Elliot had learnt from experience that Michael always expected a certain look from people otherwise they would be faced with the possibility of an acerbic verbal retribution. "I will endeavour to try and remember in the future. So have you seen *Max Squared* recently?"

"I have to say though, Elliot, and it pains me to do so," began Michael cattily, as he clutched at his throat for further emphasis, "that what you have in the looks department, you certainly lose in the brains department!"

Elliot widened his eyes in surprise at the unexpected retort, as Kristian's lips curved into a smirk.

"Oh yes, my dear," Michael started with his admonishment, "you may very well want to entertain that shocked look upon your pretty features but there is no hiding the fact that you clearly have a brain like a sieve and don't have an eidetic memory for those, hmmm…shall we call them *the more important issues* in the lives of your friends?"

"Well, I think that's a bit harsh. Don't you?" snorted Elliot.

"*Harsh?* No, not really. I think what is rather harsh is that, *yet again*, I will need to refresh your dim and failing memory, dear boy."

"Oh, this just gets even more fabulous," Kristian said facetiously. "I take it we are now going to get a history lesson from our intellectual but resoundingly camp drag queen chum, who thinks he's a neuroscientist, who in turn likes to believe he is masquerading as a competent genealogist."

Surprisingly, Michael ignored Kristian's comment as he had already begun to mentally transport himself back over two years previous.

"I know it will be a tall order but cast your minds back to the opening night of *Secrets* in Putney, when we were all gathered in my dressing room…"

"Well…" began Michael, clearly itching to divulge all the latest gossip. "The gorgeous Max is now married to the most divine of men. They are quite the stunning couple. I mean, I just cream my knickers every time I visit them and really, I don't know who of the two causes me to get so moist! I know that you," he glanced knowingly at Elliot, "were a gorgeous couple when you were together…but I mean, really, that woman will end up losing me as a friend if she keeps on getting all the Adonis's falling at her size five feet!"

Both Elliot and Kristian shook their heads incredulously, realising that absolutely nothing had changed about Michael. They knew that he could still be the life and soul of any party, if the guests could understand and appreciate his particular style of comicality.

"Do you see much of Maxine then?" asked Elliot, genuinely intrigued.

"Oh, my darling petal," Michael said, as he began to pack away Queen M'Kay-La's personal items. "I do believe you still have a soft spot for our little Max, don't you?"

Elliot grimaced, as he instantly remembered that Michael had the unenviable ability to drive the proverbial nail into where it would hurt the most without giving a second's thought to tact.

"If it makes you feel any better," Michael went on, oblivious to Elliot's discomfort, "I do still see her quite often. In fact, I seem to be seeing a lot more of her than her husband actually does! I only wish that it was the other way around, if you know what I mean." He winked at Elliot suggestively.

"What's he like?" asked Kristian.

"Who? Max's husband?"

"Yeah."

"You'd never believe that his name's Max too. He's Max Beresford, she's Max Wyatt. It's just too much to cope with. I have affectionately dubbed them as *Max Squared*."

Both Elliot and Kristian looked at each other quizzically.

"I can tell by the perplexed expressions you're both exhibiting that my mathematical genius is completely wasted upon the both of you. So let me explain…it's simply because it's Max to the power of two, hence it would naturally become *Max Squared*."

"Very clever," said Elliot sardonically.

"Ah, *now* the numismatic token of a diminutively fiscal nature irrevocably plummets," Kristian said with haughty derision.

Michael looked at them both through narrowed eyes, pursing his lips in a contentious manner before he decided to continue with what he thought as his perfunctory discourse. "He is just as outrageous as she is and really ever so nice. I'm pretty sure that you'd both really like him if - or rather, hopefully when, is what I meant to say - you get to meet him. Unfortunately, there will be no chance of history repeating itself, if you know what I'm saying." He looked at Elliot, who blushed slightly.

"How on earth do you manage to remember all of this in such fine detail?" asked Elliot, bringing Michael back into the present day.

"I guess it's just one of God's little gifts that he bestowed upon me in his infinite wisdom."

"So," began Elliot, with a keen desperation to steer the subject away from him and his history with Maxine, "please tell us more about this mysterious boyfriend of yours."

"What do you want to know?"

"You know – the usual stuff. How old is he? What's his name? Where did you meet him?"

"His name is Steven Cronje. He's twenty-seven and I met him at *Tutti Frutties*. He's from South Africa originally and oh…that accent of his just melts me. I could just listen to him talk nonsense to me all night long and I would feel that I was in heaven."

Elliot and Kristian listened intently as Michael relived the moments which bought him and Steven together, describing each nuance and every exploit in profuse detail. The more he got involved in telling the story, the more animated and excited he became, making less and less sense in what he was saying. As far as they could make out from his nonsensical ramblings, he got talking to Steven at the *Tutti Frutties* nightclub and it was *he* who was making all the moves on Michael. Apparently, nothing happened on that night other than the de rigueur goodnight kiss, which Kristian found incredibly hard to believe as Michael had, at college, constantly boasted about speedy his conquests. Steven had called Michael the following day and arranged to meet for a picnic but still nothing on an intimate level happened save for a hug or a kiss. It wasn't until nearly a month after their initial meet that they actually slept together.

"I can tell you this much, it was certainly well worth the wait," smiled Michael, remembering the day clearly, as though it had only occurred the previous night.

"It certainly sounds like it," said Elliot.

"So why didn't you bring Steven along with you?" asked Kristian.

"Because he's visiting his parents."

"You'll have to bring him around some time, so we can meet the man who's captured the heart, mind and soul of Michael Hart and probably, no doubt, momentarily stilled the vicious tongue of Queen M'Kay-La."

"The heart, mind and soul bit is true but I doubt anyone or anything could silence Queen M'Kay-La. But, you won't have long to wait before you can meet him because he's actually coming to London tomorrow. I'm staying at the New Regent Hotel and I've told him to meet me there."

The Absence of Friends

"No, no, no, no, no!" exclaimed Kristian, almost choking on his defiant excitement. "We absolutely won't hear of it. Why on earth don't the two of you come and stay with us? Surely it would make much more sense, rather than having to fork out for extortionate hotel rates."

Elliot nodded acquiescently. "Sure, it's a great idea. You can ring Steve and we can pick him up at Victoria station when he arrives."

"We wouldn't want to impose."

"Michael!" Kristian bellowed firmly. "As you yourself know, you are a very imposing character anyway. However, there is plenty of room here, so it wouldn't be an imposition at all. So, why don't you hush up, give Steve a call and let him know the change of plans?"

"Thanks guys," said Michael, as Elliot passed him the phone.

Having spotted Steven walking down the platform, carrying a small suitcase, Michael jumped up and down with the excitement befitting that of a child who knew they were about to get an ice cream.

"There he is," he yelled, running up to him and greeting him with a huge hug before realising he needed to introduce him to Elliot and Kristian.

"It's so nice to meet the two of you," Steven said warmly, shaking their hands with an almost vice-like grip. "Mike has told me so much about you both. So it's great to actually meet you."

"Likewise," they replied in unison.

Kristian mouthed "Mike?" to Elliot, allowing himself a few moments to absorb the disbelief that Michael would allow anybody the opportunity for hypocorism.

Michael had always been incredibly pedant about people calling him Michael. He didn't understand why people felt the need to shorten his name, as he considered it to be a lazy form of communication. There had been many occasions that both Kristian and Elliot had witnessed Michael taking umbrage at being called Mike, Mickey or even worse, Mick, but seemingly this ardently preserved rule didn't apply to Steven, unless Michael hadn't actually noticed in his excitement of meeting him.

"Ooh," Michael squeaked friskily to Steven, "please don't say no, but you just have to say something really gorgeous and beautiful in Afrikaans."

"Iets regtig pragtig en mooi in Afrikaans," Steven smiled, granting Michael his zesty wish.

"What did you say?" asked Michael with proliferated enthusiasm, clapping his hands in gleeful impatience.

"I said exactly what you wanted me to say, *something really gorgeous and beautiful in Afrikaans.*" Steven replied officiously.

Michael rolled his eyes back and sighed heavily. "Oh, seriously Steven? *That's* what you took from that request? I give up, really I do. I would have thought you would have at least said something far more provocative and stimulating than just *that*." He let out a long, drawn out sigh once again. Shaking off his disappointment, he turned to Elliot and Kristian, asking: "Well, it wasn't much to go on but...anyway, didn't I tell you? Isn't that accent just to die for?"

Steven Cronje's appearance, demeanour and his effortless ability to abruptly steer a conversation away from Michael and his ludicrously unconventional effeminacy, genuinely surprised Elliot and Kristian, as he was really not what they had expected. In fact, when they first met him, he was the exact opposite of what they had mentally conjured up as Michael's partner. Although he didn't tower above Michael's stature, he was easily over six feet tall, with a very well built frame - although not overly muscular - and rugged, masculine features. He had an incredible thick head of strawberry blond hair, which was perfectly groomed into a side parting. It could have been their imaginations but his emerald-like eyes and pearl-like teeth seemed to glint and glisten in a certain light. It was perfectly clear to the two men that Steven was keen on taking a great deal of pride in both his physique and with his physical appearance. He was impeccably dressed, wearing a pair of smart navy blue trousers with a crisp, sharp seam that were more than likely to be a part of a two, or even a three-piece suit. His light blue shirt looked as though it had literally been put on straight from the dry-cleaners, as it didn't appear to show a single crease from the day's wear and was completed with what appeared to be rather quaint, sapphire-like cufflinks. Steven would never dream of wearing a dress shirt without a tie and so opted to wear a silk one with stripes in several shades of blue. The look wouldn't have been complete without a pair of sensible, black brogues that had naturally been polished with the utmost rigour in order to compete with the sparkle of the cufflinks. Comparatively, both Elliot and Kristian considered themselves to be extremely underdressed and unkempt in their comfortable jeans and sweatshirts. They couldn't quite comprehend how Michael and Steven were suited but who were they to voice such an opinion publicly.

Notably, Steven was a particularly shy person, as it took him some time to relax and join in with any of the myriad of topics that were discussed on the journey back. "I'm so sorry," he apologised. "For some reason, I find it really difficult to be able to dive straight into conversation with people that I don't know...unless I've had a drink or two!"

"Don't you worry yourself about it," said Kristian with assurance.

"We want you to relax, take it easy and treat this as your home," said Elliot.

"Thank you so much. You guys are amazing…no wonder Mike talks about you all the time. I can see why!"

And there it was again. Elliot and Kristian both noticed Steven's use of shortening Michael's name once more and were awaiting his inevitable fractious tirade, as there was no way that it could have gone unnoticed this time. They were more than a little surprised that Michael didn't even pre-empt a predicted reaction; not even with the slightest hint of an antagonistic batting of his eyelids.

"Right then," began Michael, completely over-looking his own golden rule about how he should be correctly addressed, "what was the name of that place that you said we were going to tonight?"

"*The Grand Duchess*," said Elliot. "We'll be meeting up with Luke and Scott there."

"Is that Luke, the singer?" asked Michael.

Kristian nodded.

"Yes," said Michael, unusually phlegmatic. "Wasn't he the young man that you wanted to introduce me to on a couple of occasions? For the life of me, I really can't quite remember why but for some reason it never transpired."

"That's right," added Elliot.

Regaining his effervescent spirit, Michael added: "I'm sure there was some plausible explanation as to why it didn't happen…but that will clearly be rectified tonight." Turning to Steven, he asked: "Would you like to go?"

"Sure. I'm fascinated to see what London has to offer in terms of entertainment."

Elliot and Kristian attempted to make Steven feel as comfortable and relaxed as they possibly could, bringing him into their conversations subtly and gently. Although Steven was the bigger built and more than likely the strongest of the four of them, he was certainly the most timid and definitely the quietest, which, when Michael was around, wasn't a remarkable accomplishment. When he did eventually begin to join in with the various topics being discussed, Elliot and Kristian noted that whilst he was eloquently spoken, there was a real mellifluous quality to his voice.

When questioned by Michael later on about what he thought of Elliot and Kristian, Steven said that he liked them instantaneously. To justify his summation, he cited that they made him feel as though he belonged within an already established group and not as the outsider, as he had experienced many times before with previous partners and being introduced to their friends.

"I was originally born in South Africa," he said, when questioned on his background. "My mother is from Pretoria and my father, from Jo'berg, although I grew up in Cape Town. I guess I was just coming into my teens when we moved to England, as my father had secured himself a job as a principal lecturer in design and technical drawing. My father is one of those men who wants his son to follow in his footsteps. Well, more *expected* than wanted. I had absolutely no interest in technical drawing or teaching. For many years, we never really saw eye-to-eye, quite simply because he wanted me to conform to his ideals but I was having none of it.

"My mother, however, had a totally different outlook. She encouraged me to do whatever it was that *I* was interested in, although I was very unhappy that this ended up causing many bitter arguments between my parents. At one point I found it really unbearable to live with them, so I moved out when I was probably about seventeen. The good news, though, is that our relationship seems to be a lot stronger now, as my father has somewhat mellowed the older he has become. They are actually very happy for me that my career has taken off, though sometimes my father does keep telling me that I would have made an excellent teacher."

"So, did you end up moving back in with your parents, then?" asked Kristian.

"No, I didn't. But I do live in the same town as them though."

"Oh? Where's that then?"

"Gosport."

"Ah, that's in Newcastle, right?" chipped in Elliot.

"Wrong, I'm afraid," replied Steven, with a smile. "You're thinking of Gosforth. Gosport is actually in Hampshire."

Elliot noticeably blushed at the fact that someone who had only been in the country for about fifteen years, corrected him on his geography.

Kristian smiled at Elliot's faux pas. "It's nice there," he said. "We went there a few times when we visited Portsmouth and Southampton, eh Michael?"

"That's right."

"Luke's from Southampton, so he will probably know Gosport quite well."

"Do you know Southampton much, Steven?" asked Elliot.

"Fairly well. There's quite a nice nightclub there that I used to go to sometimes, called *The Magnum*. I guess the easiest way to describe it would be that it's a smaller version of *Heaven*, here in London. It has three floors: the first one is purely a bar. It's nice just to sit there if you want to have a quiet drink and talk with friends. The second floor plays Hi-NRG and commercial music and the third floor is rave, techno and house."

The Absence of Friends

"Sounds wonderful," said Elliot. "Ten years ago, I might have been there every weekend."

"Well, if you went there regularly, you might actually have a different view of the club. Don't get me wrong though, it was always very busy and people did rave about the place but these were generally the youngsters who had only just entered into the world of clubbing. The place sounds a lot more glamorous and sensational than it really is."

"It's true," Michael chipped in, with a nod of his head. "It's a good place for an occasional night out with some friends but other than that, nothing more exciting or exotic than you've already got in London. I suppose that's one of the main reasons that we want to move to London…because there is so much more available to you in the way of culture and diversity."

"Um…hold on just a second," said Kristian, shaking his head slightly and displaying a confused frown. "Can we just rewind there, please?" He paused for a little more dramatic effect. "Michael! This cannot be an on-the-spur of the moment decision. Unless I am losing the plot, I don't remember you telling us that you were planning on moving. When exactly were you going to tell us?"

"I've just told you," he grinned. "Anyway, it's not quite definite yet. We are seriously considering it but whilst we're here, we are going to go property and job hunting. Dependent on that, will be the catalyst to moving."

"It's going to be just like our college days."

"Oh God, I hope not! You *are* joking, right?"

Kristian shook his head.

"Oh, my darling boy! You are totally different now, to how you were at college. How can I put this without hurting your feelings? You were about as exciting as a dirty nappy!"

"I don't think we really need to get into that," said Kristian, willing the conversation to rapidly take a change in direction. Kristian would have been extremely mortified if Michael had regaled stories from their college days. He seemed to have the ability to verbally back people into a corner, without any hope of getting away.

Kristian breathed a sigh of relief when Elliot announced that they should think about getting ready to go out for the evening.

By the time the four of them had arrived at *The Grand Duchess*, Luke was already on stage. Elliot spotted Scott near the front and motioned the other three to follow him. The introductions were rushed, as they sat down at the table to watch Luke.

"Good. Isn't he?" Michael asked Steven.

Steven nodded at Michael but didn't verbalise an answer, as his eyes were resolutely transfixed upon Luke, where he was unable to take them off him.

This was not because he thought that Luke was the best singer he had ever heard, as he had listened to some absolutely stunning singers in his time, nor was it because he thought he was good looking, which he did. The mesmerising gaze was more to do with the thought he was adamant that he recognised him from somewhere, although he couldn't quite recall where. He was convinced that the name of Luke Faraday sounded familiar to him when it was mentioned earlier and now, with his eyes fixed firmly upon him, he was wracking his brain to remember exactly why that was.

When Luke had finished his performing, he immediately made his way to the table to greet his friends, with the new introductions being made once more. Conversation flowed as freely as the drinks did, whilst the men bonded, as though they had always been a group of six.

"Now I remember where I know you from," said Steven, after Luke had mentioned that he had appeared in musicals.

"Oh?" said Luke with intrigue, thinking that Steven might have been a punter at a bar he had performed in many moons ago. There was a degree of curiosity and speculation about at what point in Luke's history he had crossed paths with Steven, as he felt that he was normally very good in never forgetting a face. He had to admit defeat as he didn't recognise Steven in the slightest.

"Yes. You probably actually know my friend, rather than me, as I guess you've auditioned against each other on many an occasion."

"Just how small *is* this world?" asked Michael. "It's highly incestuous, as everyone seems to know everyone else, through someone or other."

"What was the audition for?" asked Scott, equally intrigued as Luke.

"It was for a musical in the West End, if I remember correctly. Oh god, what was the name of it now?" He drummed his fingers against his forehead, as if this would dislodge the memory he was hoping to conjure up from the deepest recesses.

"Well, if you tell me who your friend is," said Luke with an air of graceful panache, "I will probably be able to remember what musical it was that he was in."

"Emilio Lopez," said Steven with a smile.

The colour drained from Luke's face. "*Him*," he spat, beginning to see red mist forming before his eyes. "And you can take that fucking smile off your face too!"

Nobody at the table, least of all Steven, understood why Luke suddenly launched into a tirade of abuse, with expletives dominating the majority of words that came out of his mouth directed predominantly towards Steven.

"That's quite enough, Luke," Kristian said firmly, standing up from his chair and placing his hands squarely on the table as if to drive into Luke that he meant business. "Steven is a friend of ours. Your behaviour just now is not only reprehensible but to be honest with you, downright disgusting and offensive."

Michael had tears streaming down his cheeks, utterly shocked by the misfortune of what he had just witnessed. Steven comforted him with a strong arm, pulling him in tight as if to shield him from any more of the horror that they might be bombarded with.

If Scott could measure how mortified he felt, it would be off the scale but his anger was still plainly shown on his face. "What the hell is wrong with you, Luke?"

"Why don't you ask *him?*" hissed Luke, pointing an accusatory finger in Steven's direction.

"No!" Scott snapped back. "I am asking *you!*"

"Emilio fucking Lopez. That's what wrong with me," Luke growled, baring his teeth like a rabid dog, ready to puncture any foolhardy challenger with an insidious bite.

"What? You're not making any sense."

"Maybe I'm not making any sense but I bet it's all very crystal clear to the whiter than white Steven Cronje. You and your *friend* - the unscrupulously parasitic bastard - Emilio are out to destroy my career!"

"What?" said several voices in confused unison, all a couple of octaves higher than their usual tone.

"It's so laughable, that it's not even funny. The guy was an utterly talentless moron and completely inept. His acting and singing - if that's what you could call it - was nothing more worthy than shit," cried Luke manically, "and he managed to steal *that* musical away from me. Now along comes this guy," he pointed forebodingly once more at Steven, "who is no doubt conspiring with him to steal my venues." Laughing hysterically, he continued: "And you lot seem to think that it's me who is being unreasonable! So called friends of mine. Well, you can all go to hell for all I care."

Had the group been given the opportunity, they may have been able to calm Luke down long enough to get him to see sense and realise that Steven had nothing at all to do with Emilio getting the part in the musical nor that anybody was out to destroy his career.

However, before anybody had the chance to convey their palatable rationales, Luke had already fled from the bar.

Humble pie, in copious quantities, would be on the menu for Luke in the days and weeks that lay ahead of that incident, as he sought the forgiveness from the five people who had sat at the table that night. Some, though, would require more than just the one serving.

CHAPTER TEN

"Scott," Luke whispered softly, with a trembling lump caught deep within his throat. "I'm HIV positive." He hung his head like a shamed child, anticipating an inescapable punishment for doing something wrong. He certainly felt that the diagnosis was punishment in itself, as he had every reason to feel thoroughly ashamed of himself.

"Don't even joke about things like that. It's not funny!" said Scott sternly.

"Am I laughing?"

"Are you sure?" he asked, softening his tone slightly.

"Yes. I got the results a couple of weeks back."

"Whatever made you go for the test on your own anyway? We normally go together."

"You did, Scott."

"Eh? What are talking about?"

"Well, wasn't it *you* who had the affair? And wasn't it *you* who caught gonorrhea?"

Instinctively, although bizarrely hallucinatory, Scott saw his arm rising up to lash out at Luke and his hand striking him hard across the face but his befuddled mind didn't register that it was actually him who was carrying out the deed. It was only the sting from his palm and seeing Luke wince in pain that he understood what had just occurred. He paced the room back and forth like a caged animal, scratching his head occasionally as if this would help him to think with further clarity, whilst Luke sat tacitly on a chair, inert other than to wipe the tears from his eyes with his handkerchief that was already soaking wet.

"Oh God," said Scott eventually, still unable to believe what Luke had told him was the truth. "I don't believe it."

"Please don't shut me out, Scott. I need you more than ever now," sobbed Luke.

"Jesus!" was all Scott could say, massaging his forehead soothingly as though he had an intense headache. "How…? When…?"

"I guess…it was probably when I first came to London."

"What are you talking about?" said Scott, becoming irritated.

"I was a rent boy, Scott."

"Fuck me!" Scott sucked in his breath. "You never told me about that."

"It's all in the past. I thought…"

"In the past?" yelled Scott. "It's far from in the past. Your past has just caught up with you now. Jesus, Luke! What the hell were you thinking?"

"Scott, I was a scared eighteen year old kid, with no money and nowhere to live. What did you expect me to do? Besides, it was only for a short while." He wiped the tears from his eyes again.

"Have you told anyone else?"

"No. It's not exactly something I take pride in telling everyone."

"Don't be sarcastic."

"Remember, when I told you I was first raped, by David, all those years ago? It might have been then," Luke stuttered.

"Yes, I remember." Scott paused for a moment. "Now, how about telling me the *real* truth? You may think it but I'm not stupid, Luke…there's no way you would have only just been diagnosed from something that happened all those year ago. It *has* to be much more recent than that."

Luke could only hang his head in abysmal shame once again.

It suddenly dawned on Scott what Luke had just said. "And what exactly do you mean when you said the *first* time you were raped? I want the truth, Luke and I want it now."

Luke drew in a deep breath, letting out a long, slow sigh. "Okay," he said, wringing his hands tightly. "Remember a few weeks back, when I totally lost it with Steven, when we were at *The Grand Duchess*?"

Scott nodded. "How could I forget? It's taken nearly all this time for things to turn back to normality. There were some real frosty reactions from everyone for quite a long time."

"Anyway," Luke continued. "I left the bar in an absolutely foul mood…"

"Understatement."

"Scott, please! Let me finish. This isn't easy for me."

"Okay."

"So, I ended up leaving the bar in an absolutely foul mood, where I was feeling decidedly acrimonious and highly-strung, to say the least. I guess I was feeling a gargantuan amount of resentment towards everyone…including you! I suppose, thinking about it now, the anger that I felt for you brought back the memories of your one-night stand with Ben Richards and made me all the more embittered. The way that I was feeling at that point, I was in the right frame of mind to really have it out with someone…anyone really, I guess, who gave me just cause to start on them.

"I remember you telling me that he worked as a barman at the *Golden Gate* pub by Turnpike Lane tube station, so that's where I found myself heading, not even having a clue whether he was actually going to be working that evening or not. But by that time, I didn't really care. I didn't even know what I was even going to do when I saw him. *If* I even got the opportunity to see him.

"By the time I arrived at the pub the anger in me had more or less subsided, so I thought I might as well just get totally and utterly drunk. I don't really know how much I actually had to drink but I guess it was a fair bit, as I think I was just knocking back one after the other. There was a guy who honed in on me, feeding me all these corny and clichéd one liners about how good looking I was and how horny I made him feel, constantly touching me and groping me. Whenever I turned around, he was always there…with arms and hands everywhere!"

"Ben!" stated Scott.

"Yes, Ben! Once he told me his name, I realised immediately who he was but I told him my name was Pete, or Paul…I can't remember exactly what name I used but I didn't want to give him my real name in case he put two and two together. If I'm being perfectly honest, at that point, the thought *did* cross my mind about fucking his brains out…just to see what it was like for you."

"That's really not fair, Luke!"

"But it's how I felt at the time, Scott. Anyway, I guess that Ben must have been the duty manager who was scheduled on that evening because the next thing I knew, it was just me and him left alone in the bar. He asked me if I wanted to have some fun back at his place but quite frankly, all I wanted to do was go back home and take myself off to bed.

"He had obviously locked the door when I wasn't looking, or when I had gone to the toilet because when I tried to leave, I couldn't. I asked him to unlock the door so I could go and his reply was that if I really was determined to go home, then the least he could do was to send me on my way with a shot. I know if I continued to argue with him, it would have been a fruitless exercise, so I agreed to have a quick shot…after all, it was only going to add a couple of minutes more.

"He obviously had only one thing on his mind at that point, as he was continually rubbing himself up against me, trying to get my cock out of my trousers. I tried to stop him, really I did but…I was drunk and he was sober… so it didn't take much for him to overpower me. I thought he might have stopped after he had given me a blowjob."

"Did you give him…?"

"No, I did not! I didn't do anything to him, Scott. He had me pinned down and totally immobilised, even though I was struggling to get away. He obviously wasn't going to stop what he was doing until I had cum in his mouth. I thought that after that had happened he would finally let me go home but he said that it wasn't fair that I had cum and he hadn't. I suggested that he

The Absence of Friends

should just finish himself off with a wank and let me go home. Clearly, that wasn't good enough for him and he said he was sure we could find a far more satisfying way *together* to make him cum."

"So he…?"

"So he fucked me! Not just the once…but twice! I think he was so into reaching his own climatic gratification that he didn't even realise that I had been physically sick."

"Did he use…?"

"No! He didn't use a condom, even though earlier on in the evening he professed to be an advocator of safe sex. I only realised the true horror of what he'd done…or rather, what he hadn't done, when he came inside me. In no way am I condoning what he did but I'm not even sure he registered that he'd actually forced himself upon me because he told me that the only reason he managed to cum twice was 'cause I turned him on so much. I felt rather bilious when he said I was sensational; especially so when he expressed his hope that I had had as much amazing fun as he had. He even had the audacity to suggest that we must do it again.

"I spent the next few hours wandering aimlessly around, cursing my own absolute stupidity for *all* the events of that evening, until I came back here in the morning."

"And of course, that's when you told me that you had stayed with a friend, who had managed to calm you down enough to be able to see sense."

"Right," Luke sighed heavily, relieved that the truth had finally come out but still harbouring the overwhelming feelings of guilt and shame.

There were a few minutes of deathly cold silence whilst Scott digested everything that he had just been told. The persistent ticking of the second hand on the clock made Luke feel like he was a condemned man, awaiting the judge – being Scott – to pass sentence. Every second that the clock ticked, appeared to create its own anguished eternity.

"Oh my God," Scott said finally, causing Luke to abruptly recoil. "What if I've got it? Shit!"

"I think you're jumping to rather tenuous conclusions there."

"Am I? *I* don't think so…we haven't exactly played it safe ourselves, have we? Are you sure you've only known for a couple of weeks?"

"For fucks sake, Scott! What the hell are you trying to suggest?"

"I really don't know, Luke. You tell me."

"I really hope to God you're not insinuating that I've deliberately tried to infect you just because I have it. Seriously, Scott, do you honestly think I would be that callous? After all we've been though together, I would have hoped that you'd thought more of me than that."

"To tell you the truth, I really don't know what to think anymore."

Luke rose awkwardly from his chair and walked with stealth towards Scott, feeling totally drained of emotions. He had, at least, hoped for a different reception to the one he had just received. In his diminutive anticipation he thought that he might earn a sympathetic and supportive ear from Scott rather than be made to feel like a cantankerous but angst-ridden child who was about to be severely reprimanded for doing something reprehensibly iniquitous. As he neared Scott, he put his arms out to embrace him. Scott backed away, unable to hide his fear or his disgust because Luke was unable to determine exactly what it was that Scott was actually feeling.

"Scott, please will you give me a hug."

"You've got to be joking. I'm sorry, Luke, but right at this moment I just don't know what to do."

"Give it some time. Please," Luke pleaded.

"I really don't think I've got any time for you right now. I need it for myself 'cause I've got to think about what I am going to do."

"Scott! Please! Don't leave…"

Scott didn't hear Luke finish his sentence, as he had already walked out the door, obstreperously slamming it behind him.

The mercilessly spinning sensation that Luke felt in his head, was patently ineffable, which prevented him from being able to sink in what had just gone on. He desperately needed someone to talk to; even if it was just to be there with him. Although he was usually a fiercely strong-minded individual, he was not loathe to admit that he didn't have the strength to work through this alone. The only issue that tormented him was that he didn't want too many people becoming aware of his new status.

He came to the conclusion that his most favourable course of action would be to ring Elliot and Kristian. He knew that no matter what happened, they always made him feel better whenever he felt demoralised or had a problem. He dialled their number judiciously but only succeeded in obtaining their answer phone message. Despairingly, he slammed the phone down, back on to its hook.

The only other recourse left available to him was to follow the path of his next best option, which was the only thing he could think of doing; going out and getting himself blind drunk. At least, then, he wouldn't have to think about anything and he could allow the alcohol to take hold of all the negative emotions that were burning within him. At least, for a short while, as no doubt he would be faced with them once more when sobriety would ensure that they resurfaced. If nobody could give him the answers that he was seeking, or be there for him in his time of desperate need, the drink would always be there to console him. He put on his jacket and walked for what seemed like hours, before taking himself into a bar.

"I'm pregnant," Maxine announced with exuberant joy.

"Congratulations," said four voices simultaneously.

"When's it due?" asked Elliot.

"Mid-September. So another six months."

Elliot threw his arms around Maxine, hugging her tightly to him and permitting himself to kiss her gently on the cheek. "I'm really pleased for you. It's a shame this is only your first, 'cause I know you've been wanting a child for some time now."

"I know. But it has been fun trying," she giggled.

Everyone in the room smiled at Maxine's suggestive comment.

"I bet Max is pleased," said Kristian.

"He's completely over the moon," answered Maxine. "Though he does fuss like an old woman. *Don't do this* and *you mustn't pick up that*," she mimicked.

"I hope you're going to name him after me," said Michael flippantly.

"What if *he* is a *she*?" asked Maxine, interested to hear how he would answer.

"Makes no difference. You can still name her after me."

"Have you thought of any names?" asked Kristian.

"I have, actually," she said matter-of-factly. "If it's a boy, Max said he wants to call him Pierson. If it's a girl, I want to call her Thalia."

"Thalia," repeated Steven. "I really like that name. So I, for one, hope that it's a girl."

"As long as the baby is healthy and has ten fingers and ten toes, I'm not fussed whether it's a boy or a girl."

"I see nobody's *that* hooked on the name Pierson. How on earth did Max come up with that?" asked Michael.

Maxine scrunched her face, recalling why Max had chosen that name. "I think it's a slight alteration on his best friend's father's name, who was called Piers. Max idolised him. So, how's the house coming along, Michael?"

"It's looking really nice now. Elliot and Kristian have been a great help with the decorating. I'm useless at those sorts of things. You know how it is, Max, you just can't be ruining your hands with all this DIY nonsense. It's a real bitch when your nails keep breaking!"

"Oh God, Michael," sighed Steven.

"You needn't have fretted, Michael. You could always have borrowed a set of my false nails," said Maxine, with a smile.

Michael smiled. "I don't deserve friends like you, Max. If I didn't know you better, sweetie, I would think you were being a trifle bitchy."

"Who, me?" she giggled. "I wouldn't dream of it."

Scott sat pensively upon a bench in St James' Park, watching the numerous couples walk by him hand-in-hand. He recalled the first day with Luke, when they had had a picnic together; his eyes were fixed on the spot where they sat. They had been through a lot in the two and a half years that they had been together. He had been planning on buying tickets to Paris, for their third anniversary; spending a romantic two weeks there, possibly spending some time with Vince, who would have treated them like royalty in his restaurant. This idea would now have to be put on hold, if not completely forgotten about.

His mind wandered from Simon, to James, to Luke. He couldn't understand why, when things were going so well for him, something had to happen which would end up spoiling it. With Simon, it was the affair; with James, it was his career and now, with Luke, it was his health. He had lost most people who had mattered to him, including his father and mother and now, he was going to lose Luke.

He decided that he needed to get away from London for a while, so he could be on his own to think things through. His mind felt as though it were ready to explode, due to Luke's bombshell revelation and he himself being overly reflective in response to this. He rang both his brother and sister from the nearest phone box, to see if he could stay with either of them for a few days. Eve, his sister, revealed that she was going on holiday with her husband and two children, to Portugal the day after tomorrow and wouldn't be back for a couple of weeks. Marcus, his brother, readily agreed to put Scott up for as long as he needed. No sooner had he stepped out of the phone box, it began raining, gradually becoming heavier. He recalled hearing on the radio earlier that rain was to be expected and regretted not bringing an umbrella with him.

It took him nearly an hour to get back home, opening the front door rather cautiously in case Luke were there, for a good few hours had passed since he had left and he didn't know what state Luke might be in.

He was relieved that Luke was not around, as he couldn't face another confrontation like before. One in a day was bad enough. Had Scott not been in such haste to pack himself a bag of clothes and much needed bare essentials, he might have spent a moment to ponder on where Luke might have gone. Even though the revelations were a great shock to Scott, he didn't want anything terrible to happen to him. After he had finished packing, he left Luke a quick note. He explained that he was going away for a few days – to have some time alone to think – not revealing where he was actually going to, as he knew he wouldn't be able to face Luke ringing, or even coming to his brother's house.

Luke had been drinking rather heavily for the past few hours and staggered uncontrollably outside the pub. Due to the amount of alcohol he had consumed, his equilibrium was more than a little askew; not that he particularly cared because any sensibility he had prior to his alcohol-induced marathon had long since left him. He was aware that his clothes still felt uncomfortably damp after being caught in the torrential downpour earlier; not that he had taken any great deal of effort to shelter himself from the rain. His tear-stained face was conspicuously evident that the drink had in no way resolved or even helped his problems but actually succeeded in making them worse. Now, more than ever, he needed someone to talk to. He clumsily flagged down a taxi and managed, between several incoherent slurs, to inform the driver of Elliot and Kristian's address. He only just managed to scrape together enough money to pay for the fare, although he wouldn't have particularly cared if he hadn't. He made a lackadaisical attempt to thank the driver, as he stumbled to his friends' front door.

Kristian answered the door, drowsily, to Luke's desperate ring on the doorbell, still half asleep. "Luke!" he exclaimed, when he saw the figure in front of him. He rubbed his eyes and took a moment to refocus in case it was an apparition and he was still actually asleep in bed, in the midst of a deep dream. He wasn't, as Luke was still standing there in front of him, swaying with his inability to stand up straight. "What on earth...? It's one o'clock in the morning."

"Oh! Is it, really? I didn't know that," Luke garbled, not having any real concept of the time but just wanting to be with someone.

Kristian caught a waft of the strong, stale smell of alcohol and recoiled to catch a breath of fresh air. "You're drunk!" stated Kristian, the annoyance in his voice clearly audible.

"Maybe," Luke giggled intemperately. "I've only had a couple, so possibly... I'm maybe...just the teeniest, tiniest, little bit tipsy."

Kristian's voice softened when he saw the state of Luke's face, as he stepped into the light. "Have you been crying?"

"I do believe that I have," Luke nodded lethargically to his friend's question, wanting to let everything out into the open and paradoxically hoping he wouldn't have to submit to a barrage of questioning, like a prisoner.

"Come on...come inside." Kristian took Luke's arm and led him into the living room, sitting down in an arm chair. "Now, tell me, what's wrong?"

Luke tried, as coherently as he could, to explain that he and Scott had had a bitter argument that had ended in Scott storming out of the house and as a result, he was apprehensive in going home in the current state that he was in. There were a lot of pauses, whilst Luke tried to get his head and his tongue around several words that wouldn't immediately spring to mind. Kristian was unable to understand a lot of what Luke was trying to say, as all he could hear was a lot of loquacious mumbles and slurring noises in between the rasping sobs.

"Okay. Well, it's pointless in you going home right now in the state that you're in. You might as well stay here for the night." He took Luke to the spare bedroom, removing his shoes and jacket before pulling the covers over him and tucking them in with neat precision. No sooner had he done this, Luke was fast asleep.

Kristian returned to his own bedroom, relaying everything to Elliot about what had just happened. Elliot suggested he should phone Scott, just in case he was worrying where Luke might be. Kristian agreed. They were concerned when they didn't get any answer from Scott, hoping that nothing serious had happened. They were obviously not going to get any proper answers until the morning, when Luke would awake with the mother of all hangovers but at least, sober.

Luke finally emerged from the spare bedroom shortly after midday and was greeted by Elliot and Kristian, who had been awake, showered and dressed for a good five hours, barely having slept much more than three hours. They were too busy mulling over in their minds both solely and together about what might have led Luke into such an intoxicated state. They were also concerned about Scott's whereabouts - wasn't he worried about Luke?

"Good morning," said Kristian cheerily. "How are you feeling? I guess you've probably got a monstrous headache."

Luke coughed uncontrollably. "I feel absolutely awful," he said breathlessly, rubbing his eyes in a bid to make him feel more awake.

Elliot gave an admonishing grin. "I'm not surprised you feel awful. You were drunk last night...in fact, you were *very* drunk!"

"I don't mean the hangover...no sympathy required, as it was self-inflicted. I think I might have caught a cold. I keep on coughing so much that it hurts my ribs and makes me feel terribly breathless." He sat down in the armchair and drew in a couple of deep breaths.

"I'll get the thermometer and take your temperature," called Elliot, already making his way to the medicine cabinet in the bathroom. "We've got some cough mixture too, so I'll get that too," he continued to holler.

"Were you out celebrating last night, or something?" asked Kristian, fishing for the answers to last night's questions that hadn't been pursued.

"No," replied Luke flatly.

"Oh, okay!" Kristian knew he needed to tread carefully with his interrogative autopsy of last night's debacle, so as not to cause Luke any further distress. In order to get to the root of the issues, he would have to garnish enough information from him so optimum potential could be reached in dissecting all suitably appropriate solutions. Luke, he thought, had done some very irrational things in the past few months but getting himself into the state that he was last night, was certainly something that he just did not do. "So, was Scott with you then last night?" he asked tentatively.

"What is this, Kris? Twenty questions?"

"Sorry. I was just trying to make conversation."

"No, I'm sorry…I shouldn't have snapped at you…I know you're being what a good friend is meant to be. It's just that I feel really awful and I guess it's making me really irritable."

Elliot returned with the thermometer, handing it to Luke, whose hand was visibly trembling as he took it.

"Keep this under your tongue for a couple of minutes," Elliot instructed.

Luke placed the thermometer under his tongue and looked pathetically at his friends, like a bedraggled cat returning from an all-night escapade and seeking solace in familiar surroundings.

There was silence until Elliot removed the thermometer from Luke's mouth and read it carefully. "Well then, young man, it's straight to bed with you. You have a temperature of one hundred and two."

The two men helped Luke up to the spare bedroom and by the time they got him into bed, he was totally breathless.

"Do you want me to call a doctor?" asked Kristian.

"No! I don't think that's necessary. I'll be okay after I've had some rest. I just feel completely and utterly exhausted."

"I'll go and get some extra blankets," volunteered Elliot, leaving the room. Whilst he was gone, he decided upon giving Scott another call. He had already tried earlier on that morning, before Luke had awoken but still hadn't obtained any answer. He dialled the number and was even more surprised when there was still no answer. He retrieved a couple of blankets from the cupboard before returning to the spare bedroom. He placed them over Luke, who shivered as he did so, even though he was sweating profusely.

"Are you going to be okay?" asked Kristian with fraternal concern, realising afterwards that it was a rather pathetic question to ask.

Luke nodded.

"We'll leave you to get some rest now," cooed Elliot.

They both gave Luke a gentle kiss on the cheek before leaving the room, closing the door quietly behind them.

"I've just tried to ring Scott again," Elliot whispered softly, after the bedroom door had been closed.

"And…?"

"There's *still* no answer."

"Things are definitely not right with those two…something is drastically wrong. Luke apparently went out last night and got ridiculously drunk without Scott. I'm wondering if Scott might have given cause to upset Luke in some way, leaving him to drown his sorrows in the drink…he had obviously been crying but for what reason…it still remains a mystery."

"It's got to be something pretty serious for Luke to have been in the state that you said he was when he came here last night, or rather the early hours of this morning. I only wish he would talk to us."

"We'll give Scott another try later. Hopefully, he will shed some light on what's going on if Luke doesn't talk to us."

Despite the whispering, the two men were oblivious that they had the type of voices that carried no matter what volume they were pitched at. Luke had heard the majority of what his friends had said outside of the bedroom. Tears began to roll down his cheeks, as he turned over and willed himself to drift off to sleep.

Scott was finding it increasingly difficult to gain any real quality of sleep, constantly tossing and turning throughout the entire night. There was only one persistently fanatical thought that played upon his mind: Luke. He wanted to be able to hold Luke tightly in his arms and tell him how much he was loved. Yet, contradictorily, he couldn't quite bear the thought of being anywhere near him. This cataclysmically unsolvable quandary that Scott found himself facing was more than a mere conundrum that could be conquered with some precocious rationality. Whichever direction his thoughts took him in, the outcome would always lead to unpredictable consequences. What the hell was he going to do?

Scott was conscious of the fact that, although he was family, he would have been an imposition upon his brother, Marcus, by being put up in his cottage. He wasn't naïve to think that Marcus would have had to make a few minor alterations to his diurnal and nocturnal regimes in order to accommodate him. Scott didn't waste any time telling Marcus that he was grateful.

"I know we haven't had the kind of close *brotherly love* relationship that mum and dad would have liked us to Marcus, but that aside, I *do* really honestly appreciate and value the support you're giving me at this time."

"Putting our relationship history of recent years aside, Scott, I'm not going to let my little brother down in his hour of need."

"I don't actually know when and how things began to go wrong between us."

"I'm not convinced that it's going to be particularly conducive for us to rake over old ground and analyse who said what, when and why. I think we should just let history stay where it belongs…in the past…and let ourselves concentrate on the here and now. To be honest, we can't claim back what's already passed between us but what we *can* do, is use this time together, constructively, to rebuild the foundations of our relationship."

Since the two brothers had moved away from their parents' home, the contact between them had been very little to non-existent. Scott wasn't sure if this was the aftermath of some form of sibling rivalry, or they naturally just drifted apart over time. Still, as Marcus had pointed out, there was no real benefit on dwelling on the past. Scott's current predicament with Luke seemed to be the catalyst that broke any and all barriers that might have been built up between them both, bringing them closer together and ensuring their relationship could only grow stronger from this point on. Just having someone to talk to that wouldn't pass any judgment on him made Scott feel instantaneously better. He had bottled up his feelings for far too long by himself but now the relief he felt, after talking with Marcus, seemed like a ton of bricks had been lifted from his shoulders.

"So what do you think you are going to do now," he asked Scott.

"To be perfectly honest, I really don't have the first clue."

"Maybe talk to him…and I mean really *talk*…not shout, holler or scream. That might be a good place for you to start. Don't you think?"

"I just can't bring myself to be near him at the moment," Scott sighed.

"I do think that, maybe, you're being just a little too hard on him," suggested Marcus, looking over the rim of his glasses. "We're not perfect you know…we all come with our own little flaws…our own unique design faults, for want of a better way of putting it. It takes a good person to look beyond someone else's flaws but a stronger person to help conquer them."

"I completely understand what you're saying, Marcus but I think I just need some time on my own to be able to put my thoughts into some kind of perspective."

"I appreciate that, really, I do...but just take a moment to think about what must be going on in Luke's head right now though. I probably wouldn't be far wrong in guessing that he must be feeling rather confused, maybe even a little frightened but most certainly very alone without the person he loves giving him that extra strength he needs."

"I know, I know, I know," Scott said, putting his hand up to signal that he was easily surrendering to Marcus' input, as well as his own thoughts that had been spinning inside his head. "What you are saying makes absolute sense and I do feel exactly the same way myself. I just don't think, at this precise moment in time, with the way my head is mixed up with all these emotions, that it's going to be particularly helpful to either me or Luke, without dealing with them first."

Marcus pondered for a few moments before offering his brother another solution, which he thought might hold more appeal to him. "If you feel that you can't speak to him just yet, then why don't you speak to one of his close friends? I know it's not the typically conventional way of resolving any relationship issues but it might be an easier way for you to approach this from. Mind you, having said that, you *will* have to face him sooner or later...you can't keep putting that off. Even if you come to the conclusion that you aren't able to continue with the relationship, he at least deserves to be told that by you face-to-face."

"Again, you're probably right. I know that he's very close to Elliot and Kris, who are good friends of both of ours, so I might give them a call in a day or two."

Marcus nodded. "I think you're doing the right thing."

Scott shook his head dubiously and bit tentatively upon his lower lip. He was still not completely convinced of the appropriate course of action and the way forward for his relationship with Luke. He rose from his chair and left the room. *Am I being unreasonably selfish*, he thought to himself. Marcus had seemed rather zealous in hammering into Scott's head that he would be throwing away, through his own stupidity and selfish pride, someone who was clearly of huge emotional importance to him. Granted, it was definitely a lot to be turning his back and walking away from, he pondered, yet he couldn't allow it go ignored. He knew that when it came to it, his brother wouldn't have the courage to ring Elliot and Kristian but Marcus would see to it that he did.

Scott confined himself to his bedroom for the rest of the day, thinking of nothing else but Luke.

"Well, hi there. How is the patient feeling now?" asked Elliot with concern but attempting, a little unsuccessfully, to retain an upbeat ambiance.

"I feel worse, actually," said Luke with laboured breathing. He covered his mouth with his hand in attempt to stifle a deep, chesty cough.

"I've bought you something to eat," said Kristian with a smile, as he entered the room.

"What time is it?" asked Luke, feeling a little bewildered.

"It's nearly ten o'clock," said Kristian.

"Really?" Luke was surprised at how long he had been asleep for. He tried to hoist himself up onto his elbows and inch his way to sitting up. Elliot gave him some assistance when he saw the effort that it was taking him.

"The bed is absolutely soaked!" exclaimed Elliot.

"I'm really sorry...I've been sweating something chronic."

"No need to apologise," said Elliot, "but I guess we need to get you out of that bed and into a bath."

"I'll put some clean sheets on the bed whilst you run the bath," Kristian volunteered, as he placed the tray of food on the bedside table.

Elliot supported Luke into the bathroom, as he put one of Luke's arms around his shoulder and one of his own arms around Luke's waist. He was very surprised and incredibly concerned at how weak and pale Luke had become. The dampness from Luke's clothing, from his persistent and profuse sweating, felt very uncomfortable against Elliot's skin. He silently reprimanded himself for not giving Luke a spare set of pyjamas and allowing him to sleep in the same clothes as he had the previous night. Elliot managed to steer Luke onto the chair in the bathroom, sitting him down so that he could turn his attention to drawing the bath.

As Luke began to slowly undress himself, Elliot said: "Leave your clothes in a pile by the door and I will wash them for you."

Luke signalled for Elliot's help to get him into the bath. "Thanks," he gasped, desperate to get his breath back.

"That's okay. If you need anything, or when you've finished, just give one of us a holler and we'll come straight away."

"Sure. I'm sorry to be such a nuisance for you both."

"We'll have less of that talk, thank you very much. You are not a nuisance in any shape or form and you don't want to let Kristian hear you talking like that because you know that it'll upset him."

"Sorry...it's just that..."

"Hush! I'm just going to get you a fresh towel and a set of pyjamas for you to wear."

"Okay. Thanks."

Luke returned to the bedroom after spending a considerable length of time soaking in the bathtub. He noticed the clean sheets on the bed and fresh pillowslips. In fact, the whole room looked as though it had been subjected to a thorough tidy whilst he had been gone. Elliot and Kristian helped him into the bed, as he was struggling to get in by himself.

"Why don't you have something to eat," said Kristian, taking the tray from the bedside table and placing it on the bed.

Luke pushed it away, with a nauseous grimace. "Sorry, I'm really not very hungry."

"But you haven't eaten anything all day."

"I'm honestly not hungry. I guess this flu has taken away my appetite."

"Please try something," insisted Elliot. "Even, if it's just half a sandwich. It'll make you feel better."

Luke unwillingly picked up a sandwich from the plate, hesitating before he took a bite from it. He chewed for ages, swallowing with a look of discomfort across his face. "I can't eat anymore. I'll be sick if I do."

Elliot looked at Kristian anxiously, as he felt Luke's forehead. "You're freezing."

"But I feel really hot."

"Are you sure you don't want me to call you a doctor?"

"I'm sure. It's probably just one of those forty-eight hour bugs that I've got."

Elliot looked worried. "I wish we knew where the hell Scott was."

"Guys," Luke began, taking a deep breath. "There's something I should tell you." His friends sat on the bed, each holding one of his hands. By the look of anxiety on Luke's face, they could tell it was going to be something extremely serious he was about to tell them.

Although his speech was, at times, breathless and awkward, Luke reminded them about the time Scott had had the affair with Ben Richards. He followed this by telling them about what happened on the occasion he had the misfortune to also meet Ben.

"When Scott had caught gonorrhea from Ben," said Luke, "I decided that I should go to the clinic and get tested for it myself, after my encounter with him. When I got there, they asked if I wanted to be tested for anything else. You know how much I hate all the long, drawn out spiel they give you, so I just agreed to have all the tests, so I could get out quicker.

"I couldn't be bothered to ring for the results, completely forgetting about them until I received a letter from the clinic asking me to come in." He began hyperventilating, trying to control his breathing by taking slow, deep breaths until he felt able to continue. "When I arrived at the clinic, I was told the HIV test had come back as positive. They attempted to give me some counselling but it just wouldn't sink in.

"As you can probably imagine, I was shocked and terrified. The only way I can describe how I was feeling at that moment, was as though time had frozen around me and I had been slapped in the face a thousand times. I really couldn't bring myself to tell Scott until yesterday. He went completely berserk and walked out on me. I have absolutely no idea where he might have gone but he obviously hasn't come back, which is why you're not getting any answer from him when you call.

"I don't know when he'll come back…if he'll even come back at all. He was very angry and upset…to say the least."

Kristian stroked the back of Luke's hand, gently and softly. He spoke in a soothing tone. "You know that you can stay here as long as need be."

"I'm pretty sure that Scott will calm down soon enough and then he will realise just how much he needs and loves you. Remember, he's been through quite a shock too and probably needs some time to get his head around it all," Elliot said temperately.

"Oh God…I really wish he was here now. I really love him." Luke finally let the tears flow that he had fought back for so long to hold off.

Elliot cradled him to his chest, almost fraternally protective, stroking his hair. "You know, whatever happens, you will always have us…Kris and I love you, like a younger brother and you will never lose that. Stay here, with us until Scott returns from wherever he is and then, you'll have the three of us. You'll see…it will all work out in the end."

"Thanks," he sobbed into Elliot's chest. "You guys mean the absolute world to me and I couldn't bear to lose you too."

"Well, I can assure you, that's never going to happen, Luke. Hell would need to freeze over first and the way that Elliot and I feel about you, hell's fires will be burning ferociously for all eternity," said Kristian poignantly.

Luke's eyes smiled at his friends, even though his lips wouldn't curve to compound the same emotion.

"You must get some rest now," said Kristian.

Luke nodded, as he allowed his friends to tuck him into bed. Elliot had brought a dampened flannel from the bathroom, wiping the tears away from Luke's eyes and mopping the perspiration from his face, neck and chest. They kissed him affectionately on the cheek, once again reassuring him that they would be there for him if he needed anything.

It was a weak smile but a smile nonetheless, as Luke closed his eyes and allowed himself to drift off into the darkness.

Kristian removed the tray of barely touched food back into the kitchen, whilst Elliot sat on the bed for a few more moments until he was sure that Luke was fast asleep. He took hold of Luke's hand and whispered: "Don't ever forget that we both love you, Luke. You will always be like a brother to us...don't give up...be strong and fight this. You don't want to lose us...well, we don't want to lose you either." He wiped away the tears that had formed in his eyes.

Having returned from the kitchen, Kristian poked his head around the bedroom door. "Come on, Elliot. We should leave him now. He needs his rest."

Elliot rose from the bed, joining Kristian in the hallway. "I tell you something for nothing," Elliot murmured softly, "If he's not better tomorrow, I'm calling the doctor. No matter *what* Luke says."

Scott, yet again, had another restless night. This time, it was because he was replaying over and over in his mind how the phone call might go that his brother would ensure that he made to Elliot and Kristian. The sheer prospect of the unknown scared him to his wits end. He wondered how they might react when he finally built up the courage to call them. He found himself speculating about whether they might have seen Luke since he had left. If so, how much information would Luke have volunteered about what had happened? Scott desperately tried to think of other things - anything - so his madness wouldn't continue to torment him but inevitably, his train of thought would always return to the phone call and Luke, haunting him like something from the supernatural. At times, his thoughts were so vivid and realistic, he was reduced to tears.

Marcus, at times, could hear his brother's persistent sobbing and knew, no matter how much advice he could offer Scott, only he himself would be able to put things right. So, the question on Marcus' mind was, would Scott actually be able to take that leap of faith without having to be pushed? He knew, cast in the role of conjecturer, that his theories and suggestions could be construed as negligible, which irked him when he was fully aware of how stubborn Scott could be. Once his brother's mind was fixed on something, nothing and nobody seemed able to convince him to change it. For as long as he could remember, Scott had always followed this trait. Still, this never deterred Marcus from trying to do so. Even as a young boy, he would continually rise to the challenge, which would almost certainly make Scott all the more adamant not to change his mind.

With the benefit of hindsight and the knowledge of foresight, Marcus knew that he had to tread carefully with what he was about to do.

The Absence of Friends

Marcus could already see, by the battle that was being fought inside Scott's head, that it was beginning to destroy some of his more magnetic characteristics and there was no way that he was prepared to sit back and witness these being annihilated. What kind of brother would he be if he allowed this to happen? He was fully prepared for the inevitable consequences, as Scott would be irrepressibly livid when he discovered that he was about to contact Elliot and Kristian, as he found their phone number in Scott's personal address book. Nevertheless, he thought, it had to be done and he was fully prepared to take that consequential risk.

It really couldn't be put off any longer.

He walked past the phone, several times, almost picking up the receiver on a couple of occasions but the nerves were beginning to get the better of him. The confidence that he had managed to build up to carry out the deed was rapidly beginning to shatter, the longer he procrastinated in making the call. He began to understand the emotional torment that Scott must be facing, yet his own fear and waning confidence were on a much smaller scale to that of his brother's.

Marcus reasoned with himself that he was only in this position because he was aware that it was more likely than not that Scott would come up with some tenuous excuse to back out of phoning his friends.

It was now or never.

He picked up the telephone and dialled the number, his hand shaking with the fear of not knowing what to say or what to expect.

The engaged tone sounded like a drum, continually beating in his ear.

He waited a couple of minutes and tried again.

The sound of the telephone ringing at the other end, loud and clear, made his heart beat fast with building trepidation. He was about to hang up the receiver, as it seemed to ring for an eternity, when he heard the faint sound of a man's voice answering. Quickly, he returned the receiver once again to his ear.

"Hello?" said the man's voice on the other end, slightly anxious, partly because nobody was answering. "Hello?" he repeated, with more aggression in his voice.

"Hello," replied Marcus. "Who am I speaking to, please?"

"Elliot Hayden," said the voice with the same level of anxious aggression. "Why? Who is this?"

"I don't mean to intrude, but I had to call." He paused to regain his breath. "My name is Marcus Delaney. I'm Scott's brother. You see, I…"

"Oh my God," said Elliot with relief. "I'm so glad you've called." Elliot recounted to Marcus everything that had happened to Luke over the past couple of days, omitting nothing, even the incident that happened a few minutes earlier.

"Jesus Christ!" exclaimed Marcus, as he dropped the receiver onto the sideboard where the phone rested. He didn't realise that in his panicked haste, one of his ornaments was knocked to the floor, causing pieces of shattered china to be strewn across the floor, around the vicinity of the sideboard. He was already halfway up the stairs, calling out his brother's name.

Scott rushed out from the bedroom. "What's wrong, Marcus?"

"It's…" he tried to regain his breath, his hand held over his heart, as though to prevent it pounding right out of his chest. "It's Luke."

"What?" exclaimed Scott, shaking his head in stunned confusion.

"Something really terrible has happened."

Luke awoke the following morning to what felt like a lead weight on his chest. His hair was soaking, as though it had only just been washed, clinging to his forehead. He felt the pillow, sheet and quilt with his hand and they too were saturated from his excessive perspiration. He got himself out of bed, holding his chest as he did so but nearly keeling over from the lack of breath. His breathing was very shallow and erratic, as he took short, quick gulps of air into his lungs. To anyone who saw him, they might have drawn the conclusion that he was perfectly acting the part of a drowning man, complete with convincing sound effects, flailing arms and an ashen face.

Luke's eyes widened with sheer panicked terror, with his pupils dilated to their fullest, as he found it increasingly more difficult to sustain a regular and comfortable pattern of breathing; even more so when, every so often, it was aggravated further by an intense coughing fit. Only one thought dominated his mind: he had to get to Elliot and Kristian…and quickly! He struggled to open the bedroom door, almost ripping it off its hinges in his pure desperation to get out; every movement he made became an extreme effort as his chest was in excruciating pain. By the time Luke managed to reach the base of the stairs, each step being like its own individual obstacle, it felt as though he had no breath left within his body. Maybe if he shouted out to them, he thought, they would come quickly to his aid but his shouts turned out to be nothing more than virtually silent gasps and rasps. Tears began to flow from his eyes as hopeless despondency set in. Had he had the ability to think logically and clearly, he still wouldn't have been able to say how he had finally managed to get himself into the living room.

The Absence of Friends

Kristian spotted Luke coming through the door, almost as if it were being played out in slow motion. "Luke?" he cried out desperately, "What's wrong? Are you okay?"

Luke carried on shuffling his feet, holding onto one of the display cabinets when he reached it. He was still clutching his chest when he struggled to get the words out. "Kris," he said in a panic-stricken gasp, "I…can't…br…" Luke was unable to finish his sentence, as he slumped weightily to the floor, sending photos and books crashing from their locale along with him.

Kristian moved with lightning speed to his friend. "Elliot!" he screamed desperately, with almost blood-curdling horror. "Call an ambulance! Quick!"

Everything that happened seemed to unfold in a matter of mere seconds; from Luke coming into the room, until Elliot had phoned for an ambulance. Literally moments after he had finished with the call with the emergency services, the phone rang again. Tentatively, Elliot picked it up, answering it with an anxious "*hello*". At first, he thought it might be the emergency services phoning him back for some reason but nobody answered at the other end. He really was in no mood to be dealing with some pathetic individual who might think it hilarious to be making a prank call. He answered "*hello*" again, with a slight degree more aggressive firmness, intent on hanging up if there was still no response from the other end.

"Hello. Who am I speaking to?" asked the voice that seemed to have a nervous quiver to it.

"Elliot Hayden," he said, still feeling that anxious aggression, especially as he didn't recognise the voice of the person on the other line. "Why? Who is this?"

"I don't mean to intrude, but I had to call." There was a pause. "My name is Marcus Delaney. I'm Scott's brother. You see, I…"

Elliot allowed himself to calm a little, as he was relieved that finally, someone who was connected with Scott had managed to contact them. Had Marcus left making the call another few minutes longer, he would have missed speaking to them, as Elliot and Kristian would have gone with Luke to the hospital.

Knowing that time was against him and therefore preciously limited, Elliot attempted to be as innocuous as he could possibly muster, as he hastily revealed to Marcus all that had happened with Luke: the fever, night sweats, the lack of appetite and the difficulties with his breathing. He also told him that he had just collapsed and they were awaiting an ambulance to take him to the hospital.

"Jesus Christ!" Marcus exclaimed with alarm, as he felt the hairs on the back of his neck rise.

"Marcus? Marcus?" Elliot called fervently but there was no answer from him. Initially, he thought something might have happened to Marcus, as he heard a walloping thud and the smashing of glass or crockery. It wasn't until he heard the faint voice of Marcus calling Scott's name that he concluded that Marcus must have dropped the phone and in his haste to relay the recently divulged information to his brother, the phone, or he, must have knocked something over, causing it to break.

After he heard Scott's name being called a couple of times, there was total silence.

"Elliot?" said Kristian softly, almost inaudibly.

If not for the deathly silence at the other end of the line, Elliot wouldn't have heard his partner's voice. He put down the receiver and turned to face Kristian, whose face had completely drained of colour.

"What?" he asked questioningly.

"Oh my god! Oh shit!"

"Kris? What's wrong? What's happened?"

"Elliot! Luke's stopped breathing!"

CHAPTER ELEVEN

The man flicked the pages back and began reading from the black leather-bound diary with the owner's initials on it. It was not actually his diary but his partners, who had asked him to record everything that had happened.

This is how the man remembered it:

I watched as the doctor came closer to me. Every step he took seemed to take longer than the previous; almost deliberately slow as if to prolong the pain and anticipation I was feeling, making me dread the speech I was about to hear. I could see the doctor's face clearly, his vacant expression making me feel very uncomfortable and somewhat disconcerted. The doctor couldn't have been more than twenty-five years old, with an almost childlike face. I noticed the wedding ring on the doctor's left hand and shook my head dejectedly. I tried to imagine how he might act if our roles were reversed, toying in my mind the numerable scenarios that were possible.

I couldn't quite comprehend how doctors managed to keep their emotions calm in these types of situations. I felt the perspiration coming through my shirt, which was only a minor discomfort to what I was feeling now. The doctor, it seemed to me, had only moved about two paces forward. Why on earth was he taking so long? It felt as though somebody, somewhere, was playing a cruel prank on my existence by keeping their finger firmly on the slow motion button, which didn't impress me in my current fevered anxiety. I just wanted to run up to that doctor and ask him what was going on but my feet felt like concrete, keeping me firmly glued to the spot I was in. If someone out there in the great beyond did want to punish me, they were doing a bloody good job of it!

I'd been pacing around the waiting room for goodness knows how long; like I was an irascible animal, imprisoned within their cage, becoming increasingly ravenous for the information I was impatiently waiting for. I looked upon the doctor as though he were my prized prey, ready and poised for a graceful pounce if he should dare to come too perilously close to me. If I am being perfectly honest, it was the feeling of total helplessness that was the worst. I wanted to feel useful, to be able to actually do something, yet all I was able to do was to pace the room and wait…and wait…and wait! I had a sense of perception about what the old adage it's like waiting for an eternity *actually meant. I can't put into words how frustrating that can be!*

I've absolutely no idea nor reason as to why my brain was predominantly allowing itself to think of various hackneyed clichés but another age old expression came into my mind: "No news is good news". Not in this case it wasn't, as I was going totally out of my mind. I needed to know what was happening. Had people been deliberately avoiding me? Maybe it was my paranoia working overtime but it felt as though I had been kept in the dark for days, rather than hours.

Studying the doctor further, I found everything about him looked neat and clean. His short, dark hair had either been gelled or waxed into place, though it looked to me as if it had only recently been cut short. The doctor's skin appeared smooth and well looked after; whether he ever had a problem with acne was seemingly not apparent. He had an almost European look about him; either that, or he had only recently returned from a holiday abroad with an even tan, which no doubt would have made his colleagues green with envy. His overall was a brilliant white, with not a crease to be seen anywhere. I guessed he must have only just recently come on duty. What a way to begin a day's duty, I thought to myself. As the doctor drew nearer, I could begin to see his name badge clearly. It read: S.J. Roberts, Senior Nurse. I found myself smiling, thinking how easily I had come to the conclusion that the man approaching me was a doctor, rather than a nurse.

My mind, in its inexplicably infinite wisdom, began attempting to guess what the initials S.J. stood for. Simon James? Stephen Jacob? Stuart Justin?

I breathed in deeply, as the nurse was now stood in front of me. My palms were sweating, so I wiped them on my trousers several times to ensure they were dry. "Well?" I asked the nurse in a soft, almost inaudible voice.

"It's not good news, I'm afraid," the nurse said in as gentle a tone as he could muster. I could tell he hated this part of his job; telling the partner of a patient that the news he had to deliver was not good. In his mind he would have probably attempted to work out exactly what he would like to say to them prior to meeting but inevitably, I guessed, it would never quite work out the way as he would have planned.

Even though I was desperately wanting to know what was going on, as S.J. Roberts had begun to tell me what was happening, it seemed as though it were not actually me he were talking to. The only way that I can possibly explain it, although I will still be considered as pompous, was as though I were in the midst of a somewhat transcendentally phantasmagorical experience. (Even if I do say so myself, what fabulously descriptive words, which I know my partner would love to read and will no doubt still probably say something condescendingly patronising because of it...still, it's me who's writing this diary entry and not my partner!)

Anyway, I am digressing…I could hear every word that S.J. Roberts was saying to me but it didn't seem like it was my ears that were hearing the words. It was a peculiar sensation, which caused a shiver to creep up my spine. I could feel the escalating shiver travel throughout my entire body. Even though it was particularly warm in the waiting room, I felt an unearthly coldness.

I desperately tried to fight the tears back, as the nurse continued to tell me the bad news. The more I was told, the harder it was to keep the tears from flowing; until I could hold back no more. I took the handkerchief from my jacket pocket and wiped away the tears. "Can I see…?" I sniffed, feeling the gargantuan lump in my throat that was making it an effort for me to speak.

The nurse nodded. "Please make it brief though."

"Sure."

I made my way to the ward that the nurse said I would need. Opening its door rather tentatively and I am not ashamed to say, with a fair degree of trepidation, I looked around the room to see nearly every bed was occupied. It was like walking into a sea of macabre sadness, feeling people's negative emotions wash over me like a strong tidal wave, ready to sweep me away with it.

I looked at each occupant of the beds and at their respective visitors, feeling despondent and empty until I realised there was another room near to the end of the ward. Wondering if I might find my partner behind that door, I opened it, wholly expecting to see a complete stranger.

And there she was.

"Hi," I said, trying to make out that I hadn't been crying. "How are you feeling?" I watched as she shrugged her shoulders. I could tell she was feeling as bad as I was, but was trying to be strong. We hugged each other tightly, not wanting to let go. I felt her pulling back, and she smiled, although the tears showed it was a smile more for my benefit.

"I'm going to lose the baby, Max! Aren't I?"

It had been a few weeks since Vince had last heard from Scott. Admittedly, he was just as much to blame, as he had neglected to either write or phone. He decided it was high time that he put pen to paper and write a few words, possibly suggesting that he should go over and visit Scott and Luke.

Before sealing the envelope, he re-read the letter he had written:

Andrew R. Hamilton

Dear Scott & Luke,

It's been quite some time now since we last heard from each other, so I'm making a positive effort to tell you what's been going on with me recently. I must apologise, actually, for not writing a lot sooner but you know how it is when things start to get on top of you and all the tasks and chores you know need to be done, or the things you feel you want to do just seem to take a back seat. You're probably in the same boat as me I suspect. What, with being a Headteacher, you probably don't get a great deal of spare time to do the things you really want to, or you know you really must do…and naturally, Luke's diary must be filling up quicker than a bucket in a torrential downpour

The last thing that I remember hearing from either you or Luke was when he was recording his album. I really hope he was pleased with his efforts. I'm surprised, actually, that you never even sent me a copy of the album but I suppose it comes down to the fact of being too busy again even though you know it's one of those things that you really want to do. So here's a gentle reminder…don't forget me!

I truly do hope that relations between the two of you have vastly improved and that things are going swimmingly for you both…just don't be having any more silly one-night stands! Your relationship is worth far more than that. I don't think I particularly need to say this but Luke is a really lovely chap and the two of you look so enviably good together. It really is rather silly to jeopardise something - or indeed, someone - so precious for something with no real value or worth but you already know about that anyway, as it's all in the past. Water under the bridge, if you will.

So, I hear you ask, what's been happening with me then? Well, I am going to be moving away from Paris soon. I know that I haven't been here all that long but I'm going to be opening another of my Shepherd's ∏ restaurants, which I am very excited about. This time, it will be in Germany. I can't quite remember if I told you that I was going to Düsseldorf for a little holiday, but that's by-the-by. Anyway, whilst I was there, I saw this rather lovely property for sale. So, after I'd viewed it and thoroughly mulled over the 'could-I, would-I, should-I' scenarios, I decided to buy it so I could expand upon the Shepherd's ∏ chain.

The sale, I have to say, went surprisingly smoothly and so, all being well, the new Düsseldorf Shepherd's ∏ restaurant should be opened and operational by the end of this year. God, if I continue in the way that I'm going, who knows, I might be opening Shepherd's ∏ restaurants all over Europe.

I've already managed to buy myself a rather lovely flat in Düsseldorf although I'm not going to be moving in until the end of November, which

The Absence of Friends

gives me a month to settle in before Christmas. You and Luke should come to Germany some time, after I have managed to settle myself in; it's really stunning and absolutely beautiful there. I couldn't believe how truly picturesque a place could really be.

The restaurant in Paris is proving to be very lucrative. It's making quite a healthy profit now. I did have my doubts for ages if it would ever take off, as it never seemed to break even. Do you remember I had every confidence that it would break even by the end of 1999? Well, when it didn't, I seriously considered about selling up, giving up and just returning to London. I thought I would give it just one more year, to see if Lady Luck might smile down upon me. So, you can imagine my joy and relief when it eventually did break even. It's given me more far more confidence about the Düsseldorf venture. I'm actually very excited about the prospect of opening another restaurant.

Don't get me wrong though, as in a way, I will be sad to leave Paris. I've become rather quite fond of the place but we can't have everything, can we? You know me, I was never content with staying in one place for too long; I get itchy feet too quickly to be able to settle down anywhere permanently.

Whilst I was in Germany, I did actually meet someone. His name is Félix Weiss and, well there is no other way to say this, but he is absolutely gorgeous! He's thirty years old, with a mind for business and a body for sin, if you know what I mean. He's a professional cook, so I hired him, with the mind to manage the Düsseldorf restaurant and he's agreed. It all just seems so unreal to actually be true.

I'm constantly pinching myself at the moment…just to make sure that I am not actually dreaming.

So, what's been happening with your good self and Luke? Is there any hint on the horizon of Luke recording a follow-up album? I hope so. I really do enjoy his singing and he has such a wonderful voice. I trust that you're both keeping well and looking after each other.

Do you know, it's been nearly two years since we last saw each other? This really must be rectified…soonest, Scott. Why don't I come over for Christmas? It would be really nice to see you the two of you again. It's only about four weeks until I move, so you'll have to let me know soon if you do want me to come over for a visit.

Do take good care of yourself, Scott and give my love to Luke.
All my love, Vince

He felt pleased that he had finally put aside some time and made the effort to write a reasonably comprehensive letter. He did, especially when he had a lot to say, prefer to phone, as it added more of a personal touch than a letter did but since he didn't get any answer from either Scott or Luke when he phoned at various times over the past couple of days, he assumed they must be away on a holiday. He knew that Scott would be keen for him to come over, as he had so much more to tell them both that he just didn't want to write about in a letter. He was almost certain that they too had a lot of news to share.

Michael sat patiently in his seat, thoroughly digesting the programme he had purchased, while he awaited Steven's spectacular entrance. He stopped, admiringly, at the article about Steven's stage career that was illustrated with a professionally taken headshot, which Michael considered to be a luscious representation of how attractive Steven was. The article itself wasn't particularly lengthy, as this was only Steven's third casting in a stage performance but with the length of time Michael had spent reading it, drinking in every letter of every word, it would have appeared to others that it was an article spanning several years. He raptly studied the piece, thinking how little an insight into Steven's life anyone else reading it would really have.

His reverie was abruptly disrupted by an elderly couple wishing to pass him, in an attempt to reach their seats. They smiled appreciatively at him, apologising for disturbing him but he dismissed the notion of being disturbed with a return smile. He watched as the couple took their seats and noticed, with dubious intrigue, that the woman had taken off her shoes and placed them in her handbag, which she placed under her seat. He shook his head irreverently at what he considered to be rather bizarre behaviour but did ponder if this might have been rather ritualistic, although the couple was completely oblivious to his derisive act.

As if being involuntarily drawn into some morbid fascination, Michael glanced once again at the couple and saw that the man held the programme in his gnarled hand, which he ultimately surrendered to the woman after she had said something to him. He decided, although it was merely a presumption, that the woman had to be his wife. Every so often she would point something out to her husband from the programme that had clearly captured her interest. What was far more apparent to Michael was the superfluous apathy in her husband's face. If he had been a betting man, Michael would have predicted that the woman was the archetypal nagging wife, irritating her husband no end, like an incessant dripping tap.

Taking a moment to scan the theatre from the comfort of his own seat, Michael noticed that there were a few seats still empty. He hoped, for the

The Absence of Friends

actors' sake, that the majority of these would be occupied by latecomers, who had purely lost track of the time. Then, of course, there were those individuals who he thought would have purchased a ticket and not been well enough to come out to enjoy an evening's entertainment. Through his correlated musings, Michael offered a perfunctory, albeit arbitrary, get-well wish to those who might have fit that particular category.

He wouldn't have been the slightest bit shocked at the result, if he could have measured the decibels from the general noise of people conversing and those who laughed with irrationally hysterical mania, laced with the continually irritating rustle from packets of confectionary, or the mechanical flicking of the pages of the programme. Michael allowed himself to smile inwardly, thinking that it was interesting just how much commotion could be made prior to a play commencing but then, as the curtain rose, you would be able to hear a pin drop, bar the odd cough or sneeze throughout the auditorium. What mortified Michael the most was the magnitude of people who couldn't, or wouldn't, follow the rules of basic hygiene etiquette. Each time he witnessed someone blatantly violating these simple codes of conduct, he pursed his lips and shook his head with contemptuous belligerency.

Michael continued to look around to see if he was able to catch sight of anybody famous, as he remembered Steven telling him that celebrities from film, television and music, sports personalities and possibly even royalty would almost certainly be in attendance at the premiere of any stage production. As he gazed optimistically around the theatre, though not from a particularly prolific vantage point, he was almost certain that he could spot a couple of his all-time favourite singers. He had to bite his tongue in order not to squeal out with delight, when he was convinced that he had caught sight of a former No. 1 Wimbledon champion, hoping that his eyes weren't deceiving him. He had a fleeting moment of indignation, as it reminded him that he had missed watching the Wimbledon women's singles final on television, which was the first year he had ever done so since he became an avid fan of the grand slam tournaments. The royalty were easily pin-pointed, as they had obviously taken residence within the royal box but from his position, he was unable to determine exactly which of the royals were gracing the theatre with their presence. He was a little disappointed that he couldn't spot any other celebrities, except a particular comedian, whose show Michael and Steven had been to a few weeks ago - he found himself intuitively giggling as he ruminated and reminisced about some of the anecdotes that were told, especially the ones that were in bad taste - but Michael conceded that the man, who had had his sides aching from laughter, looked rather dashing and handsome donned in a tuxedo.

He did momentarily pause to consider if it would be rather infantile to go touting for celebrity autographs after the show had ended. Somewhat dejectedly, he concluded that it would probably be a futile and puerile exercise and no doubt frowned upon within the civilised nature of the milieu.

Only another five minutes to go until the curtain rises, he thought to himself, as he checked the time on his watch. He knew, unequivocally, that Steven would be exceedingly nervous, though Michael had every confidence in him that he would be nothing short of outstanding. He scolded himself for not having told Steven just how proud he felt of him. It had taken several months of rehearsals, late nights and early mornings for this production and Michael was sure all the hard work would have paid off.

He took another look at the odd couple again. The woman's face had taken on a very stern look; Michael presumed she was probably chastising her husband for doing something no doubt quite innocuous but nonetheless, a cause of concern to her. He watched, intrigued, as she brushed the shoulders of his jacket with her hand and took a guess that she more than likely henpecked her husband, treating him like an incompetent child. His thoughts once again journeyed into what their private life might be like, as he wondered if they had any children, or even grandchildren and how they might be treated. His extraneous thoughts were interrupted by the lights dimming and so he pulled himself bolt upright in his seat, settling down for the eagerly awaited performance.

"I'm really angry with myself," said Steven with a look of despondency, after the performance had finished and he was once again reunited with Michael.

"Why?" asked Michael, undeterred by the vehement tone Steven was using.

"Because it was an absolute nightmare. I was terrible."

"No you weren't," Michael argued. "I thought you were absolutely terrific," he continued, with a reassuring look.

"I know you're only trying to be nice but…I forgot my lines, Michael… twice! That's really unforgivable."

"Don't be so hard on yourself. The thing is, as an audience member, I couldn't even tell. So, it can't have been that noticeable. Only *you* would notice if you had forgotten your lines but you must have covered it up by adlibbing, or creating a dramatic pause."

"I guess that's the nature of the beast in my line of work…if it's not perfect, then it's a disaster."

The Absence of Friends

"Remember, this is only the debut performance, so you're bound to get a bit of first night nerves. Besides, I bet you weren't the only person who believed they had made an error with their performance."

"You always know the right things to say, to cheer me up," Steven said, allowing his very infectious smile to return to his face once more.

"Still," continued Michael, "you *did* get a standing ovation, which surely must count for something and I wouldn't be at all surprised if the theatre critics cite you as an exceptional performer."

"Really?"

"Yeah, really."

Once again, Steven showed off his perfectly shaped and brilliant white teeth in a smile that would have made the Cheshire Cat incredibly proud.

"I am not at all ashamed to admit that I was an emotional wreck…in a complete flood of tears when you, and of course we as the audience, were led to believe that your unmitigated love for Diana was left unrequited. That, my darling, was heart-wrenching enough in itself to handle but then…because of this diabolical misapprehension, you thought there was no other alternative but to commit suicide 'cause you couldn't live and wouldn't be complete without her…that was the straw that broke the camel's back and enough to ensure the floodgates were well and truly opened. When she saved you in time and declared her undying love for you, well…" He put a hand on his chest and took a deep breath, hoping it would cease the potential for another emotional outburst that he felt building up inside him, as he re-lived the scene. "Sweetie, you were just marvellous."

"Well, thank you for that…it really means a lot to me. Now, however, we need to get our skates on and go because we've got a table booked for eleven o'clock."

"Okay. It's such a shame that Max wasn't able to come. I know that she would have loved it. Although, having said that, you would probably have found us huddled together in a blubbering mess in some corner. You know, we really *must* visit her some time."

Steven nodded, as he hurried in the direction of the car park.

Max turned over the page of the diary and carried on reading what he had written:

"I'm really terrified, Max. You remember what happened to my mother?"
"Please don't think like that," I said, taking hold of my wife's hand.

Maxine wiped the tears from her eyes. The doctor had told her she was suffering with Pre Eclampsia, explaining that it was an hereditary condition. She was assured that her baby would be monitored closely by the tests that would be done. This did not stop her from contemplating the loss of her baby's life, or even her own; the exact scenario of her mother. She was given tablets to stabilise her blood pressure but the anxiety was clearly shown in her face.

I couldn't bring myself to admit to Maxine that I felt equally as anxious as she did about history repeating itself. I knew I had to be strong for the both of us, assuring her that everything would work out okay. It was the usual thing that most people would say in these difficult situations, as there is nothing else you really can say other than: "Everything will work out fine", but who actually really believes it? I know, through my own fears, I didn't and I'm sure, no matter how many times I tried to reassure her, Maxine didn't either.

I tried to sound as convincing as possible, as I said: "You know that the doctors will do everything possible for you. They are monitoring both you and the little one's progress. Really, there is no need for you to worry."

Maxine could read me like an open book and knew I was only saying these kind words in order to comfort her, not truly believing them myself. The smile she gave me was more to comfort me, than to reassure me she believed everything would be okay.

"Will you do something for me?" she asked.

"Anything. Just name it."

"Will you write the next few entries in my diary for me? You know how much the diary means to me, especially as Michael and I have been doing this for several years now."

"Sure, no problem. I can do that for you."

"The key to the diary is in my jewellery box that's on the dressing table."

"Okay."

The nurse, who had seen me earlier, stepped into the room. "I'm sorry but I'm going to have to ask you to leave now, Mr Beresford."

It's a bitterly cruel world that we live in. I didn't want to leave Maxine alone again. I had waited all this time to see her and only after what appeared to be seconds with her, I was asked to leave. There was so much we could have talked about, yet, when a limitation of time hangs over your head, you forget the majority of what you really wanted to say.

"One second, please," *I said to the nurse. I turned to my wife and spoke in a soft voice.* "I love you, Maxine, with all my heart."

"I love you too." *She smiled warmly at me.*

The Absence of Friends

> *"Remember, you have our baby to bring home with you. There are so many people looking forward to meeting the new addition to the Beresford family."*
>
> *The nurse tried to look as though he weren't listening to what was being said and gave us both a respectful smile, as he closed the door behind me as I left.*

That was the last entry Max had made in the diary for that day. He didn't know what had happened after he had left the room but naturally, he wanted everything to have turned out okay. This was how the events transpired:

As Max left the room, S.J. Roberts pulled out a bottle of tablets from his overcoat and placed them on the bedside table, pouring out a glass of water from the jug. "Okay then, Mrs Beresford, it's time for your medication."

"Can you tell me how everything's going?" she asked, taking the tablets from him.

"Everything's going fine. We are monitoring the progress of your baby extremely carefully and with these drugs, your blood pressure appears stable at present."

"Thank God for that," said Maxine, heaving a sigh of relief and falling back onto her pillow with emotional exhaustion.

It was only a matter of hours after S.J. Roberts had left the room before Maxine felt severe stomach cramps, worse than that of her monthly period. In fact, she had never felt anything quite so excruciating in her life as this pain. "My baby," she screamed chillingly, pressing the panic button fast and furiously, knowing it was her only line between life and death. "My baby," she screamed again, her lungs feeling as though they would almost explode, like a wine glass shattering from an intense resonance. "My baby's dying. Oh God, help me…please!"

Although it was only a space of two minutes before she was rushed out of her ward and into the operating theatre, to Maxine it seemed as though agonising hours had painfully and slowly gone by. She clutched her stomach tightly with her arms and writhed about the bed as if some incorporeal force were wrestling with her. Amidst her terror and unbearable discomfort, she could hear the voice of a doctor explaining what was happening to her but the words word not sink in to her reasoning, as her only interest lay in the welfare of her unborn baby.

"Mrs Beresford," explained the doctor ceremoniously, "the foetus has gone into, what we would call, severe distress. This means that it has actually stopped moving and its heart is beginning to beat faster and faster…"

"No!" she yelled, lashing out with her limbs. "You're killing me. My baby's dead. Stop! Please God, stop!" Her anger, fear and distress washed over her, making her feel as though she were drowning in the sea of her own emotions, as she desperately tried to gasp for air.

"I need you to try and focus, Mrs Beresford," the doctor said soothingly. "I know that you're panicked and obviously fearing the worst but I need you to try and remain calm. It's not going to help you or the baby if you allow your distress to worsen…focus on me and my voice and follow my breathing. I know you're in a lot of pain but please try…"

Maxine bit down on her lip with such force, that she managed to draw blood. She focused her eyes upon the doctor and desperately tried to match his rhythm of breathing. "Please don't let my baby die," she sobbed.

"We will do everything we can to save your baby. It's still alive but at the moment in terrible trouble. We will have to operate now though because if we leave it too much longer, the chances of success will drop. We are going to have to perform a caesarean."

It seemed as if her entire world were crushing in on her. What had happened to her mother was now going to happen to her. They would operate on her, manage to save the baby but she would never wake up from the anaesthetic. How could life be so cruel, she thought. She wanted to tell Max that she loved him more than anything in the world. *What would he be doing right now?* she continued thinking, *probably pacing up and down the waiting room.*

"I need you to count to ten, Mrs Beresford," said the doctor, after he had injected her with the anaesthetic.

"One…two…" *I want Max to be here with me. If I am going to die, he's got to be here.* "…three…four…" *Don't let me die. Don't let my baby die.* "…five…six…" Maxine didn't get any further than six, as she pictured herself drifting down into the blackness of an eternal sleep; never to awaken again.

Then there was nothing but total darkness.

Luke had been rushed immediately into the hospital when the ambulance arrived at the home of Elliot and Kristian.

Kristian came to the realisation that in his debilitating panic, it must have appeared that Luke had stopped breathing. Regardless of his erroneous diagnosis of Luke's condition, he still remained in shock, with the fragility of his nerves being paramount in his current state of distress. The thought that Luke had actually died was just too much for him to cope with. Elliot,

The Absence of Friends

who was equally shocked, tried desperately to calm Kristian down, until the ambulance had arrived.

"Isn't life just a total bitch?" Kristian sobbed.

"Eh?"

"Well, first of all we get all this worry with Luke and Scott…then, we get a call from Max, telling us that Maxine has collapsed and she's also in hospital. These kinds of things always happen in threes…don't they?"

"Oh Kris, that's just superstitious nonsense, clearly designed by the sanctimonious fanatics who relish the idea of people subscribing to the idea of not wanting to tempt fate. Frankly, I'm a non-believer…incredulous to the notion of all this tenuous claptrap. You need to stop worrying yourself into a state. Luke's going to be fine. He's a fighter and won't give up that easy. You know though, that he'll need us to be strong for him."

"I guess you're probably right about all that superstitious mumbo jumbo. I just need to pull myself together and like you say, stay strong for not just Luke but Maxine too. I'm sure Scott and Max will probably be banking on our strength to help them through this difficult time as well."

"Exactly. Actually, talking of Scott, I'm going to phone him again and let him know we're on our way to the hospital and see if he wants to come along with us."

"Okay. Good idea."

Elliot was about to pick up the receiver of the phone when it rang, causing him to jolt in fright. "Jesus!" he gasped, sucking in a deep breath to try and calm his fast-beating heart and regulate his breathing. He picked up the receiver and breathlessly said: "Hello?"

"Elliot?"

"Yes? Is that you, Steven?"

"Yes," came the panicked response.

"What's wrong? Are you okay?"

Steven earnestly recounted in detail what had happened with himself and Michael. Elliot, in turn, informed Steven that he and Kristian were just on their way to the hospital to see Luke.

"I don't suppose you've heard that Maxine is in hospital too, have you?"

"Yes," said Elliot quietly. "Max phoned a few minutes ago. I was just about to phone Scott to see if he wanted to come to the hospital when you phoned."

"Oh! Okay, I'd better let you go then."

They said their obligatory farewells and Elliot had put down the receiver. No sooner had he done so, Kristian looked up inquisitively. "What's happened now?"

Elliot's face was still pale from Steven's news. "It's Michael. He's…"

"I knew it! I just bloody well knew it!" Kristian felt a cold shiver run down his spine. "Didn't I tell you these things always happen in threes?"

Steven held the pen tightly in his trembling hand, unwilling to let go of it at any cost. The pen became a symbolic object to him, as though it were representing his salvation; to drop it would mean that his whole world would implode and he would probably lose all meaning of sense and reality.

The handkerchief that he held in his other hand was clean before he had sat down at his beautifully varnished, mahogany desk to write. Now, it was filled with his tears from endless crying. He noticed that some of his tears had fallen onto the pages of the diary and smudged the writing.

The diary.

Michael's diary.

The black, leather-bound one with his initials on it in gold lettering.

He felt his eyes begin to well up with tears again and wiped them away with the already sodden handkerchief, as he relived the events he had just etched into the diary:

> *It's rather funny, isn't it? Not funny as in hilarious you understand, but funny as in strange. What I mean to say is, how the different aspects of your life can fall neatly into place, so much so, that you begin to take them for granted. Your job. Your home. Your partner. When all three seem to run smoothly and in sync, you just know that disaster is around the corner and that it's going to strike somewhere…sometime, when you least expect it. Never can the three run in harmony, for an eternity, with each other.*
>
> *Life's a bitch and then you die…a clichéd irony if ever I heard one. To be honest, I really don't care if what I write makes sense or not…I really just need to get my thoughts down on paper, or I know I'll go mad keeping them bottled up.*
>
> *Why the hell did it have to be Michael? What harm did he ever cause anyone? I know that he's considered eccentric in his mannerisms by some people but seriously, he wouldn't even hurt a fly. God knows that I love the man, even though there are occasions when he can drive me to complete distraction but I never got a chance to tell him before…*
>
> *…Well, I'm telling him now. "I love you, Michael and I know that I could never stop loving you, regardless of what could ever happen."*
>
> *Not that it makes much difference now. He's still not here. If only I hadn't…*

The Absence of Friends

Although Steven was feeling quite emotional after reading the first part of what he had just written, he found himself intuitively half-smiling. He knew, that if Michael were there with him now, he would have undoubtedly made some bad-taste joke, or come out with one of his distinctively quirky and spontaneous phrases. In his imagination, he could hear Michael's voice whispering into his ear: *and just what kind of warped world do you think you are living in, sweetheart, writing this convoluted pleonasm?* just to diffuse the depression that hung in the air like a stale stench.

He read on:

I know that it's human nature to do so but really, we can't keep living our lives around the could-a, should-a, would-a scenario. It's easy to say now, with the benefit of hindsight but what's happened has happened. My mother always used to say to me: "There's no point in crying over spilt milk, Steven." But I can hardly equate Michael to spilt milk now, can I? I know that I am never going to be able to forgive myself...

...but anyway, about what happened...

...I had just finished my debut performance and was feeling rather despondent because I thought that I had given a performance below my capabilities. Michael, naturally, told me in his own unique way that I was brilliant but then he would, he's Michael for God's sake. He would have this knack of always being able to pick up on the good points of the most atrocious film, or music, without ever sounding the slightest bit insincere. I know he just wanted to make me feel better; to reinstate my confidence. I suppose I should have listened to him but I am not the sort of person who would suddenly agree with someone else's analysis if there was any shadow of a doubt in my mind. Although I am thankful for his faith in me, I had already said that I didn't feel my performance was up to scratch and I wish he had just left it at that.

The previous night, I had booked for us to have a celebratory meal in one of my favourite restaurants, straight after the performance had ended, so had made the reservation for eleven o'clock. We were already running late and I knew, from my past experience, that the restaurant was not very keen on holding your table more than a few minutes after the booking time. I know I should have realised that I was being unrealistic in booking a table half an hour after the show had ended but here I find myself again...as they do say that hindsight is such a cruel bitch of a mistress. Once more I find myself coming back to the old adage: "There's no point in crying over spilt milk."

Maybe it was due my fatigue - not that I should be looking for any particular excuses - but I was becoming rapidly infuriated with Michael because he was fully aware that we were in a hurry and I wanted to...

...I feel an overwhelming sense of guilt in saying this about Michael, when I know that he is...

Steven rose from the desk and selected a clean, white handkerchief from the cheap MFI chest of drawers, thinking it was high time he upgraded them into something slightly more glamorous than MFI. Maybe he could find a beautiful antique one if he looked hard enough. He remembered watching Michael attempting to assemble it; how he had laughed like a hyena when Michael was working himself into an exasperated state, as he couldn't quite manage to follow the instructions to enable him put it together.

"This is just completely ridiculous…absolute utter nonsense…I'm pretty sure the devil himself must have written *these* instructions. Bloody hell!" he yelled, slapping one of the parts as though it were someone's face. "Damn this un-gorgeous piece of bargain basement crap to the depths of hell, back to where it belongs."

"Do you want me to give you a hand?" asked Steven, with a grin.

"No! I will not give up and be defeated, Steven, sweetie. Even if this pathetic excuse for a chest of drawers causes me to break all ten nails, I am not giving in!" His tone was unquestionably inexorable.

"Are you sure?" Steven asked, biting hard on his lips so he wouldn't break into irrepressible laughter. "I'll help if you want me to."

"Steven! I can manage."

"Okay, okay," said Steven, "I concede to your unequivocal determination." He waved his hand dismissively as his form of submission. "I know when I need to raise the white flag and I'm certainly not going to argue with The Bitch From Hell."

"Well, quelle surprise…I've vanquished the wicked witch of the west without even having to bat a false eyelash. Judy Garland, eat your heart out, darling!"

Steven couldn't hold it back any longer and burst into uncontrollable laugher.

"And what's tickled you then, mister?" asked Michael indignantly.

"Nothing…absolutely nothing. I'm just being silly. I'll…um…leave you alone to your own devices."

"Well, thank you sweetie. That's all I ask for…I don't ask for much in life. Come back in an hour or so and I will have it erect."

Steven raised his eyebrow at his own interpretation of the ambiguous statement. "You never take that long with me."

"Don't be so vulgar, Mr Cronje…certainly not when I'm working! One hour is all I will need to finish this. One hour!"

"In one hour, I will more than likely come back and find you in a huddled mess in some corner, sobbing your heart out in defeat to the devil's victory."

Michael twisted his face at the sarcastic comment. "If you're going to be a bitch, darling, at least do it with a phrase of your own…don't steal mine."

It took under half an hour for Steven to assemble the chest of drawers when he came back over an hour later to see an infuriated and confused Michael poised over the instructions and an item of furniture that resembled something Picasso would have created. It might have taken him half the time if he didn't have to undo the imitable creation of Michael's abstract art.

"There we are," said Steven, admiring his handy work. "One-nil to the wicked witch of the west, I think."

"Oh, why don't you just do me a favour and go and take a hike on your broomstick?" said Michael petulantly.

Steven returned to the mahogany desk with a fresh handkerchief and continued reading from the diary:

Michael didn't seem to notice that I was becoming increasingly agitated. It seems that whenever Michael goes off on a tangent when he is in one of his talkative streaks, nothing or nobody can ever seem to bring him out of it until he has reached his natural conclusion. He was going on about something to do with Max and Maxine and scolded me when I hadn't referred to them as the obligatory Max Squared. I wasn't particularly listening to what he was saying, as I was too busy concentrating on driving because the weather conditions were less than favourable.

"…and Max Squared weren't sure if they would be able to do it or not but if that's all it takes to flummox them, don't you think we could do so much better? What do you think, sweetheart?"

I didn't actually hear the question in its entirety and instead of asking him to repeat it, which I wish had done, I said rather brusquely: "Michael! Please, will you shut up!"

(Note: I wonder if this was the point where our fates became sealed. Upon reflection, if I had acted differently, it would definitely be Michael sitting here writing this entry in his diary).

"Sweetie," Michael said in his casual way, "you mustn't be angry with yourself still. I told you, the play was gorgeous and you were even more gorgeous." He leant over to give me a kiss.

"Michael! Not now! I'm driving for God's sake. It's pouring with rain out there and I need to concentrate. Now, please will you show me some respect and be quiet for a few minutes?"

"Sorry, sweetie. I just wanted to…"

"Michael!"

I should have made an executive decision there and then and just forfeited the idea of going to the restaurant but instead, I carried on. I kept my foot on the accelerator, watching the speedometer rise.

Michael tapped me on the shoulder and once again, if I had noted the serious tone in his voice, things might have turned out differently. "Steven, watch your speed, please. It's very slippery on the road."

What the hell came over me at that point, I don't think I will ever fully understand. I just seemed to totally freak out, temporarily forgetting that I was driving the car. I verbally lashed out at Michael, yelling at goodness knows what kind of thunderous volume.

"Steven! The car! For fuck's sake," he shrieked, trying to grab the steering wheel to control the car.

It may have been the blindingly glaring headlights, or the loud, monotone noise of the horn from the oncoming truck that snapped me out of my temporary psychosis but I grabbed at the steering wheel and swerved hard, causing us to skid over a steep grass verge.

What actually happened after that is really hazy and unclear. I think I must have managed to roll from the car after I had struggled with my seatbelt and opened the door. Only me and the darkness heard Michael's hauntingly petrified screams as the car continued careering on its destructive course.

Whether it was immediately, or I had passed out and then regained consciousness, I really couldn't be sure. I called out Michael's name several times but elicited no response. The final call of his name was more like a terrible realisation that Michael hadn't survived the crash.

With a lot of effort and debilitating pain, I somehow managed to raise myself onto my elbows. Before my eyes were able to focus and drink in the scene around me, I watched in hapless horror as I could see billowing smoke coming from my car.

I must have lost consciousness, as my last thought was that Michael was trapped inside the car, which was going to burst into flames at any moment.

CHAPTER TWELVE

Elliot reluctantly handed Kristian a flimsy, polystyrene cup full of lukewarm liquid that resembled something more out of a washing up bowl, rather than the eagerly awaited hot, strong cup of tea he was hoping for. Nothing could ever beat a homemade cup of tea but as their throats felt decidedly parched, they chose to risk using the hospital vending machine.

Both men wondered why a hospital often opted for the cold and dispassionately sterile look, instead of having a more friendly and welcoming appearance to them. It was a bad enough experience having to enter a hospital in the first place without the added oppressive atmosphere of clinical blandness. A little decoration or uplifting colour here and there might not have gone amiss, which probably explained why people were so eerily quiet whenever they were in a hospital. It was almost as if an individual would undergo a desolate transformation as soon as they stepped through the doors.

"Has he gone in to see Luke?" asked Elliot.

He, was Scott.

Kristian nodded. "Yes, he has." He took a sip of his tea and grimaced at the taste. *Still, at least it is wet and warm*, he thought.

When Elliot finally got to make the phone call to Scott earlier, offering to give him a lift to the hospital to see Luke, Scott thought it might be a far easier option and less time consuming if he made his own way there. He decided upon phoning for a taxi and wasn't happy that he would have to wait about twenty minutes for one to arrive. He cursed the fact that he had turned down Elliot's offer in favour of what constituted as a grossly erroneous calculation of saving time.

Elliot and Kristian were already in the hospital waiting room when Scott eventually arrived, looking quite flustered and perturbed, as though he were considerably late for a highly important meeting. As soon as he came crashing through the doors, he stopped suddenly in his tracks as if to ponder on whether he should really be there or not.

"Oh, thank God, you've arrived," sighed Kristian. "We were beginning to wonder what had happened to you."

"Bloody taxis," Scott said succinctly.

"Ah," acknowledged Elliot.

Scott grabbed Kristian's arm and squeezed it a little too tightly, causing Kristian to wince. "How is he?" he asked, his voice tense, with a trace of dread.

"We don't know anything yet," said Elliot, answering for his partner. His eyes showed empathy toward Scott, as he knew he loved Luke a great deal but was unable to cope with the knowledge that he had been diagnosed as HIV positive.

"Is he…?" Scott swallowed hard to prevent the tears from falling. "Do you think he is going to die?"

Kristian, being conscious that Scott looked as though he were about to pass out from the heavy burden of anxiety he was carrying, led him to a seat. "Luke's a fighter," he said, dodging the question but knowing that Scott had only voiced everyone's fear.

"He can't die! He mustn't die!" Scott couldn't hold back the tears any longer and collapsed into the seat.

Elliot knelt down in front of Scott and took hold of one of his trembling, cold hands. He rubbed it between his own, hoping to awaken his blood flow and create some warmth into his body. "Hey…just remember that whatever happens, Kris and I are always here for you."

Kristian spoke: "That's right."

"Thank you. That means a lot to me."

"I'll go and get us all a cup of tea. Okay?" Elliot offered.

"I'm okay, thanks," Scott whispered.

Kristian indicated that he would like a beverage with a nod of his head. A bad cup of tea was better than no cup of tea, he thought to himself.

Elliot had only been gone for a couple of minutes when a doctor came into the waiting room, looking authoritative by bearing a clipboard in one hand. As he drew nearer to Kristian and Scott, they noticed his dishevelled hair and thick-rimmed glasses, making him look like someone who would be cast as a classic accident-prone character in a comedy, rather than a person you would take seriously within the medical profession. The doctor couldn't have been any more than 5'6" and so rotund, that he looked like an over-blown football. He wasn't a young man by any stretch of the imagination, as his thinning hair and bushy moustache were drained of any colour other than white. Peering over his glasses like an eccentric politician, rather than a doctor, his piggy eyes focused on the few people sitting in the waiting room area.

"Mr Delaney?" he enquired with a thin, tinny voice that didn't particularly fit with his physical appearance. He tapped at the clipboard with his pen as he awaited a response from one of the strangers seated in front of him.

Scott wearily looked up to where the voice was coming from. "Yeah, that's me."

"Good afternoon Mr Delany. I'm Doctor Fenwick," he said with an almost robotic monotone and mechanically proffered a hand for his introductory handshake. "If you would like to follow me please," he continued, already making his way back through the door he had just appeared from but courteously holding it open for Scott to follow him through. The robotic façade melted away as Doctor Fenwick smiled sympathetically at Scott with his thin, pale lips. The glimmer of warmth from Doctor Fenwick didn't last long before he peered over his glasses again, his eyes narrowing, making it seem that he was eyeing Scott in an unjustifiably suspicious and dubious manner.

"Am I going to see Luke?" Scott enquired cautiously.

Doctor Fenwick nodded. "He has been asking for you continually since he regained consciousness."

Scott thought it would be rather prudent of him to stay silent until he reached the ward where Luke was. He didn't relish the idea of engaging in a lengthy discussion with the doctor about what might, or might not, be wrong with Luke. It was a task in itself to come to terms with Luke's diagnosis without adding confusion into the mix about not being able to understand half the medical terminology that the doctor would no doubt have used. He began to let his mind deliberate whether doctors intentionally set out to confuse other's with their over usage of extensive medical terms.

Elliot returned to the waiting room with the cups of tea and handed one to Kristian. "Has he gone in to see Luke?"

Kristian nodded. "Yes, he has." He sipped on his tea, as Elliot sat down on a seat next to him.

"Elliot? Elliot Hayden?" came woman's voice from behind them.

Both Elliot and Kristian swivelled around precipitously in their seats, to be greeted by an attractive woman behind them. She was roughly the same age as the both of them, give or take a year or two. Her fiery red hair flowed like lava, down to her shoulders, with the fringe coming perilously close to her deep, hazel eyes that she kept flicking to the side. The crudely low-cut, white t-shirt she wore revealed an ample amount of cleavage that left nothing to the imagination. The black trousers covered her stupendously long legs, which she had crossed, showing off her Jimmy Choos

"Rachel?" asked Elliot with slight uncertainty, as he guessed at the woman's identity. "Rachel Thorne?"

The woman shook her head, smiling, as she said: "Sorry but you just failed the million dollar question. I'm afraid I'm not Rachel Thorne…I am, though, Sue Thomson." She flicked a wisp of hair away that had fallen over her face, obscuring her vision.

Suddenly realising who she was and with a cacophonous squeal, Elliot jumped out of his chair and embraced her with such enthusiasm, he was like a python with its prey. "Sue! Oh my God! I haven't seen you for…well it's been simply ages, hasn't it? How the devil are you?"

"Good grief, Elliot," Sue gasped. "You're nearly squeezing the life out of me!"

"Sorry," he apologised, releasing his almost death-like grip. "It's just that I'm so pleased to see you again after such a long time."

Kristian interrupted. "For a brief moment there, when I first laid my eyes upon her, I thought Julia Roberts might have been in the same room as us… until that fantasy was shattered by the revelation of her name. Do you know this rather fine specimen of a woman, Elliot?" He realised that his question was somewhat pathetic and redundant. *Obviously* Elliot knew her, he reasoned.

"Yeah, I do. We trained at the same dance school together, as well as appearing in a couple of shows. We lost contact a few years back when Sue auditioned for a company that was touring their show around parts of Europe and Asia. Jealousy didn't even remotely cover what I was feeling when I found that out." He winked at Sue.

"So…God…Elliot, what's been happening with you, after all these years?"

"Oh, you know…the same old, same old…just a little bit older, a little bit fatter and a little bit less hair. I do the occasional dancing in a show here and there but obviously, I'm not as flexible, nimble or agile as I used to be all those years ago! Predominately though, I'm now a dance instructor, tutoring young teenagers to follow in our footsteps."

"And this is…?" she motioned towards Kristian.

"And this is my boyfriend, Kris. I can't remember if you had already gone abroad when I met him but we're coming up for our tenth anniversary this Christmas."

"I have a vague recollection that you were in the foetal stages of a relationship and if my memory serves me correctly, he was all you would ever talk about…and I remember telling you back then, there was more to life than just men!"

Elliot blushed. "You would say that though, wouldn't you?"

"Hi," she said, smiling at Kristian, revealing her perfectly white teeth.

Kristian returned the greeting.

"So what do you do, Kris? Please don't tell me that Elliot has you as a kept man and you're enjoying a life of blissful leisure."

Kristian grinned. "I wish…but unfortunately not. I own my own garage. So if you have a fetish for greasy car mechanics, then I'm your man."

Elliot rolled his eyes disparagingly. "Well, I think that's the perfect point to stop talking about us," he said to Sue. "What's going on with you?"

The Absence of Friends

"Well, I've just been given a six months contract for a show that's opening in the new year, in Oxford. I'm really looking forward to it and very excited because it will be my first leading role."

"Good for you," said Elliot.

"It's not called *Alone In The Dark*, is it?" asked Kristian.

"That's right," said Sue, a little surprised. "You've heard of it then?"

Kristian felt better that he was not the only one who asked silly questions. "Yeah, I've heard of it. I saw an advert for it in a magazine somewhere, I think. I read the preview and it sounded really good. Our kind of show, Elliot."

Sue beamed at Kristian's comment. "If it's your kind of show, you should definitely book tickets. I know you'll really enjoy it."

"We might just do that," said Elliot.

"So…what are you two doing here?"

Another silly question, Kristian thought, *two-one to me*. "We're visiting a friend of ours," he said solemnly.

"Luke Faraday?" she asked plainly.

"How the…? You know him?" *Oh God, another silly question. No, not another one but the same one! Two-all.*

"Oh yes, I know him," she gloated, as if Kristian should already have been aware of that. "I was in a musical with him a few years ago and have also been for auditions at the same time he has…for the same show…but obviously for different parts…as if I really needed to tell you that. I recognised the other man who was with you, from photographs. That's his boyfriend, isn't it?"

"Yes, that's right," confirmed Elliot. "Who have you come to visit?"

"My girlfriend."

"Oh? What's wrong with her?"

Sue blushed slightly, hanging her head ashamedly. "It's a bit embarrassing…"

"Oh, come off it," said Elliot, folding his arms contentiously to goad her into continuing. "If I remember rightly, nothing and I mean *nothing* embarrassed you. Your puritanical demeanour might have washed with me years ago, missy but knowing the stuff you've gotten up to in your time, you'd have to try a whole lot better than that."

"I guess I can't argue with that really, can I? As you have such an eloquent way of putting things, Elliot, I suppose I can put you out of your misery and tell you. It's Sarah's birthday today…"

"Sarah's your girlfriend I take it?" asked Kristian, clearing away the possibility of any confusion.

Sue nodded and continued: "Well, Sarah has always had a fantasy about bolognaise. Don't ask me how or why…and God knows I have been involved some freakishly bizarre activities in my time but…anyway…it had to be vegetarian bolognaise, mind you." She watched as Elliot and Kristian raised their eyebrows in bewildered awe. "We're both vegetarians, you understand," she added rationally, as if the two men were specifically confused as to why the bolognaise should be vegetarian. "Well, I thought it would be nice to turn her fantasy into reality for her birthday…I know it sounds a little archaic but you know what they say, a little experimentation can sometimes add a whole new spicy dimension."

"Oh God," was all Elliot and Kristian said in unison, expecting the obvious and fearing the worst.

"Yes. I don't think I really need to go into any graphic description of what happened because I think you can already work it out. Suffice to say, the bolognaise was too hot and now she's got internal burns." Somewhat inappropriately, she giggled, able to see the funnier side of the events. "It wasn't a pretty sight, I can tell you that much…nor was the words that were coming out of her mouth. Let's just say, that we're not going to try that one again!"

Elliot apologised for both he and Kristian laughing. "I'm really sorry. It just sounds so surreal that you can't help but laugh."

"Oh, that's okay," she said reassuringly. "I would probably have laughed if someone else was telling me a story like that…just the sheer absurdity of it. I mean, really, what *were* we thinking?"

"You always were into rather obscure and outrageous activities," Elliot sniggered.

"I know…but I guess that's half the fun of it," said Sue, licking her lips. "It only stops being fun when you're on the receiving end of something like this."

"Miss Thomson?" came the shrill voice of Doctor Fenwick.

"That's me," said Sue, vacating her seat. She said her goodbyes to Elliot and Kristian, giving Elliot her phone number and asking him to ensure that they stay in touch this time. "And do make sure you come along and see the show when it opens."

"Definitely," they said together.

"Well, take care then," she said finally.

"And you too, Sue. Hope Sarah gets better soon."

"Thanks," she called back, following the doctor out of the waiting room.

Luke was propped up comfortably in his bed, with four pillows behind his back. He watched, warily, as Scott fidgeted uncomfortably on the chair beside him. When he first saw Scott walking into the ward, he initially felt a sense of relief that finally, he had come to see him but this quickly turned into feelings of awkwardness and embarrassment.

Scott broke the silence first. "So…how are you feeling?"

Luke couldn't quite bring himself to look Scott squarely in the eye. "Okay, I guess," he said softly. He didn't really like the idea of Scott seeing him in this state.

"That's good to hear."

Luke plucked up the courage to start the conversation flowing. "Look, Scott…I want you to know that I'm…"

Scott placed a finger on Luke's lips. "Shh…you don't need to say a word. I've done a lot of thinking over the past couple of days and heaven knows I've had *plenty* of time to do nothing else *but* think. I guess what I'm trying to say is that I owe you an apology for the way I over-reacted at the time when you told me. I'm really sorry, Luke…I didn't mean to hurt you. You have to believe that."

"I do believe it. I'm sorry too…sorry for being the cause of all this worry and stress for everyone."

"Don't be silly. We're all just glad that you're okay. So you have absolutely nothing to apologise for."

"Thank you, Scott…Thank you for not turning your back on me. I'm not really sure what I would have done without you."

"Well, there's no need for you to think like that anymore," Scott began, with poignancy, "I would have bought you some flowers, or something but I came here in such a rush that I…Oh God, Luke…I am so happy that you're okay and truly, I am sorry for behaving like a complete twat when all you wanted was a reassuring hug to know that everything would be alright, so…" He hugged Luke for a few moments.

Luke rubbed Scott's back comfortingly as he surveyed the room and watched people's varying reactions to seeing two men hugging each other in more than a fraternal manner. Scott sat back on his chair and took a tissue from the box on Luke's bedside table, wiping the tears from his eyes.

"Hey, come on. What are the tears for?" Luke held the side of Scott's face with one of his hands and wiped the wetness away with his thumb.

Scott forced himself to smile, for Luke's sake. He could tell that Luke was putting on a brave face for both their benefits. "Would you like me to bring anything from home, for you?"

"Yes, please. The book that I had started to read, which is on my bedside table. I think it's called *Death In The Jury* or *Murder In The Dozen*…but something along those lines anyway. The author is A.R. Hamilton."

"It sounds a delight. What's it about? Obviously a murder mystery, I should suspect."

"Yes, it's a murder mystery, set against the backdrop of a room of jurors, one of whom gets murdered. I'm quite intrigued by how the author will and does carry *that* storyline off, without patronising the reader by insulting their intelligence."

"Is that all you want me to bring?"

"No, no. A fresh pair of pyjamas would be great. Oh, and Feltcher."

"What?" said Scott, genuinely surprised.

"Feltcher…the teddy bear that you bought me."

"Ah! Okay."

Scott recalled how Luke had become in possession of the bear that he had grotesquely named *Feltcher*. They had been shopping in IKEA for new furniture for the flat, with the sole purpose of buying shelves and wall lights to go with the new wallpaper that had been bought a few months earlier. It ended up that they had spent nearly two hundred pounds, leaving the store without either the shelves or the wall lights. Scott had bought the teddy bear for Luke, after he had spotted it and become rather attached to it.

Max found himself compelled to chew aimlessly upon a cheese and pickle sandwich that he had purchased in a small café nearby to the hospital. He hadn't been eating at all well since Maxine had been admitted but from the little he had chosen to consume of his own volition, it wasn't especially healthy. He wasn't feeling particularly hungry at the current time but he was eating more from necessity, than through hunger. It was either that, or take up smoking again and he hadn't touched a cigarette for more than six years, when he was considered a moderate smoker; not that he hadn't been tempted to buy a packet, on more than one occasion. When he had paid for his sandwich, to his surprise he found himself virtually wandering into the newsagents next door. He was taken aback that he had been seduced by temptation far enough to even imagine what his first cigarette would be like after so long. Would he enjoy it, or would he hate it? It was only the vivid images, conjured within his mind's eye, of Maxine's disenchanted face that prevented him from actually buying any cigarettes.

He had been unable to keep his mind on any train of thought for more than a few seconds, without it continually wandering back to Maxine and what might happen to her. The woman who had served him in the café had asked him several times what type of bread and filling he wanted, before he had finally managed to snap himself out of his trance and the dream-like world he allowed himself to become trapped in. He had never really been a keen lover

The Absence of Friends

of cheese but as that was the first thing he saw on the counter, he mindlessly found himself asking for a cheese and pickle sandwich.

As he sat edgily in the hospital waiting room, nibbling at his sandwich, his eyes wandered thoughtlessly to the posters on display, for the hundredth time. Or was it more like the thousandth? The clock, hanging on the south wall in the guise of Mickey Mouse, seemed to be leering at him, as though it were painfully taunting him by deliberately making time go slow.

A nurse wandered through into the waiting room, snapping Max out of his monotonous phase. "Excuse me," he said to her, as he raised himself out of his seat.

"Can I help you?"

"Yes. I was wondering if there was any news on Mrs Beresford."

"And you are?" she asked inquisitively.

"I'm her husband."

"Okay. One moment, Mr Beresford and I will get someone to see you."

"Thank you." Max sat down again, watching the nurse disappear through a door and hoping her figurative use of *one moment* didn't actually mean an hour. He picked up a magazine - that had obviously seen better days – from the table and desolately flicked through the pages. He stopped at an article that gave women useful hints and helpful tips on how to make their pregnancy and the birth easier. He threw the magazine back onto the table with abhorrence. *And how would they have made Maxine's pregnancy easier for her?* he thought. In his irascible condition, he was becoming increasingly agitated at how long the nurse was taking to get someone to see him. He looked at the clock again convinced that Mickey Mouse's leer had become more prominent. *Go screw yourself!*

"Mr Beresford?" came the familiar honeyed voice of a man.

Max looked up in the direction of the voice. It was S.J. Roberts. Max was already of the mind that S.J. Roberts was about to deliver bad news and wrung his hands nervously. "Yes?"

"Would you follow me, please?"

Max picked up his coat from the chair, slipping his finger through the hook and flinging it over one shoulder. He followed the senior nurse outside the waiting room, unable to stand the trepidation any longer. "What's happening with my wife?" he asked urgently.

S.J. Roberts looked at Max with sympathetic eyes. "As you know, your wife had to undergo a caesarean, due to the complications…"

Max nodded impatiently. "…and…?"

"…and she gave birth to a girl. Because she was born prematurely, we had to put her into an incubator, as a safety precaution. You see…"

"What do you mean *a safety precaution?*" Max snapped. "Just cut the crap and tell me if she's going to be all right. She is going to be all right, isn't she?"

"It's uncertain at the moment. You see, it's normal procedure for a premature baby to be placed in an incubator, as some of the organs may not be fully developed. We will be able to monitor her progress carefully from the incubator over the next few days. It would be way too risky and highly inadvisable to discharge her at the moment."

"And what about my wife? How's she?"

There was an air of awkward silence, as the senior nurse diverted his gaze to the floor.

Max interpreted the silence as the outcome he had been dreading. "Oh my God! She's dead, isn't she?" He braced himself, waiting for senior nurse's response to his outburst.

"No, she's not dead. However, we are having problems…"

Max cut him short and snapped. "Problems? What kind of problems?"

"We are experiencing difficulties in reviving your wife from the anaesthetic."

"Oh, shit!" Max felt a cold shiver run up his spine and shuddered. Everything that Maxine had feared about the hereditary recurrence was now becoming a reality. Max could feel the anger, the bitterness, the despair all rising within him, as he felt betrayed that history would so cruelly repeat itself and for having been kept in the dark for far too long about what was happening. "I have been sat in that bloody waiting room all this time," he yelled, "with not one person being genial enough to let me know what was happening and now, you have the audacity to tell me *this*."

S.J. Roberts shuffled uncomfortably on his feet. "I can only apologise, Mr Beresford. We are and will continue to do everything we possibly can."

Max snarled like a rabid dog. "You're damn right you will. I will not have anything happen to my wife because God help me, if anything does, I will hold you personally responsible."

"Mr Beresford, although your wife is unconscious at the moment, she is very much alive. She may very well come around imminently but there is also the possibility that it may be a protracted period." S.J. Roberts thought it prudent not to antagonise Max any further by adding that he might have to prepare himself for the possibility that his wife may never regain consciousness.

Max had an overwhelming compulsion to strike out at S.J. Roberts for what he construed as the senior nurse being excessively placid and spuriously disingenuous regarding matters that really should have been treated with a great deal more tact and urgency. If S.J. Roberts wasn't to be at the receiving end of Max's wrath, which he knew would only result in regrettable consequences at his own cost, then the Mickey Mouse clock would damn well get it instead; only if to wipe that derisive leer off its loathsome face.

"Oh, you are sweet and adorable, my Angel! But, anyone who might have read this would probably have thought I had died."

"Well, I thank God that you didn't because life would have been so empty and boring without you around." Steven took the diary from Michael's hand and put it back into the drawer of the sideboard. "Besides, I'm way too young to be able to carry off the funereal look convincingly…so if you have to eventually depart the world in *this* manner, please do it when I'm old, grey and wrinkled."

"Ooh, I do think that some of the Bitch From Hell's persona is finally rubbing off onto you," Michael grinned, with a hint of narcissistic pleasure.

Steven inhaled deeply and exhaled just as deep. "So, how are you feeling?"

Michael had his arm in plaster along with varying degrees of grazes over his body. "Well, apart from this," he held up his plastered arm, "and the fact that I ache all over, I'm fine, I guess."

"Anyway, my little B.F.H.," said Steven returning to the subject of the diary, "I didn't actually know, at that point, whether you *had* died or not. Any person with the slightest degree of emotional intelligence or integrity would be able to determine that I was missing you terribly. So, clever clogs, in a way it was like you had."

"Okay, okay," said Michael, holding his injured arm between himself and Steven like a protective barrier, "I'm not going to argue with you."

"Good. Remember what the doctor told you? You have to relax and take it easy. So none of this larking around like an excitable child that you're prone to do."

Michael relaxed into the comfort of the armchair, closing his eyes and began to recall the events of the accident. He remembered, lucidly, that Steven had totally freaked out and given him the mother of verbal lashings. The car was precariously swerving from side to side, so Michael grabbed at the wheel in, what he unequivocally considered to be a valiant effort, an attempt to keep it under control. Michael could almost re-experience the blindingly bright headlights of the oncoming truck, with its piercingly loud, monotone horn that had snapped Steven out of his uncontrollable state of mind. Michael unwittingly predicted that the car would tumble over the steep verge and so, tried to yell "jump" to Steven but the word didn't come out. He was unclear, even now, how he had managed to think straight in order to undo his seatbelt and throw himself clear from the car as it was going over the edge, but he did.

He seemed to roll for an eternity before finally knocking hard against a tree, which must have rendered him unconscious.

The next time he had any real awareness of what was going on, was when he woke up in a hospital bed, with his whole body aching. Apparently and much to his incredulity, he had been unconscious for two days. The doctors had thought him to be extremely fortunate to have survived the crash with only a broken arm and a few grazes to show for it. They told him that, if he hadn't made the split second decision to eject himself from the vehicle, his chances of survival would have been practically nil. Michael took this as a sign, from the powers that be within the heavens above, that his time on earth was not yet done.

He was told by Steven that it was actually the driver of the truck with which their car was about to collide, who stopped and called the police, giving them the details of what had happened. When the medics and the police arrived at the scene, both Steven and Michael were found unconscious and taken to the hospital. Steven had been discharged after several hours, with a few superficial cuts and minor bruising.

"Obviously the Gods still want me around to antagonise more people," Michael had joked, when he eventually regained consciousness.

When Steven had come to meet Michael at the hospital, he couldn't stop apologising enough to him for causing the accident. He told Michael that he felt incredibly guilty and completely responsible for the whole accident.

"As you put in my diary, *there's no point in crying over spilt milk*. So, please stop apologising and feeling guilty about it. We must look to the future," Michael cooed, upon reading Steven's rather verbose diary entry on the incident once he had arrived back to the familiar surroundings of his own home.

"Well, at the moment, that's easier said than done."

"Is there any further news on Maxine yet?" Michael asked apprehensively.

Steven thought that it was more than his life's worth not to divulge to Michael, at his earliest opportunity, the deplorable events with Maxine's pregnancy. He knew that it would cause Michael far more distress by withholding this information until he were suitably recuperated and therefore, would far rather risk the condemnation from the doctors than Michael, by doing so.

Steven pondered on Michael's question for a moment before answering. "Max actually called me yesterday and said that they had to perform a caesarean section. Naturally, he sounded extremely worried and didn't really make a great deal of sense in what he was saying but I suppose that's understandable. The poor guy's got a lot going on in his mind."

The Absence of Friends

"I do hope that she's okay. Max and I are practically like sisters...we're both intuitive, almost as if we are mentally and emotionally synchronised... and, of course, we tell each other literally everything. You know, she told me one day that this is exactly what happened to her mother when she was pregnant with her. Only her mother didn't...I really do hope she and the baby are going to be okay."

"Oh...look, Michael, there's no point in worrying yourself unnecessarily." He really didn't know what else he could say, other than acknowledge Michael's concerns about his *sister*.

"I shall honestly bitch-slap that girl if she continues to torture me further with any more mental anguish...I don't think I can take much more...just look at the lines it's bringing out on my face!"

Steven was aware that Michael's inappropriate remark was not said with any form of malice but more to do with indomitably preventing himself being dragged into a bottomless pit of despondency by means of a person whom he loved and cared for unconditionally.

"Would you like something to eat?" Steven asked, hoping to take Michael's mind away from Maxine.

Michael took a moment to consider his array of options. "Smegma on toast is what I feel I fancy."

Steven's face contorted into one of revulsion. "Michael! That's just disgusting!"

"Well, it's either that, or I fancy going for a fast drive in the rain."

"Michael, you really are quite an impossible man."

Scott bade Elliot and Kristian goodbye, leaving them at the hospital to see Luke. He would have stayed there, to secure himself a lift home with them but he felt claustrophobic and needed to get outside and into the fresh air; although fresh air in London was somewhat of an irony. As he gave them both a farewell hug, he acknowledged how much he valued their friendship and that they had been exceptionally good friends to both himself and Luke. In retrospect, he wished he had told them this already, before something as unpleasant as what had happened to Luke finally made him realise just how much his relationship with them meant to him.

He opted to take the bus back home to Ealing, drinking in the surroundings that he usually took for granted. He vowed to himself at that point that he could no longer allow himself to take anything in his personal or professional life for granted anymore.

As he stepped inside the front door to his house, he noticed the letter from Vince lying on the mat. Picking it up and making himself a coffee with long-life milk, as the fresh milk in the fridge had long since gone sour, he sat down to read the letter. No sooner had he finished, he picked up the phone and dialled Vince's number in Paris. The connection took a few moments.

"Bonjour?" came a man's vocal gravitas at the other end of the line. It was a deep, throaty voice that reminded Scott of a voiceover artist on a movie trailer who sounded very sexy and quite erotic. The man didn't sound particularly French to Scott but he couldn't quite place its origin, although he was convinced it was somewhere in Western Europe. The fact that the man was putting on a faux French accent was the cat amongst the pigeons, proving it difficult to actually place.

"Oh! Bonjour," replied Scott, adopting a superlative French vernacular to rival that of his fellow conversationalist.

"Que désirez-vous, monsieur?"

"Je peux parler à Vince, s'il vous plaît?"

"Oui, bien sûr. Veuillez patienter, pendant que je lui me pour vous. Qui je lui dirai que c'est?"

"Merci. S'il vous plaît dites-lui que c'est son ami, Scott, de Londres."

"De rien. Bonne journée"

"Et à vous de même!"

So, has the saucy bugger gone and got himself a sexy, male secretary? he thought, as he held on for a few moments, intrigued to find out who the man behind the voice was that answered the phone.

"Scott? Is that you?" came the familiar voice of Vince.

"Vince, you sly, old fox! Who the hell was that who answered the phone? Have you employed a resident PA, or something?"

"That, my dear boy, is Félix, who I told you about in my letter. I'm presuming you've received my letter; hence your phone call to me now. He's been staying with me for the past few days but is going back to Germany tomorrow."

Germany! I was right that he was western European, thought Scott to himself. "Ah, so that's the illustrious Félix. Well, I have to say, Vince, he sounds very sexy."

"That's nothing," boasted Vince. "His body's even sexier!"

"Too much information, Vince…" Scott fiddled with a pen on the table top. "…So, how are you doing? You already guessed that I got your letter…it arrived today. I'm glad to hear that you've managed to get yourself hitched at long last. I *was* beginning to think you were doomed to remain a spinster for the remainder of your years. And of course, congratulations are in order for

The Absence of Friends

your new enterprise in Düsseldorf…I am really pleased for you. It sounds as though things are going really well for you."

"They definitely are, Scott. You wouldn't believe it. Sometimes I feel like I'm caught up within a dream and one day, I will wake up and find I'm back in the East End of London."

"Well, if this *is* a dream, I hope that you never wake up!" Scott could sense the excitement in Vince's voice and was delighted that things were, at least, running so smoothly in somebody's life. "So, when is that you are actually moving to Düsseldorf?"

"Well, it was supposed to be in a couple of weeks' time but, I have quite a few things to sort out in Paris first before I can move. So, it looks as though it's going to have to be postponed until early next year now."

"I know how much of a nuisance these things can be but just as long as it's not too much of a hindrance on the German side of the restaurant's development."

"No, it should be okay. Anyway, how are things with you and Luke? I tried to call you several times over the past few days but never got an answer. Have you been away on holiday?"

"No, I'm afraid not. Luke's been in hospital."

"What? Why?" came Vince's shocked voice.

"It's a long story, Vince but I really do need someone to talk to. Elliot and Kris have been an absolute godsend and a great comfort to the both of us. I can't help but think, though, that it must be a lot of pressure on them to mediate and counsel, if you will, for the both of us."

"That all sounds rather commendable, Scott but I am still at a loss as to what's going on. What's actually happened?"

Scott inhaled a deep breath before telling Vince the details. "Well, Luke's been diagnosed with HIV. I reacted really badly to it and walked out on him…I went and stayed with my brother, Marcus, for a couple of days. It was really helpful and he was ever so good but it's just not the same, talking with a sibling about personal matters of the heart. But anyway, having said that, he did phone Elliot and Kris for me and that's when they told him that Luke had collapsed and stopped breathing…"

"Oh my God," gasped Vince. "He's not…?"

"No, he's not dead. Thank God. Kris was in a total panic and thought that he had stopped breathing. I went to the hospital and saw him today…oh, Vince, he looks awful. His face is so gaunt and he looks terribly pale and thin. The awful thing is I don't really know what to say to him."

"Hey, I'm not surprised you don't know what to say. You've been through an awful shock and obviously need some time to readjust. It doesn't just happen overnight," said Vince softly.

"That's only the half of it."

"What? I don't understand all this ambiguity, Scott."

"Well, before I took off to Marcus', I went and got myself tested. I'm not ashamed to say, Vince, but I am shit scared of it coming out positive. I am so confused about what's happening at the moment…and it gets worse…

"…When I was at the hospital earlier on, I overheard two doctors talking about Luke's condition. They seem to think that his condition could be psychosomatic but they're not sure. He's got all the symptoms of developing the AIDS syndrome."

"And what exactly does that mean? What's the prognosis?"

"I'm not quite sure myself. I don't fully understand it all. From what I can gather, I think that basically yes, he's HIV positive but it's possible that he's just got a chest infection and because he's so worked up about the possibility of it developing into AIDS, he has developed these symptoms psychosomatically, I guess. Anyway, they said that it was only a possibility so we're still very much in dark about it all."

"And what *is* the likelihood that it's only psychosomatic?"

"I don't actually know. I guess that they need to run some more tests, or whatever it is that they need to do in order to satisfy their suspicions."

"I'm sure that everything will work out just fine."

"Vince…?"

"Yes…?"

"Would you like to come over and stay with me for a few days? I really could do with the company right now. I'm not sure if I'm ready to face Luke on my own just yet."

"Sure thing but I won't be able to get there until late tomorrow afternoon."

"That's okay. I don't think they'll discharge him for another couple of days, at least"

"Right, that's settled then. I'll go and book my flights online straight after this call and I will see you early tomorrow evening."

"Thanks Vince. This means a lot to me."

"Don't mention it. Sleep well tonight and I will see you tomorrow. Bye."

"Bye Vince." Scott heard Vince put down his receiver down and held his own to his chest for a few moments before replacing it back onto the hook.

Feeling particularly ravenous, he ambled into the kitchen to make himself a sandwich and looked longingly in the fridge to find something that might take his fancy. He opted for the oak-smoked ham and picked it up, searching

The Absence of Friends

for a use-by-date. With disgust and a degree of annoyance at wasting good food, he tossed it into the bin when he discovered it had passed its date by over a week. He took out the margarine and a packet of cheddar cheese, toasting a couple of slices of bread from the loaf of bread that was in the packet. The use-by-date on the bread was only the previous day but he couldn't be bothered to go to the shops and buy some more. Having made himself another cup of coffee, he sat down in the lounge to devour his little feast.

After polishing off the toasted sandwich and coffee, he climbed the stairs to his bedroom and stripped himself of his clothing and took a fresh towel from the airing cupboard before nonchalantly taking himself into the bathroom. He turned the tap and allowed the water to run for a minute so it became hot enough; he wasn't a believer in brutalising yourself with all this nonsense about having a cold shower in order to galvanize the body into a plethora of vitality. No, he liked to enjoy the heat of the water against his skin, which he found far more invigorating. Stepping into the shower, he closed the door behind him and scrubbed himself for twenty minutes, with such ferocity; it was as though he were caked in dirt from head to toe. He left the shower and rubbed himself down with his towel, with equal vigour as he had washed himself, then wrapped it tightly around his waist.

As he was about to enter his bedroom, the doorbell rang. *Who the bloody hell could that be?* he thought, annoyed at being disturbed. *If it's those damn Jehovah's Witnesses, they'll get a piece of my mind.* He reached for the dressing gown on the back of the bedroom door. It was Luke's. He hesitated, momentarily, before deciding to put it on. He tied the sash as he made his way to the front door, opening it languorously but ready to tell anyone who wanted to push religion down his throat to "piss off".

It was Elliot and Kristian who greeted him.

Instantly losing his prior antagonism, he greeted them both cheerily. "Hi. Come on in."

"Thanks," they said.

"I'm sorry about this," he apologised, pointing at the dressing gown, "but I've just come out of the shower."

"That's okay," Kristian reassured.

"So, what can I do for the two of you?"

Elliot and Kristian followed Scott into the lounge and flopped themselves down on the sofa. Elliot spoke: "We thought we'd pop round to see if you're all right."

"Oh, as well as can be expected, I guess."

"We didn't really get the chance to talk to you properly at the hospital. So, I hope you don't mind us coming round unexpectedly."

"No, not at all. To be honest, I'm quite glad of the company. I just want the two of you to know, though, that I am really grateful for all the help and support that you've given to both me and Luke."

Elliot gave a magnanimous smile. "What sort of friends would we have been, if we didn't help our friends in their times of need?"

Scott felt slightly ill at ease and managed to find a way out of the conversation and the direction he knew it would be going in. "Would either of you like a drink? I quite fancy a cup of tea myself."

"Oh, a tea would be lovely, thank you," said Elliot.

"A tea as well, please," added Kristian.

Both Elliot and Kristian shot each other a half smile knowing exactly what the other one was thinking. They were looking forward to a *proper* cup of tea, rather than the abhorrent rubbish they had had at the hospital; so much so, it was almost as if they had been offered a glass of their favourite wine.

Scott left the room, relieved that, at least for a few minutes, he wouldn't be drawn into the topic of Luke. It was obvious that they had come round to talk to him about Luke but he wished that they would raise another topic of conversation rather than the inevitable. Still, he convinced himself, it wasn't their fault because Luke clearly played a big part in all three of their lives and currently it was *him* who was a naturally controversial and provocative subject to raise. He still loved Luke a great deal but it was difficult to try and forget everything that had passed in the last few days. He knew he would have to try, if only for Luke's sake and that would probably be made easier with Vince being around.

He returned to the lounge after a few minutes and offered the two men their tea, to which they thanked him.

"Ah," groaned Kristian with gratification, "I really needed this."

Elliot nodded. "After that dreadful concoction in the hospital that they had the cheek to label as tea, I am more than grateful for a decent cup at last."

Scott eyed Elliot and Kristian for a moment before speaking. "You both look totally exhausted."

Kristian rolled his eyes. "You wouldn't believe what's happened over the last few days. A good friend of ours had to be rushed to hospital because of complications with her pregnancy."

"I'm sorry to hear that," Scott said deferentially. "I hope that she and the baby will be okay. I feel for her partner, he must be tearing his hair out at the moment."

"We haven't heard from her husband today but, as far as we know, she's still there and the situation is very touch-and-go at the moment."

The Absence of Friends

"Then, of course," added Elliot, "there's Michael as well. Do you remember Michael and Steven?"

Scott nodded. How could he forget those two? The first time he had met Steven, Luke had nearly provoked a fight between the two of them.

Kristian continued: "Well, they were involved in quite a nasty car crash. Michael nearly didn't survive but fortunately, he's been discharged from hospital now. We're just waiting to hear some good news on Maxine and the baby now."

"I'm really sorry," Scott said humbly. He was beginning to comprehend just how much consternation, emotional stress and resentment the two men had been forced to face, with three of their friends being hospitalised simultaneously. He admired the fact that despite, ostensibly, the amount, the intensity and the level of anxiety being dealt to them, they still managed to remain resolutely solid for those who might be crumbling around them.

Before one of the other two could, Scott decided to broach the subject he wanted to evade himself. "So, how was Luke when you left him?"

Kristian looked at Elliot with an air of worry about him. It was Elliot who did the talking. "He still thinks that you're angry and upset with him."

"I'm not!" he almost shouted, more from defiantly trying to make his point than because he was actually angry, although this was how the two men interpreted it.

"Yes, we know that," said Elliot, as he put a supportive arm around Scott's shoulder, "but I'm not entirely sure that Luke is convinced of that. You've both been through a very traumatic experience and it's going to take some time to get things back to the way they were between the two of you." He deliberately avoided using the words *back to normal*. After all, what *was* normal anymore?

Scott revealed that he had also been tested for HIV and what he had overheard the doctors saying at the hospital earlier that day. He pleaded with them not to tell Luke anything about these revelations; not under any circumstances because he didn't want Luke to feel any worse than he already was.

Reluctantly, they agreed to his wish.

Max, feeling undeniably elated and euphoric, jumped in the air and whooped with delight, as if he were the victor of an exigent battle of the wits. In a way, that's exactly what he felt he was. He attracted the attention of the other patients who were in the waiting room, not that he particularly cared what they might have thought of his physical and vocal outburst because he had just had some really good news. No, not *good*, as that didn't give the level of news any real justice. It was absolutely, bloody fantastic news.

S.J. Roberts had come into the room and informed Max that his wife had recovered from the anaesthetic and was asking for him. He had stepped back, startled, at Max's outburst. The other visitors and patients had looks of wariness about this man's strange behaviour, or smiled on his behalf as they guessed he had received the news that he was longing to hear.

"Thank you ever so much, Sebastian," Max said over and over, forcing himself to stop short of giving him a vice-like hug, or even a kiss of familiarity. The formalities of addressing S.J. Roberts by his designation, or by his surname were totally discarded, as the need for that kind of protocol didn't seem to exist in Max's current state of ecstasy.

He had discovered what the S of S.J. Roberts' name stood for when he overheard a conversation between him and a woman, whom he presumed to be his wife, the previous evening. At the time, because Sebastian was in civilian clothes, complete with an overcoat, Max thought the woman had come to pick him up because his shift had finished for the day and to take him home. He imagined that the woman would have prepared a deliciously home-cooked meal, ready for them both to enjoy when they arrived at the family homestead, possibly with even a glass or two of wine.

Sebastian happily led Max to the Recovery Room, where Maxine had been transferred to. Max followed him into the room, still a little unsure and nervous as to what to expect. Even after being given the wonderful news about Maxine, he entered the room with bated breath, still opting to expect the worst. When he entered the room, he saw that his wife was sitting up comfortably in bed.

"Hi," he said with a warm softness.

"Hi," she echoed.

He sat on the bed next to her, taking her into his arms and with loving tenderness, kissed her gently on the lips.

"Nurse Roberts took me to see Thalia on my way to see you. She's so tiny."

The smile on Maxine's face abruptly disappeared. "The doctor told me that she's still in a critical condition. How could this happen to us, Max? Have we done something so terrible in our lives that we're being punished for it?"

Max looked at his wife with concern. "Don't upset yourself, honey. She's being well looked after and before you know it, she'll be home with us."

Maxine's face showed that she didn't share the same level of optimism as her husband, as a confusing web comprising an abundance of thoughts was being spun in her head. No sooner had she herself come out of danger, than little Thalia's life was put on the line. How could life be so cruel to an innocent

The Absence of Friends

and defenceless child? *If* there was a God, how could he let her and Max suffer so much?

She took a long look at her husband, seeing his tired, dark eyes and unkempt look. "How long have you been at the hospital? You look really tired. Are you getting any sleep?"

"I've probably been here most of the time since you've been admitted and no, I've not had much sleep at all."

She held her husband's hand, squeezing it tightly to show that she valued his strength and support at this time. "I love you, Max."

"Why, thank you. You're not so bad yourself."

"Oh, you're such the romantic," she said sarcastically.

"The good news is that you can come home this afternoon. They are happy for you to be discharged."

"What about Thalia?"

"They want to keep her here for a few more days, just to observe and monitor her progress. The doctor was quite adamant that he wouldn't be happy to discharge her prematurely."

Maxine remained silent. Although she really couldn't wait to get out of the hospital, as her association to them was less than favourable, she was far less keen on the idea of leaving her daughter behind. She couldn't manage to find the appropriate words to express to Max how completely overwhelmed she felt that she hadn't suffered the same unfortunate fate as her mother. Like an antagonistic persecutor resiliently keeping its victim within their grasp, so Maxine's adversely negative thoughts continually taunted her, convincing her that leaving her daughter at the hospital would prove only to be a bad omen.

Max stretched across the bed to kiss his wife on the lips as he bid her goodbye, telling her that he would be back later in the afternoon so he could take her home. He left the hospital with a feeling of relief about his wife but a continued anxiety for his daughter. He didn't wish to voice own his concerns and fears to Maxine, although he was aware that he felt exactly the same as she did. What he felt he needed to do was to be strong for Maxine, just in case the moment they were both dreading became a reality; just in case their daughter didn't survive.

Arriving back at home, Max threw his car keys carelessly onto the kitchen table and sat upon a stool at the breakfast bar. He rubbed his overly tired eyes, feeling the effect of the stress and tension since his wife had been admitted to hospital, starting to take its toll on him. He decided to wash and dry the neglected, dirty dishes that he had left stacked on the draining board. His hands were still shaking from the anxiety he still felt, that was coursing through his veins like cars on a Formula 1 racetrack, causing him to break two glasses and a dinner plate. After each of the first two breakages, he yelled: "Goddammit!" but after the third one, it was too much for him to bear as he threw the tea towel at the sink and slumped to the floor, weeping.

When he finally managed to compose himself, he made his way to the drinks cabinet in the living room and poured himself out a large whisky and soda, falling back on to the sofa. He noticed that the answer phone was flashing, signalling that he had a message waiting for him to listen to. He placed his drink on the coffee table and rewound the tape on the machine, pressing the play button.

"Hello my darling Max, you sweet, precious, gorgeous and may I say, rather luscious hunk of man candy," came the irrefutable owner of the recorded voice. "It's Michael, if you hadn't already managed to guess that. Well, just to let you know that I am out of hospital now with only a broken arm and a few grazes to show for that rather tragic escapade recently. Apart from that, though, I'm all warm, bubbly and wonderful. How's my *other* darling Max? She is so wickedly, wickedly naughty for putting us through all this worry. So, when she comes to her senses and decides that she's had enough of wasting time in a hospital bed and gets herself back home, where she belongs, she is going to be faced with a very severe telling off from yours truly! Anyway, mucho amor from me and Steven. Give us a tinkle when you can, sweet cheeks, or pop round if you want some company. I really must dash now, as it's time for my obligatory face pack. Kisses to you both. Ciao, ciao, ciao....byeeeee."

The machine beeped, indicating the end of the message and switched off.

Picking up the receiver, Max dialled Michael's number.

Steven answered. "Hello?"

"Hi, Steven. It's Max. I just got the message that Michael left."

"Hey, Max! How are you?"

"I'm doing okay...apart from being really tired."

"Yeah, I bet."

"What about you? How's things with you both?"

Steven sighed, which Max took to mean that Michael was being his usual trying self.

"Like that, is it?" Max said, light-heartedly.

Another exasperated sigh. "Yeah, I'm afraid so. What's the latest on Maxine and the baby?"

"We have a baby girl."

"Congratulations to you both," said Steven with joy. "Don't tell me... you've named her Thalia?"

"Uh-huh." There wasn't the same enthusiasm in Max's voice as in Steven's.

"What's happened?" asked Steven with unease, noticing the lack of joy that should have been so apparent in a new father's voice.

Max let out a tired groan, rubbing his eye with his free hand. "Thalia's in a critical condition. They've put her in an incubator…to monitor her progress, you understand. I'm not sure she's going to pull…"

Steven cut him short. "Hang on there just a minute," he said firmly. "You can't allow yourself to think like that. While she's under the care of the professionals and being monitored, there is every chance that things could improve. You're not going to do yourself, Maxine or even the baby, any favours if you allow yourself to be consumed with these negative feelings. I understand that you're anxious and fearing the worst but that's only because of a possibility…there is an equal possibility that the exact opposite will happen."

"I do understand what you're saying. I'm sorry, it's just that…"

Steven heard Max's sniffles. His voice was gentle and compassionate. "But Maxine's okay? Isn't she?"

"Yes. Maxine's doing okay, although she's obviously upset about Thalia. I'm going to be picking her up later this afternoon as she's being discharged today."

"Well, there you go," said Steven encouragingly, "that's a piece of good news in itself and hopefully, the beginning of a trend for you. You know, if you want to talk further, you are more than welcome to come round…I'm pretty sure that Michael would be more than happy and very capable of obliterating all those negative thoughts you're carrying and replacing them with more positive and uplifting thoughts."

Max, although very tempted, declined Steven's kind offer of company, saying that he was really tired and wanted to try and get a couple of hours sleep before returning to the hospital. He readily accepted the offer of dinner sometime soon for himself and Maxine at their home.

"Take care, Max and be sure to give Maxine our love."

"I will. Thanks Steven and please pass on our love to Michael too."

"Sure, no problem. Bye."

"Bye."

Max placed the receiver back on the hook and made his way into the bedroom upstairs. He threw his clothes carelessly on the floor and flopped himself into bed. Reaching over to the clock, he set the alarm to go off in just over two hours, which he thought would be more than enough for a decent rest and still give him plenty of time to get to the hospital. Falling back onto the pillow, he closed his eyes, allowing himself to drift off into a deep sleep.

For some unknown reason that left Max bewildered, he slept right through the alarm. He turned over and looked sleepily at the clock. Three seventeen.

"Shit!" he moaned at it. His mouth felt particularly dry, as he thought that he must have been considerably more tired than he first thought and really needed the sleep; though it was very unusual for him to ever oversleep. Throwing the covers off the bed in a belligerent manner, he swiftly showered, shaved and brushed his teeth. Selecting a smart, dark blue suit, a crisp white shirt and a light blue tie, he dressed. He took a quick glance at himself in the mirror, thanking the fact that he didn't have any hair to fuss about with and waste any further time. He looked once more at the bedside clock. Three forty two. If he hurried, he could still make the hospital a few minutes after four o'clock. Grabbing Maxine's diary from her dressing table, as he was sure she had asked him to bring it and retrieving the keys he had thrown on the table earlier, he ran out the door and into his car.

Just as he had predicted, he arrived a few minutes after four o'clock, even with the stop off at a florist to buy some carnations. The hospital appeared unnaturally empty as he began to wander the corridor to the reception area. Max felt uneasy, as he realised the place resembled a ghost town. Nobody was around and this didn't sit very well with him. The doctors and nurses he normally saw rushing about their business were nowhere in sight. He thought that he might have seen the smiling face of Sebastian, pleased that he was finally taking his wife home and also, to give him the opportunity to enquire as to the welfare of his daughter. He thought it incredibly odd that the receptionist wasn't at her post either, especially as the switchboard phone was continually ringing.

Feeling confused, Max scanned the room. *Had hooligans been here?* The posters were hanging off the wall, ripped to shreds. Mickey Mouse had gone, *thank God for that*. The chairs and tables were overturned, with all the leaflets scattered over the floor. *What the hell is going on?* He wasn't sure that anybody would come along and tend to his needs, so he decided to make his own way to the Recovery Room. He wandered the maze of corridors, unable to recall the way, as they weren't at all like the ones he remembered. Surely he couldn't have been *that* tired that he had driven to the wrong hospital? He didn't think he was but something was drastically wrong. After what seemed like an hour of despondently meandering the endless corridors, Max finally stumbled upon the Recovery Room. He began to envisage Maxine wondering where on earth he had got to. He threw open the door, ready to greet his wife with an apologetic kiss.

It was empty.

Where the hell was Maxine? Max hoped to God that she hadn't had a relapse.

The Absence of Friends

He ran the matrix of corridors, not knowing exactly where he was going, desperately calling out his wife's name. Each time he called for her, there was no response. His heart was beating so fast with panic and fear, he assumed that it was the adrenalin coursing through his body that was the only thing preventing him from collapsing. He stopped running, to allow himself a moment to take in a few deep breaths and regulate his breathing. He looked up and down at the mass of corridors, undecided which one to investigate next. Making his choice, he noticed once again the door to the Recovery Room. Had he really been running around in a complete circle? Warily, he strode to the door and turned the handle, opening it slowly.

The sight that met his eyes caused them to open wide with deathly horror. What the hell was happening to him? He didn't, no, he *wouldn't* believe he was so exhausted that his mind was cruelly playing hallucinogenic tricks upon him but nothing was making any sense to him.

The Recovery Room was no longer a room in the hospital where his wife had been but a graveyard with only two large headstones in the centre. His ever-growing consternation didn't prevent him from tentatively edging his way into the room, in order to take a closer look but when he read the inscriptions, he wished his fear *had* held him back.

One of the headstones had his daughter's name on it and the other, his wife's.

He walked over to the graves, his whole body trembling with fear, as he forced himself to peer into them.

They were empty.

Hearing a noise, he looked up from the graves and noticed Maxine walking towards him, carrying their child in her arms.

"She's dead, Max," she said in an icy tone.

Maxine gently placed the body into the smaller of the two graves and tucked a blanket over it, as though she were only putting her daughter to bed. Pulling a gun from her hospital gown, she placed it against her temple.

"I'm sorry, Max. I love you but Thalia's dead and I really don't see the point in living anymore."

Max could only watch with frozen horror, as Maxine pulled the trigger and fell back into her named grave.

"No!" It was a blood-curdling scream that came from him, which seemed to resonate long after he had stopped. He turned his back on the graves and dropped to his knees, weeping at his loss. The commotion that followed a few minutes later made him alertly jump to his feet and spin around with such speed, he almost lost his balance. Standing by the gravesides were Elliot, Kristian, Steven, Michael, Maxine's father and her step-mother.

Andrew R. Hamilton

And himself!

He saw that he was still knelt by the two graves, with his hands covering his weeping eyes. Was he dead? How? He could see that everyone was pointing at his other self accusingly. Elisabette walked over to his double and spat various statements at him: "If only you'd gotten here sooner", "you shouldn't have overslept", and "look at what you've done; what you've caused."

The piercing noise from the alarm clock woke him with a start. Breathing heavily, he surveyed the surroundings to ensure that he wasn't in a graveyard. He let out a relieved gasp, as he slowly began to realise that he was still in his bed and had only been trapped within a terrifying nightmare. His heart was pounding furiously in his chest and his entire body was covered in perspiration. He looked at the clock on the bedside table. It read: 14.02.

He showered, shaved and dressed, opting for his black 501s and a slate-grey shirt, so as not to tempt fate. Driving to the hospital, he thought of nothing but the terrifyingly vivid dream, hoping to God that it wasn't some kind of gruesome premonition.

CHAPTER THIRTEEN

Vince looked at the familiar surroundings of London that had once been his home town. How unattractive it looked to him now. After Paris and soon-to-be Düsseldorf, most places in London looked decidedly ugly and unappealing. He hailed a black cab, waving his arm in the air like a maniac. One cab totally ignored his signalling. *Well, fuck you*, he thought. Another black cab approached and he resumed his manic waving again. The cab stopped this time. He asked the driver if he knew of the road in Hammersmith that he required. For some reason, the driver felt offended and refused to take Vince. As the cab sped off, Vince raised his middle finger at the departing vehicle, shouting out "bastard!" The third driver stopped, confirmed that he knew the road and agreed to take Vince there. Satisfied, Vince stepped into the cab. He threw his suitcase on the seat beside him, as he reached over to the door and closed it.

In Paris and Düsseldorf, he thought, although quite feisty, the cab drivers were not as rude as the ones in London. He had forgotten how rude some of them could be and was displeased that he was unpleasantly reminded. The journey to Scott's took about forty minutes, with the driver confirming a couple of left or right turns with Vince. Climbing out of the cab with his suitcase, Vince paid his fare and thanked the driver. The driver incoherently grunted something back to Vince, who didn't have the inclination to establish exactly what it was the driver had said.

Vince thought how depressing and soulless everything looked. The air had a heavy smell of rain and the dull, grey sky looked as though it was threatening to rain again. What was left of the leaves on the trees, had turned ghastly shades of brown and withered to almost their last breath of life. Picking up his suitcase, Vince followed the path to Scott's front door.

He rang the bell.

Scott opened the door and greeted his friend with a cheery "hello", ushering him out of the cold, damp air.

"Shall I leave my case here?" asked Vince.

Scott nodded. "You couldn't have timed that much better, as I've literally just put the kettle on. Would you like a cup of tea?"

"Oh, yes please. I could murder a cuppa."

"You should have called from the airport. I would have come and picked you up," said Scott, making his way into the kitchen.

"I just thought it would be easier for me to catch a cab," he said, following in Scott's wake.

"So, how was the flight?"

"It was quite awful really."

"Why? What happened?"

Vince took the mug of tea that Scott offered him and moistened his dry throat by taking a sip before responding to Scott's question. "Well, there was this guy, who when I come to think of it, was probably completely terrified of flying. At the time, I felt quite sorry for him actually because he was adamant that the plane was going to crash; he was becoming more and more agitated and restless the further into the flight we were. So, you can probably imagine that quite a few of the other passengers became panicked and freaked out, especially the youngsters."

"God, I'll say. Mind you, I'm not the best when it comes to flying, so I would probably have been one of those who ended up freaking out! It sounds like it would have been a total nightmare both for you and those who were panicking."

"You said it. You think that these kinds of incidences only ever happen in the movies. You don't expect to be faced with them in reality."

Scott blew on his tea. "So how did they calm him down and regain the peace?"

"It was actually one of the stewardesses who did the deed. I think her name was Sylvia or Cynthia…something that ended in *ia*…anyway, that's beside the point. For arguments sake, let's call her Sylvia. From my experience with Sylvia on the flight, she was a real charmer and knew *what* to say, *when* to say it and *how* to make it sound. She had one of those really soothing and genteel kind of voices, you know - the sort of voice you could have talking to you for hours, just to keep you calm and relaxed. Anyway, I would imagine she probably worked her magic and charm by talking some sense into this passenger."

"Was that all it took?" asked Scott, a little surprised.

"Well, not exactly," smiled Vince. "I think there was probably a little bit of help from *another* kind of magic involved in the process. When the man came back to his seat, let's just say, he wasn't totally compos mentis. So, putting two and two together, I would hazard a guess that the stewardess, in her wisdom, gained a little extra help from one of her friends, Jack Daniels or Jim Beam, if you follow my meaning!"

"Ah," said Scott, realising and making a drinking motion with his hand.

The Absence of Friends

"To be honest, I wouldn't be at all that surprised if airlines might have cleverly secreted themselves away a little stash of their very good pals, for this very reason and possibly learnt from past experience."

They finished their teas and Scott suggested that they retire into the living room. Vince readily agreed, stopping in the hallway to pick up his suitcase. Scott was already sitting down in an armchair when Vince entered the room, dragging his case behind him.

"I've bought you back a little something from France," he said, placing his suitcase on the floor. "It's nothing extravagant, just a little token." He undid the various belts, clasps and zips that had fastened the suitcase as if it were Fort Knox, which also included a combination lock that Vince momentarily struggled to remember what it was. Rummaging through t-shirts, underwear and other various articles of clothing, he eventually found what it was he was looking for. Passing the wrapped package to Scott, he said: "There you are… don't expect too much, then you won't be disappointed," he grinned.

Scott took the gift and beamed like a small child would at Christmas. "Thank you," he said, undoing the wrapping and taking care not to rip the paper, as was his usual custom with any gift.

When all the paper had been carefully removed, Scott was holding a red box. Slowly and deliberately, in order to retain the suspense for as long as he could, he removed the lid from the box to reveal the contents inside. It was a porcelain statue of a man, which looked as though it had been meticulously hand painted with beautiful and intricate detailing. The man himself was holding a miniature brass Eiffel Tower in his outstretched palms. "It's really lovely," said Scott, admiring the gift.

"I was going to have an inscription put on it, like: *I promised you the world but all I could manage was the Eiffel Tower*. It sounded really quite tacky, so I thought better of it. I think it seems just right as it is. Don't you?"

"I think it's perfect."

"I've got one for Luke too…it's quite similar to your one but instead, he's holding a miniature Arc de Triumphe. They're just some little Objets d'Art I picked up in a shop, in a quaint little area of central Paris, which is probably quite similar to The Lanes in Brighton."

"Vince, you shouldn't have."

"Well, it's too bad," said Vince, "'cause I have."

"Well, thank you," said Scott once again. He placed the ornament on the mantelpiece and stepped back to admire it. "It looks quite good there, don't you think?"

"Beautiful," replied Vince. He neatly replaced the contents of his suitcase and began to re-fasten a couple of the belts so nothing would spill out when he picked it up. "Do you mind if I take a shower? Travelling, for some reason, always makes me feel really dirty."

"No, not at all. Treat this house like your own…you don't need to ask if you want something."

Scott showed Vince to the bedroom where he had stayed on the previous occasions that he had come to visit his friends. It was exactly the same as it was on his last visit, almost as if they had left it as a shrine to Vince himself. The room was plain but warm and homely looking. Three walls were painted in First Light white, with one wall painted in Angie pink, as a focal wall.

Vince remembered back to his very first visit to Scott and Luke. He had asked why they had chosen to paint one wall in pink, of all colours.

"To match the bed, of course," said Luke with a smile, as if there were nothing else to add other than that.

"Eh?" said Vince, neither his curiosity nor confusion satiated with merely a smile.

"Well, because it's a queen-sized bed…" began Scott.

"…it means that you should be able to fit into it perfectly," continued Luke.

Vince shook his head and rolled his eyes. "You've designed a palatial bedroom, purely for me. Well, I'm touched…really, I am."

"It's a delicate room, fit for a delicate queen, who doesn't necessarily have a delicate outlook on life," grinned Luke, continuing with the theme.

"Okay, okay. I get the picture. The royal décor doesn't really quite fit with my persona but I will play along…Queen Shepherd commands that her subjects bow before her and show her the bloody respect that's due!"

The bed was adorned with a fiery-red quilt, with matching pillow-slips. On the floor, beside the bed, was a sheepskin rug, laying invitingly for the occupant of the room to run their bare feet through. It stood out, quite strikingly, against the plain, burgundy carpet. There was a matching bedside cabinet and wardrobe, with a set of built-in drawers, both of which were empty of any contents, save a few hangers in the wardrobe. On the bedside table were a simple lamp and an equally simple alarm clock.

After Vince had showered, dried and sprayed himself with the latest eau de cologne that he had purchased from the Duty Free shop on the way to London, he selected a clean pair of jeans and shirt to wear.

They caught the tube into the West End later that evening, choosing to dine in China Town. Instead of selecting separate dishes, they opted to order a variety of different dishes and share the lot between them. Scott opted for a prawn dish and one with beef, whilst Vince plumped for a dish with chicken and the other, with pork. To say it was a pleasant reprieve for Scott, from the goings-on of the last few days, was an understatement, as the two men

The Absence of Friends

found that they had plenty to talk about whilst they ate. He didn't see Vince anywhere near as much as he would have like and so, at least temporarily, he wanted to forget about any of the negatives and all of his anxieties and just allow himself a brief moment of decadence. When the bill arrived at the end of the meal, Scott generously offered to pay for the whole lot. Vince kept refusing, saying that it was *his* intention to treat Scott. After a few minutes of disputing and refusing each other's offers, Vince finally relented and allowed Scott to pay.

"I see you haven't lost that stubborn streak of yours," joked Vince.

"And I see yours has gotten worse!" replied Scott.

If they had known that there were problems on the underground when they were ready to make their way home, they might have chosen an alternative mode of transport. However, due to signal failures at both Earls Court and Barons Court, all the trains were travelling at an agonising snail's pace. Feeling a little agitated that they were going nowhere fast, Scott suggested that they disembark at Knightsbridge, which was the next stop and catch a cab for the rest of the journey. Vince wholeheartedly agreed, wandering if they might receive the same frosty and ill-mannered reception as he had with the cab drivers earlier.

When they eventually arrived home, albeit with Vince somewhat surprised that Scott must have hailed the most friendliest cab driver in London, Scott marched straight into the kitchen to make them both a cup of tea, which they took with them into the lounge. He selected a CD of Vivaldi's *Four Seasons* and slotted it into the player. He had to readjust what he called *daytime volume*, to *night-time volume*, so as not to aggravate the neighbours. He sat down in the armchair, pulling up the cushion to support his back and opened up the conversation that had been on the two men's minds practically all evening but neither one daring to broach the subject.

Luke.

Max couldn't really have been any more pleased to have seen the leering face of Mickey Mouse greet him when he arrived at the hospital several minutes before four o'clock. All the familiar posters, the words of which he knew by heart, were still hanging in one piece on the same notice boards as he remembered.

When he reached the desk, the receptionist greeted him with an acknowledging tilt of her head, as she pushed her glasses back up from her nose. Her immaculately coiffured hair refused to fall even the slightest bit of out of place from any movement she made. Had Max been a betting man, he would have wagered a large amount of money that this was more than likely due to the excessive use of a firm-hold hairspray.

"A good afternoon to you, sir and with what may I help you today?" she asked in a tone reminiscent of what Max harshly referred to as someone adopting their *Cadbury's voice*. It was a voice that was annoyingly over-jovial, unnaturally high-pitched and insalubriously sickly-sweet, hence the epithet.

"I…ah…" he stuttered, momentarily unnerved by the woman's lavish exuberance. "My wife is being discharged today. I've come to collect her."

"Not a problem sir. What is your wife's name?"

"Mrs Beresford. Mrs Maxine Beresford."

The woman typed what seemed like a mini epistle onto her computer, in a matter of seconds, before she studied the screen - her perfectly formed smile never once dissolving from her meticulously made-up face. "Yes, Mr Beresford. They are expecting you on the ward momentarily. If you would like to take a seat in the waiting area, Nurse Roberts will attend to you shortly."

Max thanked the receptionist as he took his seat in the waiting area, feeling as though he had just ingested a thousand calories from the saccharine voice of the woman.

As he had anticipated happening from his nightmare, Sebastian emerged from the door, to greet him with a beaming smile and pass on his best wishes to both him and Maxine. Max continually thanked Sebastian for all he had done for his wife and revealed how ecstatic he was at the prospect of finally having her back at home with him.

"Mrs Beresford has been talking of nothing but that since we told her she can go home today," said Sebastian, with a pleased smile. "We will take very good care of your daughter and hopefully, she will also be at home with the two of you before you know it."

Maxine was surprised at how Max tried to hurry her out of the hospital, although she was overjoyed to be out of the place. "I'm so glad to be going home," she said, climbing steadily into the car and fastening her seatbelt. She let out a whimper as she felt the belt catch where the incision had been made.

"So am I," grinned Max, as the car pulled out of the car park.

"All I want to do is put my feet up and have a hot cup of tea."

"I will ensure that that is the first thing that happens when we get back home."

"Has anything been happening while I've been cooped up in that dreadful hospital?"

"You'll be pleased to know that Michael is back to his usual effervescent self. Although, he's acting as though nothing actually happened. Steven's quite worried about him."

Maxine tutted. "I'm sure he'll be okay…there's very little I'd imagine, that would prevent him losing the traits of his usual gregarious and grandiose ego. I would hazard a guess that, if he is playing at being upset, then it's probably because he's not the centre of attention. You should realise that with him by now."

"Well, he's very upset with you for causing him *a tremendous amount of worry and concern* is what I think he said. I think he's on the warpath with you too…"

"What! Why?"

"If my memory serves me correct, he said that you were extremely naughty for putting him through all this unnecessary worry and that he would tell you off severely when you got home."

"He's a fine one to talk," she chortled. "As long as I can get my cup of tea first, he can do or say what he likes."

"Oh," said Max, suddenly remembering another snippet of the conversation. "I nearly forgot to tell you…We've been invited to dinner with him and Steven tomorrow night. Do you think you might feel up to going?"

Maxine smiled. "Sure. I don't see why not. As long as Michael remembers that I won't be able to do any twisting and shaking, like he normally wants to do. He will have to realise that I can't do these weird and wonderful contortions until I've healed properly."

Max told his wife about the awful nightmare he had had, telling her that it seemed so real, which was the most frightening thing about it.

"Oh, darling, that must have been dreadful."

"It was. It seemed so believably real at the time."

"We're obviously more in tune than you think."

"Sorry? I'm not following your meaning."

"I also had a really awful nightmare earlier on."

"Really? Oh God, what was yours?"

Maxine thought back to her terrifying dream, her blood running cold as she relived those moments:

I'm lying in my bed, in the hospital. Everything around me seems unnaturally cold but no matter how tightly I pulled the blankets around me, I cannot seem to get myself warm. The chill in the air, that grows heavier with each passing minute, cuts through me as though I were lying on a bed of ice. I want to get out of the bed…to move around and try and get my blood flowing to warm me up…but no matter how much I try, I just cannot seem to move. The only way I can describe it was that it was like I had become a part of the block of ice; almost as if I had fused together with it.

I notice that the door to the room is opening slowly and eerily, like something out of a horror movie and I am just waiting for the inevitable terrible thing to happen. Even though the logic in my head does not want to play the typical part of the damsel in distress, my heart beats fast, anticipating the compulsory scream coming forth. It's a very strange sensation that I'm feeling because, even though I was trapped in whatever it was that was about to happen, it also felt that I wasn't actually there, partaking in the horrific scene I was convinced was about to unfold.

It is my mother who walks into the room, looking heavily pregnant. I look at her, confused, shocked and apprehensive.

"Oh, my poor baby girl," she says. Her eyes sad and lifeless.

As she approaches nearer the bed and sits on it, I take another look at her and see that it's not my mother but Elisabette, who possesses my mother's voice. She moves her head nearer to my cheek, as though she is going to kiss me but doesn't. Instead, she whispers into my ear: "Siobhan," she says in my mother's voice but with a disconcertingly malevolent edge to it, "it's all your fault. You killed me. If I hadn't gotten pregnant with you, I would still be alive now."

I try to speak to Elisabette and tell her that there was no way it could have been my fault but I can't get any words to come out of my mouth. I know what I want to say but the words seem to be lost along with the undiscovered reasons for the icy atmosphere. Elisabette looks at me with pure hatred in her dark eyes. "I should have had an abortion, whilst I still had the option," she hissed.

Noticing that I am pregnant, she laughs hysterically. "Well, well, well…" she cackles, "…isn't revenge just the sweetest thing? Wouldn't you say, Siobhan?"

"Leave my baby alone, you bitch!" I scream.

"Now, now, Siobhan," she croaks, stroking my hair with a strange kind of tenderness, with an almost soothing feel to it. "You really mustn't work yourself into a state. It's not going to do any good for the baby, is it? And of course, you don't want to put yourself in a position where you might lose the baby, eh? What would Max say? I know exactly what he would say…he would blame you…and he would never forgive you." She leers at me with her snake-like eyes.

I can feel the anger rising in me, ready to burst at any moment, as Elisabette repeats again and again that I will the one to cause the loss of the baby. I cannot contain my anger any longer. Exploding into a rage, I yell at Elisabette: "Listen to me, you evil bitch. You can say what you want to me, like the vile, odious excuse for a human being you are but I swear to God, that if you dare to even lay one finger on my baby, I will kill you!"

"Maxine?"

Elisabette is no longer sitting on my bed, as she has been replaced by you Max. You're looking confused, as you stroke my hair, just as Elisabette had done earlier.

"She says that I'm going to lose the baby…and that I will be the cause of it," I whimper.

"Who said that?"

"Elisabette."

"What! Why the hell would she want to say something so malicious?"

My eyes widen in complete horror, as I see Elisabette standing behind you, with Thalia cradled in her arms. Her expression is full of contemptuous desire, with her eyes daring me to carry out my deathly threat. With the baby in her arms, she knows she has successfully defied any vocal or physical attack that I might have tried to throw her way.

Behind Elisabette, I can see Michael and Steven standing there, although they are dressed as priests. Between them, they are holding a colossal bible and mouthing the words of the last rites. Even though they are mouthing the words, I can hear the low drone of every single word floating towards my ears and it feels as though they are actually screaming them directly into my ear. Each word that I hear takes me further into a state of dumbfounded terror.

Throwing off the bed covers, I scramble to grab Thalia off Elisabette, who drops her. I'm not entirely sure whether she deliberately dropped her, or if it was because of my actions but when Thalia hits the floor, she smashes into little pieces, like a china doll.

All I can hear Elisabette saying is: "I told you that you would be the cause of losing your baby. Didn't I?"

A piercing scream comes from my mouth.

"It was at that point that I woke up," she said to Max, shivering at the memory.

Max put his hand on Maxine's. "She's going to be okay. We have to believe that. We can't allow ourselves to be drawn into these dreams we're having… it's just our minds trying to play tricks on us, as they try to make sense of everything that's happening."

Maxine nodded at her husband's optimism.

When they arrived home, Maxine had her eagerly awaited cup of tea and tried to rid herself of the pent up stress she had carried by continually sighing deeply. Max prepared the bathroom whilst Maxine undressed herself. He had brought a chair from the kitchen, putting towels on the seat of the chair and underneath it and placing the chair next to the bath. Without thinking, he put some Radox into the bath, which he had half-filled. When Maxine entered the bathroom, she took her place on the chair and sat there as if she were posing for nude painting. Max sat on the side of the bath and tenderly sponged Maxine, taking extreme care around her stomach. There were a couple of winces from Maxine not because Max had hurt her but more because she was anticipating the pain.

As Maxine was drying herself, Max searched the wardrobe for the clothes she had asked him to get for her. During his search, he thought how bizarre the two dreams were, hating the fact that they seemed so real. Changing his shirt to a blue, denim one, he went back to the bathroom to check on Maxine.

"Finished?"

She nodded.

After Maxine had finished dressing, she joined her husband in the living room and began drinking the cup of tea he had made her.

"You had some post while you were in hospital. I didn't think to bring them with me on one of my visits but you would probably have preferred to read them at home, with your feet up."

She took the envelopes and studied each one individually before opening them. One was a bank statement of her personal account. Another was a letter from Francesca Sacchetti, her friend in Italy, asking her and Max to come over to Italy for a holiday sometime soon. Enclosed with the letter was a photograph of Francesca's son, Antonio, who was nearly fifteen years old now.

"Goodness me, doesn't he look quite the young man now?" said Maxine, passing the photograph to her husband.

"Where do all the years go?"

"I know. It only seems like yesterday that he was born. Now, he's not that long to go before he leaves school!"

The third letter was from her father.

"Oh my God," Maxine said suddenly, clasping at her mouth with shock.

Max looked up from the newspaper he was reading. "What's wrong, sweetheart? Please, no more bad news!"

"This letter," she said, holding it up to Max. "It's from my father. He wants me to phone him when I've had the baby, so he can come and visit his new grandchild."

"Okay. Is that such a terrible thing?"

"No, *that's* not. However, he wants to bring Elisabette with him…and *that* is!" Her voice took on a more worried tone, as she said: "Max, I really don't want her here. When Thalia comes out of hospital, I do not want that woman in this house."

Elliot concluded that both he and Kristian needed some cheering up after the events of the last few days. He rang Sue's number and arranged to meet her in *Harpos* bar in Earls Court, in little more than an hours' time. Kristian whole-heartedly agreed to the evening out; he could always rely on Elliot's assumptions, as invariably, he would be correct more often than not. Wrapping themselves up in their jackets and scarves, they braved the bitterly cold winds to their car, parked a little way down the street.

"It's so bloody freezing," said Kristian, stating the obvious.

"I've put the heater on but it'll take a few minutes to warm up," said Elliot, turning the ignition key. The car spluttered with a little life before it gave up. He turned the key once again and this time the car sprang into life.

The drive to Earls Court was very uneventful, as both men remained silent for the duration of the journey. The lack of places to park added a further ten minutes to the journey, especially as they had to leave the car two blocks away from the bar and face the cold winds once again.

Elliot looked at his watch. "It's nearly eight o'clock. I don't think that's bad going, really, as I told Sue to meet us at the bar at around eight."

"Oh, I hate to burst your little bubble, Angel but really, you haven't done anything particularly outstanding. You phoned Sue just before seven o'clock, saying that we would meet her in an hour. Well, an hour from seven o'clock would be eight o'clock. So well done, babe," Kristian said, with a sarcastic smile. "Had you done it in thirty minutes, I might have been impressed."

They walked at a brisk pace to the pub, not wanting to spend any more time than necessary in the cold night air. Both smiled warmly at the stocky bouncer standing at the door, who greeted them for the start of their evening's entertainment.

"I'm just going to the toilet," stated Kristian. "You go and find Sue and I will join you in a minute."

"Okay. I'll get the drinks in too. Will you be driving home, or am I?"

"You can drive, I really fancy a drink."

Kristian made his way to the toilets, as Elliot searched for Sue. He found her sitting alone at a table in a corner.

"Hi," he said as he approached her table.

She looked up. "Hey, Elliot. Where's Kris?"

"He's gone to the toilet."

"Oh, right." She stood up and gave Elliot a friendly peck on the cheek.

"I'm just about to go to the bar. Would you like a drink?" he asked, noticing she had almost finished her pint.

She sat down again. "Um," she hummed thoughtfully. "A pint of Guinness, please."

Elliot strode to the bar and waited for a few moments before he was served.

Spotting Elliot at the bar, Kristian strolled over to him. "Sue not here yet?" he asked.

"Yeah, she is," he nodded, pointing at the corner table where she was sitting.

Kristian took his drink, while Elliot carried Sue's and his own to her table. He handed her the drink, as he and Kristian pulled up a chair to the table.

"How's Sarah doing?" Kristian asked with concern.

"Not so bad, thanks. She's at home now. I've given her strict instructions to rest and take it easy. With Elliot phoning me, it gave me a good reason to get out of the house for a couple of hours, just so we can both have some peace from each other."

Elliot thought it was great fun to catch up with Sue and all her activities since they had lost contact with each other. Kristian thought it was far more fun hearing the odd outrageous story from his partner's history that Sue was willing to divulge. Sue listened intently about stories both Elliot and Kristian had to offer the conversation.

Hearing one of his favourite dance tracks being played, Elliot asked Sue if she would like to have a dance. They got up and danced by the side of the table, rather than making their way onto the dance floor. Elliot put his arms around Sue's waist, who in turn, put her arms around his neck. She rested her head against his shoulder as they swayed with the rhythm of the music. Kristian smiled as he watched the two of them act like a loved-up couple.

"What the hell do you think you're doing?" came the angry voice of a man behind them, who couldn't have been more than twenty-five years old. He had his hands on his hips, looking directly at Elliot, with malice showing in his eyes.

Elliot spun around to face the young man and responded simply with, "Get lost!"

The man raised his hand as if to strike Elliot but Kristian jumped out of his seat like lightning and grabbed the young man's arm, pulling it behind his back.

"Who the fuck do you think you are?" Kristian snarled.

The man looked from Kristian, to Elliot and then finally to Sue and said: "I'll tell you who the fuck I am. I'm her husband."

Steven was busy preparing the food in the kitchen, whilst Michael offered his assistance by setting the table with his one good arm. As the pièce de résistance, he chose to bring out the exquisitely ornate Lalique glass vase that he had purchased in Paris several years ago, after a friend had raved about how fabulously chic and voguish Lalique items were. He carefully positioned the

The Absence of Friends

base in the centre of the table, which he had filled to the point of almost over stuffing it, with carnations: yellow, pink and white.

He stepped back from the table to admire his artistry. He began to let his mind wonder onto the subject of roses and their apparent romantic significance, questioning himself as to why he never had any roses in the house. He knew, of course, that Maxine was allergic to them but he couldn't quite recollect his own reasons why he refused to have them. His response whenever Steven had brought up the topic was because they were a complete waste of money and really, a rather pointless symbol of showing someone that you loved them. He thought harder about the reasoning behind his dislike of roses and came to the conclusion that it was just that. He didn't like roses. They were plain and dull and did nothing to entice his romantic inclinations. Nothing beat a lovely bunch of colourful carnations, which, he thought, were far more romantic than a bunch of roses.

Positioned around the vase, he had three sets of three candles that mirrored the colours of the flowers. He didn't wish to put them so perilously close to the vase that there would be the possibility the flowers might catch alight. He glanced at the clock on the mantelpiece. Seven thirty. It would be too early for him to light the candles just now.

Managing to find four complete sets of matching cutlery, he placed them by each person's matching place mat, along with a matching Swarovski handcut heart wine glass. How he had managed to perform origami on the napkins into a particular design with his one hand, he wasn't entirely sure but they did look impressive. He displayed the newly folded napkins onto each of the placemats. How proud he felt of his little display. Michael always had the view that if a job was worth doing, it was worth spending those extra few minutes to ensure that it was done properly. Most of the time, his artistic talents went completely unnoticed, which he tried hard not to let bother him. Fortunately, this would not always be the case, as he would often ask people what they thought of his handiwork.

Steven's voice emanated from the kitchen. "Have you wrapped up the present yet?"

"No, I haven't" Michael yelled back. "I'll go and do it now."

"Okay but don't be too long because Max and...*Max Squared* will be here soon."

"Even if I do only have one workable hand," he whispered to himself. He strolled into the kitchen, asking: "How's the dinner coming along?"

"Everything seems to be running smoothly, I think," said Steven, slicing the carrots on the chopping board. "Hopefully, by the time they arrive, everything should be just about done...then maybe I can sit down and relax for five minutes...if I get the chance."

"By Jove old chum," Michael began, adopting a classic public schoolboy accent for reasons known only to him. "I do believe you've done a rather spiffing job, if I do say so myself. Rather mighty fine, don't you think, that you aren't one of these laggards who would leave everything until the last minute. Verily, I offer thee felicitations on a job well executed, as I do believe we shall be in for a rather rambunctious evening."

Steven looked up from chopping the carrots and gave Michael one of his *you better behave yourself tonight* looks.

Acting like a reprimanded child by his father, Michael continued to play along with the accent. "Oh crikey, I rather think Pater's on a bally. Drat, botheration and curses to you. Well if you must insist on spoiling all my fun...I promise you, Pater, one shall be on their very best behaviour tonight."

"Don't be cheeky, Michael," said Steven, brandishing the knife playfully, albeit with menace.

Still in his public schoolboy voice, Michael tutted and said scornfully. "Oh, cripes! Mater always insisted that one should never play with knives. And why? Because you could do someone a rather nasty injury, that's why."

"Out!" yelled Steven. "Before I really *do* do someone a nasty injury...and it won't be me!"

Michael skulked out of the kitchen, dragging his feet as he did so.

"Michael! Stop shuffling and pick up your damn feet! You've only got an injured arm, not injured legs!" Steven called out.

He heard Steven's laughter as he climbed the stairs. It made him smile that Steven could take his asinine antics and clowning around with a pinch of salt. Once in the bedroom, Michael switched on the radio and proceeded to wrap the gift they had bought for Max and Maxine.

The doorbell rang just as the jingle leading into the eight o'clock news blasted from the radio. Michael jumped up from the floor, flicked the off switch on the radio and breezed down the stairs at such a pace, he would nearly have taken flight. He flung the door open with such fierce excitement, that Max and Maxine stepped back from the porch with a look of shock on their faces.

"Hi Michael," they gasped in unison.

Michael grinned incandescently at his friends. "Hello, my gorgeous sweethearts." He gritted his teeth, puckered up his lips and ran his one good hand through his hair, in a crude attempt to emulate a model. In a lusty voice, with a hint of an Eastern European accent he said: "And welcome to the humble bordello of Michael Hart and Steven Cronje. Please do feel free enter...although you may wish to with caution."

The Absence of Friends

Max grimaced and Maxine tittered, as she asked: "You do know that you just referred to your home as a house of prostitution?"

"Oh, did I?" he asked, hastily resuming his normal stance. "What kind of dopey mare am I? Of course, I meant to say *abode*!

"Are you feeling okay, Michael?" she asked.

"I suppose that all depends on where in the world I am really," he said thoughtfully, ushering them inside and taking their coats.

"Sorry? What? Am I going mad, or is there some profound hidden meaning to that?" Max still became easily confused by Michael's nonsensical ramblings.

Michael hung the coats on the hat stand. "I thought it was rather quite simple to understand. If I were in America, I would feel a million Bucks. If I were in France, I would feel a million Francs and if I were in Germany, I would feel…"

"A million Marks," Max finished off. "The Pfennig finally drops!"

"Exactly," said Michael, pointing at him.

"How would you possibly manage to cope with feeling a million lads called Mark?" quipped Maxine?

Michael opened his eyes wide, doing his best Eartha Kitt impression. "Don't try and be smart with me, lady. That was a cheap, throwaway line… with the upcoming introduction of the new Euro, my analogy wouldn't have had quite the same impact!"

"I'm really glad to see that you're still your bubbly, cheerful self," Maxine smiled.

"Once I have arisen from my prostrate position, there's just no holding me back."

"Really?" said Max, raising an eyebrow at his self-made innuendo.

"Talking of prostrate positions," began Maxine," how *is* Steven?"

"Oh my darlings…I only have to look at him and my knickers are so moist, they need changing!"

Maxine tutted, while Max rolled his eyes at Michael's frankness.

"That is not what I meant," Maxine chided, "as well you know, Michael."

"I thought I heard my name being taken in vain. What are you three doing out here, anyway?" said Steven, as he made his way from the kitchen.

"Oops," said Michael, twisting his lips in case Steven should chastise him again. "Don't worry Angel, I shall be the hostess with the mostess right now… we can't have *Max Squared* dehydrating through lack of alcohol consumption, can we?"

Throughout the evening there were barely five minutes that passed where there wasn't a burst of raucous laughter, or someone yelling out: "Michael!"

It was after the meal had been finished and the plates cleared away, that Michael decided to give Max and Maxine the present that had been brought for them.

Maxine's eyes widened, as she was presented with the gift by Michael.

"Well, go on…open it," he said impatiently, as though he had no idea what was contained within the wrapping paper.

Gingerly, she took off the paper and opened the box. Inside were several items of clothing for a newly born girl. Maxine's lips slowly emerged into a smile, even though a couple of tears forced their way out of her eyes. "Oh guys," she cooed, wiping the tears from her eyes. "This is so lovely. Thank you so much."

"She *will* come home…and she *will* get the opportunity to wear these," said Steven with a warm sanguinity. "I know that with the brains and brawn of her father and the beauty and bravado of her mother, Thalia will be an amazing little girl, a wonderful young lady and when she reaches womanhood, an absolute force to be reckoned with. She will tread in her parents' footsteps but leave her own unique footprint upon the world."

Tears were streaming from Maxine's eyes, touched by Steven's eulogy. "Thank you, Steven. Those words were beautiful…and meant so much to me."

"There really are no words to describe how much the two of you mean to me, so I am not even going to try and attempt to find any…sufficed to say, I love you both very dearly and you mean the absolute world to me," Michael said solemnly to Max and Maxine, his eyes misting over at Maxine's reaction to the gift and Steven's speech. "There is no limit to our love and so there will be an abundance of love awaiting Thalia, to absolutely smother her with. She's our little Princess Thalia." He glanced at Steven, who enthusiastically nodded in agreement.

"Michael," sobbed Maxine, "that was wonderful." She threw her arms around him and squeezed him.

"Besides," said Michael, his jovial tone returning once more, "although she will clearly inherit the brains, the brawn, the beauty and the bravado from her actual parents, with two Queens as surrogate co-parents, she will also learn how to be comical, feisty, convivial and really, someone quite precocious."

Max and Maxine beamed proudly, knowing that with so many people wanting to look out for Thalia, their little miracle was going to have a great start in life and master so many quality attributes.

The Absence of Friends

The man who had claimed to be Sue's husband was called Jason Simpson, who currently worked on a building site in Hackney. He was somewhat of a peculiar looking individual, as his entirety looked as though he were put together from several different entities, much like Frankenstein's infamous creation.

For a manual labourer of twenty three years old and from the string of expletives that had spewed forth, with ease, from his mouth, both Elliot and Kristian were surprised at how baby-faced Jason looked. Before they were told of his age, they did have their doubts that he had even reached puberty, let alone begun the manly art of shaving. His round, chubby face looked rather strange perched upon his thin - and debatably - malnourished body.

Either Jason didn't care, or lacked self-pride, as he was a particularly untidy and dirty looking person. His matted, sandy coloured hair looked like an untended rose bush that was in dire need of pruning. Neither of the two men would have been the slightest bit shocked if they had learnt that Jason's hair hadn't seen a drop of shampoo in weeks. The clothes that he wore hung loosely from his body and looked as though he had slept in them; probably for as long as his hair had remained unwashed. The two men couldn't ascertain whether Jason had intentionally bought clothes far too big for him, or he didn't have any dress sense whatsoever; they concluded the latter possibility was probably the more likely.

To top off the whole oddly inexplicable ensemble and persona, Jason had a strong Australian accent, despite his trying to disguise it by putting on an English one.

Sue took out a packet of cigarettes from her breast pocket and offered the packet to her husband, who took one. Elliot and Kristian both refused the offer. She lit Jason's cigarette before lighting her own and took a long drag from it.

"I'm really sorry," Jason apologised, still trying to disguise his native accent. "I wasn't going to start a fight. I just think it's funny sometimes when I suddenly announce that Sue's my wife."

"And is she, then?" asked Elliot, eyeing Jason suspiciously.

Sue spoke: "Yes, I am."

Kristian looked confused. "Sorry? Have I missed an episode or two here? Can we rewind a bit for someone who's clearly not astute enough to follow the storyline. What's a straight, married guy doing in a gay bar, looking for his wife, who is apparently a lesbian?" He raised an eyebrow in anticipation of the answer but spoke before he received it. "Or are you bisexual?" he asked, directing the question toward Jason.

Jason smiled, showing his stained, yellow teeth. "No, I'm not bisexual… and I'm not straight either."

I'm guessing that the toothbrush and toothpaste are obviously still sitting on the supermarket shelves, along with the shampoo, Kristian thought to himself.

"So, a marriage of convenience then?" offered Elliot.

"That's right," Jason confirmed.

"We've been married for nearly three years now," said Sue.

"Three years next Friday," Jason added.

"We keep meaning to but we just haven't got around to filing for a divorce yet."

"So," began Elliot, suddenly becoming interested in the topic. "Did you get married because you have a boyfriend here in the UK?"

Jason nodded.

"It's rather interesting that you still stay in contact with each other, even after this length of time. I know you said you haven't yet filed for divorce but I thought that most marriages of convenience stopped the façade after a year or so," Kristian presented clinically.

Jason looked at Sue, a quirky smile creeping across his face. "Shall I tell them, or do you want to?"

Sue leant across the table, as though she were going to whisper a closely kept secret. "He's going out with Sarah's brother."

Kristian rubbed his forehead, feeling as though he had completely lost the plot. "This gets worse."

"It's a small world! Right?" Elliot grinned.

"Sure is," piped Jason, in an accent which now sounded vaguely American. He put his cigarette out in the ashtray. "Anyone for another drink?" he asked, showing off his rotten teeth once again.

The other three gave their orders, which Jason repeated back to them before bouncing off to the bar.

"What on earth made you decide to marry him? He's…um…well, he's quite the character, to put it mildly," Elliot asked, when Jason was well out of earshot.

"It wasn't my idea," she said, as though she had been accused of an immoral act. "It was Sarah's!"

Scott reached for the box of tissues on the table. Grabbing a couple of them, he wiped his eyes with one and blew his nose with the other.

Vince had left the room and announced that he was retiring to bed, not because he was particularly tired but because he thought it may help Scott if he was left alone to think about the conversation they had just had. He guessed that Scott would have plenty to think about and decided it was best if he left Scott alone with his own thoughts to mull over.

The conversation they had, focused mainly on Vince prompting Scott into think about what he thought the future might hold for him and Luke. If he could see a future for the both of them together, he would have to consider how they would progress from this point.

"Luke is a human being too, Scott," Vince had said. "He has real feelings and real emotions, the same as you and I. He is probably just as shit-scared of all of this as you are. Even more so, as he is the one who has to live with it."

"And you think I don't already know that? I have thought constantly about that day, wishing to God that I could turn back time and have dealt with the whole situation in a totally different way. I regret ever walking out of the house now and wish that I had given him the love and support that he so desperately wanted."

"So, what's preventing you giving that love and support to him now? Really, Scott, you should be telling *him* all of this, rather than leaving him to wonder what exactly it is that's going on in that head of yours. He's not a mind reader, so unless you speak up and tell him what it is that you're feeling, he will always be kept in the dark about it."

It was at that exact point that Scott started his long thought process. He was so wrapped up in his own thoughts, he was completely oblivious to Vince leaving the room and announcing that he was off to bed.

His glazed eyes focused upon a picture that was hanging proudly on the wall. It was a blown-up, framed photograph of him and Luke, taken at Luke's twenty-seventh birthday. As far as Scott could recollect, it was taken shortly after Luke had made the announcement that he was to be recording his debut album. They were both so incredibly happy at that point in their lives; nobody and nothing seemed possibly capable of being able to tear their love apart.

Remembering the circumstances of the whole scenario with crystal clarity, Scott found himself sneaking a smile. They had been sharing an intimate embrace, with Luke displaying that demure smile of his that Scott simply could not resist. Out of the blue, someone had come up to them and broke the tender bond of the moment by saying "smile", before the flash of the camera made either of them realise what was actually happening.

The result of that one moment in time being captured was now displayed in the living room. The man who had been responsible for taking the photo had somehow managed to capture the true essence of their love, along with the charming shyness within Luke's eyes. Scott was under no illusion that if the photo had been taken a couple of seconds later, another story would have been told, as their faces would have taken on a permanent look of shock.

How happy he and Luke had been in those days.
All Scott wanted was for those days to return.

Even though Luke had been informed by the doctors earlier on that evening that he was going to be discharged the following day, he felt nothing but numbness. There was no spark of excitable happiness within him that people would have expected. The realisation that he was going home filled him with mixed emotions.

He felt a sense of relief that he was finally able to leave this god-forsaken excuse for a hospital and finally be back in familiar surroundings. He felt a new kind of fear he had never experienced before, as he didn't know what the future might hold for both him and Scott; if indeed there even was any future that featured them together. The most overwhelming of his feelings was that of sadness; a sadness that was slowly pulling him further and deeper into a pit of depression, where he knew he would languish until he was going to die.

Ever since he had told Scott that he was HIV positive, all Luke ever wanted was the emotional support that he had hoped Scott would give him. If he had anticipated the reception that he actually got, he might have thought twice about telling him. He knew, deep down, that was not at all true, as he was not the sort of person to keep a major event of his life hidden from the person who meant the most to him in the world.

He was pleased that Elliot and Kristian had been there to offer him help, support and their undeniably strong love and friendship but Luke had wanted the love of his partner. He couldn't expect either of his friends to hold him in their arms tenderly, kiss him with heartfelt passion and stroke his hair soothingly in the way that Scott could.

Now, though, he felt incredibly alone and isolated. The feeling of bitter loneliness was the one thing that he didn't want to experience. The emotions were sweeping over him with a severe intensity.

He pondered on how much his life had changed over the last few years. Meeting Scott had been the most wonderful thing that had happened to him. Not even the emotions he had experienced when he found himself in the recording studio putting together his debut album compared to what he thought when he had settled himself into his relationship with Scott.

It was far from wonderful now, he thought, as he stretched over to the cabinet next to his bed, to take a tablet. His hand shook unsteadily as he attempted to pour water from the jug into the glass, spilling most of it onto the cabinet and floor. His eyes welled up with the sheer frustration of everything.

He hated his life now. *Life! Huh, what life?* he thought.

He would rather have endured the beatings from his father, than sit in a hospital bed, contemplating his impending death. He wracked his brains, torturing himself, in an attempt to find some rational explanation as to what it was that he had done so terribly wrong in his life that he was being punished in this way but the depression which had sunk so deeply into him, prevented him from doing so.

Wiping his tear-stained face with his hand, he lay back on his pillow and had only one thought constantly going through his mind.

He wanted to die.

CHAPTER FOURTEEN

If anyone had been dreaming of a white Christmas, just like the one's Bing Crosby had sung about, then their dreams had come true. There were three inches of thick, crisp snow lying on the ground, carpeting as far as the eye could see like an explosion of marshmallow, tantalisingly inviting hoards of children to invade the peaceful and harmonious tranquility. The only thing that had spoilt the perfectly smooth snow, were the birds that had done their early morning Christmas dance, fruitlessly searching for their festive delicacies.

Shakin' Stevens' *Merry Christmas Everyone* was emanating from Elliot and Kristian's house, marking the beginning of Christmas Day, as they shared a cuddle, tucked warmly under the duvet. Not that Kristian had a great deal of the duvet to be wrapped in, as Elliot had cocooned himself in the majority of it. However, it was more that Kristian was cuddling Elliot, who refused to open his eyes; moaning about his hangover from the excessive amount of alcohol he had consumed the previous night.

They had been out to one of their favourite clubs, *Guyz & Girlz*, which they had always known as *Whirlwind* under the previous management and still continued to call it so. Kristian had won himself free tickets on the gay radio station, as three of his favourite boybands were all performing there. He knew that the place would be absolutely heaving, as all three bands were currently riding high in the singles charts, so the only way he could possibly ensure guaranteed entry into the club was securing the VIP tickets. As the radio presenter, Dan Hewitt, had called it, it was "a Christmas feast trilogy to be savoured and enjoyed." Not only had Kristian wanted to be heard on the radio, which he had asked Elliot to record but he also had a secret desire to meet Dan Hewitt. He thought Dan sounded really sweet and sexy; though Elliot reckoned he was just your average, every day, smooth-talking radio presenter. Kristian squealed with unmitigated delight when he had won the prize, rushing to tell Elliot of his escapade to the treasure. Anyone listening to his excitable ramblings would have thought he had won a prize worth several hundred pounds and not two tickets worth less than thirty.

The night went painfully slow for Elliot, who spent most of his time at the bar, ordering drink after drink, whilst Kristian remained goggle-eyed at the young men featuring in the *Christmas Feast Trilogy*. Elliot couldn't abide the stereotypical, manufactured boybands, as to him, they were all just singing the same songs, looking like exact carbon copies of one another with the only difference being the name of the band itself. Every flexed muscle, every

The Absence of Friends

contrived dance move and every flash - no matter how brief they were - of the artists' abs and pecs, made Kristian's eyes widen further, allowing himself to sink deeper into his own private desires.

It did put a slight dampener on Kristian's festive spirit, as Elliot would go out of his way to get drunk, making it more of a major task to wade through the sea of bodies: drunk, stoned and half asleep. Elliot always seemed to succeed in upsetting Kristian whenever he got ridiculously drunk, which, over the past few weeks, seemed to become more of a regular occurrence.

As he lay snuggled up to Elliot in bed, rolling his head around his torso in order to find the most comfortable position and playing with the hairs on Elliot's chest, he thought about the Christmas dinner in store. They had invited Luke and Scott, who were bringing along Vince, Michael and Steven and of course, Max and Maxine. Initially, Kristian had the wonderful idea of starting on Christmas Eve by inviting them all to *Guyz & Girlz*. They had all politely declined, as they were planning on doing their own special thing with their respective partners, although they did mention how much they were looking forward to the Christmas dinner.

"Steven and I are planning on having a quiet night in," Michael cooed, during his particular phone call. "We will probably have a sherry, or something, just to be at one with the festive cheer. However, the dinner tomorrow," he said, lightening his tone, "if nothing else, it will save me having to cook…and of course, my delicate hands just don't take to that kind of mass of washing up."

"We might have come to the club with you tonight, but we've only just put Thalia down to sleep and there's no way we would be able to find a babysitter at this late stage," said Maxine apologetically, on her phone call. "But…What a wonderful idea for the Christmas dinner tomorrow. All of us together. All of us celebrating in the one house. Maybe, next year, Max and I can host a Christmas dinner…we'll have to try and get in there first before Michael claims that honour," she giggled.

"I'm not sure we'll be up for going out tonight, guys, as Luke's still feeling quite low to be honest," said Scott in his phone conversation. "He's not sure if he's in the mood to be going out clubbing, so I think it's probably better to play it safe and take a rain check on that one. I'll see how he feels later and if he *is* up for going out, we may see you down there but going by the acts that are on tonight, we will be lucky if we even get to make it in. I'm pretty sure that, tomorrow, having all the people together who love him will be just what he needs in order to lift his spirits once again. I think it's going to be a wonderful day and I can't think of another group of people I would rather be spending Christmas with. Would it be extremely cheeky of us to bring along Vince too?"

Elliot stirred slightly and opened his eyes, adjusting them to the light. "Merry Christmas, darling," he said, trying to get some moisture flowing in his bone dry mouth.

"Merry Christmas, you drunken pisshead," Kristian replied, with a sarcastic smile before giving Elliot a kiss. Climbing out of bed, he reached for his towelling dressing gown hung on the back of the door. "A cup of tea and doughnuts okay for you, for breakfast?"

"Sure," said Elliot simply, through half-closed eyes.

"And you'd better not be asleep when I come back up…it's a nightmare trying to wake you up at times."

"Fret not…I don't want my domestic goddess getting into a tizzy. I shall be ready and waiting for you when you come back."

Kristian watched as Elliot rolled over onto his side, knowing it would only be a matter of seconds before he was fast asleep again. *How perfect*, he thought, as the next Christmas tune came on the radio - he turned up the volume, to allow Mariah Carey to blare into Elliot's ears. Without even turning over to assess his aim, Elliot threw a pillow in Kristian's direction, accompanied with a grunting noise. The pillow naturally missed its expected target but hit the mantelpiece instead, sending Christmas cards floating helplessly onto the floor.

Kristian returned to the bedroom about fifteen minutes later, with a large selection of doughnuts and two mugs of piping hot tea. The steam from the mugs rose and met, dancing mysteriously in time with the music from the radio, which Elliot had lowered to a more acceptable volume for someone who was nursing a nauseating hangover.

Seeing Elliot sitting up, he smiled. "So how's the head then?"

Elliot gave Kristian a look, which suggested to him not to bother to continue pursuing the subject.

"Don't worry," said Kristian, answering his own question. "I've brought a couple of painkillers for you." He put the breakfast tray carefully on the empty half of the bed, then dropped his dressing gown, letting Elliot see his naked body standing in front of him.

"Are you going to get back into bed, then? Or are you just going to stand there all day, freezing?"

Kristian winked suggestively at Elliot, passing him the tray so he could climb back into bed. "Have we ever done it with doughnuts before?"

Elliot raised an incredulous eyebrow. Speaking quite flatly, he simply said: "No!"

"Do I take that to mean that you don't want to give it a go?"

"Yes!"

"Oh, come on, I thought it was a prerequisite to have a bit of festive fun before the day begins. Where's your sense of adventure?"

"Here," said Elliot, holding up the painkillers. He popped a couple into his mouth and sipped his tea.

Kristian looked at the clock. "You've had a lucky escape there, Mr Hayden because I must put the turkey on soon, or else it won't be cooked in time." He ravaged a chocolate doughnut.

"You're a pig!"

"Oh baby, talk dirty to me."

"Honestly," Elliot sighed, "you're really quite disgusting."

After the majority of the doughnuts had been devoured - mainly by Kristian - and the tea drunk, the tray was placed onto the floor. Kristian snuggled up to Elliot again, rubbing his stomach softly with the tips of his fingers. He knew this would arouse Elliot and waited a few minutes before crawling under the duvet, manoeuvring his tongue expertly over Elliot's smooth body, not allowing himself to stop until practically every inch of his body had been covered.

Their lovemaking had begun.

Kristian nearly always climaxed first, finding it more pleasurable to help Elliot reach orgasm, than himself. He watched, wide-eyed, as Elliot shot across his own chest, feeling the sticky moisture run slowly down his stomach and filling the well of his navel.

Breathing heavily, Kristian gasped: "Christmas present number one unwrapped and fully enjoyed."

They lay there, in each other's embrace, for a few minutes before Elliot threw back the duvet. "Are you coming for a shower?" he asked suddenly.

"I've only just cum," joked Kristian.

Elliot groaned. "How many times have used that joke? It stopped being funny about a thousand times ago."

"Oh, I'm so sorry, Ebenezer." Kristian pulled a face, meaning he wouldn't use the joke again if it were no longer funny.

Whenever they showered together, inevitably they would end up making love. Indeed, today was no exception.

As they dried themselves, Elliot broke the silence. "I do love you, you know. I know I probably don't tell you as often as you would like to hear it," he said with romantic poignancy. "So, as of today, I am going to make more of an effort…beginning right now…Kristian Leon Irwin, I love you with my heart, my soul and my all."

Kristian winked at him. "I know you do and I love you too. You know… we've still got time to make it a hat trick if you want."

"Oh God, I'm knackered!"

"Just joking," Kristian smirked.

Like a playful but mischievous kitten, Elliot slapped Kristian lightly on his bare behind. "Get dressed will you, you sex-mad maniac."

Maxine woke to the sound of Thalia's raucous cries. The clock read: 5.52am.

Ever since Thalia had been discharged from the hospital, Maxine was lucky if she would manage three hours of pure, uninterrupted sleep. Her intuition told her that Max was only pretending to sleep whenever there was a sound coming from their daughter's cot. She knew only too well, that if a feather were to fall on the bed, Max would awaken with a bolt, as it seemed as though her husband had added a whole new dimension to the meaning of being a light-sleeper.

Why should Max get off scot-free each time Thalia needs tending to? She prodded him in his ribs. "This time, it's your turn," she said.

He grunted, as he rolled over to face his wife. "Eh? What?"

"It's no use pretending, Max, 'cause you've got away with it for far too long and I'm not falling for it anymore. Your daughter is crying, so it's about time you began doing your duties as a father."

Begrudgingly, he crawled out of bed and sauntered heavily to his daughter's cot. He peered over the side, putting a finger into her tiny hand, which she grabbed with surprising tightness. In a baby-like voice, Max cooed: "What's the matter with Thalia then? What's upsetting my darling girl?"

He picked her up out of the cot and no sooner had his hand slid underneath to cradle her, he knew exactly what the problem was. Thalia gurgled excitedly, as though she were amused by the fact that her father would need to change her soiled nappy. Max held his nose, his face contorting into one of real discomfort, which he made sure Maxine caught sight of, pleading with his eyes that she should be the one to rectify the case of poo-gate.

Maxine shook her head. "Oh no you don't," she began, "I've shown you more than enough times. It's about time you did it for once…then you'll realise just how unpleasant this chore is for me each time."

Max sighed as he left the room to fetch a clean nappy.

"You'll need to clean her bottom too," called Maxine. "*Properly* though… not just a quick wipe down, as you normally do in the kitchen when you're *cleaning* the surfaces!"

"I know," replied the stale voice of her husband.

The Absence of Friends

Maxine giggled inwardly. She quietly reprimanded herself for not getting Max to do his fatherly duties when she was more awake to appreciate and enjoy him making a dockyard job of something quite so simple, which she was confident, would be exactly what he would do.

Max returned to the bedroom with an armful of ointments and creams. Maxine looked at him with unbelievable confusion. "What do you need all those for?"

"To clean her with, of course."

"It's okay," Maxine huffed. "I'll do it. This time…watch me!" She climbed out of bed, to her daughter's cot. It took less than two minutes for her to complete the task. When she had discarded the dirty nappy, she said: "So, now you can make me a cup of tea, while I have a shower. Or do you need me to show you how to do that too?"

"Very funny," quipped Max, as he handed his wife her dressing gown. "Would you like Earl Grey or English Breakfast?"

"Don't we have any Darjeeling?"

Max forced himself not to rise to the bait. "I'll have a look," he said, through gritted teeth. "And if we don't?"

"Oh," Maxine sighed, pondering upon the choices, as if it were life or death dependent. "The Earl Grey, I guess."

Max feigned a smile before leaving the room.

Maxine picked up her daughter and cradled her in her arms, caressing her daughter's cheek lovingly with her fingers. "It's so easy to tease daddy, isn't it?"

A smile emerged on Thalia's face, as if to agree with her mother's rhetorical question.

"And daddy was being very silly about changing your stinky nappy, wasn't he?"

A jovial gurgle was the response this time.

"Mummy's going to take a shower now." She placed Thalia carefully back into her cot and stroked her cheek. She watched as her daughter clasped and unclasped her tiny fingers, as if she were waving her mother goodbye.

Stepping into the shower, Maxine sucked in her breath at the heat of the water. Due to the cold air, it didn't take long for the room to become enveloped in a sheet of steam. She felt invigorated with the water falling over her body, relaxing her tense muscles. She began singing a Christmas carol - the more relaxed she became, the louder she sang. To her, the noise of the falling water became the musical accompaniment that she needed. As she turned herself around in the shower, so the steam turned with her, taking her deeper into her own musical fantasia.

It was her husband's holler that he had made breakfast and fed Thalia that had bought her out of her fantastical dream world. She stepped out of the shower and dried herself thoroughly, enjoying the softness of the towel against her cleansed skin. Afterwards, she lightly talcum powdered herself, using the talc that she would have used on Thalia. Maxine had the view that the body had to be pampered and treated like a temple and she was damn well going to look after her body.

Selecting what to wear became more of a major task for Maxine. She liked to look good as well as feel good. She opted for a sensible but chic outfit, selecting her black 501s, a white t-shirt, the deep scarlet cashmere cardigan that Max had bought for her birthday and a pair of sensible, flat, black shoes. A quick look in the mirror was all she needed before she joined her husband downstairs. His reaction to what she was wearing would be the final approval to herself that she was happy with her outfit. Her hair didn't look quite right, so she brushed the offending areas, until she was satisfied.

Max looked up, as Maxine wandered into the dining room, cradling Thalia in his arms. He let out a long, low whistle. "Doesn't mummy look absolutely beautiful!" he said to his daughter, making it sound more of a statement than a question.

Thalia gurgled her reply anyway.

Maxine sat down at the table and said: "Thank you. You are looking rather handsome yourself."

It was rather fortunate that the house boasted a downstairs shower, as Max had his usual five minute shower, whilst Maxine's lasted over four times longer. This gave Max plenty of time to feed Thalia, prepare the breakfast and get dressed before Maxine had even emerged. He had also opted to wear his black 501's, selecting a light blue, thick cottoned shirt that had enough of the top buttons undone to show off a wisp of his thick chest hair. With shaving his head the day before and his brilliantly white smile, Maxine could quite easily picture him on the front cover of a woman's magazine.

"Merry Christmas to my beautiful baby girl...and of course, to my handsome and sexy husband. I love you both, very much."

"And we love you too, don't we Thalia?"

Thalia jumped up and down on her father's knees, flapping her arms wildly as she gurgled her excitable response.

Steven woke to find Michael singing to him the lyrics to *Merry Christmas, Darling* by The Carpenters.

The Absence of Friends

"Merry Christmas darling," he crooned, "*We're apart that's true. But I can dream and in my dreams, I'm Christmasing with you.*"

"That's…um…very nice, Michael but the song's about two lovers who aren't actually with each other, hence the dream and the fantasy of being together."

"Oh, Steven! Do you *have* to be so literal? Can't you just try and indulge me when I am trying to have a romantic moment with you?"

"I'm sorry," he apologised. "It was very beautiful. Merry Christmas to you."

"Merry Christmas, sweetheart." Michael gave him a big, slobbery kiss.

"You need a shave, Mr Hart."

"What I actually need, Mr Cronje, is a blow job," Michael corrected, in a crass tone.

"You had one last night."

"Oh, am I on rations now? Ah well, you can't blame a boy for trying."

Michael had bought two cups of coffee to the bedroom, placing them on his bedside table, as he lay back down on the bed. He handed Steven one of the cups before reaching to turn the radio on.

He was looking forward to starting the day with the comedy version of *A Christmas Carol* that he had seen advertised in the *Radio Times*. A string of popular comedians had been cast into the roles of narrator, Scrooge and ghosts of Christmas present, past and future. The magazine had described the festive production as: *The classic Dickens tale has been given a rather humorous makeover that will have the listener wishing they had their own hilariously hedonistic journey into the past, present and future by three amusingly unorthodox ghosts.* Neither man was disappointed with the production, as they were in fits of uncontrollable laughter. Not solely because there were side-splittingly funny parts throughout but because of the actors who had been cast into the roles and their own unique portrayal of the characters.

"This is just as outrageously camp as LaSandra DeSouza's show," Michael chuckled.

Steven nodded in agreement.

LaSandra DeSouza was the up-and-coming Afro-American, lesbian comedienne, whose comedy act centred mainly on racial prejudices, body image and sexuality. Her show had the two men laughing so much that they ached. The show had been advertised as: *This is pure comedy entertainment at its very best - we guarantee you will leave the show with your sides splitting and your mouth aching from all the laughter*, which had them both doing just that. Even after they had arrived back home, there was still the odd burst of laughter coming from one or both of them, when they thought of a particular line from the show, which they ended up reciting to each other, word-for-word.

"Oh my God!" Michael exclaimed, in almost a shriek. "Will you just look at the time!"

Steven looked at the clock. "Hell! It's five past ten."

"We've got to get our skates on, sweetheart, or else we'll be late."

The two men were so absorbed in the radio programme that they forgot about the time. They were meant to be at Elliot and Kristian's for midday. If they didn't hurry, they would almost certainly be arriving there late, especially as Michael took delight in spending an eternity in the shower. Steven was never quite sure what he did in there for so long. Whenever they showered together, it never took longer than fifteen minutes, as neither was particularly turned on by making love in the shower or the bath. The kitchen table and the living room sofa, however, were a completely different kettle of fish.

"We'll shower together," suggested Steven, knowing that this would save them a considerable amount of time.

"Sure thing," said Michael, sensing Steven's anxiety.

Thirty minutes later they were showered, groomed and dressed.

"What do you want for breakfast?" asked Steven.

"I was just thinking about that very dilemma," replied Michael.

"And what was your conclusion?"

"I really fancy a fruit salad."

"A fruit salad? Don't you want something a little more substantial?"

Michael shook his head, whilst patting his stomach. "My weight, Steven. Remember, I'm trying to lose some weight."

Steven nodded. He remembered that Michael had sworn to stick to a stringent diet after his weight had shot up by well over a stone. Michael was very particular about his weight and rued the recent times where he had indulged himself in one too many takeaways and cream cakes. Food items that were really meant to be a once-in-a-blue-moon treat and not part of his regular diet. Steven, on the other hand, concluded that Michael couldn't have been *that* particular, or else his weight wouldn't have gotten into such a state that he found it necessary to go on a strict diet.

"So, are you not eating anything, sweetie?" asked Michael, diving into his fruit salad and watching Steven pack a bag with the presents they had bought for the others.

"I'll have a slice of toast in a minute, I think."

"And there you were talking about me having something more substantial."

When Michael finished his breakfast, he washed and dried the dishes. Steven was pleasantly surprised by this, as it was usually he who ended up doing all the washing and drying. He thought it only fair though, as it was usually Michael who was responsible for cooking the meals.

Satisfied that everything was in order, Michael asked: "Are you ready to go then?"

Steven scanned the room to make sure they hadn't forgotten anything. "I think so."

"Do you need to go to the toilet before we set off?" Michael joked, mimicking the banal phrase of a stereotypical mother before a journey.

Playing along with the charade, Steven spoke like a young boy. "No, I went for a wee tinkle just a few minutes ago…and yes, I *did* remember to wash my hands!"

"Well then, let's go."

Steven picked up the bag of presents, leaving Michael in charge of locking up the house.

Vince could hear the rhythmic banging of the headboard from Scott and Luke's bedroom. He wished he were with Félix in Germany, caressing his beautifully bronzed body and smothering him with festive kisses, as no doubt there would be mistletoe hanging above the bed. Feeling himself becoming aroused, he decided to dismiss any further thoughts of Félix. It was frustrating enough knowing that Scott and Luke were making love in the room above him and he only had the potential comfort of his right hand, which quite frankly, he thought, was no real comfort at all, nor was it any consolation. In fact, it was damned annoying.

He chose to watch a DVD to take his mind off his current train of erotic thoughts. The DVDs were stacked neatly under the television, in a made-to-measure mahogany cabinet. It was nice to see that they were all alphabetised, with the self-recorded films clearly marked with the name of the film and the main star. A comedy was what Vince was in the mood for, so he selected *Death Becomes Her*, which starred Goldie Hawn and one of his favourite actresses, Meryl Streep. He popped the DVD into the machine and grabbed the remote control unit from the table, as he made himself comfortable on the sofa.

Meryl Streep's character had just broken her neck by falling down a flight of stairs, when Scott walked into the living room. "Merry Christmas," he chirped at Vince.

"Ah, you're up."

"Very perceptive of you," said Scott, with sarcasm.

"Is Luke up too?"

"He's in the shower just now, so he'll be down in a few minutes."

Vince was only half listening to Scott, as well as trying to keep track of what was happening in the film. He decided it was a futile task in doing both and so switched the film off.

"Have you had any breakfast?" asked Scott.

"I had a bowl of muesli."

"Would you like a cup of tea, or coffee?"

"No, thanks. I really must think about having a shower and getting dressed. It's almost ten o'clock and if I don't get my arse into gear, we will end up being late."

"Is it really that late, already?"

Vince nodded, as he picked up his cup and followed Scott into the kitchen. "Why don't you sit down and I will make you a cup of tea before I hit the shower," he offered.

Scott sat at the table. "Thanks."

"Shall I make Luke one, whilst I'm at it?"

"I think so, please. He should be down in a minute or two."

Scott had convinced Luke that it would probably do him the world of good to get out and let his hair down for a few hours, rather than stay cooped up in the house all night. The three men had, therefore, chosen to go to *Secrets* for their Christmas Eve night out. Luke had spent most of the night sitting by himself at the table, toying with each drink he had, while Scott and Vince danced and chatted the night away. They had both noticed that Luke had become increasingly introvert since leaving the hospital and whenever the subject of his medical incarceration had arose in conversation, he would become progressively more upset, clamming up and refusing to talk. Vince wasn't overly convinced that it was the best idea to bring Luke out for the evening, suggesting to Scott that they should have let him come to terms with his traumas in his own time. They had tried on several occasions during the night to engage him in conversation but he wasn't showing any signs of interest in pursuing any of the topics raised. It was becoming apparent, or seemingly apparent, that although Luke preferred to be in the presence of company, he would rather be left alone to his own thoughts.

Luke had also become prone to bouts of depression, which could last anything from a few hours to a few days. Scott was becoming more and more concerned the longer these episodes lasted. Due to Vince's prompting, he sought professional medical advice. The doctor had given Scott two options: either for Luke to seek help from a specialised counsellor, or to have a psychiatric evaluation done, dependent on how severe the bouts of depression were affecting him. Scott posed these options to Luke who wouldn't have any

The Absence of Friends

of it. He promised Scott that he was fine, not that Scott fell for Luke's pretence in the slightest.

The doctors at the hospital were almost certainly convinced that Luke's condition was purely psychosomatic but he still had to take good care of his health. Luke, on the other hand, was not convinced that his health was as stable as he was being led to understand; believing the doctors were only trying to placate his fears. Scott trod carefully, attempting to explain to Luke that there was nothing wrong with developing the symptoms psychosomatically and really, there was absolutely nothing for him to feel embarrassed over. Nothing that anyone said to Luke seemed to make one iota of difference to him.

Plain and simple, he was convinced he had developed the AIDS symptoms and that he was going to die. It was just a matter of when.

While Vince was waiting for the kettle to boil, he said: "I really enjoyed last night."

"It was fun, wasn't it?"

"...and didn't you think it was ever so funny when Mr Show-Off fell off the stage? He really loved himself, flexing his muscles and leering at everyone. The look on his face after he fell was a complete picture," said Vince, still reliving the memories of the previous night. The kettle clicked its switch off, making Vince aware he could proceed with making the drinks.

Scott continued with the memory, saying: "I really thought that someone was going to hit him. Everyone was getting thoroughly annoyed that he kept knocking into them."

"Well, that's why I ended up walking off...I needed to get as far away from him as I could, otherwise it would probably have been *me* who was the one to hit him," explained Vince, stirring the drinks.

"Oh, right."

"You were probably too pissed by that time to actually realise."

"No, not at all! I remember you walking off. I thought it was just because you didn't like the song that was playing," Scott chortled.

Vince settled the drinks down on the table, adjusting his dressing gown as it had become loose. "Scott, listen...if a queen walks off the dance floor when an Abba track comes on, then there has to be something seriously wrong with them. If there's nothing wrong with them, then that's just a sad state of affairs to be in. Don't you think?"

"Oh, a suicidal travesty, for sure," grinned Scott.

"Listen, you can bet your bottom dollar that if a *total* screaming queen were busting for a slash, they would still be able to hold off long enough to allow themselves to bop to a classic Abba track...come to think of it, the same rule applies to Kylie's, Madonna's and even Steps' tracks. God alone only knows how they would manage it if all four artists' records were played consecutively."

Scott sipped his tea. "Oh God," he began, as another slice of memory came flooding back to him regarding Mr Show-Off. "When you walked off, you missed the best bit…"

"Why? What happened?" Vince asked with unmitigated interest. "Please tell me that someone finally got round to wiping that smug look off his face? Oh," he shuddered, "that fake, perma-grin of his still completely grates upon me."

Scott retold the story with accurate precision, almost as if he were back in the club, giving an account of the events as they were playing out. "…it was quite obvious that he had had far too much to drink, going way and beyond his own limitations. You know the typical kind of person who likes showing off to their mates, drinking way more than they can actually handle? They feel they have to prove some masculine one-upmanship, for whatever reasons that are floating around inside their pea-sized brains.

"Well, I guess all that exaggerated moving and shaking he did which, I have to point out was totally lacking any real rhythm with the music, didn't help matters. Not that I felt the slightest bit sorry for him. Anyway, it looked more than a little obvious that he was about to throw up. I guess he tried to make a mad dash for the toilets, in order to save himself the embarrassment and retain his self-proclaimed macho image that I can only assume someone like him would want to preserve."

"So, what did you do?" asked Vince, hanging on his every word.

"Well, naturally I followed him. And let me tell you, he didn't quite make it!" He laughed before continuing. "Though, I did feel sorry for the poor sod that had to cut their night short because he was unfortunate to be in the idiot's way. Maybe if he wasn't so shocked and mortified, he would have been the one to have decked Mr Show-Off."

"That's awful," said Vince, with empathy. "That happened to me in Paris once. Some little twat, who thought he was Mr Wonderful and…well, it's basically the same thing that happened. He threw up. I was in his way. I can tell you, I was not amused. What happened to the guy anyway?"

"He was unceremoniously thrown out and barred."

Vince nearly choked with laughter. "Excellent! Although he deserved everything he got, don't you think that's a bit of harsh result? Just for being sick!"

"There's probably more to it than that. I wouldn't be surprised if several people had complained during the course of the night about his behaviour. I could see by the looks on some peoples' faces and their reactions to his bloody-mindedness that could easily have happened. I would love to know what his mates made of the whole thing…I bet they'll give him a real ribbing."

Both men laughed.

"What's so funny?" came Luke's voice from the open door.

"I was just telling Vince what happened to Mr Show-Off last night."

"Oh, him," Luke spat. "What a complete and utter twat he was. Losers like him deserve anything and everything that comes their way in the form of retribution."

"Exactly," said the other two in unison.

"He nearly knocked over the whole table that I was sitting at, when he fell off the stage. He was very fortunate that he wasn't covered from head to toe in beer."

"It would have served him right if he had been," said Vince.

"What is fortunate is that he didn't fall on top of you," offered Scott.

"He was built like a brick shit-house and would have flattened me like a pancake if he had."

Vince yawned and stretched his tired limbs. "Anyway, enough of this frivolity. Time is ticking on and I'm going to have a shower and get myself dressed."

"Okay. See you in a few minutes," said Scott.

"That's for sure," came Vince's voice, already ascending the stairs.

"Vince made you a cup of tea," Scott said, handing Luke the cup.

"Thanks." Luke took the cup and drank it in half a dozen mouthfuls.

"How are you feeling?"

"All the better for having a shower."

No sooner had Luke spoken, they heard Vince's throaty, totally out-of-tune singing come floating from the shower room. He was singing one of Luke's songs from his album, entitled *Love Never Dies*, which Vince had pointed out to Luke, was his favourite song from the album.

"…*even in dreams, they are filled with my love. To the ends of the earth, to the skies up above. It is everlasting, 'cause there is no measure. Like diamonds and gold, love is the treasure. It is everlasting, 'cause there is no limit. Distance cannot quench it and death cannot claim it. Love never dies even with my last breath…I will whisper your name.*"

"Talk about murdering a beautiful song," croaked Scott.

Luke was glued to the spot, listening intently to the words he had written.

"…*Love is what we make it, truly forever. Held by your arms, binding together. Believe when I say, love never dies. Love never dies even with my last breath…I will whisper your name.*"

"Don't you just abhor his singing?" asked Scott, a little too bubbly.

"I wrote that song for us, you know."

"Yes, I know." Scott kissed Luke, showing his appreciation. "It's a beautiful song. I absolutely love it."

"But do you *believe* the lyrics?"

Scott pondered upon the question for a few moments. "I guess so. Why?"

The tears fell from Luke's eyes, stinging them.

"What's wrong, Luke?" asked Scott gently.

"I *don't* believe the lyrics. How can I not believe the words that I wrote? What's happening to me, Scott?

"Hey. Come on. It's okay. I know you're upset by what's happened recently but *love is what we make it*, right?" He took hold of Luke's hand, staying quiet for a few moments.

Their moment of silent unity was shattered, like being woken from a beautiful dream, as Vince stepped into the room. He noticed them pulling their hands away from each other. "I'm sorry," he apologised, "I can come back in a few minutes if you want some time alone."

"No. Don't be silly," Scott reassured him.

"I guess we ought to leave now anyway. We'll be very late if we don't," said Vince pragmatically.

Scott sucked in his breath, as he looked at his watch. "Oh God, you're right."

They moved hastily, clearing away the dishes and collecting the things they needed to take with them.

"Everyone ready then?" asked Scott.

The other two murmured, nodding their heads.

"Good," stated Scott. "Let's go and have ourselves some fun." He rattled the car keys as if to finalise the decision.

CHAPTER FIFTEEN

Elliot and Kristian had slaved away for what had seemed like an eternity, in order to turn their dining room into one with a slight French, post-medieval look and a subtle hint of fairytale camp.

"Really?" questioned Elliot, when he realised what Kristian was intent on doing. "You honestly want to mix a classy, post-medieval theme by being over-indulgent with a bit of Disney-style camp?"

"Yes, I really do," said Kristian, feeling slightly indignant that Elliot would question him. "You see, apart from Max and Maxine, it's going to be a room full of queens," he said. "So, I thought it would be a good idea to dilute the butch serfs and wenches feel that we've currently got going on, with some high-class camp."

"Okay, if that's what you want. Personally, I don't think the two themes will mix very well. To be honest, it's really only Max who is the stand alone person; the odd man out if you will. Not that I'm calling Max odd, you understand...not by any stretch of the imagination. He's far from being *odd*."

"What on earth are you wittering on about?" snapped Kristian.

"Well," Elliot began to explain, "when you put both Maxine and Michael in the same room together, she can be just as camp as he is...sometimes it's hard to tell the two apart when they're both in full swing."

"Apart from the fact that she's got boobs and Michael hasn't!"

"All I'm saying is, she has to be made an honorary queen because, quite frankly, I do feel that she's really a gay man trapped in a woman's body."

"Maybe that explains why you were attracted to her all those years ago!"

It was Christmas Eve and both men had just finished putting the final touches to their themed room. Kristian, particularly, was incredibly proud and thrilled by the end result. He had placed little homemade place names at everyone's designated position at the table. Hours had been spent meticulously designing something unique, personal and poignant to each individual in the hope that these diminutive niceties would be noticed and appreciated. It was a foregone conclusion to Kristian that on no account were any couple permitted to sit together. He wanted the group to be completely mixed *not* matched.

Surveying his handiwork on the new-look dining room, Kristian asked: "So, what do you think?"

Elliot had his arm around Kristian's waist, giving him a one-armed hug. "I think it looks great," he said, sucking in his breath, wondering if Kristian wanted him to expand any further on compliment he was clearly fishing for.

He decided that it was probably prudent to add something extra. "In fact, I'd even go as far as to swallow my previous reservations, as it's so much better than I thought it would be, when you first suggested you were going to do this."

Elliot had not been entirely convinced about the idea when Kristian had originally come up with it. He left his partner to his own creative devices, as he began to ponder over drawing up the shopping list of what he thought they might need in order to make the day as great a success as they could manage. He did, though, completely understand Kristian's reason for wanting to do something completely different this year, as he was more than a little bored of carrying out the same old boring routine that they had to contend with year after year. He just thought, without seeing the finished result, that Kristian's particular choice of idea was not the best one that he could have come up with.

They had both been out shopping over the past few days, in order to purchase all the items that they believed they needed for their Medieval Christmas extravaganza. They had shopped from morning until night, in order to find just the right objects d'art and various materials for the room. All their modern pieces of furniture and other such bric-a-brac would have to be stored elsewhere, temporarily.

The first major task was to clean and scrub the room from top to bottom. Kristian suggested he start at the ceiling and work his way downwards, while Elliot would start at the skirting boards and work his way up, until the met in the middle. They were both surprised that the room took nearly an entire day to thoroughly clean, realising that it was probably a good idea that they took the few days before Christmas off work, although Kristian's idea of repainting the walls was immediately balked at and dismissed by Elliot. If they had left all the work to do during a weekend, which is what they had originally planned to do, they wouldn't have been able to complete it all on time. Everyone would have arrived for their day of festive fun, to what would have looked like someone moving house.

Thankfully, for their pièce de résistance, an intricate and beautifully carved Louis XVI dining table was found and picked up from a shop in Brighton that majored in period furniture and clothing. Even though it was only a reproduction, it was surprisingly inexpensive. Neither man was prepared to spend several thousand pounds on a mere whim, which was roughly what they discovered the cost to be in their initial research. Nevertheless, both men fell in love with the piece of furniture instantly, especially as they found it easy to picture taking centre stage within their dining room and indeed, that was exactly where they had positioned it.

Elliot, as a final straw, decided to put his foot down when Kristian suggested that they strew wood chippings and sawdust over the floor, just to give it that extra authentic look.

"Are you serious?" asked Elliot, not making any attempt to hide his shock.

"Why? What's wrong with that idea? Do you think it's a bit over-the-top?"

Elliot gave and exasperated sigh. "Um…just a bit."

"But I bet nobody else has ever thought of doing anything like this."

"I wonder why," stated Elliot. "For starters, there is absolutely no way that I am willing to ruin the carpet, just so you can have sawdust and wood chippings down for a couple of days."

"What if we take the carpet up?"

"Are you really serious with these questions? Are you hearing how silly the whole idea sounds?"

"Why? You're making me sound like I'm abnormal."

"No, *you're* not abnormal but the whole idea absolutely is." He gave Kristian a dismissive shake of his head. "I don't mind buying the furniture, the candelabra and even a few odds and sods here and there to make the place look authentic but really, there is just no way I am going to entertain the whole sawdust and chippings on the floor business. The idea is just completely absurd."

The chairs were also cheap imitations, to match the table that Kristian had found, advertised in a newspaper, although he had to go to Hertfordshire in order to collect them. He knew the others would think they were completely mad after all the trouble they had gone to but as they were genuinely excited about their little enterprise, they didn't let it bother them what the others might think. There were seven more people coming to the Christmas dinner and they were fortunate enough to be able to buy ten matching chairs. Elliot thought it wise to buy an extra one, just in case any unforeseen accident might happen and then, all bases would be covered.

"Perfect," said Kristian, as though he had created something outstandingly special but, to him, he had.

The candelabras and other objects d'art were picked up in various junk shops and antique fairs that they managed to discover within a reasonable travelling distance. Not that they would have minded travelling a bit further because both were thoroughly enjoying the whole experience. The material they used for the faux drapes was picked up in a shop they stumbled upon in a backstreet in Kent, which used to trade as a costumier.

Their efforts had definitely paid off, as the room looked as reasonably close as to what they had originally envisaged.

"It's gorgeous," said Elliot, smiling as though he were the cat who just acquired some cream.

"So you really do like it? I know you weren't keen on the idea initially."

Elliot's eyes smiled, to match the curvature of his lips. "Yeah, I really do like it. I think we've done really well. Actually, I'm so impressed with our efforts, I defy anyone to say the room looks terrible."

Kristian sighed deeply, as exhaustion of his efforts finally set in. "Good."

"I don't know about you," began Elliot, "but I think we should have a drink to celebrate."

"Another reason for you to open a bottle, you mean?"

"Please don't nag me again, will you?" Elliot puffed.

There one-glass celebration turned into a lot more. Elliot had nearly drunk his way through three bottles of Tocai Friulano, an Italian wine full of peachiness and minerality, which was fast becoming one of his favourite to have stocked in the house. Kristian managed a glass from each of the opened bottles, sipping daintily and swishing the liquid around his mouth as though he were an established wine connoisseur but of course, there was absolutely no way he was going to follow in the footsteps of the real experts by using a spittoon.

"Babe, please don't get drunk tomorrow," Kristian pleaded, picking up from the earlier conversation. "You'll end up embarrassing both yourself and me, beyond what is obviously unavoidable." It was becoming extremely tiresome for Kristian to keep asking this of Elliot time and again whenever they hosted, or were invited to a dinner party but he felt it needed to be said. He pictured himself like a mother, telling her child on their way to a party, not to forget to say please and thank you. Kristian had found himself in a few embarrassing situations due to Elliot's drunken escapades, when he was in one of his stupors and he wasn't prepared to put up with it any longer. If Elliot wanted to get drunk at home, or even if he went out on his own and got drunk, fine but there was no way he was going to continue to keep apologising and making excuses for Elliot's behaviour, which he found totally inexcusable anyway.

Keeping Elliot from drinking all the alcohol before Christmas Day was becoming almost a full-time job for Kristian - his tact for ensuring that this could be achieved was to deliberately leave buying it all until as late as possible. The drinks cabinet was full of various alcoholic drinks, including a selection of red and white wines. They even persuaded each other - not that they were really looking for an excuse - to treat themselves to a couple of bottle of expensive champagne.

The Absence of Friends

"Elliot!" Kristian would exclaim every time he caught him at the drinks cabinet. "This is not meant for general consumption. If you keep drinking it all like water, we'll have none left for Christmas."

"Will you please stop nagging me, Kris," Elliot moaned.

As Elliot had told Kristian, everyone who arrived on Christmas Day gasped at the dining room, commenting on how impressive it all looked.

"Well, this is basically what you would call your average queen of minimalism's objets d'Art central," said Michael, as he began to semi-plagiarise lines from the script of a previous series of *Absolutely Fabulous*, and then claim it as his own material. "But Jesus Christ, Elliot! This little lot must have cost you quite the pretty penny. Tell me, how on earth did you manage to pay for it all? Did you have to cancel your aromatherapy, your psychotherapy, your reflexology, your osteopath, your homeopath, your naturopath, your crystal reading, your shiatsu, your organic hairdresser…and then, have to postpone Kristian's re-birthing until next year?"

"When someone feels the need to repeat scripts, almost verbatim, over-and-over again, it really does begin to grate on your nerves," said Steven, who winced at Michael's recital. "I mean, don't get me wrong, *Absolutely Fabulous* was indeed just that but sometimes, I wish it had never been on. At least then Michael wouldn't be reciting lines at any available opportunity. To be honest, it's becoming a bit of a nightmare - and rather boring, to say the least - wondering when and where he's going to break into an Edina-ism or Patsy-ism."

Maxine interjected. "Ah! Leave the poor lamb alone." She put her arms around Michael and gave him a hug. "There, there, there," she said, patting his head as though he were a young boy.

"Watch the hair," he warned Maxine, combing it with his fingers, hoping it wasn't creating any further damage.

Michael was particularly fussy with his hair. It had to look perfect before he was entirely happy about it. He always told himself that his hair was very important when wanting to create an impression. "Hair tells someone a lot about you," he said to the group. What it actually *did* tell people, he didn't have the slightest idea. Michael was the sort of person you could play a practical joke on and he would be gullible enough to believe it. It was actually Scott who had told him the story about the hair and that people could determine a lot from it. Michael, being Michael, began to take a great deal of interest in what Scott was telling him.

"…You can't let it grow too long," Scott had said, "because people would then think that you were lazy and also very untidy. Even if you had your hair long but it was kept neat, people would think you were a hoarder; the sort of person that hung onto things, regardless of whether they were needed or not."

Michael opened his eyes with full interest. "What if I have my hair really short?"

Scott shook his head. "Oh, goodness! No! You mustn't have your hair short. Short hair represents someone who will only make do with the bare essentials. They feel that they don't deserve to have nice things around them and that material wealth is something that cannot be revered."

"Oh," said Michael, genuinely surprised.

"That's not all," continued Scott. "A person with short hair is not someone who is spontaneous. An impromptu activity would go against everything they believed in, as they need structured planning and time to prepare."

"What about a parting?"

"If you're a compulsive cleaner and obsessive about tidying up then that's what a parting would represent."

"Dyed?"

"Only if you have something to hide! Those people are deceitful and devious, continually wanting to cover up the truth. Like the hair, what is the point of not showing your true colours? The dye grows out, the hair gets cut and then, the true colours are shown once more! There really is no hiding with dyed hair."

"What about gelled hair, then?"

"Ah, now you're talking. Gelled hair shows that you are a risk-taker. You're not afraid to take on a challenge and try something new. It shows that you're solid in your beliefs and will not be compromised for anyone…of course, the more gel you use, the more prone you are to being the kind of person to bounce back from life's little trials and tribulations."

Michael stocked up on plenty of hair gel after this conversation.

It was clear that Michael had believed every word of what Scott had told him. It only dawned on him that what had been said was nothing more than a complete fabrication, when he visited his barber at the salon.

Raphaël, who was Michael's usual barber, was twenty-seven years old. He was born on the Côte d'Azur, in the south east corner of France. Having originated from the Mediterranean coastline, Raphaël boasted beautifully smooth and rich, olive-skin, which many other men envied. Not Michael though, as Max had told him that darker skin ate all the nutrients in the body, leaving it lethargic and elastic by the time you hit your forties. Of course, Michael, in his gullible naiveté, was completely taken in by Max's believable tale.   Michael really liked having his hair cut by Raphaël, not only because he enjoyed hearing his thick, French accent and charming pronunciations of

The Absence of Friends

English words, but he seemed to get a more personable and intimate service from him, than with previous barbers he had been to. Raphaël's hands were extremely soft and gentle, whenever he touched Michael's face in order to move the position of his head. Michael thought they didn't quite fit the ruggedly masculine look, along with his designer stubble, or *barbe de plusieurs jours*, as Raphaël had once told him, but this only added to the mystical allure.

"Dommage," Raphaël sighed wistfully, when Michael didn't wish to entertain any of his suggested hairstyles for him.

Michael confided in Raphaël on why it so important for him to want his hair to look a specific way and that it should be exactly right.

Raphaël laughed at Michael's explanation, having to bite his lip in order to contain himself. "Vous êtes très drôle, Michael. Someone, I think, has been telling you very silly stories."

"What?" Michael said with incredulity, confused and feeling slightly abashed that Raphaël had found his explanation so hilarious.

"C'est vrai, je crains. Yes, your hair will tell people nothing about how you would live your life. Je suis désolé. So sorry."

Michael felt extremely foolish. How many times had he fallen for one of the others' jokes? Hundreds, he imagined. This was just another one to add to the long list of many, of his failed realisations that a joke was being played upon him.

Maxine apologised for messing Michael's hair up and he accepted graciously, as though he were about to receive a knighthood, rather than a simple apology. The others just looked at Michael with gratuitous disbelief with how he acted.

"Well, I for one," began Vince, "think you've done a great job on your dining room. I really like it."

The others nodded in agreement.

Elliot said: "Kris was really worried that you wouldn't like it."

"There was absolutely no need for him to think that. It looks wonderful… and it's certainly different from what you'd expect to see at this time of year," offered Steven.

"Thank you," said Kristian.

"It must have taken you ages to get all the right materials and little bits and pieces you've got going on here," suggested Scott.

"Once we put our minds to it," said Elliot, "and knew exactly what we wanted to do, everything we needed just seemed to materialise in one way or t'other." He winked surreptitiously at Kristian. They decided it wise not tell the real, convoluted story of how they had managed to attain the "unequivocal stunningly gorgeous furniture," as Maxine had referred to it.

Max offered his piece and said: "It certainly is different. The atmosphere it creates seems to be more relaxed and calm. Did you know that Michael?" He turned to Michael, to make sure he was listening.

"Did I know what, sweetie?"

"That different atmospheres in a room can enhance a particular mood?"

Michael was not going to fall for another of their wind-up games. "Oh, sure Max. Like everyone here is experiencing the same mood. Get real! I'm not falling for one of those pathetically fatuous games again."

The others laughed.

"It's true," said Steven and Maxine, almost at the same time.

"He is actually right," offered Vince.

"It's a known fact," chipped in Elliot.

"Sure it is." There was a strong note of sarcasm in Michael's voice. He had been fooled once too often by one or more of those who stood in front of him - he was not about to allow himself to be fooled again, no matter how many people tried to persuade him what Max was saying was, as Scott had put it, *the God's honest truth.*

Max continued pragmatically: "Well, results of research studies have revealed that rooms with a bright light, for example, either natural or artificial, can improve outcomes of health, such as anxiety, depression and sleep deprivation."

Kristian's voice rose above the noise of the others wishing to put in their contributions. "Hey! Give him a break will you. This *is* Christmas, after all. We should all be drinking and having fun."

Elliot joined in. "Who wants to crack open some wine?"

The noise that came after Elliot's suggestion gave him the answer he required, as he selected a bottle of white wine and searched for the cork screw within the cutlery drawer in the kitchen. This always happened to him - never being able to find the damn thing whenever he wanted it. If only he could remember where he had put it the last time he used it. He recalled placing it down on the drinks cabinet which, he thought, would be the most likely place for it to be. Sure enough, hidden amongst the many bottles of various alcohols, there it lay.

Assuming the role of waiter, Elliot found a silver tray and placed the full wine glasses onto it. He meandered through the others, offering a drink to anyone who cared to have one.

Luke watched the various scenes playing out before him, after he had taken a drink from the tray and thanked Elliot. Everyone seemed to be in their little clique, excluding him from their jovial conversations. It seemed to

The Absence of Friends

Luke that they were deliberately trying to avoid acknowledging his presence and even his very existence.

He studied each of the groups carefully.

Michael was being his usual over-the-top self, with Maxine laughing mechanically at anything and everything he said. If they didn't tone themselves down, he thought, they would wake Thalia up, who was blissfully unaware of the goings-on beneath her. Just as well, he thought, as he really couldn't be coping with a screaming baby, as the noise level from all the adults was enough already.

Then there was Max, Vince and Kristian having what seemed like a very intense discussion about the possibility of various taxation rises that were imminently coming into play. So much for the Christmas celebrations, he thought, as he couldn't think of anything more mind-numbingly boring to talk about than the state of the economy and political differences.

Lastly, there was Steven and Scott, who had just been joined by Elliot. God only knows what drivel they were talking about, as they were a little too far out of his range to be able to hear properly. However, try as he might, he desperately focussed on the group, straining to shut out the noise of the others, attempting to decipher what the content of their riveting conversation might be. He was able to pick up the odd word here and there like, "…another album", "…prognosis", "…depression", "…treatment" and "…his own time". *So they don't mind talking about me*, he thought, *but nobody thinks to talk to me*.

With Michael and Maxine constantly screaming and the increasingly loud, heated discussion regarding Government increases, it was a wonder that Luke could hear himself think at all.

The more he gazed upon everyone's smiling, jovial faces, the angrier he grew. He hadn't particularly wanted to come along to the dinner party, and had told Scott so. Reading a book in front of the fire had held far more appeal to him, although Luke knew, deep down, that this wasn't actually true. He was feeling increasingly distressed about his illness and predicting - by self-prognosis - that his future was likely to look very bleak. He guessed that it was this reason why everyone had chosen to ignore him. A cunning little plan was beginning to formulate inside Luke's head; if people were going to brush him aside, they wouldn't after what he was intending on doing. He was opting for an attempted suicide bid as the easiest way to make people stand up and take notice of him. He would get a knife from the kitchen, maybe scream and shout a little and tell everyone that they would be a whole lot better off if he was dead. *Knowing Scott*, Luke thought, *he would make a mad dash for me and grab the knife before he believed I would slash my wrists. Everyone would be completely shocked, but at least it would finally get me noticed.*

That was how Luke's initial plan had started out before he sat down to dinner with the others. Watching everyone laughing and joking together put his rational thinking out of all proportion, as he decided that he would actually do it for real. *They seem to be having a great deal of fun without even acknowledging me, so I might as well be dead*, he thought.

The meal that Elliot and Kristian had prepared was going down a real treat with the guests at the table. They began with Vichyssoise soup and sesame toast, which was swiftly followed by prawn cocktail with a special sauce concocted by Kristian, who was very reticent about revealing his secret recipe to Maxine when she asked him for it. The main course was a choice between Duck à l'orange or Coq au Vin, accompanied with perfectly roasted potatoes, garlic and herb stuffing balls, sausages wrapped in bacon and a selection of various vegetables.

The choices of dessert were highly tempting, where most of the guests found it difficult to narrow their decision down to just one and so opted for two, or for the more adventurous of the group, all three. Firstly, there was the traditional Christmas pudding, topped with either rum sauce, brandy sauce or custard; or again, for those who found it difficult to choose, a combination. Then there was the sherry trifle, with a delightfully moreish topping, which this time was made by Elliot. Finally, there were homemade cinnamon biscuits, served with rum 'n' raisin ice cream that both men had worked on making together, as a first attempt. For those who tried the third option, both Elliot and Kristian received continual compliments, especially from Michael, who bit his lip suggestively, with a mock expression of *I really shouldn't but I simply can't resist*, when he asked for seconds.

For anyone who felt they had any room left, there were savoury biscuits, with an assortment of cheeses from around the world. To finish off the perfect meal, coffee and brandy was served by Kristian.

Everyone thanked Elliot and Kristian in their own little way, with either a kiss, a handshake or a hug.

"We've got some gifts we'd like to give out," said Elliot, as he patted his full stomach lightly with his hand.

Every member of the group commented on how full they were, or that they couldn't actually eat another morsel, or how wonderful the entire meal had been. Regardless of these statements, some kept dipping their hands into bowls of nuts and other nibbles, or even the occasional chocolate. Luke sat silent, watching the scene with hatred and distaste growing like a snowball being rolled down a hill. His anger and depression seemed to dominate and take precedence over the rest of him. He decided that he would slip into the kitchen unnoticed while everyone retired to the living room to open their

The Absence of Friends

presents. They would be extremely sorry to see him end his life like this but what did he care.

True to Luke's calculations, Kristian suggested they all retire to the living room. Michael squealed something about the dining room being too impersonal to engage with all the gift-giving.

How Luke truly hated Michael - with his camp, effeminate voice and overworked Brummie accent, which sometimes he would screech at in a pitch that was unknown to either man or dog. And those constantly bitchy comments - how he loathed those bitchy comments that weren't even in the slightest bit funny, or clever.

He despised Michael's boyfriend, Steven. Ever since he had first been introduced to him all those months ago, he had never really taken to him as a potential friend. Who the hell did he think he was to have been in league with Emilio Lopez, trying to destroy his career?

Vince. Vicious, vindictive and volatile Vince. No, there was nothing admirable or warming about him, especially when he was the one that Scott ran to whenever there was an issue to be discussed. Vince was always there to offer his opinion and theories, violating Luke's privacy.

Max and Maxine were hardly known to him but that was reason enough for him not to feel any real emotional connection to them. Besides, they were good friends with Michael and Steven, so that in itself was reason enough for him to dislike them instantly.

Then, of course, there was Elliot and Kristian. Supposedly, his best friends for many years but seeing them now, he began to wonder if they ever were truly his real friends. They seemed to look far more at ease with Scott, than ever they were with him. Of course, they always had to be the heroes - the modern day saviours, whenever there was a crises or predicament that needed to be resolved.

Last but not least, there was Scott.

How Luke hoped that Scott would regret his suicide the most. He loved Scott, with all his heart, with every fibre of his being - but after the way he had been treated since he told Scott that he was positive, he sincerely hoped that he would really suffer. *Wouldn't it be funny if it were the other way round?* he thought. *If Scott were to die instead of me...huh, I bet everyone would take notice then.*

He watched, eagle-eyed, as everyone filed through the door, disappearing from the dining room one-by-one, like cygnets following their mother.

As soon as the last person had left the dining room, Luke crept into the kitchen and rummaged through the various drawers and cupboards in order to find himself a suitable weapon - he wanted the job done quickly and without too much fuss, as there was no point in drawing out the inevitable, like they would in the movies.

"If you're gonna shoot him, just do it!" he would shout at the television. "Why the bloody hell would you waste time by talking about it? 'Cause you know damn well that the bad 'un is gonna take that opportunity to rip the gun right outta your hands!"

Luke found an exceptionally sharp knife in a ceramic pot, where various sized wooden spoons and spatulas were kept, just next to the cooker. Taking the knife slowly from the pot, he leant with back against the cooker.

He became strangely reflective and ruminative, pondering on the various aspects of his life, where major incidences had occurred - from being beaten by his father, to becoming a rent boy, to being raped, to meeting Elliot and Kristian, to meeting Matthew, to being dragged into Matthew's suicide, to meeting Scott, to meeting the other's in the group and finally, to being diagnosed as positive.

Was his entire life just a jigsaw puzzle put together and made up of tragic episode after tragic episode of gloom, doom and despondency? What really was there to live for? Nothing! He felt that his life was much like a computer game - him being the only player and everyone else around him, his opponents - designed so, that no matter what he did, what he said or who he met, the end result would always be the same. A no win situation, with his character standing no chance of surviving until the end.

He studied the knife that he clasped tightly in his hand. There was still a chance for him to back out if he wanted to. He could just slip into the living room, without anyone having realised he had gone missing for a considerable length of time.

No!

He was determined to see this through. He had made up his mind that he was extremely unhappy with his life and there was nothing left to really live for. His past was enough to make him thoroughly ashamed of what the future might hold - not that he was willing to give himself the possibility of a future to look forward to.

It was at this point, that he suddenly gained crystal clarity as to why his mother had constantly begged him to continue with his life alone. He could relate to and understand why she didn't want him to be a part of the shame, torment and humiliation of her past - though it had left him dubious as to whether his past was responsible for the shaping and controlling of the present. How could anyone possibly look forward to a bright and wonderful future, if they weren't happy with their detrimental past?

The Absence of Friends

He wasn't in the least bit surprised that nobody was aware he wasn't present in the living room. He could hear the different voices floating from the room, in response to the various gifts that were being exchanged. There were shocked gasps, mortified giggles and sickly sweet comments. Wasn't it enough that he had to suffer the day with these people, pretending that he was enjoying himself? And for what?

Nothing!

Luke had become so angry with his own life, as well as that of the others, he didn't realise he was screaming and shouting. "Tell me why the fuck I *should* live? Huh? My lover's so humiliated by me, he doesn't want to be near me. My best friends have turned against me…"

As the anger in him began to boil, his face turned puce and his whole body began to shake but he continued with his tirade: "…and would you be sorry to see me go? No, I don't think so. I'm probably doing you all a great favour.

"You all think you can just…" He stopped in his tracks, as he realised that he had attracted the attention of everyone. They were all standing at the entrance to the kitchen, with various expressions of shock and horror. Unbeknownst to Luke, this had caused him to smile manically.

Luke continued with his nonsensical diatribe: "So…now you want to acknowledge my existence, do you? Come to watch me and gloat, have you? Luke, the no-hoper, who is going to end it all…and of course, all the farm animals have to come and watch, to cheer him on. Or do you all think he's going to mess this up, like he has done with the rest of his life?"

Vince tried to talk with him. "Hey Luke," he began, carefully. "Listen, I know you're upset because of what's happened to you recently. It's difficult, sometimes, to be able to deal with a life-changing experience. But it's all very understandable that you feel the way you do."

"What do you understand, Vince? How the hell can you really know how I'm feeling?"

"True. A fair point. In all honesty, I don't understand how you're really feeling. What I meant is, that *we* understand and acknowledge the difficulties you're experiencing with your diagnoses."

"*The difficulties…?*" Luke spat, with a derisive laugh. "None of you really know about the *difficulties* I've been facing. You all sit there with your mightier than thou attitudes, pretending you know it all, that you've seen it all and you've done it all. In actual fact, you don't really care in the slightest about me and what I'm feeling. None of you have even had the courtesy to talk to me today - to find out what it is that I'm *really* thinking or feeling. So…really… what's the point?"

"We do care though, Luke," said Vince, keeping a watchful eye on what he was doing with the knife. "I guess we thought, albeit wrongly, that it might be better for you to try to come to terms with things by yourself. We didn't want to bombard you with questions and suggestions. Maybe it was the wrong thing for us to do…but killing yourself isn't going to help anyone." He stretched out his arm. "Why don't you give me the knife? We can have a chat together, if you like, away from everyone else."

"Never!" Luke bellowed vehemently. He swished the knife in the direction of Vince's outstretched arm - like a feral animal - who instinctively pulled it back to safety.

Luke's eyes drifted from the determined looking Vince in front of him and scanned the rest of the faces in the room:

Max had his arms around a horrified looking Maxine, the colour drained from her face as though she were about to be violently sick.

Steven was fanning Michael with a piece of cloth, or a magazine, as he looked as though he were about to execute the classically theatrical faint of a damsel in distress at any second.

Kristian was clasping Elliot's hand so tightly - refusing to let it go - the sound of breaking bones was an almost certainty if he were to tighten his grip any further.

Scott's mouth hung wide open - like the Grand Canyon - frozen to the spot he was standing, like a statue of solid ice.

"Stay the hell where you are…all of you! If any of you come any closer to me, I won't be afraid to use this!" Luke scowled, brandishing the knife. "I would strongly suggest, for your own sakes, that you leave me alone."

Whilst Vince was still desperately attempting to coax Luke into giving him the knife, one member of the group unequivocally opted to take matters into their own hands and try to surprise Luke from behind with the intention to wrench the knife out of his hand before he did any damage to himself, or anyone else from the group.

So far, it was working.

The figure had slipped away, unnoticed by Luke, although a couple of members of the group realised what was happening. Luckily, for the figure, the back door was unlocked, or the plan would have had to have been aborted instantly - it was fortuitous that the person remembered Kristian unlocking it earlier, in order to let some fresh air into the kitchen. The figure tip-toed stealthily and as quietly as possible behind Luke, not wanting to make any big or sudden movements, in case it alerted him to what they were intending on doing.

The Absence of Friends

Vince's attempts to coax Luke into giving up the knife were proving to be futile and he was fast running out of potential solutions available to him.

Luke began to be aware of what was going on when he caught sight of Vince looking past his shoulders and pleading with his eyes at something…or some*one*. He scanned the group once more and only saw six faces staring back at him - with himself and Vince, that made eight. Someone from the group wasn't there…they were missing! But his current state of mind wouldn't allow him to register who it actually was. It didn't take him long to put one and one together and work out what was happening. There was no way anyone was going to put a stop to what he intended doing.

At that very moment, the figure grabbed at Luke's arm. The sudden pulse of shock that Luke felt course through him was so intense, his natural instinct caused him to spin round with such speed so as to strike the offender in the face with all the weight of his body behind him.

"Get off me!" he shrieked. In his panicked shock, he momentarily forgot that he was still holding the knife in his hand, as he lunged at the figure with all his might.

Not knowing who it actually was that was behind him, Luke guessed where the middle of the head would be as he spun around and violently lunged out. It was not until he felt the knife lacerating the person's soft flesh, he realised the horror of what he'd actually succeeded in doing.

Screaming and shouting were all Luke heard, as he watched in frozen terror at what had unfolded before him – he could even see, in his periphery, someone bent double; no doubt vomiting at the grotesqueness of the scene.

It was an agonising couple of minutes that followed for the rest of the group, who couldn't find any motion within their legs - those two minutes seemed like a lifetime to each one of them. Their bodies had turned to stone but their minds were wired with a thousand emotions and thoughts, each colliding with the other, unable to find a point of clarity.

Luke's face had drained of all colour, turning him into a ghostly shade of white as he stood there almost frozen in time. Unable to move, he repeatedly gasped: "Oh my God! What have I done?"

His widened eyes had witnessed the body slumping heavily to the floor, with blood rapidly carpeting the surrounding area. It was almost as if some macabre and hypnotic energy had taken hold of him, refusing to allow his eyes to do anything but look at the horrifying scene he had created.

Even the sound of someone vomiting – it might have been the same person as earlier – in the kitchen sink couldn't seem to break the deathly spell that he had been cast under.

Seeing the blood-stained knife still in his hand, Luke threw it to the floor with bilious disgust. His breathing had become peculiarly irregular, as he gasped: "Oh God! I've...I've killed...No!"

He let out a blood-curdling scream.

A scream that everyone in the room would have thoroughly embedded within their memories and remember for a very long time afterwards.

It was Vince who managed to break free from the frozen enchantment and get himself to the body first. Taking hold of a lifeless wrist, he prayed that there might still be a hint of a pulse. He knew before he took hold of it that it was a futile act, as the jugular vein had been sliced. With the amount of blood that had left the body, there was nothing to actually pray for, as the wound had been fatal.

Vince looked up at the others and whispered: "I doubt there was anything that anyone of us could have done. It would have been quick."

Luke reeled backwards, knocking into a cupboard. He slid slowly to the floor, as he brought his knees up to his chest, howling and weeping. If he hated himself before, he absolutely despised his very existence now - he listened as someone phoned the police and then an ambulance, to come and take the body of a person whom he loved really deeply.

The body of Elliot Hayden.

CHAPTER SIXTEEN

The deathly silence poisoned the air – with a claustrophobic oppressiveness – dragging each person in the room deeper into the abyss of their own personal oubliette, that none could hope to find a way of escape. Their bitter panic was like the putrid stench of rotting flesh and unseemliness stinging mercilessly at their nostrils, as if by a swarm of violently angry bees.

It was hard to believe that only minutes beforehand everyone had been feverishly jubilant from booze-fuelled jokes and laughter, allowing themselves to sink deep within the festive gaiety and spirit. Anyone who had drunk too much, or had felt slightly tipsy, had certainly sobered up somewhat rapidly with the events of the last few moments. Even with the central heating on, it felt extremely and unnaturally cold in the room - or was it because everyone was still frozen in shock?

Nobody dared to utter a single word - partly because their breath had been caught in the back of their throats, rendering them temporarily mute. For most, this was probably a godsend because even if they did have the ability to muster up the courage to speak, they wouldn't have known what to say, or who to say it to.

Kristian was glued to the spot where he was standing, as if his legs were made of pure lead, staring glassily at the body of Elliot.

Steven was the first to recover from his quiescent position and looked around to find something to cover the body with. A few minutes later he returned to the kitchen and placed a sheet that he had found over Elliot. As the others managed to free themselves from their state of petrification, he noticed that their movements appeared as though they were being executed in extreme slow motion.

No sooner had Steven finished covering up the body, Kristian came to life, collapsing to his knees and howling like an animal that wasn't sure if it were doleful, angry, traumatised or just caught in a situation of utter distress. He grabbed at the sheet covering Elliot and ripped it away aggressively.

"No!" he growled, which came out as more of a tormented whine. He narrowed his eyes towards Steven. "What the hell do you think you're doing?"

Shivers ran up everyone's spines.

"He's not dead! He's not!" he said, with blood-curdling defiance.

All eyes were on Kristian, as he crawled towards Elliot's body. "You can't die on me, Elliot. You mustn't. Please don't die," he sobbed. "I love you. I don't know what I would do if you left me."

Every word that Kristian uttered seemed as though it were being meticulously sculpted into everyone's memories; the pain that he carried, being drilled mercilessly into every person in the room, through the sheer anguish of his words.

He picked up Elliot's limp and lifeless body, cradling him in his arms - rocking him gently as though he were holding a newborn baby, soothing it with the gentle motion. "He'll be alright, you know," he said with an icy matter-of-factness. "He's just resting his eyes…he's had a very exhaustive few days." Even as the words left his mouth, he wasn't convinced by what he was saying. "He'll wake up in a minute. You all know that he likes his sleep…it's always a struggle to rouse him when he's sleeping," he blubbed.

"Well, don't just stand there," he wailed. "Please will somebody help me clean this mess up?"

Maxine was the first to move. She didn't want to be the one to tell Kristian that Elliot was in fact dead and that nothing anyone said, or did, would bring him back. She filled the bowl in the kitchen sink with warm, soapy water and placed it on the floor next to Kristian, handing him a cloth. She was unsure as to whether to help him, or leave him alone to tend to Elliot by himself. She concluded that the latter option was probably the best course of action and making everyone a strong cup of tea would be a more appropriate use of her time.

Scott was far from being in the mood to indulge himself in the superstitions of the supposed calming powers that tea had to offer - he had already opened a bottle of whisky and drunk nearly half the bottle, not even feeling any of the effects by consuming a large quantity of alcohol.

"This is all my fault," he sobbed to himself, as he took another large swig from the bottle.

Vince moved toward Scott. "Don't be ridiculous," he snapped. "It's not your fault at all."

"Yes it is. Of course it is. If I had paid more attention to Luke, none of this would ever have happened."

Vince sat next to Scott, attempting to convince him that none of this was his fault. "*Nobody* is to blame for what has happened…least of all you. So, you need to get those thoughts out of your head straight away."

"Don't try and make me feel better, Vince. It won't work."

"I'm not trying to make you feel better," Vince began. "But no doubt, everyone will be finding a reason to lay blame with themselves. I suppose it's the brains way of trying to make sense of what has happened. We are all battling with our own mental confusion, wondering if we might have been able to have done something that could have made a difference."

The Absence of Friends

"I don't see how on earth anybody else could be responsible for this."

"To be honest with you Scott, if anybody *wanted* to lay blame with someone, each of us could easily come up with some reason or other that might vindicate our own guilt, or point an accusing finger at another of us."

"But this is such a terrible thing that's happened."

"Yes, I know. We all know that…" Vince's frustration took control of his usual coolness, as he grabbed Scott by the shoulders, hoping that he could shake some reason into his friend. "…But for fuck's sake, Scott, *it's not your fault*! Believe that, will you?"

Max, being the dependably level-headed man within a time of crises was the only one who tended to Luke, who had been dismissed from everybody else's thoughts with their initial numbness.

"He's in a severe state of shock," he said to anybody who cared to listen.

"Who gives a shit about what he is?" snarled Kristian, baring his teeth like a wild and rabid dog, ready to bite his tormentor, as he looked at Luke. It was the first time he had laid his eyes upon him since the knife was thrown to the floor.

The blinding hatred he felt toward Luke was exceptional, choking him as it began to consume the weaker - more humane and decent - emotions he had existing within him, in its battle to gain ultimate supremacy and develop in strength. He spotted the knife and lunged for it, with the intent to release his pain and hurt onto Luke for the heartache he had caused.

Everyone froze in horror once again.

"Kristian! Don't!" yelled Max.

Kristian saw the bloodied knife in his hand, his eyes widening with horror as the realisation of what had happened finally sank in. His piercing scream resounded throughout the entire house as he fell to the floor, sobbing uncontrollably. He released his grip on the knife, which crashed to the floor with an unusual amount of noise.

It was Michael who took it upon himself to go upstairs and check on Thalia. If the truth be told, it was the perfect excuse for him to steal a few moments away from the ardently sadistic horrors of the past few minutes, as he still wasn't quite sure if what had happened *was* actually real, or if he were trapped in a disturbingly shocking nightmare that wouldn't allow him to wake up. He peered into Thalia's cot, as if he were the doting father, ready to rescue her from any infantile anxieties she might be experiencing. He raised a surprised eyebrow, as he watched her peacefully sleeping - blissfully unaware of the tragic events that had happened below her. How Michael wished that he could swap places with the innocent and untainted world of Thalia's limited existence - to be totally naïve and oblivious to the cruel happenings of the world. He wondered how long it would be before her innocence would be permanently shattered.

Back downstairs, Maxine had filled several mugs with boiled water, to make everyone a cup of tea. She didn't count the number of mugs she used - just filled several of them, hoping she had done enough for everyone. Putting a couple of spoonfuls of sugar into one of the mugs, she placed it beside Kristian.

"Here," she said to Kristian warmly, "drink this. It will make you feel better."

Kristian looked up at Maxine - his face expressionless but his eyes cold and steely, as he laughed incredulously. "Make me feel better, you say? And just how the hell do you think a cup of tea could make me feel better?"

Maxine looked as though she would burst into tears at any moment. "I'm sorry. It was just…I was only…"

"Yeah? Well don't even bother," he snapped, picking up the mug and throwing it contemptuously across the room. "A cup of tea won't make me feel any fucking better!" he sneered, as the mug shattered upon contact with the wall and the liquid inside forming a bizarrely morbid shape as it trickled down the wall.

"Hey, hey…" began Max.

"What?" spat Kristian.

"She was only trying to help."

"Really? Is that what you call it? Well…I don't need anyone's help."

Maxine put a comforting arm around Kristian. "Come on," she said with concern. "Let's go and sit down."

"Fuck off," screamed Kristian.

Out of the two, neither knew who was the more surprised as Kristian lashed out at Maxine, catching her cheek with the back of his hand and sending her reeling backwards.

Max charged toward Kristian and slapped him hard across the face. Kristian looked shocked and stunned for several moments and broke down in tears once again.

"I'm sorry," he sobbed. "I'm really sorry."

Max comforted his wife and led her back into the living room. He directed his next statement toward Vince. "Can you keep an eye on Kris, please?" he said before leaving the kitchen.

Vince nodded.

Steven and Scott were locked deep in conversation. Scott had almost finished the bottle of whisky he was drinking - making very little sense by slurring a lot of his words. Steven sat there patiently and intently listened to what Scott had to say, whether it made sense or not. Scott just needed someone to talk to and Steven was that someone.

"…and we talked about it you know," he attempted to say. "Recently, I think it was because he wanted to clear the air."

"Okay," replied Steven warily. "Although I'm not really sure who *he* is and what it was *he* was talking about."

"Luke. He and I had a good talk about, you know, *that* show. The one that Luke thought Emilio Lopez had stolen from him…and the fact that you were out to destroy his career."

"Oh?"

"He confided in me that he wasn't overly interested in the role anyway. He felt that he wanted to seek out more challenging roles…but he went for it because he was fascinated by the storyline…"

"So his outburst in the pub…when I first met him…that was all for nothing then?"

"Yes…and no. He was quite annoyed at being rejected from the role and began to doubt his abilities as an actor. Upon reflection, he thought that because he had successfully auditioned for several roles, he had begun to expect that he would be successful in anything he auditioned for."

"And no doubt, as Emilio was just breaking into his acting career and not having established himself a strong résumé, Luke presumed the lead role would automatically have become his."

"Exactly. Because he had begun to doubt his ability as a bonafide actor, and allowed his thoughts to convince him that there were conspiracy theories afoot, this was the reason why he wasn't particularly affable or magnanimous towards you when you first met. It was a complete shock to him that he had been rejected, which brought him back down to earth with a tremendous bump. He is only human after all, you know."

"It's okay, Scott. I had forgotten all about it anyway. It's history. Long since forgotten."

"You know something, Steven. You really are a great guy."

"Thank you," he responded, his cheeks flushing slightly at the compliment.

"Michael is a very lucky man to have you."

"And I'm very lucky to have him too."

"Why the hell did all this shit have to happen to Luke? He hasn't had the best of lives. In fact, come to think of it, he's had a pretty shitty life."

Steven shrugged his shoulders. "I'm afraid I can't answer that, Scott. I wish that I could but it's one of those questions that you can't just rattle off any old excuse for. There's probably no viable explanation as to why some people have a more difficult or harder time than someone else. Life can just deal us some pretty crap cards at times."

"Huh! Luke has always been dealt crap cards."

"Now, Scott. You know damn well that's not true. He's released a very successful album. He's got you…"

"…Got me? Yeah, right! What kind of boyfriend have I been to him?"

"And what makes you think that you're so different to anyone else here? Any one of us can say that - that we haven't been a good partner to our other half, for one reason or another. Everybody can have difficult periods in their lives…nobody corners the market in that respect but partners are there to share the burden; to offer help and potential resolutions to the various problems we face in life. I know it's rather hackneyed but it's true that a problem shared is a problem halved. Aren't relationships all about sharing? The good *and* the bad."

"I guess so. I just wish that Luke and I could have been more like Kris and…" Scott couldn't say Elliot's name as he had begun to sob bitterly.

Steven handed Scott his handkerchief as he put an arm around his animated shoulders, allowing Scott to rest his head upon his own.

Luke was still slumped in a huddled mess in a corner of the kitchen, with his arms holding his legs close to his chest, gently rocking back and forth.

"It should have been me," he incessantly repeated in a low hum. "This wasn't how it was meant to be. This wasn't what I wanted…not the outcome I had planned. I'm not a killer…I'm not!"

Max had wrapped Luke in a blanket earlier, when Steven had brought the sheet down to cover Elliot's body. The colour had completely drained from Luke's face; it looked as if someone had taken a brush of white paint to his face. Nobody knew what they could or should do for Luke but Max suggested that they do nothing until the medics arrived, as it was probably safer to leave him than attempt to do anything.

"…Why did it have to be Elliot?" Kristian sobbed. "What did he ever do?"

Vince shook his head, unable to offer any explanation that might have satisfied Kristian.

"He wouldn't even harm a fly, you know. He used to scowl at me for spraying or swatting flies - he constantly told me that they had every right to live, as we did. He could never see bad in anyone and would always say, no matter how small, everyone had good in them. So again I ask, why did it have to be Elliot?"

Vince breathed in deeply as he sat on the floor next to Kristian, stroking the back of his head. Not that Kristian could feel anything - he was totally numb.

The Absence of Friends

"I guess any one of us could be asking that exact question," he eventually said in response.

"Eh?"

"Well, any one of us could have chosen to sneak out to try to stop Luke. And any one of us could have...well, nobody should have been...What I am trying to say is, that even if Luke had succeeded in taking his own life, we would all, including Elliot, be in exactly the same position as we are now - asking ourselves why and maybe finding someone else to blame, if not blaming ourselves."

Michael came back down the stairs, reticent in leaving his sanctuary of tranquillity where Thalia had been sleeping and being cruelly returned to the world of reality.

"How is she?" asked Maxine.

"She's fine...sleeping like a...well, like a baby."

She was about to ask another question when the doorbell rang, causing most people to react like they were watching a horror movie and something scary had just happened.

As Michael was the one nearest to the front door, he answered it.

Nobody actually remembered placing the phone call, as it must have been a natural reaction within their state of shock but the place quickly became overrun by police and medics. In a discussion between Michael and Maxine several months later, they thought the most likely of candidates to have placed the call would have been Max or Steven.

Most people gave their individual account of the events that had happened. Scott was too drunk for the police to get any sense out of him and was requested that he go to the station the following day to give his statement, when he was more coherent. Kristian and Luke did not give their statements, as they were both being tended to by the medics and were slightly catatonic through their shock.

Those who felt able, after being given permission, packed up their belongings and went home. Max ordered taxis for those who had wanted them.

Kristian was taken to hospital, to be treated for severe shock.

Luke, however, was initially taken to hospital for treatment, where he was placed under observation that lasted several months until his trial began. It was a foregone conclusion that didn't come as a shock to anyone that he was found not guilty of murder but guilty of manslaughter. The judge had decreed him temporarily insane at the time of the incident and sentenced Luke to ten years imprisonment for involuntary manslaughter due to diminished responsibility. He was ordered to undergo intense psychotherapy within a psychiatric ward until such time that he could be transferred to a low risk prison in order to serve out the remainder of his sentence.

Kristian watched the solitary figure at the grave, as he shielded himself behind an oak tree. He didn't wish to intrude on someone who was paying their respects, which he knew his friends would sometimes like to do - usually it was both members of the couple that would visit the grave but today, it was a lonesome figure.

It was six weeks since Elliot had died and Kristian still hadn't let the full reality of his loss sink in. The funeral had taken place just over a fortnight after Elliot's death. Everyone who was friends with him, or Elliot, had attended the funeral and he had asked them to throw a single flower of their choice onto the coffin. His eyes had misted over at the reverend's comforting words but he refused to allow himself to cry any more. His friends had told him to let go and cry, as it was not a bad thing to let the tears flow and he would probably feel better emotionally. It seemed to Kristian that he had cried for an eternity anyway and no amount of tears would ever make him feel better - he didn't think he had any tears left in him. He thanked everyone for their support over his loss.

Michael had arranged "a little tissue-essential farewell get-together", as he had called it. Kristian didn't stay long, as he wanted to be by himself, rather than be forced to socialise with everyone else. He was sick to death of hearing statements such as: "Elliot wouldn't want you to mope around like this" or "You need to carry on with your own life." He wanted to lash out at the next person who said anything insensitive about what he should, or what Elliot would have wanted him to do. He knew everyone was only trying to help and obviously had his best interests at heart but he didn't need to be told what Elliot might or might not have wanted him to have done.

As Elliot's appointed executor, Max told Kristian that he had not died intestate but had, in fact, left a will in which most of his possessions and assets were naturally to go to him. There were a few little bits and pieces that Elliot had wanted to go to other people which, Max specified, were described in fuller detail within the will. Kristian thanked Max for his kindness over the years and for overseeing the legalities vis-à-vis in dissolving Elliot's instructions of his will.

It became a bi-weekly activity for Kristian to visit Elliot's grave - always taking a fresh bunch of flowers with him, as undoubtedly the others would have begun to wilt. Usually, he went on a Tuesday or a Friday but for some

The Absence of Friends

reason he chose to go on a Sunday. As he approached Elliot's grave, he noticed the figure knelt by it and so he shielded himself behind a tree. He knew immediately who the person was, as their words carried toward him on the warm breeze.

"It's over," the voice whispered softly. "It's finally over."

Dressed smartly in a dark blue suit, the figure knelt beside the grave. It was an unusually warm day for the end of January and the sun beat down ferociously upon their back, causing little beads of sweat to roll down their face, which met with the tears coming from the deeply bloodshot eyes. Everything seemed to participate in the figure's sorrow. Birds were watching from tree branches, expressing their sympathy through sad singing. Flowers had their heads hung as a symbol of their reverence; even other animals seemed to stop what they were doing as if accustomed to this ritual whenever somebody visited the grave.

Pulling out the weeds and wrapping the dead flowers from a previous visit in newspaper, the figure laid a wreath of fresh carnations; yellow, pink and white, by the headstone. Wiping the tears or the sweat from their face, they didn't care which, the figure stared at the flowers just laid. "They were our favourite. We always had to have some in the house. We never bought anything else, especially roses. It always had to be carnations."

Opening their partner's briefcase, a leather-bound diary with the owner's initials on it, in gold lettering was produced. "Do you remember this? I've re-read it all. We had some good times together, but there were a few dark secrets in our shadows of fear."

The figure lovingly touched the diary, caressing the letters with their fingers, clutching it close to their chest, as though the person were with them at the grave side. The figure kissed it before replacing it back into the briefcase.

"I couldn't accept what happened to you, but you would have wanted me to go on as normal. You did help me find peace in myself, but now it's over for the both of us. You have to believe that I've never stopped loving you, not for a moment. I really wanted to ask for your forgiveness after the way I thought of you.

"I really wish that none of this had ever happened, as nobody deserved to die in the awful way you did…especially not *you*…and certainly not by…I just cannot bring myself to say their name!"

The tears that Kristian had been holding onto for several weeks, slowly began to fall from his eyes, when he heard every heartfelt word that Maxine had uttered.

He knew Maxine had always loved Elliot, to the very depths of her heart. Not, though, in the way that she was helplessly in love with Max - and even though she made out she wasn't devastated when Elliot finally revealed he was gay, which put an end to their romantic relationship, Kristian knew otherwise. Maxine was incredibly close to Michael and often, she would confide in him - as a sister might to their sibling - especially in matters regarding Elliot. What Maxine never knew was that Michael would always relay what he had been told back to Kristian; not maliciously or out of spite but because he believed Kristian had a right to know.

Kristian was aware that as Elliot had nearly married Maxine, he would have known about her peculiar allergy toward roses and the fact that she would have preferred to have carnations in the house. The diary she had mentioned was probably more than likely the one she had kept whilst she was dating Elliot - she would have written down all her thoughts, no matter how good or bad they sounded. This is what, Kristian decided, she was asking forgiveness for.

Feeling moved by the scene he had just witnessed, Kristian made his way over to Maxine.

She jumped with a start when she heard Kristian approaching from behind her. "Oh my God," she gasped, clutching her hand to her breast.

"I'm so sorry," Kristian apologised. "I didn't mean to scare you."

"That's okay. I was so wrapped up in my own thoughts, it was just a shock to hear someone else."

"I heard what you said just now."

Maxine's face didn't reveal whether she was surprised, mortified or pleased. Kristian rested his head on Maxine's shoulder, as he embraced her around the waist. The tears were still continuing to flow. She stroked the back of his head in a bid to comfort him, while her other arm was tightly clasped around his waist.

"I really loved him," Kristian confided to Maxine through his sobs.

Maxine felt a shiver travel up her spine to the back of her neck and shuddered momentarily. "I know you did," she whispered softly into Kristian's ear. "We *all* know you did. More importantly, Elliot knew how much you loved him."

He wiped at his eyes with the handkerchief Maxine had given him. "You know, Elliot *did* love you a great deal too - you became like a sister to him. It took him a long time to forgive himself for the pain he had caused you but the fact that he never lost your friendship meant the world to him."

Maxine smiled at Kristian's words of comfort. She was pleased that Elliot had ended up with someone like Kristian, who had a lot of love to offer, as well as being kind and genteel. Not only had Elliot become like the brother she had never had but she also considered Kristian to be like a brother too. Elliot had been extremely happy in his relationship with Kristian and that was comfort to her in itself.

Kristian looked up at Maxine, his eyes sore from the sting of the tears. "He never meant to hurt you and really believed that you would end up hating him for the rest of your days. He told me that you were and always would be very special to him."

Maxine thought she had cried all the tears she could but with Kristian's kind words, she found more falling from her already swollen eyes. She picked up Max's briefcase that she had had with her and opened it, producing a photograph of her with Elliot and Krisitan.

"Here," she said, offering the photograph to Kristian, "I'd like you to have this. I made a copy of it for myself but I had always meant to give you this. Max has carried it for me in his briefcase, so it wouldn't get damaged, until such time we got to see you again."

Kristian took the picture and wiped his eyes, which had misted over with his crying, so he could study it. He remembered the events with crystal clarity, as though it had only been taken a few days ago. The photograph had actually been taken a few years back, shortly after Maxine had met Max, who was the one who had taken it. He seemed to be frozen in time as he stared at the picture for what seemed like an eternity.

"I didn't know you came here on Sundays," said Maxine, breaking the silence.

"I don't normally."

"That's why I came today - because I thought that nobody else would."

"I know how much Elliot meant to you, Maxine and believe me when I tell you that he still loved you a great deal. When we first met, he was devastated about losing you. He never meant…" He began to choke on his tears.

"Hey…" said Maxine, hugging Kristian tightly once again. "It would have been a huge mistake if we had stayed together. I'm sure we would have probably ended up hating each other and to be honest, I would rather have lost Elliot as a lover than lose him as a friend. I suppose it's a small consolation that he died being with someone that he truly loved."

"Oh, Maxine," Kristian blurted out, flinging both arms around her as he cried bitterly.

"That's it," she said soothingly. "Let it all out. It's good for you to cry."

They spent the next few minutes hugging each other tightly, not uttering a single word. Kristian was glad for the support from Maxine - she and the others had been an absolute tower of strength that he had needed over the past few weeks.

"I didn't even get the chance to tell him how much I loved him," Kristian said eventually, breaking the tender moment between the two friends.

"You didn't need to tell him. He knew already how much you loved him," Maxine said softly.

A horn sounded from the car that was parked by the side of the road.

"Is that Max?" asked Kristian, trying to see the person who was sitting at the wheel.

"Yeah."

"Oh! I would have thought that he would want to be here with you… whilst you chatted to Elliot."

"Well, we're actually off to a business meeting shortly - Elliot was always interested in mine and Max's careers - and he knew that I wanted a few minutes alone with Elliot. I needed to say a few things that I had been bottling up for quite some time."

"I'm certain that Elliot would have appreciated it."

Kristian watched as Maxine made her way back to the car. Even after they had driven off - with Max giving a deferential wave - it was as if he were glued to the spot, unable to move. It took several minutes before he could finally summon the strength or the ability to move. He sighed deeply at the foot of the grave, whilst inside he was continually asking himself why it had to happen this way.

It was a programme on Dan Hewitt's radio station, several weeks later, which prompted Kristian to think seriously about the direction in which his life was going.

The subject of the intense debate was bereavement and coping with loss. Normally, Kristian would only ever phone in to the station when it was a light-hearted competition, with the prize of seeing a hunky singer or boyband, at *Guyz & Girlz* with whom he harboured a secret crush upon. However, on this particular occasion, he found himself subconsciously dialling the station's telephone number that had been repeated throughout the debate.

As the telephone was ringing, Kristian recalled the last time that he had called into the radio station. It was a few days before Christmas, for the *Christmas Feast Trilogy* competition. How excitable he had been on that occasion but now, his heart hung heavily in his chest, as he found himself becoming increasingly more nervous. It was one thing to call in for a competition but to engage within a serious debate, that was a totally different matter and he momentarily wondered if he should just replace the receiver rather than allow his inner most feelings to be made public and vulnerable. Had it not been for the fact that Kristian had heard Scott only a few minutes beforehand, his decision would have been made so much easier about not continuing with the call.

His trepidation had almost gotten the better of him and had the radio station answered several seconds later, they would have answered to a dead line.

"…once again, I would like to thank Dr Fiona Lester for her invaluable advice to all of our callers this evening," said Dan Hewitt in his incredibly smooth but bass voice. "Okay, let's see who our next caller is this evening."

There was a slight pause before Kristian said: "Good evening, Dan. My name's Kristian."

"Welcome to the show, Kristian and thank you for phoning in. Where are you calling from, please?"

"I'm from Ealing."

In the studio with Dan Hewitt, Dr Fiona Lester had been invited in especially for the programme. She was a trained psychologist, who specialised in bereavement therapy and was there to give advice to callers who had the courage to phone in. Many of those who called in, had spoken about their partners, friends or family members who were dying, or had died due to illnesses like cancer, or those who had been involved in an unexpected but fatal accident.

Scott had chosen to phone in after he thought about Luke having the HIV virus and the possibility that this could develop into the fatal AIDS syndrome. Then of course, he had the fear that he might even follow the same path as Luke, as he was still unsure as to whether he had contracted the HIV virus. Scott had spoken at length about Luke developing severe symptoms, albeit psychosomatically and was after some advice from Dr Fiona about the best way forward for himself and for them as a couple.

"And what would you like to ask Dr Fiona?" asked Dan.

"Well…I heard a friend of mine phoning in a short while ago…Scott, his name is."

"Uh huh," acknowledged Dan.

Dr Fiona's voice was gentle and soothing, as she said: "Take your time, Kristian. It's not an easy subject to be able to discuss openly."

Kristian's voice was noticeably shaky as he continued. "Um…well…Scott's partner was involved in my partner's death a few weeks back."

"Okay," said Dr Fiona, recognising what Kristian had said.

"He is currently undergoing counselling for his HIV status but I also know that he's receiving some additional counselling for the shock he received when Elliot died."

"Elliot was your partner?" asked Dr Fiona, ensuring that no misunderstanding could be made.

"Yes."

"Can I just ask when Elliot passed away?"

"Christmas Day…last year."

"Okay. And it was Luke who was the cause of his death, right?"

"Yes. That's right."

"Can I just ask something here? Was Luke close to Elliot?"

"Yes, he was…both of us were close to Luke. Elliot and I were his best friends. He had a really tough life when he first moved to London."

"That's what Scott had told us. It's very clear, from what we learned from Scott that Luke had been though a tremendous build-up of pressure, right from when he was a young age. Then, of course, realising that he was wholly responsible for the death of his best friend was too much for his young shoulders to bear and sent him into a severe state of shock."

"Well, yes…I agree with everything that you're saying but this wasn't a deliberate or malicious act you have to understand. I guess I have only just come to terms with realising that Luke killed Elliot by accident - he had sunk so low that he couldn't understand, or didn't feel that he deserved to keep living. If it hadn't been Elliot, it could have been anyone else in the room and I guess that is equally as upsetting and shocking as losing Elliot."

Kristian could sense that Dr Fiona was temporarily thrown off guard by this new revelation, as he recounted the details of Elliot's death - his voice quivering through various points. Dr Fiona was, to Kristian, surprisingly sympathetic as she offered him advice on how to come to terms with Elliot's unfortunate and untimely death.

"There are also some great support groups within the London area," she offered, "that are run by professionals but also have guest speakers who have been through similar experiences such as yours. After we come off-air, I would very much like you to stay on the line so I can take your telephone number and put you in touch with these groups."

"Umm," was all Kristian could say in response.

"I know something like this will seem like a big step for you but once you have taken that step, the healing process will begin - for some, it will take longer than others but the process will have begun. If it makes it any easier for you, I would urge you to go along with a good friend…at least on the first time you go."

The Absence of Friends

"Okay," Kristian agreed. What shocked Kristian the most was the advice Dr Fiona gave him with regards to Luke.

"...and we know that even for his young amount of years, he has been through a tremendous amount of pressure, shock and personal loss, spanning right back to his very early years. If you are unable to find it within yourself to forgive him for what you mentioned was obviously unintentional, it could end up taking him deeper into depression that will be incredibly difficult for even the strongest minded of people to find a way back from.

"I would suggest that by way of him receiving and accepting the counselling that had been offered him, he is showing a certain amount of regret for what he has done. At this point in his life, he needs as much love and emotional support as he can get. Obviously I am not negating the fact as do you. You told me that you and Elliot were his best friends - I would say that he still needs that strong friendship of yours. The bond that the three of you had together sounded like a very strong and solid one and if you break that bond entirely, it could cause him and you a lot of emotional damage that may be very difficult to reverse...if it all."

Although Kristian wasn't entirely convinced by Dr Fiona's analysis, he found himself agreeing to the advice he had been given by her and thanked her for it. He admitted that he needed this opportunity to put his own thoughts into some kind of clear perspective that he could digest and move forward from.

"I do sincerely wish you all the best for the future in whatever direction you choose to go," she said to Kristian. "And of course, to Luke."

Dan finished off the call. "If there are any listeners who have been unable to phone in this evening, Dr Fiona has set up a help line with specially trained counsellors who will be happy to take your call. All the information of when lines are open can be found on our website. Thank you, Kristian, for sharing your experiences with us. I would like to echo Dr Fiona's best wishes to you and of course, to all our callers who have phoned in this evening."

"Thank you for taking the time to listen to me. Bye."

"Bye," said Dr Fiona and Dan in unison.

Kristian heard them both talking about his own experience for a few moments before the programme came to an end and the pips announcing the hourly news bulletin could be heard.

Pondering for a short while about what Dr Fiona had told him, Kristian decided that it was time he sorted out his relationship with Luke once and for all.

The emotional breakdown that Luke suffered led him to begin his ten year incarceration in a psychiatric ward, undergoing intense therapy and tests. For days, Luke sat cross-legged on the floor, rocking himself back and forth whilst his eyes remained glazed and focused on one object in the room. In his catatonic state, he didn't dare to break the visual contact he held with either a wall, a piece of furniture or even a dirty mark on the carpet, other than to blink; knowing if he did, it would only bring him back into the world of reality.

Whilst he was aware that he was voluntarily holding himself captive in his newly created world - where he believed that he was safe - he knew that he wouldn't have to think about, or confront the consequences of what had happened. If he allowed himself the briefest of moments to relive the fatally tragic day, he would also have to acknowledge that the safety he currently felt was purely a temporary one that he had constructed within his mind. Then, he would come to realise that his physical environment was far from what he would normally have described as *safe*.

For several days Luke refused to eat anything. Even when, on the many occasions, he was force-fed by the interns, he would spit the food out, or send the plate flying out of the intern's hand. In these circumstances he would undoubtedly spend some time on the isolation ward - or in solitary confinement - for his "unacceptable and inappropriate behaviour", which is what the Governor had described it as. The weight loss he suffered as a result of his refusal to eat was dramatic. On Scott's regular visits to Luke, he revealed how worried he was about him.

What Scott had actually said to eventually bring Luke out of his shell, he never really knew but once Luke had exited his make believe world, he began talking about nothing but Elliot and Kristian.

Vince readily agreed to stay with Scott for as long as he wanted him to, to give him some much needed friendly and emotional support. He telephoned Félix in Germany and told him what had happened, explaining the reason for his delay in coming back home. Félix understood completely and told him to take as much time as he felt able for his friend. It pleased Vince that Félix was so understanding - he finished the call by telling him that he loved him more than he could possibly know and couldn't wait to see him again.

Scott continually urged Kristian to go and visit Luke - stressing that he was nearly pulling his hair out with his guilt. It was only after Kristian had listened to the radio programme on bereavement that he finally agreed to Scott's request of visiting Luke.

The sight that met his eyes on his very first visit was nothing short of a complete heart-wrenching experience. Kristian had to look several times at the pitiful looking creature - that was nothing more than skin clinging to bones - in front of him before he was convinced that it was Luke, as he looked nothing like his former friend. With the grubby, over-sized clothes he wore hanging pathetically from his body, his dishevelled hair and the fact that he hadn't seen a bar of soap or a razor in weeks, Kristian would have been forgiven for thinking that the man in front of him was Luke's father rather than Luke himself.

No sooner had Luke spotted Kristian, he flung his arms around him and hugged him so tightly - refusing to let to, as if Kristian were something so precious that he couldn't bear to part from it. That was the only response he got from Luke, as he sat on a chair, wringing his hands until Kristian thought they might bleed. Seeing Luke up close and personal, he realised that the clothes he wore looked as though he had slept in them. And even though he looked unwashed, the odd thing was that he smelt clean and fresh. His eyes were swollen and his face full of red blotches, which Kristian could only assume was from the endless tears that he had cried.

Kristian found that he was doing all the talking - explaining that he didn't blame Luke for Elliot's death and apologising for not visiting him sooner. Luke just sat in his chair, staring at Kristian with no emotion revealed upon his face nor uttering a single word in response.

As the visits became increasingly more regular, Kristian began to coax Luke into speaking to him. It took nearly six months of regular visits until Kristian found that he could have a reasonable conversation with him.

Each time Luke saw Kristian, he undoubtedly began their conversation with: "I didn't kill him. It was an accident."

This always succeeded in sending a cold shiver up Kristian's spine.

"Elliot thought a lot of you, Luke - he considered you to be like a younger brother. I know he wouldn't want me to give up on you."

Luke nodded his head for a considerable length of time. He hated being cooped up in the psychiatric hospital and one day he revealed this to Kristian.

"Why?" asked Kristian. "What's wrong? I know that it's not the same as having your freedom but…they're treating you okay here, aren't they?"

Luke pointed to a man who was kneeling in the corner of the room, facing the wall and banging his fists against it. Kristian could see that he had already drawn blood but this didn't deter him from his continual banging.

"Who's he?" Kristian enquired, feeling instantly skeptical of him.

"Well, some people refer to him as Mad Monty."

"Mad Monty?"

Mad Monty was somewhere in his thirties, although he looked more like he was firmly ensconced into his fifties. His hair was long and matted and his clothes looked as though they had seen better days - fit only for the dustbin. Nobody would go near him - at least not voluntarily, as he had a strong smell of excreta permeating from the rags that hung from his malnourished body. It was enough to make anyone vomit violently. The teeth that he had left were black and rotting - threatening to drop out any day. He had been sentenced to life imprisonment for multiple murder but as he had been diagnosed as suffering from acute paranoid psychosis, the psychiatric hospital would be his home for the remainder of his days.

"Actually, his real name is Stuart Connors but woe betide anyone who actually calls him that! A new intern did once - obviously he hadn't been told how to address him properly and he paid the price with a broken nose."

Kristian's mouth dropped open. "Oh God," was all he could bring himself to say.

"Stuart thinks he's an army major and that we're all his troops. If anybody doesn't call him Major Montague, he goes absolutely berserk."

"So why on earth do you call him Mad Monty then?"

"I don't…I have more sense than to call him that…especially as he wouldn't think twice about killing you just because you didn't call him Major Montague. You can get away with calling him just Major and even Monty, dependent on his mood.

"However, to return to your question as to why the nickname, there have been some very tough characters in and out of here…those who aren't scared by anything or anyone and it's one of those who nicknamed him Mad Monty. They soon put him in his place if he tried to start on one of them but if the truth be told, I think they taunt him at times just to get a reaction from him."

"You want to stay well clear of those characters then, Luke."

"Fortunately, Monty spends more of his time in solitary confinement than out of it. He's in there so often, the Governor even refers to it as Monty's private suite."

"I'm sorry to say, that he gives me the creeps and I've only seen him for a few minutes…so it's probably just as well that he's not around so much."

"He wants to kill me," Luke blurted out with real fear in his voice.

"What!" exclaimed Kristian with incredulity.

"Somehow he's found out that I have HIV - I suspect he probably overheard the interns talking about it. The one thing I have learnt about this place is that they don't give a damn about confidentiality…I wouldn't be surprised if half of the staff don't even know what the word means. Anyway, Monty thinks I'm the enemy…tormented by the fact that he thinks I have a killer virus, which I want to use in order to kill him and his troops with. He's got this theory that he has to kill me before I kill him."

"That's totally ludicrous."

The Absence of Friends

"You try telling him that, Kristian. We're all classed as paranoid psychotics in here...none of the staff want to listen to us, let alone any of the fellow inmates, who are all considered as mad as one another."

Kristian opened his eyes wide with the revelation. "Can't you ask for a transfer, or something?"

The despondency in Luke's face was visibly apparent, as he said: "Do you honestly think they would transfer a patient if they asked? They think we're all mad! I've heard them say it. If anybody kicks up a fuss about something, they think we're on a mad rampage and their solution is to put us in isolation until we calm down. As I said earlier, isolation is like Monty's second home. I know what isolation is like, Kris and believe me, you don't want to be locked in there all alone with Monty.

"Mouse was in there once with him...and now, he is in hospital with several broken and fractured ribs. The only conversation that Monty knows is totally one-sided and usually with his fists!"

"Mouse?"

"Yes. His name's actually Mickey Moss, which is obviously as close to Mickey Mouse as you can get. So he was originally called Mickey Mouse but after a while, people dropped the Mickey part and just called him Mouse. Of course, as time's passed, the nickname just stuck. He's a good lad, really...only twenty three. I think Mouse got the rough end of the deal, as we've become quite good friends and Monty used him as a warning to me.

"You know something, Kris, a lot of people in here really shouldn't be. Mouse being one of them. He just lives in a strange fantasy world...but to be honest, he's totally harmless and at times can actually be quite lucid."

"My God! I didn't realise these places were that bad."

Luke's voice had a note of trepidation as he revealed: "You don't know the half of it. I'm really quite scared of Monty, Kris."

"Has he done anything to you?" asked Kristian with concern.

"Not yet. At the moment I think he is more terrified of me than I am of him. It got me thinking, actually...who the hell do I think I am to fear for my life...?"

"What do you mean?" asked Kristian, the confusion showing by the lines in his forehead.

"Well, I killed Elliot, didn't I? You know...an eye for an eye, a tooth for a tooth and all that."

Kristian looked directly into Luke's eyes, as though he were penetrating his very being. "We'll have less of that talk, Luke. Elliot's death was an accident. Of course I miss him like crazy but I know damn well what he would have thought of me if I had cut you out of my life permanently. People might think I'm crazy for trying to re-establish our friendship but..."

Luke shook his head - not that he was disputing that it was an accident but it was more that he was resigning himself to the fact that there was no excuse for what he had done. "That's as may be but if it weren't for me, Elliot would still be alive today. Maybe I should bring it all to an end."

"Bring what to an end? You're not making any sense, Luke."

"I'm talking about suicide, Kris. You know, a life for a life."

Rubbing his eyes from the emotional strain of their conversation, Kristian said: "Luke, you shouldn't…no, you mustn't keep tormenting yourself like this. What you need to do is concentrate on getting yourself better so you can get the hell out of here."

Each time Kristian visited Luke, he was told how much more he feared for his life from Monty and how he should end his own life before Monty ended it for him. Kristian would always ask if Monty had ever touched him and Luke would always answer that he hadn't. Kristian began to wonder - taking Scott into his confidence - whether Luke *was* actually suffering from paranoid delusions. Neither Kristian nor Scott felt particularly comfortable around Monty but he had never done anything for either of them to suspect that he personally wanted to sign Luke's death warrant.

"I think the breakdown has affected him a lot deeper than we were first led to believe," Scott confided in Kristian one day.

Kristian was inclined to agree with Scott's analysis.

After Luke had undergone ten months of treatment, he was still adamant to both Scott and Kristian that Monty was out to kill him. The only difference within the last few weeks was that Luke had now been subject to some extremely violent abuse from Monty, who had told him exactly on how he was planning to kill him - on top of this he was given the usual threats that he would have to kill Luke before Luke killed him.

Scott and Kristian decided it was time to intervene when they saw Luke with bruises all over his face and upper body, apologising that they had ever doubted his integrity. After a lengthy conversation with the Governor - Max had called in a favour from a lawyer friend of his to help with the legalities - it was agreed that Luke would be granted a transfer to a more appropriate psychiatric hospital. The transfer was to take place on 18 October 2002.

"That's just before what would have been our fourth anniversary," Scott told Kristian, with a pensive look on his face.

Kristian had wholeheartedly agreed to accompany Scott from the current to the new hospital, who had already granted an immediate visit as soon as Luke had been transferred.

"The sooner he is out of that hell hole, the happier I will feel," said Scott.

The Absence of Friends

When they arrived at the hospital, just to ensure that Luke was indeed put onto the vehicle that would take him to the new hospital, the receptionist asked them to take a seat. This was something that normally didn't happen - usually they were ushered straight into the ward.

"They're probably going to bring him out to us," Kristian suggested.

This was not to be the case.

What the Governor had to tell the two men, neither of them could believe.

"Gentlemen," began the stoic man, "I am the Governor of this institution, Darius Forrester."

"Are you wanting me to sign a release paper, or something?" enquired Scott hopefully.

"No. Take a seat gentlemen, please," Darius ushered towards the chairs as he shuffled his way to sit behind his desk.

The two men sat down, awaiting whatever it was the Governor needed to tell them.

Retaining his undemonstrative tone, the Governor continued. "Stuart Connors, otherwise known to the other residents as Monty had been on a psychotic rampage last night, knocking one of my interns unconscious before he could manage to raise the alarm for help."

Both men gripped the edge of their seats, obviously fearing the worst from the opening sentence.

"When the alarm was eventually raised, it was too late…"

"Too late?" asked Scott quizzically. "Too late for what?"

"Too late for Luke. Monty had strangled Luke to death. It took six of my men to prise Monty's fingers free from Luke's neck…long after Luke had choked to death."

"What the….?" exclaimed Kristian, as the colour drained from his face.

"He said this would happen…and you did nothing about it!" yelled Scott, his voice becoming louder with each word.

Darius chose to ignore Scott's outburst, although he shot him a disapproving look, as though he were one of the inmates himself. He bit his tongue to force himself not to retaliate but chose to continue with his explanation. "All Monty was screaming was: *you have to die because I'm not going to let you kill me.*"

Both men noted that there was no apology forthcoming - there wasn't even a hint of regret in the Governor's voice that a patient under his care was killed by another.

"I cannot lay the blame entirely at Monty's feet," Darius said coldly. "There was a history of animosity between him and Luke and therefore…"

"…and therefore you are suggesting that Luke got what he deserved," finished Scott, the venom in his voice plainly obvious.

"I did not say that."

"No, you didn't have to but you are obviously inferring it," Scott spat.

He rose from his seat and hastily exited the hospital, not knowing or caring where he was actually going. Kristian followed him, frantically searching the surrounding area. He finally found him crouched by the car, his hands covering his face to hide the fact that he was crying - ashamed of his tears.

"Why?" Scott demanded.

"Monty knew that he was HIV and believed that Luke was out to kill him."

The lump in Scott's throat prevented him from speaking momentarily. "He was getting better though, Kris. Wasn't he? Or was it just my imagination?"

"Scott," said Kristian, crouching down to join him on the ground. "Luke was under a great deal of emotional strain. I never told you this but he was planning on suicide again. He wanted to end his life…he was adamant that was his only way out."

Realising what Kristian had said a moment ago, Scott sat bolt upright and asked with vehemence. "What do you mean Monty knew he was HIV? Are you telling me that he died because of his HIV anyway?"

"We'll never actually know if Luke genuinely *was* the victim, or if he manipulated events to achieve his…well, to achieve his own death wish," said Kristian softly. "Luke found out that some of the interns had been talking quite openly about his HIV status, which Monty had obviously overheard. Monty thought that Luke was out to kill *him*."

Scott's blood was boiling. "Who the fuck do those bastards think they are? That hospital killed Luke and they will…" He jumped to his feet, making his way back to the entrance of the hospital.

"What the hell are you doing?"

Scott turned round to face Kristian - the hatred showing in his eyes and voice, as he rasped, "They killed Luke. They will be sorry…and need to pay."

"No!" yelled Kristian. He raced after Scott, grabbing his arm and pulling him back to the car. "What the hell will that achieve? Nothing!"

"They killed him, Kris," Scott said, choking on his own words and feeling the tears fall from his eyes again.

"Come on. You're going to stay with me for a while."

Kristian almost had to force Scott into the car to prevent him from re-entering the hospital and adding further complications to a situation that had seen more than its fair share of heartache.

Feeling frustrated and helpless, Scott banged his fist against his leg several times whilst Kristian turned the ignition key, bringing the car into life.

"We are here to remember the life of Luke Faraday," said the priest in his obligatory monotone, funereal drone.

They were the only words that Scott heard throughout the entire service, as he thought *what life?* He was shocked, though pleasantly surprised to see Luke's mother present at the funeral. Luke had never wanted to abandon his mother all those years ago, yet she never gave him the maternal love that he so richly deserved. Scott found himself wondering if things might have turned out differently for Luke if he had never lost his mother. It wouldn't have been difficult for her to have traced him, as undoubtedly she had wanted to be at her son's funeral. After all, he was nationally famous and his illness had, unfortunately, been publicised in the press.

Caroline's face painted a picture of a thousand words. Regret for not being a part of her son's life was clearly forefront of her thoughts. She told Scott later that advising Luke to live his life without her was the single, most hardest thing she had ever had to do. Not even the endless nights of torment and torture from her husband were comparative to what she felt when she told Luke to go his own way. She revealed that she had continually followed Luke's path of success and that he was never out of her thoughts.

"If only I had…" she began, before trailing off without finishing her sentence.

Scott looked at her. "Funny really, isn't it?"

"What is?"

"How our whole lives seemingly revolve around *if only* and *what if*."

"Yes, that's true I suppose."

"We all have to make our decisions throughout our life and live with the consequences of those decisions…no matter how difficult they might be."

All Scott's friends were present at the funeral: Kristian, Max and Maxine, Michael and Steven. Vince had flown in from Austria. Scott was pleasantly surprised at the turn out, though most of the people there were more acquaintances from bars, clubs and musicals than really close friends.

The entire funeral seemed to have an eerie sense of déjà vu for Scott, as all he could think about was Elliot. When his friends approached him with their words of condolence, it was as if they were replaying their scenes when it had been Kristian standing in his position.

Scott threw a single red rose onto the coffin, as it was lowered into the ground. "This rose symbolises protection, love and strength - just like your mother showed you when you were younger, so I want to show you for your afterlife," he murmured softly, under his breath.

He found the words of Luke's song swimming around in his head:

Like diamonds and gold, love is the treasure. It is everlasting, 'cause there is no limit. Distance cannot quench it and death cannot claim it. Love never dies, even with my last breath…Love is what we make it, truly forever. Held by your arms, binding together. Believe when I say, love never dies. Love never dies, even with my last breath…I will whisper your name.

He thought to himself how true the words were that Luke had written. He had always written perceptive lyrics to his songs and this particular song was definitely perceptive. If Luke had written this song knowing that he was going to die, the words were even more powerful and Scott found himself believing every word.

"You are so right, Luke," he uttered, as the coffin began its descent into the ground. "Death cannot claim my love for you. My love for you will never die and I will keep on whispering your name."

EPILOGUE

My fingers were going ten to the dozen at the keyboard, as I furiously typed away, explaining the events of the evening, as they were still fresh in my mind. Had I been writing the diary by hand, the paper might have caught fire from the intense speed. I had just finished what I had wanted to write when I heard Max coming into the room. It was well over an hour later than he said he was coming up. I didn't mind though, as it had given me enough time to collect my thoughts and get them typed before I went to bed. If I hadn't have typed what was still very clear in my mind, my thoughts might have gone somewhat stale and I didn't want an inaccurate account in my diary. Many times I had quietly reprimanded myself for putting off my writing until the following morning.

"Hi honey," Max said with a cheery grin, as he greeted me with a kiss that tasted of the alcohol he had consumed that evening. "Sorry I'm later than I said I would be. Vince was telling me about what he has planned for us all tomorrow."

"That's okay," I replied, taking a sip of my drink to dilute the newly alcoholic taste in my mouth. "I really hope this torrential rain doesn't continue into tomorrow…plus, you know that Michael will only have a drama because he and rain do not mix well."

Max raised his eyes to the ceiling. "I don't suppose he has heard of a contraption such as an umbrella, has he?"

"Oh, you know Michael…dramas are like part of his five-a-day - he feeds off them. Steven would have packed something for this kind of weather, I'm sure."

"Anyway, Vince wants to take us all out tomorrow night…I don't know where to though, as he didn't say but he is over the moon that we have all finally got together after so long. He said that we shouldn't leave it so long next time and we should all make an effort to meet up regularly."

"What? Like an annual reunion?"

"Something like that, I guess."

"Well I'm up for that…sure, why not. It sounds like a good idea to me."

Noticing that the screen to the laptop was on, Max asked: "Are you finishing off your diary?"

"Yes. I was just finishing as you came in. Perfect timing, huh?" I offered Max my seat. "You sit down and read what I've written and I will go and make us both a cup of tea."

Max made himself comfortable at the desk, as he scrolled up to the beginning of the diary entry:

> *I remember the reservations I had when Max told me he had received a telephone call from Scott, saying that Vince had wanted us all to meet in Austria for the grand opening of the latest Shepherd's ∏ restaurant. Vince was adamant that he would pay for everybody's flights and also stipulated that there would be no need for anyone to find accommodation because his latest Shepherd's ∏ venture had included the building of a fifty bedroom hotel above the restaurant.*
>
> *Now we were standing at the entrance to the building, trying desperately to shelter ourselves from the pouring rain, as we watched Vince cut the ribbon and ever so excitedly announce that his restaurant-hotel was now officially open. He had already opened several restaurants around Europe but now, he said, he was out to conquer the States next. Félix was standing proudly by his side when Vince cut the ribbon. How excited and happy they both looked.*
>
> *The opening night was a private party just for us and a few of Vince's closest friends, who he had wanted to be present at this special and momentous occasion. It had been over ten years ago that our original little group of now seven had all been together in the same room.*
>
> *It had been a very significant time in all our lives. I suppose the fact that it was the tenth anniversary since the tragic deaths of Elliot and Luke that made it all the more surreal in its significance; ten years since we last met… ten of us in the original group (if you count Félix as part of the original group, which I do because he was Vince's partner). There might have been those who had suggested that some of us were avoiding each other since that time but really, that wasn't the case. I think circumstances drifted us temporarily apart but now, due to Vince's invitation that was no longer an issue.*
>
> *All eight of us sat together at the central table and there was the usual exclamations of: "Has it really been that long?"*
>
> *I must say, both Max and I were looking forward to seeing everyone again after such a long time. I'm sure that everyone at the table was thinking more or less along the same lines as I was.*
>
> *Vince had asked one of the waiters to take a few photos of us all, sat at the table together. They were taken with one of those digicams, that I still can't get used to - I prefer the good, old fashioned days of taking a film to the chemist to get the photos developed. (Listen to me talking about the good, old fashioned days when digicams have been around for nearly ten years…again, it's that ten year thing!) I had bought Max a digicam for his last birthday and he had cursed several times when he realised that we had forgotten to bring it*

with us. It was quite ironic really, as even on the day of our departure I had reminded him more than once not to forget to bring it with us.

"Everyone look to the camera and say 'cheese'," said Michael, as we all tried to pose as naturally as we could, with our big toothy grins.

Although I prefer the golden oldie days of photography, I thought it was quite wonderful that gone were days of having to wait for an individual to order extra prints before they could send copies of photographs out to anyone.

"I will ensure that I email these out to everyone," said Vince, as the camera was handed back to him. "Probably tomorrow morning. You will all have your copies by the time you get home."

Michael spoke again. "Okay guys, we have dealt with the niceties but now it's down to business. This is the first time some of us have seen each other for ten years. We have gossip to catch up on…and lots of it!"

I smiled inwardly - more for the benefit of the others, as I had never been out of contact with Michael for more than a few weeks…let alone a few years. I said: "No matter how much time passes, some people just don't change. Do they?"

"I hope that isn't directed toward me, Madam," said Michael, adopting his usual mannerism when he was feigning shock or offence. "Mind you, I wouldn't expect anything less from Madam Minx…so, okay, I will bite… whatever do you mean by that remark?"

"Well," I began with my response, "you always were one for a bit of a bitch and a good, old gossip. You're still the undisputed Queen of gossip and the unchallenged Madam of bitches…even after all this time. Aren't you?"

"Too damn right! How else would you manage to find anything out if you don't listen, have a good bitch and give out a little gossip?"

I heard Max give a little, hearty chortle. I could easily guess at what point he had reached to make him react in such a way. I placed the cup of tea I had freshly made for Max on the mat beside the laptop.

"Thanks," he said, taking a sip almost straight away and sucking in his breath. "Ouch, that's hot!" he exclaimed.

"It would be…it's boiling water!"

I pulled up another chair and sat next to my husband, reading the point at which he had reached, confirming to myself that he was at the part I had originally thought.

"I guess that most would have thought - or were probably hoping - that he would have mellowed through the course of time," Max said. "Especially as none of us can no longer consider ourselves as youngsters anymore."

I shook my head. "Oh no, not our Michael. He will *never* change. I still don't think of him as the oldest one of our group - considering that he will be turning forty six in a few weeks' time because he will always act as though he is the youngest."

Max remembered Kristian saying to Michael at this point: "You're still the same camp bitch that went to college with me, aren't you, sweetie?" and smiled at his recollected thought. He wondered why I hadn't included that part and questioned the accuracy of my account.

"Oh!" was all I said in return, as I took the keyboard and typed in the couple of lines I had missed. "Thank you for reminding me," I said.

"Well, I know how you like perfection in your accounts and I thought that part was quite funny."

We continued reading:

"Too damn right! How else would you manage to find anything out if you don't listen, have a good bitch and give out a little gossip?"

Kris piped up, more than keen to interject. "Yes, Michael. You're definitely still the same camp bitch that went to college with me, aren't you, sweetie?"

"Well, clutch my pearls will you. What is it with you, Kristian? After all this time, you still want to use little, old moi as a toy that you think you can sharpen your little, albeit well-manicured claws on, as well as your tongue. Well, listen to me, Sweetpea, your wit isn't half as sharp or on-the-ball as mine. So, try as you might, my claws and tongue will always remain razor sharp, which makes you no real match for me!"

"Oh, Michael!" sighed Steven, shaking his head. "You know, if bitching was an Olympic sport, you would clearly win the gold every time! Even if you lost your voice, you would still manage to out-bitch anyone else." He looked toward me and asked: "How are the twins, by the way?"

I smiled. "They are mischievous little monkeys. I swear it's Michael's influence on them."

Michael eyed me, with one raised eyebrow, pouting. "Don't you start on me again, madam! Or else this kitty will scratch, as I will release my claws on you and there is no knowing where they will stop on their vengeful streak."

I laughed at Michael's typical response, hearing others accompanying my own laughter. It was so easy to get him to come out with his 'camp' diatribe, which everyone loved and adored him for because there was no malicious or vindictive intent behind it. He was still as capable of making everyone dissolve into a fit of hysterics as he had been able to when they first got to know him.

"They're not that bad," said Max, hoping to bring some decorum and sensibility back to the conversation.

"You're absolutely right," I said. "They're not that bad at all."

I told everyone that the twins were five years old now, recounting that the pregnancy had been totally unexpected.

"If you could have seen Maxine's face when she was told that she was going to have twins," said Max, "it was a total picture."

I explained that I had been monitored extremely closely throughout my entire pregnancy and even with my admittance into hospital two months early, I did not fear a repercussion of what had happened before.

"Medical research had come up with a way to be able to monitor and control Pre Eclampsia without fear of putting either the mother or the baby in any kind of danger," I explained.

"Originally," began Max, "we were going to call them Elliot and Luke, as a tribute to both of them but we thought it might bring back to many raw emotions so we chose, instead, to go for a derivative of their names and opted for Elias and Lucas."

Both Kris and Scott said that they thought it was a real honour that the twins were partly named after their respective partners.

"It's quite bizarre really," I continued to explain, "but already they are both picking up traits of their namesakes."

"Ah, the wonders of modern science," said Max, bringing the conversation back to its significant point at hand.

"Well, that's not all science has done for health," said Kris.

"Indeed," continued Scott with the revelation. "They've found a breakthrough for the HIV virus."

"Really?" I asked, genuinely surprised but pleased at the news.

"Yes," said Scott. "They found a newer and more effective way to prevent the virus from attacking and attaching itself to the white blood cells. It's quite complex to explain in its entirety and to get your head around but the new antiretroviral drug forces the virus into retreat and then actually seems to kill off the viral cells, where they begin to disintegrate."

"Well that is indeed fantastic news," offered Michael.

"It most certainly is," said Max, agreeing with the statement as though he were back at the table listening to the conversation for the first time.

I smiled to myself. It always made me smile that Max threw himself totally into my diaries, as though he were reading a novel and imagining himself in the situation or environment that was being written about.

"I really felt a warm glow when Scott said that he was going to be fine now," I said.

Even though I had appeared to be surprised at the revelation that there was a new antiretroviral treatment to beat HIV, we both remembered hearing this great announcement on the news about eighteen months ago. The world had finally received the news that it had waited so many years for.

I took a moment to remember all the people who had not been so fortunate enough to survive the disease and witness this great achievement in medicine.

"I'm pretty convinced that it won't be too long before they find a total cure for cancer now," I said.

"I was talking to Kris later on that evening," said Max as a side-track, "and he said that neither he nor Scott could believe it when it was discovered there was a medical breakthrough.

"Scott couldn't wait to undergo this new treatment and he was one of the first hundred people in London to do so. He was sceptical at first but after a few months of the therapy, he actually felt himself becoming healthier."

"He sure does look good now - that's a good enough reason in itself to celebrate."

Max picked up the thread of the conversation. "Kris said exactly that too. He said it was reason enough to open one of their expensive bottles of champagne, to which Scott put up absolutely no resistance."

I smiled. "Good old Scott. He does like his drink. I'm sure he's still down there, trying to drink the bar dry."

Max nodded. "Félix opened another bottle of wine as I was leaving, so no doubt they will still be there drinking when we go down for breakfast. Steven and Michael retired shortly after you did, so the hardcore gang of Félix, Vince, Scott and Kris are all still there."

We returned our gaze to the screen and continued reading:

"I'm so sorry to have sidetracked there with the health news," said Kris. "You were telling us about your children, Maxine."

I nodded. "That's okay, Kris - but it was an exciting bit of news to hear. Anyway, Elias says that he wants to be a space cop when he's older and Lucas, bless him, wants to be a designer of holographic novels."

Michael laughed. "Oh dear. What are children like nowadays? They watch far too much Star Trek and Star Wars for their own good."

"No, Michael," I said dryly. "Star Trek and Star Wars were programmes made for our generation. They have much further advanced shows than that now.

"The in-thing that the twins watch now is a programme about a computer called Ted, or Fred…or something like that. Anyway, it does something weird and wonderful like teleporting the person operating it into its screen and allows them to live out their dreams in some kind of virtual reality and when they come back out, it's as though the experience was real. I'm probably not explaining the premise of the show very well because it didn't make much sense to me when I watched it with them. They love it anyway, which is all that matters."

"Mind you," said Max, "I can totally understand what Michael is saying. Elias has swapped and changed his mind a million times about what he wants to be when he grows up. He's wanted to be all kinds of things, mostly they are influenced by that programme."

Michael continued the theme. "Yes, I was always told as a youngster that I shouldn't let these programmes and films influence me. But did I listen? Did I heck! And I turned out okay."

"Like what?" asked Scott, ready to bait Michael. "Films like Superman and believing you can fly?"

"No," tutted Michael, clearly not rising to the bait. "Nothing quite so as drastic as that…"

I interjected. "Well, it obviously hasn't worked with you then, has it Michael?"

"Eh?"

"Well, you have still managed to adopt all these camp and kitsch mannerisms and catchphrases, which you claim as your own, from all the various programmes that you've watched over time."

Whenever Michael didn't have a suitably vitriolic statement to make, he would just twist his face, as he did in response to me.

"What's happening with Thalia?" asked Steven, instantly wanting to steer the conversation away from Michael before he really found his acidic tongue once again.

"Thalia is doing extremely well at school," I responded.

"She is already top of all her classes. Obviously she takes after her father," Max smirked.

"And I suppose you are going to tell us that she takes after you in the looks department," said Michael, directing his comment toward me.

I ignored his quip and carried on: "She's coming up for her thirteenth birthday this year."

"Good grief," exclaimed Vince. "Is she really that old already?" He paused for a brief moment before continuing to answer his own question. "I *guess she is really. Where on earth does the time go? Last time I saw her, she was only a mere babe in arms."*

"Wait until you hear this," I said, shuffling myself on my seat. "She gets on really well with her grandfather…and with Elisabette too."

There were a few surprised faces at the table, as I explained how Max had urged me several times to repair the rift between myself and Elisabette. He told me that it was unfair on my father to deny him in seeing his grandchildren just because of how I felt about Elisabette.

"It was shortly after the twins had been born," I explained, "that I agreed to visit my father and Elisabette. One look at the three grandchildren melted her heart instantly.

"Over the past five years we have been slowly repairing the rift that had been created between us. When I come to think of it, I am not even sure how it all began anyway…because, of course, I didn't have the beauty of referring back to old diaries in those days."

"That's really great news," said Vince with a warm smile.

"Yes. We are all getting along really well now. All that had happened between us, for all those years, is being kept firmly where it belongs…within the deepest vaults of history. The children adore their grandfather and Elisabette. I was pleasantly surprised when she volunteered to look after the children when we told them that we were coming here."

Vince hailed a waiter to refill the empty wine glasses. As he was doing so, I rummaged for what seemed like an eternity through my handbag to find an up-to-date photograph of the children, passing it around the table when I managed to find one. I smiled at the various comments I heard about how gorgeous the children looked.

"…and you know," I said, "it really is a full-time job in itself being a mother to three totally adorable children."

"So what's been happening with you guys?" asked Vince to Michael and Steven.

"Oh, you know," Michael said jovially, "still cruising along at life's happy pace."

"Come on…there must be more to it than that," said Vince, not willing to accept that as an acceptable update. "After all, you've got ten years' worth of your lives to divulge to the rest of the table."

"Well," began Steven, feeling a little nervous like he was about to answer an interview question. "I have not long since finished writing my first stage play and it's going to be given its debut run at the Edinburgh Fringe later on this year."

> There was a thunderous round of applause that was strangely deafening from only six people and congratulatory sentiments from everyone at the table.
>
> "Thank you," he said, visibly blushing. "If it's successful at the Edinburgh Fringe, there's a strong possibility that they will take it to the West End."
>
> "It's wonderful that traditional stage plays haven't been affected by all this new, fangled technology that's coming out and seemingly taking over people's lives. It never ceases to amaze me the amount of people who cannot seem to function without their head continuously buried in their iPhone or some other handheld device."
>
> "The difference between technology and tradition is that technology is neither cultured nor cultural," offered Michael, to which everyone agreed.
>
> "Mind you," Steven added, "could you imagine it running for sixty odd years, like The Mousetrap?"
>
> "…and that is still going very strong," I said.
>
> "Wouldn't it be great if, in sixty years' time, people were still going to see and talking about my play?"

I had made another drink for myself and Max whilst he had been reading, offering him the cup.

Without thinking, he took a sip immediately. "Oh my God, that's hot," he gasped, trying to catch his breath as he almost threw the cup onto the table. Surprisingly, none of the liquid spilled out.

"Oh honey, please be careful," I said. "Didn't you learn anything from the last drink that I made? It's déjà vu all over again."

"It's okay. There's no harm done…fortunately. I'm so caught up in reading your diary that I forget I can't drink a cup of tea as soon as you've made it!" He loosened his tie, making himself more comfortable.

"Wouldn't you be more comfortable if you took your tie and jacket off?" I suggested.

Max raised an eyebrow, as he removed his clothing. "Once again, Mrs Beresford, whatever you say is absolutely right."

I took the jacket from him and hung it in the wardrobe.

As I returned to Max's side, he asked: "Where were we?"

"Steven and his play."

"Oh yes," he said, easily recollecting. "He was like an excitable child. He was acting like one of the kids after they had done their first drawing for us and wanted it proudly displayed on the fridge."

"I can't say that I blame him for being excited though," I said. "He's really thrilled about the prospect that it might go to the West End. If that does happen, it's a real testament to his ability as a writer."

"We will have to make sure that we go and see it sometime very soon."

I agreed. "Especially as we have been given free tickets."

"Eh?" Max said, confused by this new revelation.

"Ah, that must have been at the time when you took yourself off to the toilet. And if I remember rightly, you were gone for quite some time, which Michael took great pleasure in making a big song and dance about in his own inimitable style…

"…anyway, Steven said that everyone was invited to come along and see his show and then he produced a ticket for everyone. If I've got the date right, it's going to be around my birthday, so we can make a mini-break of it if you like." I searched my handbag and produced the tickets to show to my husband.

Max smiled, as he looked at the tickets. "Well, that's your birthday plans sorted for this year," he smirked. "Shall we continue reading?" he asked, signalling with his head to the unfinished diary entry.

I nodded, as I sat back on my chair.

Steven was clearly stimulated by his own work. He had grown weary of solely acting and wanted to branch out into something a little more challenging and a bit different. He found himself one day, with pen in hand, and before he realised what he was actually doing, he had the beginning of a stage play in the making. It had taken him no less than three years to write the play and he was more than a little nervous about submitting it to anyone - with the emergent fear of instant rejection playing utmost in his mind. The surprise that he felt must have been totally overwhelming when the response he received was a positive one. He thoroughly enjoyed being part and parcel of the auditioning process, being extremely selective and exceptionally particular about who should be the right person to play each individual character.

"Maybe I was being a little to specific," he said. "But, having said that, I knew exactly the kind of person - both in their look and their personality - that I wanted for each role."

"So what's it called? What's it about?" asked Kris keenly.

"It's called 'Who Would Have Thought?' and the premise of the show is…well, what's the best way I can describe it without giving too much of the plot away? I suppose, it's a three-act tragedy with each act being told from the perspective of a different main character. As each act unfolds, you get thrown a bit more of the storyline. I know it'll be considered as somewhat corny and passé and I will be slated that it's been done countless times before

The Absence of Friends

but, in my favour, it's a modern day twist on the typical story of unrequited love, with the sting of bitter and jealous rivalry, which culminates in a totally unforeseen finale."

"Can you give anything else away about it, Steven? I don't want to spoil the intrigue and surprise for anyone but this sounds like it's right up my alley - the kind of show I would thoroughly enjoy," I said, allowing myself to be caught up in the drama of the synopsis.

Steven pondered thoughtfully for a moment. *"Well, one of the main characters, who is also the narrator of the first act, is called Serge and he's your typical burly, virile heterosexual man but with a surly attitude.*

"Then you have pretty and petite Monique, who is the narrator of the second act. She dreams of being whisked off her feet by a gallant and noble gentleman, straight into a fairytale romance and the perfect wedding.

"Finally, you have Andrew, who is a writer who longs for the day when he can become an established author and is the narrator of the final act. Andrew wants to share this important moment of his life, when it happens, with someone important and special to him. He keeps having this recurring dream, featuring a man whose face he can never distinguish but is supposedly the man of his dreams.

"The three characters' lives collide when Andrew sees a guy in a shop whom he doesn't know from Adam but he is convinced is the man from his dreams…"

There was plenty of impulsive murmurings coming from all quarters of the table, on how good the play sounded. Everyone agreed that they should make an effort to go and see it, with Scott daring to suggest if there might be any subsequent follow-ups written in the future.

"…well, as I said, if it's a success at The Edinburgh Fringe, then it might move on to the West End. I have promised myself that if this does happen, then I will continue to write some more stage shows."

It was at his point that Steven produced the tickets from his jacket pocket and gave one to each of us. *"If I am going to celebrate its potential success,"* he said, *"then I want you all to be a part of the celebrations so therefore, it's important for me to ask you all to come along and see why it might be so successful.*

"If it's a flop," he continued, *"then you wouldn't have wasted any money in going to see it."*

We all thanked Steven for the ticket and assured him that we had every confidence in him and the play, that it would be a great success.

Vince lit himself a cigarette. "Well, after tonight, I have decided, that I am going to quit these," he said holding the cigarette up just in case anybody had a doubt as to what he was referring to.

Vince was the only smoker in the group, so this was met with approval from the rest of us, along with statements of tremendous encouragement.

"Anyway," he continued, "that's just a small piece of news because you all know what is happening with me in terms of the Shepherd's ∏ restaurants, which I am also going to expand into a hotel chain as well. But, let me tell you, when I begin to open restaurants and hotels in America, I will begin in New York. If that's a success, I plan on opening them all over America.

"I would though, like to thank all of you for coming over to celebrate my newest enterprise with me."

"This won't come as any surprise, not as far as I'm concerned anyway," joked Michael, "but who were we to turn down a free trip and a stay in - may I hasten to add - a rather luxurious hotel?"

I noticed that Steven was not very impressed with Michael's comment, who winced when Steven gave him a slap across what was more than likely his leg.

"Of course, this is no ordinary and basic restaurant that you're sitting in having your dinner," Vince said commandingly. "Though, if I may say so myself, the food is exceptional."

There was no whiff of an argument from anyone at the table, each one of us nodding our heads as though they were all connected to one puppeteer's string, controlling our every movement.

I excused myself from the table, leaving the remaining occupants to talk about how wonderful the bedrooms in the hotel part were, as I made my way to the toilet. I heard Max saying something about how wonderful the beds were before I was finally out of earshot of any further conversation.

What Max had said was totally true though - the beds were an absolute delight. In some inexplicable way, you could select either a hard or soft mattress to suit your taste or, if you were of the more adventurous persuasion, a waterbed-esque mattress just at the press of a mere button. There was even a built-in thermostat to control exactly where the heat was needed. I smiled to myself as I thought about how we had given the bed a rigorous test of its sturdiness earlier.

As I returned to the table, it was Scott who was doing the talking: "...I think it's fabulous, Vince. Gone are the days of fumbling around in your pockets or bag for keys, especially when you're drunk." He was talking about the voice-activated doors.

Upon our arrival, at the reception desk, when we were checking in, there was a computer that we needed to speak into. This voice recognition was the basis of the command that was then transferred to the room you were booked into and most of the electrical devices in the room would respond to these vocal commands. Max and I were like kids with new toys, trying out the different things in the room.

"Of course, Félix is now helping me run these. He has been absolutely invaluable to me over the past few years…in more ways than one." He shot a cheeky grin at Félix, who himself returned an equally cheeky wink.

"And you have lost a lot of weight too," commented Michael. "Lost the pounds around your waist, only to put them straight into your pocket!"

We all laughed.

"It may all shock you to know that nothing very exciting has happened to me over the years," said Michael. He sounded almost sad that he didn't have anything to offer to the group. "I just seem to be the mental torturer for everyone. I helped Steven with his play getting off the ground and of course, I was made godfather to Max Squared's kids…oh god, now that I've said that, I suddenly feel incredibly old."

"Oh, they adore you, Michael. As well you know," I said. "They are always asking me when you are coming to visit next. You spoil them you know."

Michael smiled.

"I am pretty convinced that he would have made a terrific father," I continued. "I even told him so one day, when I saw how he interacted with my children."

I glanced at Steven. "You know, Steven, there's still an opportunity for you to adopt a child together you know. Michael might be firmly ensconced within middle-age-dom but you're certainly the youthful one in the relationship."

Steven stifled a chuckle whilst Michael shot daggers at me.

"…although Michael," I found myself continuing, "you are not being strictly honest when you say that nothing has happened to you."

For the first time ever, I think, we actually saw Michael looking suitably embarrassed. "Okay, so I'm a nanny," he said quietly.

"A nanny?" questioned Vince.

Michael explained that because he loved being with children and that it was far easier for him to go down to their level rather than drag them up to his - an analysis which the entire group had no alternative but to agree with - he had decided to set up a crèche centre for mothers who couldn't afford babysitters for their children.

"I only charge half the price that normal babysitters would. Their rates are really quite extortionate…so if the government or the providers of household amenities aren't robbing us of our hard earned money, then it's people like these."

I offered more information to the group. "He's really terrific with the kids, you know. I've seen him in action and I've witnessed some mother's having to literally prise their children away from the centre when they've come to collect them after they've finished their day at the office."

Michael explained that he had to employ several helpers, most of whom were volunteers, as the group could sometimes swarm to the point of oversubscription with children of various ages and states of hyperactivity.

"He has had a lot of input with the twins' upbringing," I said. "He's like a real uncle to them…and as far as they're concerned, he is."

"Well, someone has to keep their mother in line," said Michael. "And Thalia is already becoming as cheeky as you."

"Like mother, like daughter," was all I said in response.

"Lord help the poor man who ends up marrying her," joked Michael.

Max looked up from the screen and was surprised to notice that I was dressed in my nightwear. He was so engrossed in reading the diary that he hadn't even registered that I had showered, dried and gotten dressed into my lacy negligée. Even after all these years, Max's heart still skipped a beat when he was tantalised by my revealing, almost to the point of indecency, nightwear.

He recalled that I had sounded rather acidic and maybe even a little brusque when I had responded to Michael's comment about Thalia. Sometimes, he wondered, if Michael didn't overstep the mark a little with me. Personally, he treated most things that Michael said with a pinch of salt. He wished I would learn to do the same.

"Thalia's not really that bad, is she?" I asked with concern.

"Well, now that you come to mention it, I actually do believe that Michael is right. Mind you, it is probably *his* influence that is rubbing off on her, rather than it being a case of like mother, like daughter."

"He is extremely good with the kids though."

"Oh, I don't dispute that at all. In fact, I readily agree that he's totally amazing with them."

"And he is a great help when he takes them on outings - especially when it's a school trip that we might have forgotten about. You know, he seems to have a sixth sense about when we need a break and is readily there to take all the kids out."

"He's a little treasure really," said Max. "Totally worth his weight in gold."

The Absence of Friends

I giggled. "He sure is."

"I wouldn't be surprised if he wants to take them out straight away, when we return to England. He'll probably want to tell them all about the adventures that he and Uncle Steven have had with mum and dad."

I returned to the bathroom to clean my teeth, whilst Max got himself undressed and had his customary five minute shower before dressing himself in his pyjama bottoms and a t-shirt. We were more than a little surprised when the clock teased us with the fact that it was nearly four o'clock. We had sunk ourselves so deeply into my comprehensive account of the night that we were totally oblivious of the time.

When I had finally emerged from the bathroom, after completing my vast ritual of pre-bedtime ablutions, Max said: "You always were one to write such a thorough and detailed account."

"I guess it's more out of habit than anything else now. I have been writing these diaries for goodness knows how long…for as long as I can remember. A good twenty or twenty-five years maybe? So I guess it's second nature now that I write more than I need to, especially when I have the beauty of the computer to help with speed."

"Shall we leave reading the rest until the morning?" Max suggested.

I shook my head. "It's already morning! It'll be light outside in two or three hours and time to get up for breakfast. Besides, you haven't got that much more to read now. Plus, we are coming to the part about you." I smiled at him.

"Oh," was all that Max could muster, as his eyes returned to the screen for what he hoped would be the final time because they were beginning to feel extremely heavy and he was longing to grasp what little sleep was left to him.

It was Max's turn to "sit in the hotseat" as Michael had referred to it.

"Well, let's see…I now run my own financial management company, which seems to be achieving great success year on year. I currently have fifteen staff members but I am looking to expand further over the next couple of years. The offices I presently have, in The Strand, are really a little too small to house my future expansion plans. So, at this very moment in time, I am debating on whether to move to much larger offices, or to possibly open a whole new branch."

Sometimes I felt that Max could be a little too clinical when he was speaking, especially when it was a conversation that wasn't naturally flowing - when he was put under the spotlight, he liked time to prepare what he was going to say. It sounded as though he were partaking in an interview, with him being the one being interviewed. Mind you, on several occasions Max had been referred to, or labelled as "the sensible one" or "our level-headed conscience", more often than not by Michael.

Steven attempted to find a resolution to Max's immediate dilemma. "Open a new branch," *he suggested.* "Think big."

Max smiled at the enthusiastic response. "Well, I'm not sure. I do have some news hot off the press to add though…"

Vince and I knew exactly what Max was going to reveal and we smiled knowingly at each other.

"…Vince spoke to me earlier, shortly after we had arrived, offering me the honour of running his accounts. With the fact that he is hoping to take his restaurant and hotel chain to a multi-international level, there is obviously too much for him and Félix to cope with, as well as running the accounts. So, I have agreed."

There were more congratulations from around the table.

"Well, that just leaves Scott and Kris to tell us what has been happening with them," *said Michael, stating the obvious.*

Scott and Kris had become very close since the deaths of their respective partners, comforting each other in their times of need. It wasn't until nearly three years later that they had agreed to sell their individual properties and buy a house together. To anyone who didn't know either Scott or Kris, they might have assumed it was the beginning of a relationship of convenience but everyone at the table knew that the day they moved in together, it was the beginning of an extremely special and close relationship. Neither of them denied the other one the memories of their partners. They had, last month, celebrated their seventh year together as a couple.

"We would like to thank each and every one of you for your kind presents and cards," *Kris said.*

It was what unravelled in the next few minutes that would stick permanently in everyone's memories. I remember, as the minutes ticked by, I couldn't stop the cold shivers from running up my spine and I even found myself shedding a tear or two.

"We found something extremely interesting not long after we had sold our houses," *said Scott.*

Various exclamations of surprise and interest were heard from all the occupants of the table, myself included.

Kris carried on. "As we were packing up all our belongings, it had become quite obvious and evident that Elliot and Luke had got together on various occasions without either of us having any knowledge of it…"

There was a gasp from the table, which I think came from Michael's direction.

"No," said Kris solemnly. "It's not what you're thinking. Luke had written some new music and Elliot had written some moving scenes to go with this particular music. They were obviously collaborating on writing their own musical together, which was to be dedicated to both Scott and myself."

Scott continued. "We spoke to Steven about our findings and he strongly suggested that we find someone to finish the work. Well…" he paused to look at Kris, who nodded at him, signalling that he was happy for him to continue. "…well, we would like him to continue with it and see if he can finish what they had started."

If this proposal didn't cause the hairs on Steven's neck to stand on end and a cold shiver to run up the whole of his spine, I don't know what would have.

"We both have complete faith in your work, Steven and we would be more than honoured if you would do this for me and Scott."

Everyone's eyes were firmly fixed upon Steven, awaiting his response - it seemed like an agonising wait. Whether it was the enormity of what had been asked of him that had rendered him speechless, or the honour, he never actually revealed but it seemed like hours were ticking away instead of seconds before he finally answered.

Nobody dared to break the silence by speaking or making a sound. Although it was only a brief moment of silence, it would be a treasured moment.

Finally, Steven nodded, with not one word passing his lips.

I don't think anyone quite realised what had just happened, or even noticed that Steven had given a nod but it was Michael who piped up first. "That, everyone, translates as a 'yes'".

"As they were going to originally dedicate the musical to us, we want to re-dedicate it back to them. We would very much like this musical to be in honour of both their memories."

"That's not all," said Scott.

Everyone's eyes widened, anticipating a further revelation. I'm pretty convinced that my blood-pressure had gone askew and my heart palpitating to such a degree that I thought it would stop altogether.

"I found a lot of Luke's songs that hadn't been published and there is enough to release another album. I have talked it over with Kris and we are both in agreement that we are going to get this album released."

"I've heard some of these pieces," said Vince, "and to be quite frank and honest, they are absolutely stunning and quite breathtaking."

"Thanks," Scott said, smiling. "I thought so too when I heard them."

Andrew R. Hamilton

Several different conversations began at once, with everyone at the table discussing the impact of Scott and Kris's revelations. As we were talking, music began to play. It was obvious that both Scott and Kris recognised the music playing, as they gave each other what I could only describe as quite a memorable smile. Scott told me afterwards that the title of the song just played was going to be what the new album would be called, especially as the album was going to be dedicated to everyone sitting at the table.

Vince hushed everyone and asked us to turn our attentions toward the stage.

It was a very crude attempt at a makeshift stage. Obviously Vince, when he originally made his plans for the design of his restaurant, was not thinking about catering for an evening of musical entertainment centred upon a stage. Maybe, I thought, after tonight's performance, he might reconsider this.

I focused my attentions toward the stage and two young lads were standing there with microphones in their hand. One of them spoke whilst the introduction was playing. "We would like to sing this song for you, especially for the occupants of Mr Shepherd's table."

I am not really sure if it was merely the lighting playing tricks, or I had a mental desire for the moment I was caught up in to be true, but I could swear that the two lads bore an uncanny resemblance to both Elliot and Luke, as they had been in their early twenties. As the words of the song floated over to our table, I found myself being drawn into pondering two interpretations as to why - whether fantasy or reality - that the singers resembled our friends. One theory I had was that it was an attempt to bring Elliot and Luke back into our midst and as pointed out earlier, "to keep their memories alive". The other theory was that it added a whole new eerie and haunting dimension to the lyrics.

As we all listened to the two lads singing, we found that we had all been mentioned in some way or other within the song. Not by name but by relating to some of the lyrics. It was clearly a song that had been written from the heart. I felt a cold chill pass through me, as I realised it was a song about preparing certain people - loved ones namely - for somebody's final departure. As I listened to more of the lyrics, I came to the conclusion that it wasn't a negative or depressing song but more a song of hope for the people who were left behind with the memories; a song about those who were left behind should allow themselves to remember all the good times.

When the song had reached its climax, I noticed that there was not one dry eye at the table. That sight alone was enough to bring another tear to my own eyes.

It was Félix who finally broke the peaceful silence surrounding our table. "That was nothing short of fantastic," he said, voicing everybody's thoughts. "It's an extremely moving song, almost as if it were toasting absent friends. What's it called?"

Both Scott and Kris raised their glasses and smiled. "The Absence Of Friends!"